WAYWARD: RUNNING

WAYWARD: RUNNING

T. A. Star

Podium

Podium

Note about romance in the series

While romance is not the main overarching plot, some romantic subplots will be shown and explored, including for the protagonist.

These subplots include a variety of potential pairings (all along the gender spectrum), different relationship statuses (monogamous, polyamorous, or even anarchist), and spanning variable lengths of time (from forever-lasting to brief fancies to never getting started).

There will *not* be explicit "spicy" scenes.

Also, not every type of loving relationship explored will be of the romantic type, as this story focuses more on chosen family.

Content warning for this book

While I try to avoid any *overly* graphic depictions of gore or sensitive content, I do include or touch on the following topics that some readers may wish to avoid:

Violence and death (of people, animals, and many monsters), kidnapping and confinement, PTSD and grief, and lots of anxiety mixed with teenage hormones.

WAYWARD:
RUNNING

CHAPTER ONE

The Night Witch

It was a night like any other night, but Phoenix couldn't sleep. The cold, sterile room of the children's hospital she practically lived in was barely illuminated by the moon shining through the window curtains as she lay in the dark.

Aside from the normal anxiety eating at her about the incurable condition threatening to make tonight her last, the pain was becoming so extreme that she clutched at her abdomen and groaned.

Phoenix tried to wipe the strands of red hair from her sweat-dampened face. Her hair was the only healthy part about her, and she loved it, always had. One of her earliest memories was yelling at her mother when she was about three, yelling at her not to cut the chaotic curls that always made her seem wild. She had promised to sit still and let her mom brush them as long as they wouldn't be taken away from her.

She wished her mother was there to comfort her, but Whitney Fraser had died in a car accident almost six months ago. Her mom would never get to see her become a legal adult, since that would happen tomorrow. She was a ward of the state now, with no family left. The only visitor she expected for her special day was her government-appointed case worker.

Phoenix didn't care about her birthday, though. Turning eighteen was never really something to look forward to, aside from simply marking another year and proving all the doctors who said she wouldn't live to see adulthood wrong.

Her father had died before she was born, killed far away in a war. She still didn't fully understand the reasons for the war in the first place, especially considering that the amount of propaganda that surrounded it was dizzying. The politics, rumors, and conspiracy theories floating around the whole thing made her avoid looking too deep.

Her mom chose to raise her alone but working as a nurse in this very same hospital made things easier for them. Officially, she had been diagnosed as a child with Duchenne Muscular Dystrophy, but the doctors weren't *positive* that's what it was, as her body attempted to attack itself and slowly wasted away. The diagnosis just gave them something to work from for treatment plans.

Another spike of pain made the grip of her offhand clench around her plush green turtle that matched her eyes. It was a gift that made her mind turn to wishing for her best friend as well. Jin had been a light for her among the dreary sadness that would often permeate the hospital where so many of their young friends died.

She remembered sneaking into their room on the good days, the days she had the energy to shamble over, just to talk and tease and laugh with each other. Jin had died too, though, claimed by cancer over two years ago.

When the pain finally got past her rather high threshold, she began fumbling in the dark for the nurse call button. She hated bothering them during the night despite knowing that was what they were there for. She hated needing to ask for help, proving yet again that she needed others to do even the most basic of tasks. She *hated* being a perpetual burden to everyone around her.

The thing she hated the most, however, was getting a new nurse who would take a glance at her chart and then proceed to misgender her. Despite the long red curls that framed her pale, sallow face and the pink hospital gown she had requested, they would see that little letter *M* and proceed to call her "mister," "sport," or worse, "sir."

She knew they didn't know better until she corrected them, and luckily, most of them would correct themselves immediately as best they could, but it was still a punch to her fragile scraps of ego. A stab in her heart that she would never be *seen* as she wanted to be.

The worst was the rare occurrence when the newbie nurse was malicious about it. They would refuse to correct themselves and go out of their way to point out her birth assignment despite its inaccuracy. They would find any opportunity to remind her that she would never be able to transition her body because of how frail and sickly she was. This was one of those times.

She knew her latest tormentor would be on duty tonight. She knew they would sneer and poke and not be gentle about helping her . . . but she *hurt*. So, Phoenix gripped the clunky plastic remote and resolved herself to press the big red button.

Before she could, however, the door opened, and she sighed in relief. Perhaps one of the other nurses who knew and cared about her had come to check on her in a stroke of pure coincidence.

Phoenix froze in a slight panic when a cloaked figure with a comically large witch's hat entered her room instead. She stared in wonder at the person's clothing, which was shining like the night sky, like robes of twinkling starlight glimmering in the darkness.

She couldn't see a face under the brim of the hat that looked like it had been stolen from some fantasy cosplay convention. She asked quietly as her pain was momentarily forgotten, "Are you an angel here to take me to heaven?"

A feminine voice laughed. "No, little one. I am *far* from an angel."

Phoenix frowned, gritting her teeth as a stab in her abdomen reminded her that the pain was still there, and it didn't like being ignored. "A devil then?"

Another laugh filled the small room. "Not quite. I'm here to help you, but do not think of it as divine charity."

"Help me?" She began to wonder if perhaps the agony was affecting her brain now and causing hallucinations. She had never experienced those before, but there was always a first time for everything.

"Think of it more like making a deal," the woman said with amusement.

"A deal?" she asked, still distracted by the searing pain in her stomach. "I think you might have the wrong person." She gasped and groaned at another sharp stab before gathering enough breath to add, "I— I don't have anything to trade."

"An investment then," the mysterious stranger said more seriously, "I made this same offer to your friend a few years ago and am pleased by the results so far, despite the mix-up. Now I'm hoping you won't disappoint either."

"My friend? Who—"

"Never mind that," the voice said, cutting off her question, "I have other plans for you."

Then the stranger—who she still wasn't convinced wasn't some kind of trick her mind was playing as she was finally dying—lifted an arm towards her and whispered something in a language she had never heard before.

The outstretched hand glowed with a pale green light for a moment before that same light surrounded her, suffusing her, and Phoenix knew this *must* be a hallucination or dream now.

The pain stopped.

Phoenix couldn't remember the last time she had felt like this. No pain, none at all. There was always some, usually just varying degrees of it, but now . . . nothing. She stared at the stranger for a long moment as the green glow vanished, plunging the room back into night's embrace, before finally asking bluntly, "*Who* are you, and *why* are you here?"

It was eerie when she finally caught a glimpse of a wide Cheshire-cat grin peeking out from under the hat as it rose upward to reveal a womanly face. "I'm called Morgan now, in this world at least. I do like going by 'Night Witch,' however. It has a magical ring to it, doesn't it?"

"This world?" Phoenix asked, beginning to wonder if perhaps the pain had stopped because she actually *had* died, and this was some sort of weird limbo meant to ease her into the next life.

"Yes, little one," Morgan replied with a nod. "There are many worlds out there in the greater cosmos, some even quite similar to this one. That's what I'm here for and what I want with you, actually."

"Me? Why would you want me? I'm sick. I've barely seen anything outside of this hospital. Unless there's something you need me to code, there's not much I can help with," she said in confusion, still distracted by the feeling of *not* feeling pain.

Phoenix had managed to go to school online and even get into a technical course that filled most of her electives with computer programming. Getting a high school diploma was at her mother's request, and she was told *repeatedly* that she'd need the little piece of paper when she finally got cured and joined the rest of society. Phoenix hadn't quite seen the point of it, but she liked learning things, and it distracted her from the daily monotony.

Despite the limited time her mother allowed for them, video games were the only thing she might be considered decent at. She assumed this stranger wasn't here to recruit her to some Warcraft guild or help with her virtual farm. Other than gaming, her main hobby and favorite way to pass the time was reading adventure books. It was a love her mother passed on to her early in life, and they were often a book club of two, reading together and discussing fantastical stories and wishing for more.

"I'm not in need of a website, little one. I prefer to stay in the shadows," the witch replied as a long staff appeared in her petite hand. There was a large, sparkling diamond atop it in the shape of a star, and it seemed to glow with an inner light as Morgan began walking around the room, dragging the staff along the ground as though drawing in the sand with a stick.

Phoenix tried to sit up more to better see what was happening, but her muscles were too weak to respond to her will, despite the pain being gone. Morgan continued speaking before she could ask what the witch was doing.

"You could say I'm a seeker of souls. Special ones. Souls with . . . potential."

"Potential?"

"Yes," the strange woman said, never stopping her weird movements around the room. "Everyone is born with potential. Some squander it. Some have it smothered by others. Some have more than others. Some use it all up. And some . . . a very rare few . . . are limitless. They break the rules and are the agents of change."

Morgan stopped suddenly and turned to look at Phoenix. Making eye contact caused her to flinch as she finally saw solid pitch-black orbs in place of eyes. They seemed to be endless voids threatening to swallow her up.

"I can sense this potential," the witch said softly, then walked closer towards her, "I can help put you on the path . . . but it's you, and *only* you, who can choose to fulfill it. To go beyond all the others and shine brighter than the sun. To be a force of change for good or ill."

Phoenix paused, unsure how to reply to the unusual solemnity the conversation had turned towards. She wasn't sure what the stranger was getting at.

If she had to pick from the examples the woman had given, she would have placed herself in the category of having all her potential used up—consumed by the sickness that had been trying to kill her since birth. She had even died the day she was born, at least for a few minutes, when her heart had stopped and she needed to be resuscitated. That was why her mom had named her Phoenix in the first place.

"I don't have any potential left," she murmured, sure it had all been spent.

The Night Witch grinned again and said, "Well, I guess we'll just have to see about that." Then the woman clapped her hands together and added, "I best get on with it then. Don't want anyone realizing I healed you before I send you on your way."

"Send me? What are you talking about? And what do you mean you healed me? I can't even sit up straight," she managed to sputter out, trying to understand what was happening.

Morgan grinned wider, held out her staff in front of her, and answered, "Then I'll send you somewhere you can. Please, don't fade into nothingness. I'm expecting a good return on this investment, after all."

"Seriously, what are you—" Phoenix's words cut off as she was surrounded by sparkling stars floating in the air around her, and a multicolored glow emanated from the floor under her where Morgan had been scratching her staff against the sterilized linoleum.

Not believing the things she was seeing, she closed her eyes tightly. She rubbed them with her palms as if to wipe the illusion from her sight and once more wondered if she really had died despite not remembering actually passing.

"Good luck, Phoenix Fraser. It's time for you to make a difference in the cosmos," the witch said as the light began to shine brighter. "Oh, and try your best not to die *too* much."

The pain returned suddenly, different this time. Her blood felt like it was on fire, and her scream caught in her throat as her body tried to cry out, yet no sound could be heard. It was like lava was being injected straight into her veins through the IV that had become a permanent accessory for her.

The only thought that entered her mind through the torture was that she didn't want to die. Despite having nobody left, she wanted to live—wanted to experience *more*. Then the pain stopped just as quickly as it had begun, and Phoenix sensed absolutely nothing at all.

CHAPTER TWO

Book of Choices

Phoenix felt groggy, as if she had slept for far too long. This made her panic, thinking that she had slept through her first round of treatment for the morning. She pushed herself up to try and check the time.

The first thing she noticed was that she was not in her bed. The hard-packed dirt beneath her made that very clear. No, she appeared to be in the center of some sort of scorched symbol etched into the earth with wisps of smoke rising from it.

The second thing she noticed was that she was able to move more freely. The pain had stopped completely, and she felt better and stronger than she remembered ever feeling before. Then her memories of the previous night returned—or had it been a dream?

The fact that she was obviously not in her hospital room was the biggest indicator that it had not been a dream or a hallucination, but that she really had seen magic. Did the Night Witch truly heal her and then somehow manage to teleport her somewhere?

The smell of her new surroundings assaulted her nose with unfamiliar odors. It wasn't clean with the stinging scent of chemicals and medicines. It was much more complex and made her nose crinkle. She vaguely recognized the scent of dirt, but was this what smoke smelled like? It made her whole body tingle, and despite the danger the scent usually indicated, she thought she actually liked it.

As she finished sitting up, she looked down to assess herself. Her first thought was horror at the discovery that she was completely naked. Quickly wrapping her arms around herself, she reactively bent forward to try and get her long hair to help cover her exposed body, often using it to hide from prying doctors.

The second thought was that she must have seen her body incorrectly. This must be some cruel dream threatening to dangle her most desired wish before her eyes, only to be snatched away when she awoke. There was no *possible* way that her body could have changed *that* drastically.

When her hair didn't act as a curtain to shield her, she reached up with a hand and found that she was completely hairless. This sent another wave of horror coursing through her.

This was definitely some twisted nightmare that taunted her with fixed biology in exchange for the only part of herself that she *liked*. In her renewed panic, she scrambled away from the center of the small runic circle. She stumbled as she tried to remember how to walk; the physical therapy had only helped so much as she got older.

After tripping across the smoldering ground, she managed to retreat into the nearby brush of a forest, which hadn't been anywhere near the hospital.

What in the abyss is going on? she wondered as she hid behind a tree, still trying to cover her nakedness.

She almost screamed in surprise when a large book appeared, floating in front of her. It glowed slightly, with its open pages facing her. It seemed to be offering itself for her to read, so she did.

At the top was scrawled in a pretty script, *"Phoenix's Guide Book,"* and below that was a message taking up the center of a soft cream page of parchment.

New Quest: Choose Your Path
You have arrived in a new reality! Choices need to be quickly made.
Objective: Choose your new path in this world within the next five minutes.
Path 1: Battle against the approaching Casters and any who might seize control of your fate.
Path 2: Flee the approaching Casters and take control of your fate.
Path 3: Abstain from acting and allow your fate to take control of you.
Path 4: Capitulate to the approaching Casters and relinquish control of your fate to others.
Reward: Common dress.

Phoenix stared at the obviously magical book for a few moments, reading it over and over before asking aloud, "Guide Book?"

She was startled by the sound of her voice being much higher pitched than it normally was but was distracted by new text appearing below the quest prompt.

Natural Talent: Guide Book
You can conjure a book that guides you and informs you about parts of the world that have been touched by your Aura.

Phoenix's eyes went wide. This seemed similar to the JRPGs and MMOs she played during her alone time, except fewer video game tutorial pop-ups and more . . . well, magic Spell book.

As she reread the quest, she found herself slightly annoyed by the name of the ability and mumbled, "More like Book of Choices. There's nothing in the quest actually *guiding* me on what to do."

Despite her anxiety over the situation, she couldn't help the smile creeping across her face. Did she really get sent to a magical world? Then she asked in confusion, "Wait . . . How did I get this ability? What's a 'Natural Talent'? This *isn't* a nightmare? What *happened* to me?"

As she had hoped, more information appeared on the next page.

Note: Natural Talents are the abilities people are born with.

Name: Phoenix Fraser
Species: Wayfarer
Caste: Mundane

Attributes
Strength: Mundane
Agility: Mundane
Fortitude: Mundane
Mind: Mundane
Magic: Mundane

Natural Talents
Aetheric Transmigrator
Beacon of Hope
Collector
Guide Book
Waypoint

Aspects
No Aspects are currently bound.

No Class is currently unlocked.

Seeing her species listed as Wayfarer was only slightly disconcerting, but it made sense from a magical-world perspective. Not only was she no longer human, it seemed, but she had been completely healed and given new abilities, which apparently included a magic book.

She glanced down at her hands as though they might reveal exactly *why* she wasn't considered human anymore, but her gaze continued further down her body. It was then that Phoenix realized that it wasn't a mind trick; her body had been healed more thoroughly than she had ever dreamed possible. This wasn't a cruel dream—her body had been transformed into what she had desired since realizing it was all wrong.

Recognizing her body now matched her soul was the thing that ended up slamming home the fact that she had actually been transported to another world and transformed in the process. She began to cry as she stared at the female biology she had always wished for and now belonged to her.

She was *finally* whole. For the first time in her life, she *physically* felt like the woman she was always meant to be.

The newly made Wayfarer sat there for a while, staring and mentally sensing the changes as tears of joy and relief ran down her cheeks. She didn't even care that she was naked. In that brief moment, she felt like she no longer had anything to hide—at least not from her own eyes.

After a few calming breaths and wiping away the tears, she noticed her new magic book was floating in front of her once more with new words.

Warning! Three minutes remaining on the quest: Choose Your Path.

"Aw, crap," Phoenix muttered as she glanced over the options again and recognized the correlation: Fight, Flight, Freeze, or Fawn. She looked back around the tree to try and take in the sight again.

There was still smoke rising from the edges of the magic circle that she had appeared in, but the sounds of people moving through the forest on the opposite side of her were more worrisome. She soon saw who the book had referred to as "Casters."

Almost a dozen people wearing armor or what looked like wizard robes were soon going to swarm the area. Phoenix instantly knew that fighting was simply out of the question. Being barely better than a baby foal, she wasn't about to take on a small squadron of armed fighters and mages.

She also wasn't really a fan of becoming some sort of lab rat to be studied. She preferred to be the one doing the studying, and she figured options three and four would land her under a microscope or whatever magical scanning devices they had in this world.

That left fleeing—or more likely stumbling away—but she wasn't certain of her odds out in the wilderness, alone and naked with only a magic book to guide her. While she had read a great deal in her abundant spare time, putting what she had read to the task wasn't always easy . . . or so she had read. Maybe it wouldn't be as hard as it seemed in all those online videos people made for clicks.

What struck her as odd when rereading her quest was all of the options talking about her fate. It made her realize that at this moment, in this new world, that was the real choice she had to make. Who would control her fate? Who would be the master of her destiny?

For her whole life, she hadn't even gotten the chance to make that choice. She hadn't been strong enough to fight for control, and she couldn't just flee from her sickly body. Fawning usually ended up being the most beneficial way to get things she wanted, but even that had its limits.

Her usual stress response would be to freeze, at least for a moment, in order to give her mind time to process and decide logically on the actual best course of action for herself, but she didn't always get the time to fully research solutions before needing to make a decision. This seemed to be one of those times.

Out of curiosity, she asked her new guide, "Which choice do you think I should take that would result in maximizing the chances of my fate being what I really want it to be?"

Her attention was momentarily disrupted as she heard the voices behind her getting closer, nearing the burnt landing zone.

"Can you believe this?! The research paper I'm going to be able to write on this arrival point is going to be the talk of the OOM!"

"Better hope the AOA pricks don't try to steal whoever landed here from us. They always try to protect these Wayfarers by making them Adventurers, which usually just gets them killed before we can get any good data out of them."

She hadn't really expected an answer from her new ability, so when she turned back around, she was slightly surprised to see it had written a single word.

RUN.

Phoenix ran.

After about twenty minutes of awkwardly stumbling through the forest, getting scratches all over her exposed flesh and especially her feet, she collapsed against another tree that had a large root jutting out at its base and was covered in enough moss to not be painful for her bare backside to sit on. The moss was a weird texture to actually feel. After seeing it in pictures, she had often wondered what it really felt like, and it was spongier than she had imagined.

She took deep breaths as she tried to recover some stamina. Despite being perfectly healthy now, she was not accustomed to running through the underbrush. The heavy breaths brought a plethora of new sensations and scents. Her hands kept wandering, feeling everything from the moss to the bark and the velvety leaves. Everything was so new, and she wanted to memorize it all.

As she rested and explored with her senses, her book appeared in front of her once more to provide updated information.

Quest: Choose Your Path
Objective Complete: Path 2 chosen.
Objective Reward:
[Simple Dress] has been added to your collection.

Completion Reward:
10 [Mana Bits] have been added to your collection.

"Collection?" she prompted. "Is that another of my new Talents? I think I remember something like that on the list."

Natural Talent: Collector
- You have a personal dimensional storage space.
- You automatically loot slain enemies that have been touched by your Aura.
- Loot automatically goes into your collection.
- You can use material components for Spells, rituals, or enchantments directly from your collection.

Phoenix stared in shock at the ability. A storage and loot power rolled into one? This was definitely feeling more like a video game now. The title seemed appropriate for what it encompassed and how she normally leaned towards playing video games—wanting to collect every treasure and achievement. She was already liking her chances of survival much more as she asked, "How do I access my collection?"

Note: You can mentally access items from your collection by thinking of the item you wish to withdraw and where you wish for it to appear within your Aura's area.

"Wait, what kind of Aura are we talking about here? Is this some kind of wuxia cultivation world?" She had only peripherally dabbled in the genre, so she wasn't quite sure if the rules were similar, but she recalled most of them involving Auras and meditation.

Note: Your Aura is currently inaccessible to sense or control until you unlock an appropriate ability and is currently limited to your physical body.

"So, how do I loot things? Or make them appear?"

Try your hand.

"Is that snark? This better not be one of those snarky tutorials that all the books and games think are funny but are actually annoying when I'm in a new world with no idea what I'm doing!" Phoenix said in a miniature rant before she processed the words. Then she thought about holding the new Simple Dress that she should have just received—which she realized that she instinctively knew was there—along with her new Mana Bits, whatever those were.

Just *knowing* something that she had never learned was the oddest sensation Phoenix had ever experienced, and she had experienced some truly odd sensations in her short life—mostly involving pain.

The dress seemed to materialize in a silver shimmer in her hand, just as she had hoped, and she quickly slipped it on over her head. It was a long, green homespun dress that matched her eyes, with long sleeves that offered her much more protection from the slight chill in the misty forest. She felt immensely better now that her skin wasn't so bare.

With another thought, she focused on holding one of the Mana Bits she had gotten. What appeared looked like a smooth river stone about the size of an American quarter but thicker in the middle, like a large Skittle or M&M. However, unlike the colorful candy, it was a translucent gray like dusty glass.

Phoenix wasn't sure what these Bits were used for, so she returned it to her collection. She practiced the movement a few times to try and get comfortable with it, which was surprisingly easy to do.

Cautiously, she reached out a hand towards the book. It seemed to intuitively respond to her desires as it moved towards her so that she could hold it in her lap. The book was surprisingly solid but seemed weightless as she grasped it, and gently turned the page back to glance at her ability list again before turning back to the next empty page and asking, "What is Aetheric Transmigrator?"

Natural Talent: Aetheric Transmigrator
- Increased resistance to negative Dimension effects. Dimension abilities have an increased effect.
- You are a Natural Translator, allowing the understanding of languages you are exposed to.
- You can directly use Aspects and Spirit Gems without the need for an Absorption Ritual.

She was relieved that she wouldn't have to worry about learning the local languages, and she wondered if the natural translation was something that all Wayfarers were granted to help them survive in a magical world.

Then she wondered if these "Natural Talents" were all the same since they were something everyone was born with. Perhaps they were based on the species? That would make her less special and unique than she had originally thought. Those people earlier seemed to know what Wayfarers were, after all, and that she was one of them.

Phoenix had never heard of Aspects or Spirit Gems before. However, she remembered seeing the former listed on her profile page simply stating that she didn't have any.

She heard a noise coming from the direction she had arrived from and quickly stood up, groaning at the pain in her feet, and began moving again. Phoenix may have completed the quest to choose a path, but she still needed to get as far away as possible from the people who wanted to imprison her just for existing. The thought made her grimace and wonder if this world really wasn't that different from her old one after all.

CHAPTER THREE

Guiding Stars

Phoenix stumbled on a protruding root and barely caught herself from falling before glaring at the offending tree and continuing down what she believed to be a game trail she had stumbled across. She wished she had a compass to make sure she wasn't getting turned around and going in circles, as the sun was almost impossible to see, and the moss seemed to grow everywhere on the densely packed trees.

The place seemed reminiscent of an enchanted forest from a European fairytale, and she was pleased to spot some wild animals that *didn't* try to eat her right away. There were birds and rodents, but they didn't look *exactly* like she remembered from the pictures and videos she had seen back on Earth.

There were also creatures she had no name at all for. Some looked like parts of other animals combined in unconventional ways, while others seemed like the animal had fused with a magical element. She couldn't help but grin after seeing what looked like a sparrow made out of water flying by her, feeling a sense of wonder that she hadn't felt since she was a small child.

While she traveled, she kept asking her new **[Guide Book]** for more information about her next Talent, "What is Beacon of Hope?"

> **Natural Talent:** Beacon of Hope
> - You can unlock more than one Aura ability.
> - Aspect abilities cultivate quicker than average.
> - You can draw magic diagrams with conjured light, including ones that float in the air.

Phoenix had no idea what most of that meant for her. Were Aura abilities different from Aspect ones? She decided to ask for another hint, "What's the difference between an Aspect and Aura ability, and is one usually the limit?"

> **Note:** Aspects are magical manifestations of worldly concepts that can be used to unlock facets of one's soul. This may include the unlocking of limited ability types, which consist of Aura, Perception, Execution, or Familiar. Only one of each of these types of abilities is usually unlockable per Caster.

"Caster?" she inquired, prompted by the unusual terminology, "Is that what everyone here is called?"

> **Note:** A Caster is a person who has unlocked all four of their Aspects and gained a Class, triggering a transition into the Crystal Caste.

"Huh. That's good to know . . . I guess? Except I have no idea what Crystal Caste means. Is that some kind of tiered hierarchy system like in India? I wonder how I can unlock an Aspect," she pondered as she continued to walk. Before she could ask her next question, however, the book's writing had been updated automatically with its own prompt.

> **New Quest:** Defeat Your First Monster!
> *You have taken control of your fate in a new world full of monsters! Prove you can survive!*
> **Objective:** Kill and loot a monster.
> **Reward:** Uncommon Aspect.

Phoenix's eyes went wide. "Wait, monster? What do you mean by monster?"

As if on cue, movement in the brush ahead caught her attention. She tried to focus on the movement—expecting the worst—and gave a little gasp as a white rabbit appeared about a yard away.

"Oh," she sighed in relief. It would have been way too cliché to have a monster appear right after getting a quest to kill one.

The Wayfarer leaned forward, placing her hands on her knees as she said in a higher tone, like speaking to a pet, "Hey there, little buddy."

A moment later, she let out a scream as the rabbit roared at her with a maw full of sharp teeth. Phoenix ran again. She only turned briefly to kick wildly at the tiny monster that chased her through the woods as the noon sun shone down through patches of the thick canopy.

After only a minute of fleeing, Phoenix tripped and fell to the ground. Honestly, she was amazed that she had lasted that long before stumbling. She glanced around in a panic to find something to defend herself with.

Her hand found a branch, and she turned just in time to swing at the furry terror, slamming the thick stick into its side. It gave another roar, and Phoenix scrambled to her feet in a rush of adrenaline. Then, she began beating the little fluff ball with the makeshift weapon.

When the creature no longer moved, Phoenix stumbled backward to lean against a tree, breathing heavily from the sprint and attack. She jumped in surprise when the monster's tiny body began to turn into a pale gray dust, seemingly disintegrating into ash before her very eyes.

She suddenly *knew* that there was now a small package of bunny meat, a tiny pelt, and a single rabbit foot in her collection. She briefly wondered why there was only one foot but shook the thought from her head. The glowing book appeared in front of her once more to give her some relevant information, which it seemed extremely prone to do.

> **Quest:** Defeat Your First Monster!
> **Objective Complete:** Killed and looted a monster.
> **Objective Reward:**
> *A first-time kill bonus has increased the reward quality.*
> [Star Aspect] has been added to your collection.
>
> **Completion Reward:**
> 10 [Mana Bits] have been added to your collection.

She glared at the book for a moment, wondering if it had somehow spawned the creature in order to challenge her, just like some sort of twisted tutorial that tried to make sure she worked her way up the difficulty ladder. The fact that it had given her a monster to fight before she even had any magic powers to do so with was entirely unfair, in her opinion.

Phoenix sighed at the pointless pondering and took out her newest loot. The Star Aspect looked like a large chunk of spiky crystal that was mostly shades of blues and purples with silver specks of twinkling starlight lighting up its interior. It was beautiful, if not a little daunting, with its many points sticking out in every direction of the roughly sphere-shaped object.

It was about the size of a large fist, and she wondered aloud, "What am I supposed to do with this?"

In response, her book wrote out a brief description of the item she held.

> **Item:** Star Aspect
> *A magical aspect of the stars.*
> **Caste:** Crystal.
> **Availability:** Rare.

> **Type:** Consumable, ingredient.
> **Requirements:** Less than four unlocked Aspects.
> **Effect:** Unlocks an aspect of one's soul, granting one passive and one cultivating ability.
>
> *You are able to absorb the* [Star Aspect].
> *Do you wish to unlock the Star Aspect of your soul?*

"Um . . . yes?" she replied hesitantly, wondering if that was enough. It apparently was, as the crystal seemed to dissolve *into* her. As it merged into her skin, she suddenly felt incredibly hot. She was unable to hold back the scream when it felt like her insides were lit on fire, eventually causing her to pass out from the sudden spike of searing pain. It was *almost* as bad as when she had gotten teleported here in the first place.

The Wayfarer woke up only a few minutes later, by her guess, since the sun still seemed to be peeking through the canopy overhead and another rabid monster hadn't attacked her. She must have bumped her head when she fell since she had a splitting headache now.

Phoenix rubbed at the sore spot, wincing slightly at the pain, but didn't cry out again as she sat up. When she thought about what had just happened, she realized that she felt noticeably different. Sensing the power that had unlocked within her, it felt strange yet familiar, as if it had been a part of her all along.

Looking at the book once again, she confirmed that her **[Aetheric Transmigrator]** Talent worked and that her newfound intuition was correct.

> *You have unlocked the Star Aspect of your soul.*
> [Star Aspect] has bonded to your **Fortitude** attribute, increasing the Caste of your **Fortitude** to Crystal 1.
> *You have unlocked the Aura passive ability: Guiding Stars.*
> *You have unlocked the cultivating ability: Transversing the Stars.*
> *You have gained the capability to sense Auras and manipulate your own.*

"Aura passive? That's what I can unlock multiples of, right? What does that do?" she asked, her curiosity quickly overriding the remnants of pain she was experiencing.

> **Passive Ability:** Guiding Stars
> **Type:** Aura (magical, light)
> **Current Caste:** Crystal 1
> **Crystal Effect:** Allies within your Aura have increased stamina regeneration and will gain a **[Starlight Companion]**. Reconstructing a destroyed

> **[Starlight Companion]** expends a low amount of mana.
> Starlight Companion (construct, magical, light): A small Starlight
> Companion hovers around you, providing light and protection. This can
> intercept and negate Magical or Elemental projectiles.

"Starlight Companion?" she rhetorically asked before noticing the glow in her peripheral vision. The small orb, glowing with a faint purple light and delicate glassy pixie wings, was hovering obediently over her shoulder like a little lamp trying to illuminate the already illuminated text.

It reminded her of a particularly obnoxious fairy from one of her favorite video game series, but at least this one didn't seem to talk or beg for her to listen to it. She held out a hand, palm upward, and the small companion obligingly landed atop it for her to get a closer look. Though it had looked like a hard glass ball with fragile luminescent wings, it was surprisingly soft, squishy, and malleable.

A bright smile lit up Phoenix's face at the utter joy she felt with the adorable creature as it seemed to playfully bounce and roll around in her palms. She couldn't help the giggle that escaped her lips.

Along with the new little fairy friend, she could now sense her Aura around her as though it was both a part of her yet separate. She could mentally feel the shape and size of it, and when she concentrated hard enough, she felt it move slightly to her will. It seemed to infuse her very being while blanketing the area around her for a handful of yards yet imperceptible to all of her other senses.

Then she remembered that she had unlocked another magic ability and asked the book to verify what she also felt inside of her, the power begging to be released.

> **Ability**: Transversing the Stars
> **Type**: Utility (construct, magical, dimension)
> **Cost**: High mana.
> **Cooldown**: 5 minutes.
> **Current Caste**: Crystal 1 (0%)
> **Crystal Effect**: Construct a stargate between two locations on a regional
> scale. The destination gate must appear in a location you have an aural
> imprint on.

Her eyes went as wide as saucers as she stared at the description of her new magic power. "A portal?! I can teleport? Like actually travel across the map in an instant?!" Full of excitement, she hopped up to try it out, but realized she didn't have anywhere to go.

She was completely lost in a forest on a completely different planet in a completely different reality. If her book hadn't been lying to her, that is—which she doubted it was, considering it had proven right about everything so far.

Intuitively, she could feel that the distance of her ability was rather far, but she didn't know where to attempt portaling to that was in range. The only place she could remember was the sizzling area she had arrived in, but there was no way she was going to go back there just to get captured and probably experimented on.

However . . . there *was* that spot about three yards down the path that she could see. Too excited about actually casting a magic Spell, she released the power that had been pleading for her to use it since being unlocked.

She concentrated on the two locations for a moment. A shiny silver ring appeared, floating in the air above both spots, growing to the size of a person, and hovered slightly above the forest floor. It was filled with a swirl of dark blues and purples with flecks of silver twinkling like starlight on a clear night.

It was beautiful and probably the most magical thing she had seen yet. The sparkling sheet of night seemed almost inviting to her, as though it held the thrilling promise of wonder and adventure just on the other side.

The sensation of mana was completely new to her, along with most things, and it was difficult to describe since it didn't conform to most natural sensations. There was no temperature change, and it wasn't *exactly* like the feel of water, but it did flow throughout her. She could feel it spreading within, escaping through her hands as she created the magic in front of her, and her mind felt a bit fuzzy from losing a decent chunk of it at once.

She shook the feeling off as her logical mind began taking over. She walked around the portal contemplatively, checking out the other ring that had shown up as well, then returned to the original source one. She cautiously touched the overtly magical portal with a finger first. No pain or missing finger was a good sign. Next went the whole hand, then the rest of the arm.

Everything came back perfectly fine and intact. She took a calming breath, followed by a step of faith and a flicker of hope, as she entered the portal. The experience was weird and slightly disorienting at first, but she reappeared right on the other side of her destination portal, just as she should have.

The Wayfarer gave a whoop and jumped into the air a little bit. She hadn't actually jumped in years. Not since she had been a much smaller and lighter child that hadn't yet withered after her diseases continued eating away at her.

Another noise in the brush, most likely an animal or something disguised as an animal that would also try to eat her face off, reminded her to start moving again. Cutting off her celebrations, she began wandering through the forest again, this time using her portal every five minutes to shortcut the distance as much as possible. She quickly discovered that the previous portal would vanish on its own after the cooldown was done.

She thought over and over again about all the information she had gotten, trying to fully process the changes that had happened to her. It was a bit much to really take in, and she briefly feared again that this was all some fantastic dream.

It was too real, though. She had read enough about magic and had dreamt enough to know that this wasn't a dream. She had truly become a Wayfarer and been transported to another world, either because the strange Night Witch had teleported her here or she had died and been reborn. Most likely the former. Maybe a little of both?

Phoenix ran into a few more tiny monsters that tried to take a bite out of her, but a decently large branch she found and started keeping with her was enough to make short work of the little beasts—once she stopped panicking at the sight of them. Thinking of everything like a video game helped *immensely*.

Her book interrupted her progress through the forest as it appeared before her again of its own volition. Obligingly, she read the new text that appeared.

New Quest: In Darkest Night
You have become lost in the forest and the sun has begun to set.
Objective: Survive a night.
Reward: Uncommon Aspect.
Bonus Objective: Cook and eat a meal.
Reward: Common undergarments.

Phoenix stared at the reward. There was no way she would just gain another Aspect by doing something she was already planning to do, was there? Then she wondered just how hard not dying overnight was actually going to be.

CHAPTER FOUR

In Darkest Night

Phoenix had managed to find a few wild berries during her excursion through the mountainous woods, silently praying to whatever gods this world might have that they weren't poisonous. Thankfully, she felt fine after eating them, but it looked like they wouldn't count towards her quest's bonus objective since she hadn't actually *cooked* them.

After another hour of fighting off little monsters that didn't seem afraid of her big stick, getting plenty of additional cuts and bites, and searching for a suitable place to camp, she was about to give up since it was almost too dark to see now. It was becoming dangerous enough that she was worried about falling off a cliff or down a hole if she kept stumbling around.

During her trek, while touching and smelling everything that she came across, she also practiced more with using her dimensional storage by picking up any sticks or branches she deemed suitable for firewood in the sense that they seemed dry and sent them into her collection for later.

Finally, she noticed a rocky outcropping that seemed to have enough clear space below it to suit her purposes. She kept her eyes open as wide as she could, searching the area for any more monster threats before making her way to it.

Phoenix cleared away some of the dried leaves, not wanting to set the whole forest on fire. She moved them into a small pile and surrounded them with some of the bigger rocks she found next to the stone ledge. Then, she set some of the wood she collected on top of the leaves, just like in the movies. Now, she just needed a spark, right?

With a sigh, she tried striking two of the rocks together, but she quickly figured out that she was neither strong enough to cause a spark nor did she have the right kind of stones to easily generate one. She stared at the would-be campfire for a long moment, thinking through possible solutions.

She closed her eyes and mentally went through the assortment of random loot her Aura had collected thus far, mostly from the small furry bunny monsters she had beaten to death, and realized that the packages of meat were literally packages. She conjured one into her hand and raised an eyebrow at the waxy green paper and twine wrapping the meat.

"How is there packaging? Is this actually a video game?" she asked aloud, and her trusty book reappeared to give her a message.

> **Note**: Loot is generated from a combination of ambient magic, the remnant magic within the looted target, and your own reserves given form by the looting power.

"Huh," she said contemplatively, "so basically, magic made it what I subconsciously wanted or expected? I wonder if I can *want* myself a box of matches off the next demon bunny I find . . . or maybe a lighter?"

She'd have to ponder that a bit more and see if she could game the loot system eventually. For now, however, she retrieved the twine off the packages and two of her sticks. One stick she used to make a little bow with twine tied on either end and the other one to entangle in the bow's string and began moving it back and forth to cause the second stick to spin faster than she could have done with her hands alone.

Phoenix hoped that she hadn't forgotten a step from that interesting little survival crash course series of videos she had found online a couple of years ago after Jin mentioned going camping before being readmitted to the hospital.

The Wayfarer tried a few different things and a few different types of kindling before finally succeeding. Setting the small bundle of wood and leaves aflame, Phoenix gave out another whoop of excitement at her success. As she added a few more pieces of firewood, she took out one of the thinner sticks she found earlier to use as a skewer, put some of the rabbit meat from the package onto it, and attempted her very first campfire barbecue.

It was terrible. The meat turned out chewy and unevenly cooked, and she wasn't positive that she wasn't going to end up poisoned after eating it. She did, however, get credit for her quest's bonus objective and was happy to no longer be going commando.

Phoenix was accustomed to not wearing underwear all the time since she hadn't really needed any when her usual outfit was an open-backed hospital gown, but it was nice to at least attempt to feel like an average person for a change.

She let the fire die down to only embers before curling up against the rocky ledge and attempting to get some sleep. The tiny bundle of pelts she had collected acted as a makeshift pillow, and she found herself wishing for her bed instead of this cold, hard dirt.

It was a fitful sleep, with every noise the forest made jerking her awake in a mild panic that another killer rabbit was going to sneak up and try to eat her. Despite her exhaustion, she found her mind continually wandering and keeping her from falling back to sleep properly.

Thinking of the world she left behind, she knew that nobody was left back on Earth who depended on her or truly even loved her. There was no reason for her to even attempt going back, and she already knew she didn't want to. She was in a new world, and this felt like a new start for her, even with the monsters.

She was literally a different person now. That caused a smile to come to her face as a feeling she had never experienced before began to well up inside her: the feeling of limitless potential.

Phoenix was shaken from her drowsy thoughts by a loud roar that seemed to echo throughout the mountains just as the moonlight began to fill the sky, which she couldn't even see through the thick foliage. She couldn't make out any stars either, not knowing if they would be different from the ones she knew of.

Another roar, this time from a different direction, shook her from her starry musings. She sat up slowly, pulling her legs up against her chest and tucking her little glowing night-light between them, suddenly feeling very exposed in the dark forest. She was pretty sure that she wasn't going to be able to sleep at all tonight now, presuming there were bigger monsters out there in the night . . . *hungry* monsters.

A low growl came from above her, and she froze, not daring to breathe and hoping that whatever creature was prowling on the outcropping of rock shielding her had lackluster perception skills.

She heard a loud sniff as the predator scented the air, and she knew she wasn't lucky enough not to be noticed. It gave another loud roar that caused her to reactively cover her ears before it jumped down to sniff at the remnants of her campfire a few yards away.

Phoenix wasn't exactly sure how or why, but her Aura could *sense* the danger that the creature had exuded. She instinctively knew from it that this monster was stronger than her, faster than her, and more powerful than her in every way.

The Wayfarer wondered what kind of creature it was and almost yelped when her book appeared with the information. Her very *glowy* book. Shining with light in the very dark forest. The beast turned towards the light and hissed before pouncing towards it.

Phoenix ran . . . again.

Not stopping to look back towards her poor book that was currently being mauled by the shadowy panther-like creature. Not stopping when she heard other strange and unfamiliar sounds nearby. Not stopping even when she tripped and fell, tearing up her dress and palms. She ran as fast as her legs could go and then used her portal to run further.

While she had come across the occasional monster during the day, mostly of the devil rabbit variety, the night was worse.

So much *worse*.

Creatures from every storybook nightmare she had ever heard of seemed to inhabit the forest at night. She even stumbled upon an evil tree that attempted to snatch her up with its prehensile branches.

She counted herself extremely lucky when she managed to stumble into a non-magical tree, and instead of smearing herself along its bark, she fell through a large crack. She discovered that it was a hollowed-out trunk that apparently belonged to a monster or some forest animal that had left long ago.

Phoenix just huddled into a ball and quietly shivered in the cold night. She prayed to anyone or anything that might be listening to keep the monsters away. She had never really been a religious person, and neither was her mom. It was difficult to believe that some divine being was listening in all the time. Even if they had been, she thought they must have been either cruel or simply indifferent to ignore her while she suffered all her life. One prayer had finally been answered, though; she was healed now. Remade as a whole person.

Perhaps Morgan was magical enough to know her prayers, or some god had sent her. Either way, she found herself hoping for some kind of divine intervention, even if it only came in the form of Lady Luck helping to keep her hidden.

The Wayfarer faded in and out of consciousness as the hours passed, not able to track the passing of time at all. She wondered if time was even measured the same here. Were there even the same kind of seasons? It had been February second—the day before her birthday—when Morgan showed up, but was it still that equivalent day here? It was winter where she had lived; was that true here? It felt cold enough to be, but she couldn't be sure since she had barely spent any time outside in recent years.

The forest seemed to begin to lighten a bit, and she was informed that the night had finished when her book magically shimmered into existence in front of her once more. Apparently, it didn't matter if a monster tried to eat it since she could just conjure it again.

Quest: In Darkest Night
Objective Complete: Survived a night.
Objective Reward:
[Dark Aspect] has been added to your collection.

Completion Reward:
10 [Mana Bits] have been added to your collection.

Another Aspect down and only two more until she became a Caster, whatever that really meant. The book had mentioned getting a Class, so maybe it indicated some sort of change to her status, and she could truly begin playing the game as a full-fledged magical character.

She put the tangent thought aside for now, assuming she'd figure it out as she went, and instead asked the book, "What was that monster from before? The one that tried to eat you."

Species: Shanther (Monster)
A shadowy predator with an aptitude for Dark magic that likes to startle its prey with its terrifying roar before pouncing for the kill.
Caste: Crystal

"Huh," she said to no one, then conjured and lifted up her newest quest reward. "Well, that's different," she added, slightly disturbed by the giant black sphere her hand seemed to have become. It was like a dark cloud, a black mist covering her fist despite the fact that she could grasp the patch of darkness made manifest. Her eyes were sending signals of *wrongness* to her mind for holding something that looked insubstantial, so she tore her gaze from it to ask her book, "And is this the same as the other one?"

Item: Dark Aspect
A magical Aspect of darkness.
Caste: Crystal.
Availability: Uncommon.
Type: Consumable, ingredient.
Requirements: Less than four unlocked Aspects.
Effect: Unlocks an Aspect of one's soul, granting one passive and one cultivating ability.

You are able to absorb the [Dark Aspect].
Do you wish to unlock the Dark Aspect of your soul?

"So basically, it's the same. Good to know," she muttered, pondering the item for a moment longer, still unnerved by the dark cloud and fully expecting the searing pain again. Then she remembered the monsters of the previous night and admitted to herself, "More magic is more power, and I can't rely on luck every night if I'm going to survive in this monster-infested reality."

She gave a weary sigh and braced for the pain as she said, "Unlock the Dark Aspect."

The pain came and, unfortunately, was just as bad as the first time but with a slightly different flavor. Instead of fire crawling over her, it was like someone had turned off her sight, and the shadows themselves had come alive to tear her apart. She couldn't see anything. Not even the dead of night had been this pitch-black when the stars would shine down.

Phoenix could still move, though, writhing against the rough wall of her hollowed-out tree as the darkness attempted to hollow out her soul, drowning her in the infinite unknown.

> You have unlocked the Dark Aspect of your soul.
> [Dark Aspect] has bonded to your **Agility** attribute, increasing the Caste of your **Agility** to Crystal 1.
> *You have unlocked the Aura passive ability: Embrace of Shadows.*
> *You have unlocked the cultivating ability: Night Blade.*

That was the message she had read upon awakening, and was glad she hadn't left the safety of her little hollow yet.

When she was finally coherent again, she muttered, "I'm starting to get really tired of passing out from pain. I know I should be used to it by now, but it's definitely not something I enjoy."

Then she glanced back at her book as it seemed to wait patiently for her prompt this time, and she rolled her eyes at it. "Alright, what do my new abilities actually do?"

> **Passive Ability:** Embrace of Shadows
> **Type:** Aura (stealth, magical, dark)
> **Current Caste:** Crystal 1
> **Crystal Effect:** Allies within your Aura are obscured by shadows, making attacks against them less likely to hit. The effectiveness of the shadows scales up with the level of darkness of the surrounding environment.

Phoenix became distracted from her reading by the sensation of her Aura being greatly expanded and gaining an odd, layered effect, which seemed to strengthen and reinforce it.

It was strange to be able to feel the creatures that were within it as they scurried away from the sensation, and she wondered if normal creatures and people could instinctively sense Auras but simply weren't conscious of it. She'd have to ponder that some more, maybe actually find some civilization where she could get more questions answered.

When her attention refocused itself on her book, and she realized she had gone off on another mental tangent, she tried to refocus on the words and read about her next ability, uncertain about what she found.

> **Ability**: Night Blade
> **Type**: Utility (construct, magical, dark)
> **Cost**: Low mana.
> **Cooldown**: None.
> **Current Caste**: Crystal 1 (0%)
> **Crystal Effect**: Constructs a magical dagger that inflicts additional Dark damage and an instance of [**Mana Siphon**].
> Mana Siphon (bane, drain, magical, arcane, stacking): Drains a low amount of mana over time.

"Huh," she said absently to the air again, then focused and conjured the dagger to her hand much the same way she called items from her collection. The weapon was a long stiletto blade about eight inches long and seemingly made of glossy onyx. It fit perfectly in her grip, but she wasn't very knowledgeable about wielding a weapon of any kind, even a dagger. She didn't need to defend herself in a hospital . . . *usually*.

Phoenix felt slightly disappointed at getting a melee weapon like this as her ability, but she had to admit that it would have come in handy earlier when fighting the demon bunnies. However, a magic missile Spell would have been equally useful, if not more so. She sighed, knowing that magic missile from the *Dark* Aspect was probably absurd, but maybe it could have been some sort of Dark bolt or something.

"Well, at least it's better than a stick."

CHAPTER FIVE

Waypoint

Phoenix continued traveling after making sure nothing was near her hollowed tree. She was grateful for the decrease in monsters that appeared to occur with the arrival of the dawn, though she wasn't sure where they had all gone at first. It wasn't until she came across the evil tree monster again that she realized the monsters hadn't despawned like in a video game but had gone dormant, seeming to sleep during the day.

Not wanting to potentially wake it up, she skirted around it and continued on her way. She only got a few yards away from the tree when she almost got her head bitten off as a ball of white fur flew towards her neck with sharp white teeth. She was barely able to dodge the demon bunny and remembered her new power, conjuring the onyx dagger.

The Wayfarer watched the tiny monster carefully, attempting to time her strike with its own. As it pounced through the air once more, she swung . . . and missed. Swiping at the air cost her, though she managed to keep her head as teeth sunk into the arm that had moved too soon. She reacted in a panic, falling to her knees and slamming the rabbit on her arm against the ground to force it to release her.

When the monster finally let go, she plunged her stiletto directly into its exposed chest. Blood sprayed everywhere as she continued to stab it. She didn't halt until it stopped making noise, and her dagger fell into a pile of fine gray dust. The disturbed monster ash puffed up into the air around her, causing her to cough before dry-heaving her nonexistent breakfast.

Thankfully, she didn't remain covered in bunny blood as even that disintegrated into dust, drifting to the ground around her. It took a few minutes for her to calm down as she babbled to try and reassure herself that she wasn't murdering innocent little woodland creatures. "Like a video game. Just a monster needing to get dusted. Like *Buffy* or every other censored monster-fighting show ever."

It was the pain in her arm that helped her move again. She tore off some of the hem of her dress to wrap the cloth around her forearm and hopefully halt the bleeding that the bunny bite had caused. She really hoped it wouldn't get infected. After a few moments of rest, she pushed herself to keep moving through the forested mountain range again. She needed to find a town or something to help bandage her numerous wounds.

The Wayfarer had to take down a few more deranged rabbits and squirrels as she meandered without a destination. The area felt like a completely untouched wilderness, based on what she had seen in movies, with towering trees and high underbrush. The game trails were her only chance at making progress, and she was positive they weren't going in a straight or efficient route.

As she walked the trails, she tried out her new Aura effects and quickly discovered a problem with the two layers that seemed to conflict with each other. Her [**Embrace of Shadows**] would try to blur her form and worked better in darkness to make her even more difficult to detect, but her little [**Starlight Companion**] from her [**Guiding Stars**] Aura was a little ball of light directly countering the effects.

After a bit of trial and error, she realized that she actually had quite a bit of control over those particular effects, being able to turn either one on or off at will. Luckily, reconjuring the little companion seemed to cost a bit of mana only if it got destroyed, not if it was simply dismissed. This also made her relax about people not being able to see her constantly blurred-out form if she ever did manage to make it to a town.

She wished she had figured out how to dismiss her tiny night-light sooner, having been terrified of its light attracting more monsters in the dark. Now, she hoped that the next night wouldn't be as fear-inducing. She would just need to make sure the night-light was off and the cloak of shadows was on and then find a quiet little nook to hole up in again.

Phoenix continued to use her portal whenever she could as she traveled, marveling at the magic and hoping it would get her to civilization faster. She eventually got the brilliant idea of climbing a large tree that seemed to tower even more over the others to get a better view. She ended up cheating a bit by portaling up to one of the sturdier-looking branches before waiting for her cooldown on it to finish and then beginning to climb higher. A fall from this height would be a sure way to die, and she hoped the portal might be a life-saving solution to that.

It turned out to be a smart move as she slipped towards the top, unused to climbing, well, *anything* before. She got scraped up by a few branches before creating the portal midair and falling through it to stumble forward near the trunk, slightly disoriented by being placed vertically from the horizontal entry.

Phoenix tried twice more after brief rests while waiting during the respective cooldowns. Once she managed to reach the top, there was nothing but a sea of trees and mountains surrounding her. However, from the new vantage point, she was able to see the peak of the nearest mountain and attempt to portal herself to that next.

She was surprised when nothing happened and asked, "Why can't I portal over there?"

> **Note**: Portaling to an area requires an aural imprint of the area. Your Aura must have touched the area previously, and the destination must not have changed significantly enough to disturb the imprint.

"Well, that's inconvenient," she muttered before opening a portal back on the ground out as far as her Aura currently stretched to, then made her way towards the mountain peak she had originally been aiming for.

It kept getting colder the higher she portaled up the mountainside, and as she opened her final portal at its peak, the wind threatened to fling her from the ledge she walked out onto. The chill cut down to her bones as she shivered uncontrollably. Her torn-up dress had been better than nothing, but it wasn't exactly meant for the high altitude she now found herself at.

As she gazed across the mountains, she was disheartened to realize just how vast it was with the plethora of peaks and ocean of green trees she had no name for surrounding her in every direction. Despite the cold, she decided to huddle against the mountainside to watch the sun move, trying to at least determine a direction to head in. With noon now past, she decided to travel away from the sun, which she believed was the direction that wouldn't land her back at the point of arrival.

After a few more portals trailing a path across the mountain range, she decided to seek shelter for the encroaching night, but what she found instead was much worse. As she glanced into a cave, which she had portaled towards after spotting it from her last vantage point, she was met with a growl she recognized, followed by the set of teeth and shadowy black fur she expected to go with it.

Phoenix barely reacted in time as the Shanther pounced at her. She turned to flee, trying not to slip and tumble down the sloped mountainside while also trying not to get slowed by climbing up said slope. The large cat was much faster than her, but its powerful lunges made it harder for it to pivot as quickly as she was trying to dodge.

Her luck ran out extremely quickly when her frantic sprint across the mountain brought her to a sheer drop where it seemed like part of the mountain had broken away. She knew the fall would kill her, if not instantly, then by having so many broken bones that a monster would be sure to finish the job.

She glanced back as the Shanther seemed to understand her predicament as well, and it gave a low stuttering growl. If Phoenix hadn't known better, she would have sworn the creature was laughing at her.

The Wayfarer looked back at the drop and conjured her dagger to face the monster she actually had a slim chance of fighting. She just needed to last a few more minutes for her cooldown to be over, and she could portal away to safety.

The Shanther didn't give her that chance.

It hissed at the small dagger and seemed to turn into a dark mist that began to rush towards her, causing her to reflexively step back in a panic. Only there was no back to step onto. As her foot met only air, she tumbled backward and away from the rocky cliff.

Unable to reach out and grasp at the stone wall as she fell, Phoenix realized she had been wrong about the fall killing her. It was never the fall but the sudden and inevitable stop that did her in. There was only a moment of brief pain as her entire body crumpled against the stony mountainside, and she sensed nothing more.

Phoenix awoke to her glowing book floating in front of her face, and it took her a moment to focus on it enough to make out the script scrawled across it.

You have died.

All equipment has been returned to your collection.

[Waypoint] has guided your soul back to your designated location.

You have been reconstituted to a state of full integrity.

Twenty-four hours remain until this effect can be triggered again.

Her mind reeled.

I died? How am I alive? Where am I now?

It took her another few moments to realize she was lying down and naked again as she slowly sat up and looked around.

She was back at her initial arrival point, vaguely recognizing the intricate swirls etched into the ground around her, though they didn't seem to be smoldering anymore. Then her gaze landed on a man who was staring wide-eyed and open-mouthed at her.

Their eyes briefly met before his began to rove downward, taking in her nudity. She quickly reacted to cover herself with her limbs and thought about the green dress that she had been wearing when she died.

To her slight surprise and immense relief, it reappeared from her collection directly onto her body, and she was grateful for the ability to quickly change like that. She made a mental note to practice that more in the future.

The stranger had short, slightly wavy brown hair and piercing blue eyes that seemed to glow with a magical light. He quickly moved towards her once he got over his initial shock, and there were no longer any . . . *distractions* for him to ogle at.

Instead, he started to ask questions like she might vanish on him again. "You! Are you the Wayfarer? How did you get here? Where did you come from? What powers do you have? Can I get a sample? Were you always bald? Wait, no, I bet that happened in transit. What world do you come from?"

Phoenix felt her heart begin to pound wildly, and her mind spun at the flood of questions. She wasn't used to . . . people. Not like this and definitely not strangers whom she had never been introduced to first.

Introductions! Right. That was what normal people did first, right?

"I, um . . . I'm Phoenix," she managed to get out when the enthusiastic man took a breath between questions. Perhaps he could help give her some information, since she doubted that she could run away from someone more used to the activity than she was.

"You were a phoenix, or is that your name? You can speak our language. Translation ability? Most Wayfarers are reported to have one."

"Y-yes. A Talent translates," she managed to respond before adding, "and it's my name. Um, what's yours?"

The young man grinned at her and replied, "Call me Miles." He glanced over his shoulder with a thoughtful expression before turning back to her, "Now, Phoenix, if you would come with me, I can help you out. I'm sure you have almost as many questions as I do. I can take you to the nearest city, and we can talk while we walk. How does that sound?"

He held out a hand for her to take to help her stand, and she glanced from the hand to the direction he had looked toward. She could vaguely make out voices that seemed like a raucous group laughing and making their way closer.

Phoenix looked back at the hand and up into his slightly glowing blue eyes and asked, "What about your . . . others?"

Miles winced slightly and said, "I don't think they would appreciate your arrival as much as I would. Some of them are Hunters and Mercenaries that don't care about the real value you hold. They may not be as gentle and considerate of your ignorance as I am.

"If we go quickly, then it can be just the two of us having a nice informative stroll through the forest, yes? No interruptions or . . . well, I'm sure the other Magi will want to do a lot more tests that are invasive in nature," he added as an afterthought.

That helped make up her mind for her as she took the proffered hand and stood to be led in the opposite direction of the voices, away from her point of resurrection. She contemplated portaling away, but she wanted more answers. Not to mention, she was still feeling shaken from her death, which she was still trying to fully process. What good would portaling away do if she would just get eaten by monsters again? As much as she hated to admit it, she needed help—at least to get to a safer place.

"What's that?" Miles's voice came as he briefly halted after they entered the denser tree line. "One of your abilities?"

She glanced back to see what he was talking about and saw her book still trailing after her dutifully with the message still on display. Nodding, she hesitantly explained, "It's my [**Guide Book**]. It gives me information."

He leaned closer to read before she realized what he was doing. His eyes went wide in shock as they glanced from the words to her. "You *died*?! That's why you reappeared there so suddenly?"

Phoenix fidgeted uncomfortably under his gaze and simply nodded, which caused him to grab her hand and pull her along once more. Miles began muttering to himself, "I need to get you somewhere *much* safer and private. If anyone else finds out about you, they're sure to take you away. There's no way they'd let a Crystal like me hold onto you."

After a few more minutes of walking, the man slowed and glanced over his shoulder at her, "Alright, I think we won't be overheard at all if you want to start answering my questions."

She hesitated and asked, "Can we take turns?"

He grinned and nodded. "That sounds fair. Even your questions will be valuable information for me to record," he said, then pulled a notebook and quill pen out of a small satchel at his side.

"Is that a Bag of Holding?" she couldn't help asking as there was no way that size of book would have fit normally.

Miles quirked an eyebrow. "It is a bag that holds things, yes. My turn now. What world did you come from?"

She scrunched her face in annoyance. "Earth. A Bag of Holding is what we call a bag with a pocket dimension inside them so they can hold more things than would normally be possible," she replied and pointed at the satchel. "That was what my original question was."

"Ah, well, the answer is the same. It's a dimensional storage like you described. This one's not that impressive, though. Mainly just holds my books and notes."

She nodded and then asked, "What world is this?"

"Oh, this world is called Makera by the more . . . let's say cosmically inclined community. Now, what Natural Talents did you arrive with? Wayfarers are usually a bit of a random assortment with extremely overpowered Talents, but many themes recur within their species."

"Overpowered?" she reiterated curiously.

He shook a finger at her in a scolding manner. "Ah, ah. I asked a question first and expect an answer before I offer one to you."

Phoenix scrunched her nose again in frustration. Resigned to play his game in exchange for information and being led to safety, she pulled her book closer to her and willed the previous information to show itself. As she read off the information aloud, she included the one she had completely forgotten about earlier this time. Apparently, it was the only reason she was still standing here.

> **Natural Talent:** Waypoint
> When suffering lethal damage, instead of crossing the Veil, your soul will be transported to the last place you designated as your Waypoint. Your body will be reconstituted there, regaining a state of full integrity. This effect can only be triggered once every twenty-four hours.

"That's incredible," Miles muttered as he wrote down the information almost frantically. He then asked, "And how did you die just now?"

It was her turn to grin as she shook a finger in the same way he had, "Ah, ah, it's my turn to ask now."

A flash of anger seemed to contort the man's face and cause her to flinch back slightly, but it was gone the next moment when he shook his head. "Right, I forgot in my excitement. Go ahead."

"I, um—" She hesitated, then pulled her glowing book close to her chest as though it might act as a shield and probed cautiously, "Where are you taking me?"

He seemed to blank for a moment before giving a cheerful smile and answered, "My home in Blomstra. Where you'll be safe and protected from those who might try to steal you."

Suddenly, Phoenix realized that there were other things now that she feared more than death as the young Mage took her hand and led her deeper into the forest.

CHAPTER SIX

Not a Safe Place

So, you're an orphan?" Miles asked as Phoenix tried to explain the hospital she had come from and her world's supposed lack of magic. "Nobody left behind?" he clarified.

They had been walking for almost an hour by now, trading questions. Miles had been mostly courteous unless she forgot to let him take his turn, and he struck her as the type who was a stickler for the rules. She hadn't gotten nearly enough information, though, mainly confirming the things she already knew now.

"Um . . . yes, I'm orphaned now, I guess. The older you are, the less you're thought of as an orphan where I come from, so I never really thought of myself that way," she admitted before solemnly adding, "but I don't have anyone left that cares about me."

The lanky man stopped walking to look at her and gave her a gentle smile. "Well, you have someone that cares now."

She flushed in embarrassment at the words and asked, "So, do you have any family?"

He gave a half-hearted laugh. "Yes. Too much, honestly. I practically ran away to the Order of Magic and buried myself in research mainly to escape my horde of siblings and make a name for myself."

Miles began walking once more as he continued to lead her through the densely packed woods with more confidence in their direction than she felt. After another minute, the Mage asked, "You said you were considered older in your world. How old *are* you? You seem rather young."

"I turned eighteen when I arrived yesterday," she responded, slightly surprised to realize that she had celebrated her birthday by wandering through the forest fighting off tiny monsters.

He glanced back at her with a slight frown. "You *are* young. Most cultures on Makera don't consider you a full adult until thirty."

"Why is that? How old do most people here live to be?" she asked as she raised an arm to shield her eyes from the bright sun that broke through the trees periodically. To her, thirty seemed incredibly old to be considered an adult.

"That varies wildly, but at thirty, you're no longer barred from certain positions of authority within most societies. However, your Caste usually plays a bigger role in that factor," Miles answered as he grabbed her hand again to help her over a tree that had fallen in the path. "Did you have caste systems in your world?"

She nodded, then remembered her book mentioning that Casters were people who had become Crystal Caste and clarified, "We had social hierarchies that placed people in certain classes. We had things like nobility, which was another type of caste system."

"We have those here, too. Monarchs, nobles, and aristocrats can be found in many of our nations. If you're part of one of the various international organizations, you can raise your social status a bit through those inner ranks, like the Order of Magic, whose members are referred to as Magi—which I am one of. Then there's the Alliance of Adventurers, who are little more than thick-skulled mercenaries, though technically separate from the Mercenary Guilds. The Society of Symphonies, Alchemy Association, or the Federation of National Unity. Or even if you join one of the many clergies of the gods."

"The nation I came from didn't have a monarch, though its social class was basically determined by how much wealth you had," she managed to say before stumbling slightly on the uneven ground. As Miles helped right her, she added, "Being a very sick and bedridden orphan with no job put me at the very bottom, naturally. Can we rest here?" She gestured to another fallen tree by the trail.

The Magi glanced back in the direction they had come from with a pensive expression before nodding. He helped her sit and took the spot beside her as she asked, "You don't happen to have any food or water, do you?"

With a shake of his head, Miles frowned and said, "That was two questions, but no. I don't need to eat or drink as a Crystal Caster. The ambient magic of this area is enough to sustain me."

Phoenix scrunched her face in confusion. "How does that work?"

He laughed and shook his head. "That's three. Before I answer, can you answer some of mine?"

She nodded, and he asked, "Was it your looting power or your book that gave you your Aspects?"

"My book," she answered and then rubbed at her stomach as it gave an angry growl. "I can loot them?"

The Mage shot her a glare that she almost missed and reluctantly answered, "Possibly. What Aspects did you get? I can sense you have two or three of them, but I can't tell what they are. There's also some weird effect I don't recognize going on with your Aura. Do you know what that might be?"

"I have the Star and Dark Aspects. I'm not sure what you mean about the Aura, though. I only got mine yesterday with those passive abilities."

"Wait, plural?" He quickly went back a few pages in his notebook and muttered to himself, "Oh, right. This [**Beacon of Hope**] Talent lets you unlock more than one Aura. I didn't realize you would get multiple so soon, though." He glanced up at her with a grin. "That's fantastic. Breaking system limitations like that is extremely rare. That means you're an Aurabreaker, which is what we call your type of Limit Breaker. You're even more unique than I could have ever dreamed of."

Phoenix flushed again at the awkward compliment, not feeling comfortable with his focus fully intent on her the way it was. "Um . . . thanks? I guess . . ."

"It's lucky that you already managed to get two Aspects in just a couple of days," he said as he scribbled in his notebook once more. "They are very valuable, especially ones like Star that are harder to find. Many Mundane families will save up their Bits for years just to be able to afford a single one."

He glanced back down the path, then up to the sky, and stood again. Brushing off the embroidered tunic he wore over his traveling pants, he held out a hand for her to take again as he said, "We should keep moving. As you're well aware by now, it's not safe at night when Visku is shining."

"Visku?" she reiterated as she took the proffered hand and tried to ignore her rumbling stomach. While she was used to pain, she was not used to being so hungry like this.

"That's the blue moon that rises at night. It's extremely magical and causes an increase in magical spawn points that occur as it circles the planet. Now—" He flipped back to the next blank page in his notebook as he asked, "What are your two passives?"

Phoenix regurgitated the information for him to note down, then went back to her question, "How can Casters survive without food or drink?"

The Mage gave a reluctant nod as he explained. "Ah, well, that's a bit of a complex answer, but the simplified version is that as you increase your Caste and refine the magic within you. That magic replaces most of your bodily functions, like needing lungs, bowels, or a stomach, and starts running off mana for fuel instead of food or air. The process occurs over multiple Castes, with the digestive system being gone at Crystal, then the lungs at Sapphire, and so on.

"This whole mountain range is considered a Low-Rate Mid Sapphire Caste area, meaning that it doesn't spawn monsters often, but when it does, they have the potential to be near the middle of the Sapphire Caste or lower, which is one step up from Crystal.

"Because it's a higher Caste area than I am, the ambient magic is enough to sustain me without food. Otherwise, I would have needed another source like mana-dense food or Crystal Mana Bits."

"Wait, you eat the Bits?"

"Or trade them. They make for a nice universal currency since they're used for so much," Miles explained as he pulled a milky white stone from his pouch to hold it up for her to see. "If you have a looting power and managed to kill some of the Mundane monsters roaming around here, you should have seen some of these by now."

"I wasn't sure what they were for," she murmured as she held out a murky gray version from her own collection to compare. "What's the difference?"

He gave a slightly pained smile and pointed at the book that she had kept holding onto. "That thing gives you information, right? Does it do items?"

"Um, yes." She held out the book in front of her, opening it to a blank page, and stopped trying to walk like that after tripping again a moment later.

Miles paused with her and set the small stone he had on top of the page, causing the information to appear reactively.

Item: Crystal Mana Bit
Condensed mana of Crystal Caste potency.
Caste: Crystal.
Availability: Common.
Type: Consumable, ingredient.
Effects:
• Can be used as an ingredient for certain rituals and enchantments.
• Can be used as a mana source for certain magical items and enchantments.
• Can be consumed to replenish your natural reserves and sustain yourself.
Warning: *Consuming a Mana Bit above your Caste will cause mana poisoning.*

"Oh nice, it comes with a little warning label," Phoenix said aloud.

Miles gave her an odd look before saying, "Yes, well, that's why I can't feed you. Eating a Mana Bit when you're a Mundane can potentially kill you."

"A Mundane?" Phoenix asked as she handed back the small stone and closed her book once more.

The Magi gave a sigh and turned to start walking again as he answered, "Yes. You're not a Caster, therefore a Mundane. Some might consider you a Half-Caster because you do have some extra magic with those Aspects you have, but you're not considered a true Caster until you have the full set and gain your Class."

Miles glanced over his shoulder as he added with a slight smirk, "Until you become a *real* Caster, you have to accept your place as a Mundane. Shouldn't be much different from your position in your old world."

Phoenix felt a shiver run through her at the thought of being as powerless here as she had been there. Something about the way he had phrased his statement, though, rubbed her the wrong way, and she asked, "So if I get two more Aspects and become a Caster, then I'll move up the Caste ladder?"

"Naturally, but for right now, you're a Mundane, and I'm a Crystal Caster. People will take my word and authority over yours." He gave her a cautious look as he bent down to pass under a low-hanging branch.

His tone became more serious as he seemed to warn her, "Remember, Wayfarer. The Rule of Caste means everything here on Makera. Most people are Mundanes, and they have their own separate structures, as you mentioned. Nobles, wealth, divinity, or what have you, but *Caste*; that is what rules."

"How many Castes are there?" she asked nervously, wondering just how low her current placement was. As she passed under the branch, she suddenly found herself between it and the much taller man who felt way too close to her now.

Miles frowned again and said with a hint of annoyance, "You keep skipping my turn. It's becoming quite frustrating, you know. Here. Let me make this really clear." Then he surprised her by beginning to draw in the air off to her left with what seemed like light from his fingertip.

He drew a white line and said, "This is Crystal." Then above that, he drew a pale blue line. "This is Sapphire. Next is Emerald." He added a bright green line above that followed by a dark red line. "And this is Ruby. With how rare they are, the last is basically a legend, but there are some well-known Obsidian Casters." Then he drew a black line at the very top with more space between it and the other lines.

"The darker, the stronger," he added as an afterthought, then moved back to the bottom and drew a barely visible gray line far below the white one. "You, however, are still here. A Mundane with only enough mana to offer a few Talents and the capability to tap into other forms of magic."

She frowned at the representation, but what he had said made her curiously ask, "Other forms of magic? Like what?"

His annoyance became much clearer on his face. "Were you not paying attention? *You* are here," he said and pointed at the gray line, then back at the white one. "I am here. We're done playing this game if you're not going to follow the rules. Now that you understand the Rule of Caste, you should understand your place in this world, which is to listen to me."

Phoenix returned his glare. She wasn't about to let some random stranger try to take this new life and freedom she had just acquired away from her, and she retorted, "I'm sorry that I have a lot of questions, but everything around me is strange and new. I didn't mean to skip your turn, but you don't have to try to bully me into doing what you want."

"I'm not *trying* to bully you," he replied with a smirk, "I'm *telling* you that it's a new fact of life you find yourself in now. You. Are. A. Mundane. Until you become more powerful than me, you answer to me. Now quit stopping and start walking while you answer more of my questions."

She almost growled at the command as her anger started to get the better of her. "I don't need to answer to you. I'll just go find my own way."

As Phoenix turned to try and go back under the branch that she had her back pressed against, she felt a hand grip the back of her neck while another arm wrapped around her waist to keep her from moving.

Phoenix tried to struggle against the hold, but it was utterly pointless against the Caster. She realized that despite his bookish looks and lanky frame, he was much, *much* stronger than she was.

Miles practically tossed her over his shoulder as he said with a chuckle, "Now, now, my little Wayfarer. There's no need for any of that. This is not a safe place for you, but you'll be more secure once we get to my home. I have plenty to eat and drink. Along with some potions that will make you nice and *compliant*. No more games, just solid data for me to increase my standing in the OOM."

Oh, screw this guy.

CHAPTER SEVEN

Escape the Monsters

What Miles described sounded too much like becoming a drugged-up lab rat for Phoenix to accept. So, she conjured her magical black dagger into her hand and plunged it into the man's back, hoping to make him release her. He did so with a cry of pain followed by a stream of obscenities that she had never heard before and didn't stop to listen to. Instead of taking the path back to the other mages, she dove into the forest brush, hoping to lose the would-be kidnapper in the greenery.

He wasn't just stronger than her, though; he was faster, too. She soon found herself slammed against a tree, gasping for air as Miles held her by the throat and glared at her. "Apparently, my lesson in the rules was not thorough enough, and you need a more hands-on demonstration," he growled, pulling her towards him slightly before slamming her back into the tree. The action caused her to cry out from the pain that permeated down her spine, and she worried he might break her literally.

"I'm not about to let a Wayfarer just walk away from me, especially one that's an Aurabreaker and can resurrect. You are a *priceless* treasure, and one that now belongs to me. Do you understand, Miss Mundane?"

Phoenix felt tears prick the corner of her eyes from both the pain and the absolute unfairness of the situation, but she refused to let this man see her cry. Instead, she tried to stab him again, but he easily caught her wrist.

Miles gave a heavy sigh. "This would be easier if you just accepted your place and listened to me. Now I have to *make* you comply, which is just more annoying since you can't answer my questions with a broken jaw." He got a thoughtful look on his face and said to himself, "Maybe if I just remove your eyes. I don't think you'll need those while we travel and talk, and I can heal them when we get to my home. Yes, that should probably work—"

His words were cut off as a terrifying flurry of quills, claws, and teeth slammed into the Mage from the side, forcing him to release her as he was savaged by what looked to Phoenix like a velociraptor with bristling porcupine quills.

As Miles's screams filled the air, she felt a wave of power cover the area, then turned and ran as fast as she could. She never stopped to look back, keeping her little light dismissed and letting the shadows wrap around her, which hopefully gave her a chance to survive her frantic escape.

Phoenix almost screamed in fright as her book appeared in front of her once more to give her more information.

> **New Quest:** Escape the Monsters
> *You are not strong enough for this area. Retreat to a lower Caste biome.*
> **Objective:** Leave the forest without getting captured.
> **Reward:** Common shoes.

She almost screamed again, but in frustration this time.

No kidding! What do you think I'm trying to do?!

She suddenly realized that, in her panic, she had completely forgotten that she had magic powers now.

Focusing on the mental image of the large tree she had climbed earlier that day before dying, she opened her portal and ran through it. She slumped against the tree in her newfound safety as she dismissed the portal behind her in the hopes that Miles wouldn't be able to follow her.

It was becoming darker now, and she hated the idea of being caught without shelter as the mountains became infested with monsters once more. After a few more minutes of catching her breath, calming her terror, and letting her cooldown elapse, Phoenix portaled back to the top of the large, towering tree to watch the moon that Miles had mentioned rise.

She was surprised by the appearance of a second moon rising alongside the giant blue orb. The twin was an orangey-yellow color that reminded her of a harvest moon back on Earth, but both of them were only about a quarter full. The sounds of growls and howls began to fill the forest surrounding her. She shuddered at her growing fear of the night despite her ability to blend into it.

In desperation, she tried to use the sleeves of her dress to tie herself to the large tree branch so she wouldn't fall. She hoped that none of the monsters that could climb or fly would find her as she fell into fitful sleep. She never wanted to meet another person like Miles again, and that fear was reflected in her brief snippets of dreams.

Thankfully, she didn't die again, which would have been much more permanent. She also remembered to set her **[Waypoint]** to this new location; the only confirmation she had of it being set was a glowing rune-like symbol that appeared in the air before vanishing a moment later. She hoped that doing this meant she wouldn't have another accidental run-in with the crazy mages who thought they could just take people that were lower Caste than they were.

Phoenix hoped that the Magi were not representative of the whole of Makera, and she wouldn't find people trying to constantly kidnap her. Based on what Miles had told her, however, it seemed like her powers and very existence were rare and, therefore, desirable to people like him. It meant she needed to be much more careful about who she revealed those secrets to. Apparently, a nice smile was not enough to judge a person on.

She continued making her way east with her portal. Trying to put as much distance as she could between her prospective captors and herself. At night, she would try to find the tallest tree she could to perch in. If she came across another monster that her Aura sensed as stronger than her, she portaled back to the last tree of safety before going a slightly different route.

After the third day, she finally found a stream of fresh water and was grateful that she wouldn't have to respawn because of dehydration. Starvation wasn't off the table, though, as she tried to search for something edible that didn't require her abysmal attempts at cooking. Despite *almost* dying to a pile of what she thought had been blueberries, she managed to get by on some more half-raw, half-burnt monster meat.

She tried to follow the river as much as possible since she remembered towns liked to pop up near them. That path was made difficult by the wild animals that would visit it for the same reason she needed it. Apparently, it wasn't *just* monsters roaming this forest, and she wondered how any animals managed to survive the nights.

After having to relieve herself multiple times on her journey, she was looking forward to getting more quests that would give her an Aspect. Miles had said becoming a Caster would get rid of her digestive system, and she was looking forward to not needing to struggle with bathroom habits that she was never very good at to begin with.

This became even more pertinent when a rabid raccoon-like creature tried to take a bite out of her when she was taking a squat near some bushes. After that little humiliating brawl, she didn't concern herself with modesty in the middle of the woods and made sure she could watch out for anything that might try to sneak up on her.

Every night, she tied herself to a branch and prayed to the stars that she wouldn't get eaten. Every day, she kept walking, searching for an escape from the seemingly endless sea of trees that were both beautiful and terrifying.

On the fifth day, Phoenix ran into the wonder of the river becoming a waterfall and disappearing off the edge of a cliff to land in a pool dozens of yards below her. She had only seen them in pictures and movies before, and none of them did justice.

It wasn't just the sight that was breathtaking as light danced off the splashing water and a rainbow formed in front of her. Not to mention the wonder of the glittering rainbow fish that were literally flying up the waterfall in a mesmerizing dance that reminded her that this world was magic.

It was her other senses going into overdrive as well that truly made her feel alive. The fresh scent of the cleansed air. The sound of crashing waves hitting stone and pool far below. The feel of the spray on her cheeks and dampening her hair. The paradoxical feeling of the wet air being both light with its refreshment and heavy with splashing water dispersing into it.

The promises of wonder and opportunity filled her with a sense of renewed hope as she finished resting and basking in the beauty before portaling to a spot much further down the roaring river. Unfortunately, a hulking, leafy bear-like creature was meandering nearby and thought she might make a tasty meal, causing her to flee once more.

She had always dreamed of being healthy enough to run, but this wasn't exactly what she had been hoping for as her bare feet slipped on the wet river stones near the edge of the water and ended up drenched before managing to portal away in time to avoid becoming lunch.

The haphazard fall into the portal, however, resulted in a twisted ankle and many tears of pain and frustration. She ripped a strip of fabric from her dress and soaked it in the cold river water before wrapping her throbbing ankle in it and forcing herself to keep moving.

Phoenix gave a sob of relief on the eighth day in this new world when she finally escaped the forested mountain range and found it had given way to a vast meadow-covered hill land.

Quest: Escape the Monsters
Objective Complete: Left the forest without getting captured.
Objective Reward:
[Simple Shoes] have been added to your collection.

Completion Reward:
10 [Mana Bits] have been added to your collection.

She needed to find civilization, but there wasn't a town in sight. Phoenix wasn't sure of finding edibles among the hills since she had no idea what kind of food aside from grass and flowers grew in this kind of biome. She was famished, and her clothes were dirty tatters after trudging through the dense brush and rocky mountainsides. The shoes would hopefully help protect her bruised and battered feet, and she carefully placed what basically amounted to leather wrappings over the swollen and bleeding appendages.

As she carefully made her way across the first few hills, movement caught her eye, and she glanced over to see a small pack of creatures daintily grazing in the meadow.

They were odd ostrich-like creatures but with longer grassy fur that made them blend in fairly well and flat cobra-like heads. She had never seen anything like them before and briefly wondered if they were carnivorous like the evil furballs in the woods she had just escaped.

Phoenix crouched down slowly, trying to get closer without them noticing her. She was so hungry that she knew she had to at least try to take down one of them. The fact that they were grazing made her pretty confident that they were herbivores and would hopefully try to flee instead of trampling or biting her to death.

The Wayfarer conjured her dagger and moved closer. She focused on being careful and would freeze in order to let her Aura blend her into the shadows if it seemed like they might turn towards her. She knew that if she couldn't get the jump on them, there was no way she'd be able to give chase with her torn-up feet screaming with every tiny step she took.

As she inched ever closer, her hope kept growing, as the animals seemed completely unaware of her presence. Then, with a final burst of speed and adrenaline, she lunged at the closest animal, aiming her dagger at one of the thin throats and praying they had a jugular vein there.

She missed. *Of course.*

The creatures were much faster than she had hoped, and they fled, which she had expected. Desperate, she stumbled after them, but as she crested the next hill, she realized that even if her feet weren't wrecked, it would be futile to run after the swift beasts. She gave a loud groan of frustration before a beam of light lanced across the sky and through one of the creatures, downing it in an instant.

Phoenix knew that it had to be magic, and she quickly dropped to the ground, dismissed her dagger, and tried to back away down the hill. She attempted to move slowly and quietly, afraid that whoever or whatever had instantly decimated that fast animal hadn't noticed her presence.

She was disappointed a moment later when shiny gold-plated boots appeared in front of her. Phoenix looked up into the stern face of a blonde bearded man in full plate armor who gleamed as golden and bright as the sun. His eyes were also golden, and in the middle of his forehead was a small gold plate in a roughly diamond shape but with some curves that she didn't recognize as signifying anything.

He raised an eyebrow at her as she just continued to stare at him until she cautiously said, "Uh . . . hello?"

The man didn't return her greeting as his gruff voice asked in the same language that the Magi had, with her Talent translating for her, "Wayfarer?"

CHAPTER EIGHT

Paladin of the Purifier

Phoenix stared at the man for a few awkward moments as she tried to come up with a suitable response that wouldn't result in her getting captured or killed . . . *again*. The golden man didn't interrupt her thoughts as he simply crossed his arms and continued to stare down at her unperturbed.

She slowly stood up and tried to make herself look slightly more presentable before admitting, "I, uh . . . got lost in the woods?"

He didn't so much as move a muscle as he continued to watch and wait for her to continue. The armored man was intimidating for sure; her head only came up to his sternum, and he was as shiny as a holy knight of light. He didn't seem to be carrying a weapon, but much like herself, she thought he could probably conjure one in a moment or just blast her to bits with that massive light beam of instant death.

The stranger didn't seem to be hostile, though. The fact that he had talked to her instead of just annihilating her like the ostrich-cobra-monster meant that he wasn't inclined to harm her . . . probably . . . right?

After a few more moments of awkward silence, she offered a bit more information since he obviously already knew she was a Wayfarer. "I only arrived in this world a few days ago . . . and have been wandering through the forest since then . . . I, uh . . . C-could you maybe point me towards a town?"

His gold eyes roamed her up and down, taking her in as though assessing her, *judging* her. She realized that his appearance was immaculate, with a neatly trimmed beard that matched his blonde, swept-back hair and not a speck of dirt on his warm tan skin or polished armor, which she noticed had white as well as gold coloring. She, on the other hand, was mostly dirt with some bits of fabric covering her stained and blood-smeared skin.

The golden knight seemed to be contemplating something, but Phoenix found herself interrupting his thoughts with another question triggered by her own curiosity. "How did you know I was a Wayfarer?"

"Your Aura," he replied simply.

Phoenix hadn't realized Auras would indicate someone's species, but she supposed that made sense. She wondered what else he could make out about her from just her Aura, since she could feel so much more power coming off him than the Crystal Caster who she had escaped from almost a week ago.

Despite the vast power difference that she could feel between them, her desire for additional information pushed her to ask more. Perhaps she could figure out what his Caste actually was and just how hopeless her situation might be. Trying to stay as small as possible in case he desired to kidnap her too, she meekly inquired, "What else does my Aura tell you?"

He locked his golden eyes on her pale green ones as he seemed to carefully measure his words, "It's like a moonless night."

She frowned slightly. "Like, it's hard to see?"

The large man shook his head slightly and said with almost a tinge of sadness, "You've started down a dark path, young one."

"Oh," she said, a bit taken aback by both his words and demeanor. She hadn't really thought about the potential consequences of taking in the Aspects that she had gotten. Now, the Wayfarer was unsure if she had made the right choice, but she was fairly certain that she would have died even more if she hadn't and would most likely still be in the clutches of that overbearing and single-minded researcher.

He closed his eyes for a moment, then nodded once to himself before commanding, "Follow," as he started to walk off.

She hesitated and steeled her nerves to ask before going with the stoic stranger. "Follow where?"

"To clean," his gruff voice replied without him bothering to look back. She knew that he could sense if she tried to run or not, just like Miles had. Getting clean didn't sound so bad, though, and if she was lucky, maybe he knew where food was or could share the meat from the monster that he had killed with whatever Spell that had been.

With a sigh, she obediently followed behind the man that she knew could easily force her to comply. She'd rather avoid that since she didn't want to get hurt again, and maybe she'd get a chance to escape via portal later if she needed to. Phoenix hoped not everyone in this world was as terrible as the man she had already escaped from, but she wasn't going to bet on it.

After the newest stranger retrieved the monster that he had killed, and about ten minutes of walking with her wounded feet slowing her down quite a bit, they finally reached a small campsite near the river that Phoenix had been following downstream.

"Sit," the rough voice said, and he pointed towards a large log of bleached driftwood next to the fire pit before he disappeared into the single tent. She carefully sat on the log and waited patiently.

The warrior returned a moment later with a satchel that he stuck his hand into. Then, he pulled out two glass bottles, one filled with a glowing red liquid, and handed it to her with an order: "Drink."

"What is it?" she hesitantly asked as she narrowed her eyes at the overtly magical liquid that could easily be some sort of evil poison.

"Healing potion."

She wanted to argue that she wasn't injured but saw his gaze looking at the many cuts and gashes on her legs and down to her swollen ankle that had only gotten worse over the last few days of forcing herself to walk on it. With a tentative drink of the sweet liquid, the feeling of healing power went to work on her numerous lacerations, filling her with a weird tingling sensation.

The other vial the man had retrieved was filled with a sparkling, golden concoction that looked like liquified glitter. "Stay still," he commanded once more and unstoppered the bottle.

Before she could ask why, he tipped the bottle's contents over her head to spill onto her. Phoenix then experienced the oddest sensation of her admittedly short and sheltered life.

The liquid flowed not just down but all across her body, as if the magical glitter had a goal of its own, and that goal was to remove every ounce of grime and filth from her skin and clothes. It couldn't mend the tears in her outfit, but when it was done, she was in the cleanest state she could ever remember being in.

"What was that?" she couldn't help but ask in awe.

"Golden Shower," came the blunt answer as he returned the now empty bottles into his bag.

"What? Ew," she responded at the reminder of the first and only sexual slang she had ever looked up at her friend's prompting, refusing to ever look up another one after that. "Why is it called that?"

"The Purifier likes gold," the stranger said with a shrug, as though that explained everything, then pulled out a slightly smaller bag from his satchel, which made her realize that the main one had to be a dimensional space, like the bag Miles had, to fit both it and the potions in. He handed it to her with another command: "Eat."

Phoenix cautiously took the smaller bag and glanced into it. At the sight of the dried meat strips, she forgot all her reservations and hungrily shoved a strip into her mouth, chewing on the flavorful snack. He then handed her a fruit that she didn't recognize but looked like a mix between a cherry and a plum. She gratefully took it and bit into it, moaning a bit at the sweet tartness. She devoured it in an instant and looked up at her savior with her best puppy eyes.

The Wayfarer thought she saw the barest twitch at the corners of the golden warrior's mouth, but he shook his head and said, "Pace yourself."

She nodded, knowing he was right. It was the same advice the doctors would give to someone recovering after not being able to eat much properly. He handed her a metal canteen and ordered, "Slowly."

Phoenix nodded again, taking the item and drinking the clean water inside it. He sat down across from her then, carefully watching as she quietly ate, drank, and recovered. She, in turn, observed him observing her.

He seemed like he was a human in his mid-thirties, but she didn't know if that was accurate at all. Technically, she wasn't even human anymore, so maybe he was something else as well? Maybe that would explain the odd metal plate embedded on his forehead.

She had many questions for the stranger but decided to start with proper introductions. After all, he had healed, cleaned, and fed her. Phoenix put on her best manners and said politely, "My name's Phoenix Fraser. What may I call you?"

His eyes always felt like they were looking *into* her instead of at her . . . as if they could see straight into her soul whenever her gaze met his. She gave an involuntary shiver as she felt odd pressure against her Aura and a feeling of incredible scrutiny at that moment when he said, "Paul Wayland."

Phoenix hoped that he would give a little more information, but she seemed to catch on that the man was more of the observing type, giving as little information as possible while taking in as much as he could. "And . . . What are you doing all the way out here?"

He gave a slight frown, and she hastily added, "If it's not too, um, forward of me to ask. I, uh . . . I'm not sure where we are exactly. I've been wandering the forest for the past week. Are we near a town?"

Paul gave a nod of understanding and said, as though regretting having to use so many words, "We are in wild lands. The nearest major city is Blomstra, but we're both heading in the opposite direction, and I don't plan to visit. I'm here on a mission."

"Mission?"

"I'm a member of the Alliance of Adventurers . . . technically."

"Technically?" He simply nodded but didn't elaborate further until she asked, "Are you like a part-timer? Or some kind of contractor that only does odd jobs?"

"Clergy members usually take fewer missions due to their split duties," he begrudgingly explained.

"You're a priest?" she asked. He looked nothing like the clergy in her previous world.

"I'm a former Paladin of the Purifier," he muttered, shifting slightly in his seat.

"Former?" she asked in confusion before taking another bite of jerky.

He stared up at her coldly and said in a voice equally icy, "Yes."

She finally got the hint that it was a touchy topic and asked instead, "What exactly is the Alliance of Adventurers?"

Paul took a moment before saying succinctly, "The AOA is an organization dedicated to defending the innocent from monsters and providing contracted services."

"I see," she said lamely but was pleased by the description. The fact that Miles had spoken disparagingly of the group actually made her more inclined to hope they were the "good guys" in this world since the Magi had obviously not been.

Then he asked her his first question. "You have Aspects. Are those two Aura powers I sense?" She simply nodded in response, and he followed up with, "What abilities?"

She hesitated a moment and then recognized that he noticed her hesitation as his eyes narrowed at her. He gave her a single warning that made her shudder at whatever retribution might await her should she disobey, "Don't lie. I'll know. Your Aura reads like an open book."

Phoenix was beginning to hate not having any way to hide her Aura from the obviously powerful Caster or have any kind of poker face as she muttered, "I have a portal and a dagger."

He tilted his head again in understanding. The odd feeling of scrutiny returned in full force as it felt like her Aura was forcibly pushed back into herself. It felt like it was being held in a vice grip as he pointedly asked, "What do you plan to do in this world?"

Phoenix shivered again, unsure of what the man kept doing to her, as she answered, "I, uh . . . I'm not sure? I've just been trying to survive. I don't really have a specific goal or purpose now that I'm here. I didn't leave anything behind, and there wasn't anyone who needed me. I, um . . . I wasn't really that useful back there . . ." She trailed off, realizing the truth of her words. She could feel that ugly bitterness begin to return, clawing at her heart, as the memories reminded her that she was still just as helpless.

In the face of her newest enemies, she had been completely useless.

"Portals are useful," he stated matter-of-factly, which caught her off guard. Was he trying to comfort her?

She shrugged. "Sure, but I just got that a few days ago when I arrived here. My world didn't have any magic . . . at least not that I knew of," she explained, then hesitated, not really wanting to bring up her tragic past or the confusion of whatever magic had brought her here. "Bad things always happened back on my world. Like, really bad things. Most of the people I knew died, and I . . ." Her voice broke a bit as she admitted, "I couldn't do anything to save them. I was always useless. Barely able to walk, let alone try to heal or protect anyone else."

The mental wounds of losing her mother, friends, and home were threatening to reopen, but she was saved from slipping further when Paul reworded his question. "Do you plan to become more useful?"

She met his gaze once more and thought about the things that had happened since arriving here. Phoenix felt like she had limitless potential at times despite having been attacked constantly. She had survived, *technically*, and gained magic powers. She could revive and get stronger now. As he pointed out, she had the capability to become more useful.

Phoenix nodded with slightly renewed resolve. "I have powers now that give me a way forward. I'm hoping to gain the strength that I couldn't before so that next time, I *will* be able to save people."

They stared at each other in silence again for a few moments before the feeling of scrutiny and pressure on her Aura subsided, and Paul nodded to her. "Very well. You'll join me."

It wasn't a request. Like most of the things he said to her. She wasn't sure if he intended to be controlling, if he just wasn't a very good people person, or if maybe it was just something he was used to doing as someone with his power level.

She wondered what his position was in the Alliance of Adventurers he had mentioned. Maybe it was just his job to give orders and expect compliance. No matter the reason, though, it rubbed her the wrong way this time.

Her mind flashed to what Miles had intended for her, and this guy felt so much stronger. However, she hadn't fled through a wild mountain range and fought off a plethora of deranged rabbits and a potential slaver just so that she could let someone else decide things for her.

"What if . . ." she started, then had to swallow down her anxiety once more as she clutched the tattered fabric of her dress. She stared down at her lap as she asked quietly, "What if I don't want to join you?"

Silence hung between them for a long moment before she dared to glance up at him. He looked . . . *amused?*

Phoenix felt confused and began to feel her panic start to rise again as she continued in a rush, "I—I know you're more powerful than me. I can tell you're at least two or maybe three Castes above me, but—" She clenched her fists as she proclaimed, "But I *won't* be taken prisoner."

After another heavy moment, he let out a low chuckle. "I'm not planning to imprison you, young one. I'm planning to protect you, at least until I can drop you off at the AOA and let them deal with you."

"Oh," she said, slightly embarrassed, but he was so hard for her to read.

"Where did you get your Aspects?" he asked suddenly.

"Huh? Oh." She scrunched her face in thought as she said a bit of a half-truth, "I, uh, found the first one in the forest after fighting a monster on my first day here, then the second one the next morning."

"A looting Talent?"

She hadn't meant to imply that but nodded quietly, knowing that she couldn't deny it either. Realizing that it might have been an unusual power from the thoughtful look he gave her, she asked, "Is that uncommon?"

"Not for Wayfarers," he said, leaving the insinuation that it was uncommon for everyone else.

Paul stood. "You were right. I am an Emerald Caster," he said, and then he began deconstructing his campsite.

Phoenix shivered at the knowledge that he was *three* tiers above her in the Caste hierarchy and wondered if he thought that he could do whatever he wanted to her, just like Miles had believed was only natural.

After swallowing the wave of fear, she offered to help, but he waved her off, telling her to just eat. As she sat there, watching him work and chewing slowly on the last of the jerky, a thought crossed her mind, and she asked, "Why do you even carry food rations and water if you're Emerald Caste? I, um ... I was informed that once you become a Caster, you don't need food, water, or, um, toilets. That mana sources sustain you instead."

He didn't look away from his work, and he replied as though it was obvious, "Most of the people I save are not Casters."

Considering the situation she was currently in, she fully believed him. That alone went a long way in convincing her to trust him and his intentions, at least a tiny bit. Another question pressed at her to give it voice. "What kind of mission brings you out here in the middle of nowhere? Are you hunting a monster? That's what you said Adventurers do, right?"

Paul still didn't look at her or even respond until he finished packing and hoisted a large backpack over his shoulder before turning to face her. "Yes, they are monsters. Located near, or inside, a nearby Reality Rift. My mission is to wipe them out."

The golden Paladin looked her over once more in that appraising way, then his entire demeanor softened slightly, and he asked, "Will you join me?"

Phoenix was surprised that he had actually asked her this time, and then they were both surprised by her glowing **[Guide Book]** shimmering into existence for her to read.

New Quest: Mysterious Stranger
A mysterious man has helped you and offered for you to join him on his quest.
Objective: Follow Paul Wayland to the Reality Rift.
Reward: Common tool.

As the Adventurer looked between her and the overtly magical book, she sighed, realizing that there was no possible way she could keep this ability a secret with it popping out whenever it felt like. She grabbed the book from the air and turned it to face him so that he could also read the message.

After a moment of processing the words, and poking around her Aura a bit more, he displayed his intelligence as he asked, "The Aspects in the forest?"

She nodded. "Both were quest rewards."

"Lucrative," he observed simply. "So, you are joining?"

She looked from him to the book then nodded her consent. Then, before she could even process what happened, she was being carried in his arms in what she knew as the "traditional damsel" style. The only words she could get out were, "Um . . . What?"

"You're slow," was the single explanation he gave before taking off in a run that felt more like she was suddenly on the highway in a convertible with the top down . . . At least, she assumed that's what it would feel like, given the insane speed they were moving at.

CHAPTER NINE

Ends Without Redemption

Despite their absurd pace across the grassy hillocks, they eventually paused to eat after a solid three hours of . . . *jogging*? Was he seriously only jogging that whole time? He didn't even appear to be sweating, only pausing because he knew that she needed to eat and drink more. For his part, Paul simply slipped what looked like a glassy, green, mostly flattened marble in his mouth with a slight grimace, and she assumed it was an Emerald Mana Bit.

He didn't make camp; instead, he just set her against one of the few trees in the biome and handed her the metal canteen once more and another bag of food. This time, it was some bread and cheese that she had never tasted before but enjoyed, and she thanked him sincerely for it.

Phoenix was accustomed to being the silent one in a group normally, but this stoic stranger made it quite clear that he would *not* be the one to offer conversation. She didn't mind the silence, having remained that way for their whole *jog*, but she had questions and desperately wanted answers. "So if you're not going to that Blomstra place you mentioned to turn in your mission, is that where it came from?"

"No."

When he didn't expound, she asked, "Then where did the mission come from?"

"Teok Lun."

"Which is where?" she prompted.

Paul gave a heavy sigh, obviously taking the hint that she wanted information. He couldn't be as simplistic in his answers as he could normally get away with since she knew nothing of this place. "It's a smaller city to the south. That is not where I will be returning to, however. This mission's Reality Rift is just on my way."

"What exactly *is* a Reality Rift?"

He assessed her again before adding, "It's what it sounds like. A Rift in this reality that joins it to another, usually much smaller and less complete, one."

"Huh," she said thoughtfully before asking, "so where are we going after this pocket dimension?"

The former Paladin looked slightly surprised by her assessment, then answered, "Tulimeir. It's much farther northeast, located in the northernmost center point of the Tulim Duchy."

Phoenix wished, not for the first time, that her book could provide her with a map. It probably wouldn't help her current situation, but she felt much more lost and adrift because she didn't know where she was in relation to other places. She continued asking her slew of questions between bites. "What are we going to be doing in Tulimeir?"

He looked down at her from where he stood surveying the area and asked with a raised eyebrow, "We?" She shrugged, and he continued with a hint of flint in his voice. "*You* will be dropped off at the AOA, or just the city gates if that is your preference, for you to find your own path. My business is my own."

Phoenix was able to see the clear signal and felt a bit down when she realized that she was just another burden to the man. A random civilian in need of saving. She paused her questions, going silent, and didn't want to ask something else that might result in an answer she didn't like or reiterated how useless she was at the moment.

The Wayfarer could feel his gaze on her, and before she could become too uncomfortable, he asked, "Do you have any combat training?"

She shook her head and gave another shrug. "I was bedridden before coming here. We didn't have magic or healing potions, remember? The only fights I've been in were against killer rabbits and other smaller monsters in the forest since arriving eight days ago."

"Killer rabbits?"

Phoenix wondered if her **[Guide Book]** had some kind of combat log and thought of asking her book about what kind of monster it had been when it suddenly appeared in front of her with the information present.

Species: Caerbannog (Monster)
A white-furred carnivorous monster that attempts to decapitate its enemies with its sharp teeth.
Caste: Mundane

The Wayfarer stared at the description, something about the name tickling the back of her mind, but she shook off the thought and said, "It's apparently called a Caerbannog."

She noticed him looking at her book contemplatively, and he stated more than asked, "That ability grants information as well as quests."

Phoenix nodded, uncertain of what he might have been getting at, but a breath later, he made his disapproval clear. "So you knew it was a Dark Aspect before you bonded to it?"

Shifting uncomfortably under his piercing golden gaze, she admitted, "Um . . . yes. Is that . . . really that bad?"

"Depends on what you choose next," he replied.

"What are your Aspects?" she asked, then added in a rush as he frowned at her, "If you don't mind sharing, that is. You, uh, you don't have to tell me anything you don't want to . . ."

"I know," he said bluntly, and she was once again reminded of the immense gap in their power levels. After a few moments of the once comfortable silence becoming awkward, he spoke simply, "Light, Fire, Sword, and Zeal. With the Wrath Blade Class."

Her eyes widened a bit as she looked up to finally meet his gaze and responded without thinking, "Paladin of the Purifier indeed. That sounds like a very holy-smiting combination."

His eyes narrowed as he responded with, "Indeed."

She looked away again, making herself a bit smaller as she took another bite of food and mumbled, "I can see now why you don't like my Dark Aspect . . . you must think I'm some sort of *tainted* soul now."

He surprised her by giving a slight sigh and shaking his head. "No. Darkness itself is not a taint, merely the balance to light."

Paul looked out towards the horizon again. His next words came a bit softer and seemed full of regret. "I have seen truly tainted souls."

The former Paladin looked back to her and said a bit more conversationally, "No, there is nothing particularly wrong about the Dark Aspect on its own, but it is one of the paths that can branch off into truly terrible ends. Ends without redemption."

"So, you're saying I should be careful about what I choose for my other Aspects because the Class might turn out evil?"

"Evil is not a state of being but a series of actions," he said resolutely. He then expounded, "There are some Classes and Aspects, however, that corrupt so deeply that they seem to force the user to perform those evil actions. Make no mistake, young one, if your chosen Aspects are one of those that are known to corrupt, I will not hesitate to purge you from this world before your actions can be made manifest."

That was the most words she had heard the man ever say at once, and Phoenix could feel her heart thudding loudly against her chest as he unflinchingly declared his intent to kill her should she make a wrong choice. Perhaps he had some powerful ability to keep her dead. Then the thought of being turned into some evil, corrupted monster by using the wrong Aspect and then *not* being killable, doomed to an endless tortured existence, seemed like an even worse fate than him ending her.

She reflexively swallowed and asked quietly, "Will you at least warn me before I might choose the wrong one?"

He watched her a moment longer before nodding and looking out to the distance again.

Paul continued jogging with her in his arms until the sun began to set that night. Phoenix was stiff from remaining in that position for so long, and her face felt a bit raw from the wind against it. Though, now that they were stopped, she realized there wasn't really that much of a breeze.

The Adventurer worked quickly to set up the camp for the night, and she was somewhat delighted to see him pull out a spit roast and a huge chunk of meat to cook over the fire. She hadn't had a warm meal in over a week, and she wasn't counting her sorry excuse for "cooked" rabbit. She expressed her thanks for the meal and dug in ravenously.

It was fascinating to see Paul's armor disappear in a flash of golden flames, leaving him dressed in a plain white shirt and cream khaki traveling pants that he must have been wearing under the heavy-looking armor.

"Was that a magic item? How can you move so fast in plate armor like that? It must weigh a ton," she observed, then chomped down on the leg of meat, wincing as it burned her tongue slightly.

"A passive ability," he answered simply. She was starting to become accustomed to the short answers as he helpfully included, "No added weight."

"That seems useful," she commented, being more careful with her next bite as she blew on it to cool it down a bit. Between her next bites, she managed to ask him, "How much longer till we arrive at the Reality Rift?"

"Tomorrow afternoon," he said before taking a bite from his own bone laden with tender meat. Phoenix found it curious that he was eating food like she was but didn't ask why. After seeing his reaction to eating the Mana Bit, she assumed he simply wanted real food like she did. The newly healed Wayfarer remembered what bland hospital food tasted like and wouldn't begrudge anyone wanting a more flavorful meal.

"Eat, then rest," Paul said, interrupting her thoughts as he gestured towards the tent that he had finished setting up earlier.

She looked between the single bedroll and back to the powerful stranger, then swallowed her bite of meat before nervously stammering, "I, um—I don't need the bed . . . You can have it."

His eyes narrowed at her obvious discomfort, and he said disdainfully, "I don't prey on children."

"Oh, right. People under thirty are children here. I forgot. That just seems so old to still be considered a kid," she said, thinking out loud more to herself than her golden companion.

Paul's gaze became razor-sharp at her words, and she felt that uncomfortable pressure against her Aura again when he asked, "Where did you learn that?"

Dread flooded her as she realized her mistake, and she stared back at him like a deer caught in the headlights. She froze in her sudden panic. Even the air seemed to go deathly still as the powerful Caster stared at her intently. Her mind raced, weighing the pros and cons of telling the truth versus attempting the lie.

"I, um . . . Well—I don't . . . I—" she stammered, glancing around the camp for an idea to come to her.

"I can read deceit in your Aura," Paul reminded her, his gaze never leaving her as he paused eating his meal.

"I . . . I don't want to say," she murmured honestly.

"Why not?"

Phoenix wrapped her arms around herself, the mostly devoured drumstick forgotten as she whispered, "I don't want you to send me back."

"Others found you first," he deduced. "Was it the Magi?"

The Wayfarer refused to meet his eyes as she nodded and said, "They showed up after I arrived. One of them . . . he . . ."

Paul glanced at the tent as if trying to connect her earlier behavior to her story, and she felt a tremor ripple across her Aura, which she thought came from him, but it was an odd sensation she wasn't familiar with. It made her go silent, though, in fear that she might have already said too much, and he would return her to the people who had tried to claim her.

"Did they hurt you?" the former Paladin asked with more softness than she would have expected from the gruff man.

She bit her bottom lip, not wanting to say more and potentially cause more trouble. When she finally looked at him, though, he tried to reassure her by offering information. "I'm not going to send you back. This is why the AOA tries to bring in Wayfarers. To help protect them from exploitation and harm, often by making them strong Adventurers in their own right.

"However, the OOM prize Wayfarers for their otherworldly knowledge and unique abilities. Their organization also has better means of detecting when and where Wayfarers arrive in our world. If one of them managed to get you alone, I can only imagine the lengths they would have gone to in order to . . . *secure* you," he explained. "Did he tell you his name?"

She didn't look away this time and showed her gratitude for the information by whispering, "Miles. He was going to take me to his home in Blomstra. He . . . he, um . . ." Her story trailed off as she remembered the way he had grabbed her, had tossed her around like a doll, and had nearly broken her back to try and make her submit.

"He hurt you," Paul stated as though answering his own earlier question, and she nodded in confirmation. The golden warrior glanced back at the tent and then stood, dusting off his pants and tossing the now clean bone into the crackling fire as he said, "I don't need as much sleep as you do. Rest while I keep watch. Nobody will hurt you while I'm near. You have my word."

He walked away from the camp then, not too far that she couldn't see him atop the nearby hill, but it was far enough away that he made it clear that he intended to give her space for the night. She glanced down at the remaining food still clutched in her hand and silently finished it off, not wanting to waste a single bite.

After tossing her own cleaned bone into the fire, she practically crawled over to the tent and quickly passed out, glad to finally have something slightly softer than cold dirt to sleep on.

No monster howls woke her from her dreamless sleep that night.

Reality Rift

In the morning, the odd pair continued as they had the day before, crossing the vast hill lands, which slowly began to level out. The sun had just hit the midway point in the sky above them when she noticed an even brighter light in the direction they were heading. She wanted to ask about it, but she didn't dare distract the man carrying her as they sped across the terrain.

It turned out that the swiftly growing light was their destination. A huge portal that was shining with a bright golden light seemed to be embedded into a giant rocky formation jutting up in the dry grassy area they arrived in. Phoenix didn't see any monsters around, so she assumed they were in the Rift, as Paul had mentioned.

When he set her on the ground about a dozen yards away from it, her book appeared again with an update.

Quest: Mysterious Stranger
Objective Complete: Followed Paul Wayland to the Reality Rift.
Objective Reward:
[Sewing Kit] has been added to your collection.

Completion Reward:
10 [Mana Bits] have been added to your collection.

New Quest: Another Other Reality
Your new companion has arrived at a Reality Rift and plans to fight the enemies inside; join him in the adventure.
Objective: Explore the Reality Rift.
Reward: Rare Aspect.

Phoenix could sense Paul shamelessly reading over her shoulder, even admitting as much when he gave a slight huff and muttered, "Definitely lucrative."

She glanced up at him and asked hesitantly, "It won't tell me the type of Aspect until it rewards me, but whatever it offers should be okay to use, right?"

He frowned and pointed out, "It sent you down the path of darkness."

The bald Wayfarer scrunched up her face in mild annoyance as she muttered, "Right . . . I don't know how or why it gives what it does."

Paul went silent once more, then looked from her to the book, then to the portal before them, and asked without a hint of his own preference, "Will you be joining?"

She replicated his own movements as she looked from his stoic face down to the book, then up at the portal before slowly nodding. "Yes. Aside from going down the path of the Sith, this book has guided me pretty well so far and tried its best to keep me alive . . . I think," she said before giving her book a side glance, wondering even more now how it worked. Was it trying to keep her safe by keeping her close to Paul? Or was it trying to off her with the monsters waiting for them inside?

The warrior gave a curt nod, and his gleaming armor materialized around him as he strode forward to lead the way. She followed closely behind the Emerald Caster, hoping proximity would be enough to shield her from whatever danger awaited them.

As they approached the Rift in reality, the air continued to get warmer. She had noticed the area, in general, warming up as they traveled throughout the day, and now she wondered if this portal was the reason. The heat was reaching uncomfortable temperatures as they walked up and entered together.

Passing through the barrier into the other pocket dimension felt extremely similar to using her own portal ability, so that didn't disturb her as much as the blistering heat and blinding light that met them. Hot wind scorched her pale skin and almost stole her breath away.

When her eyes finally adjusted to the searing brightness, she discovered that this particular alternate reality was home to what she equated to the planet Arrakis, and she briefly wondered if the monsters they would be fighting were giant sandworms. There seemed to be nothing but rust-colored sand dunes as far as her eyes could see, only matched in their monotony by the pale blue sky above them.

"Stay close," was the only thing Paul said before making his way down the large sand dune they were currently standing atop. She scurried after him, struggling not to fall as she followed. Eventually, she noticed there were actually two suns in the sky, which made her reassess that maybe they were on Tatooine instead.

About fifteen minutes of walking passed when Phoenix asked, "How do you know which way to go? There's nothing out here but sand and sun." She was fairly certain her pale bald head, which had barely begun regrowing a layer of red fuzz, was going to burn terribly under the merciless twin orbs of fire.

The tanned man didn't look back as he replied simply, "Auras."

She rolled her eyes. Of course it was Aura senses, which she was once again reminded she sorely lacked any skill in. It was only another fifteen minutes when she almost ran into Paul's back as he paused and then gestured for her to lower herself to the sand. They peeked over the top of the dune they were on, which was the tallest she had seen so far, to gaze down at what Paul had noticed.

The viewpoint allowed them to see quite a way into the distance, and the Adventurer pointed towards a small group of moving figures. They were dark shapes against the brightly lit sands, and she couldn't tell how many were there, but it seemed like they were surrounding a large glowing sphere that she couldn't make out details about.

"What kind of monsters are they? It's too bright. I can't see well from here," she whispered quietly to the former Paladin.

He seemed to debate telling her for a moment, then said, "The weakest ones are magically altered monsters. Are you familiar with Soul Reapers?" She shook her head in the negative, and he continued quietly, "They're invaders from outside of our reality. This group, in particular, has been a menace trying to sabotage our world's Reality Rifts for the last couple of months."

"Sabotage?" she asked in confusion.

"They destabilize them somehow and cause them to collapse. It has a devastating effect on our world, completely annihilating the surrounding land and disrupting the magic of the area."

"They turn the rifts into bombs in the hopes of destroying your world enough to take over?" she said, trying to piece together the information in wide-eyed horror.

Paul gave her a pointed look. "Your world too, now," he said and looked back at the group in the distance. "The altered monsters, which we call Caged, are usually stronger than the original and dumber for it, but they can easily stand against someone of equal Caste. The Reapers themselves are the smarter and bigger threat. The strongest down there is just a high-level Sapphire, however, with only a handful of lower Sapphires to help. The Caged all seem to be Crystal Caste. The low Castes are why the AOA let me take the mission alone."

"Is strength and smarts the only difference between the Caged and the Reaper monsters?" she asked in a hushed whisper, still trying to get a better look at the creatures in the distance.

"No more questions now," he said with a shake of his head, shutting down her questions on magic. He then gestured to the dune closest to the group that was between them and commanded, "You will wait there once I move in and engage. You will stay there and not draw any attention to yourself. You will not move closer to that sphere until I call for you.

"If by some bad stroke of fortune, I am incapacitated, you will return to the portal and travel east until you hit a river, then follow it north till you hit a town. If you make it that far, then it most likely means I have failed, and you will inform the local AOA branch of such. Do you understand everything I've just instructed?" His piercing golden eyes never left hers as he made his orders clear.

Phoenix nodded and adrenaline started to surge through her body at the thought of the approaching danger. She had really wished that he had explained all of that *before* she had agreed to enter the desolate wasteland of this pseudo-reality, but she wasn't going to turn back now.

With no further words, Paul turned back and slowly led them across the sandy expanse towards their target. He whispered a few words she couldn't catch and then seemed to vanish in front of her eyes. The next moment, there was a deafening explosion from the direction of the monsters, followed by a cacophony of screams, shouting, and roars.

The sounds brought back a wave of memories of the last week in the monster-infested wilderness, and she covered her ears, trying not to return to the panic of that first night. Tears streamed down her dust-covered face, unbidden. She wasn't used to having to battle monsters and hated the feeling of weakness the loud roars instilled in her.

A sudden slam from the side knocked her from her fear-laden thoughts and caused her to tumble down the sandy dune in a wave of pain. She only had a moment to look back up, trying to catch her breath that had been forcefully knocked from her lungs. What she saw was a terrifying creature that looked like a mix between a pangolin and a tarantula carved out of a sandstone boulder that was even taller than Paul.

Its armor-plated back and head seemed to offer formidable protection, while its piercing spear-like legs and sharp mouth pincers seemed to cover its offense. It seemed so heavy that Phoenix wasn't sure how it didn't sink into the sand without some sort of magic power.

She wasn't given more time to ponder the odd composition of the monster, though, as its large, spiked tail started bearing down to smash into her again. She reactively lunged to the side in a rolling dodge.

Phoenix conjured her Dark dagger and held it in front of her, rapidly trying to think of a way to take down the monster without getting skewered in return. She could hear Paul still fighting on the other side of the dune and assumed this one must have been blasted far enough away by his initial attack that it caught sight of her and saw a snack.

As the monster turned, she realized that its armored bulk made it slow and awful at pivoting, and she began to run to the side, trying to maneuver behind it.

She was pretty sure that the initial attack had cracked a rib or two and knew that she couldn't hope to match its strength. So, she had to aim for speed and smarts and pray it would be enough.

She wasn't sure if the creature actually had some of the weak points that its Earth equivalents were supposed to have, but she could only assume so as she managed to get behind it and plunge her dagger towards the base of its tail, trying to get between the rocky plating.

Almost instinctively, she could tell that her dagger's ability to apply a Bane on the creature that would siphon mana took effect as she felt her well slowly start to replenish. It was as if the magic itself was letting her know in the same way she could tell what loot was in her collection.

The shriek that came from its maw caught her off guard, and one of its stalagmite legs struck her in the chest, sending her flying backward. She forced herself to get up, coughing out sand and the blood that pooled in her lungs from the strike and faced her enemy once more.

Having lost her grip on her dagger from the blow, she conjured it again. The black stiletto vanished from the monster's hindquarters, causing blood to flow freely from the puncture wound. It was good to know that was how the ability worked, and she tried a new tactic, throwing the dagger as hard as she could at the creature.

Of course, it hit at a bad angle and fell harmlessly into the dune that was shifting with their movement. She mentally berated herself and conjured the dagger again, making it disappear from the ground and reappear in her hand once more. She didn't have time to try throwing it again, however, as the monster charged in fury.

Phoenix barely managed to duck down in time and thrust her dagger upward underneath it as it almost impaled her on one of its legs. Its underside turned out to be much softer than the sandstone-plated back, and its own momentum helped her small dagger slice open its innards as she suddenly found herself painted in blood and guts.

The added heat and gore caused her to lose the contents of her stomach as she lurched to her hands and knees, attempting to use one of her hands to wipe her face of the disgusting fluids while the other shakily kept her from falling into her own puddle of bile.

In a last-ditch effort of pain, anguish, and rage, the creature swung its large stone tail and hit her prone form with all its power. That single blow crushed the left side of her body as she tried to wipe the blood from her eyes. The pain was unlike anything she had experienced before as she felt her arm shatter in multiple places at once, and she was knocked back several yards to impact against more of the hard-packed sand. She didn't even have time to gasp, let alone scream, as her vision went black, and she felt no more.

CHAPTER ELEVEN

Ritualist

When Phoenix regained consciousness, it was to the sight of dark canvas above her, the sound of a crackling fire, and the smell of meat roasting. She slowly sat up, carefully testing out her left arm to find it fully healed. However, the memory of the pain had her wincing slightly. When she confirmed that she was, in fact, still alive and intact, she carefully made her way out of the small tent to join Paul by the fire.

It was dark outside, even with the twin moons shining high in the sky above the glow of the campfire. Paul was dressed in his casual clothes once again, pausing his writing in a small leather book in his lap as his eyes swept over her, assessing her condition, while she sat down across from him. Sitting carefully on the grass, she asked quietly, "What happened?"

Once he seemed satisfied with his visual examination, he explained simply, "You were severely injured, but the beast died before it could finish you off."

The older man went silent for a moment longer, and his gaze seemed to be searching for an answer to a question he didn't feel like asking as he continued, recounting, "Once I finished with the others, I was able to feed you another healing potion and brought you back out here to clean you up."

Phoenix nodded in understanding and wrapped her arms around herself as she said sincerely, "Thank you."

He gave a huff of discontent. "Your gratitude is unnecessary. You shouldn't have been in that situation in the first place. It was a miscalculation on my part," he muttered. In a rare show of emotion, he scratched his bearded jaw with chagrin and added, "I apologize for failing to keep my word."

Phoenix was caught off guard by the admission of blame and guilt he displayed. She fell silent, not sure what to say before finally deciding on her words, "I knew there would be risks with following you into a place where you were planning to fight monsters. It was my choice. My quest," she said firmly.

Her book decided to materialize once more at that point to update her about said quest.

Quest: Another Other Reality
Objective Complete: Explored the Reality Rift.
Objective Reward:
[Moon Aspect] has been added to your collection.

Hidden Objective Complete: Defeated a Crystal Caste enemy.
Bonus Reward:
[Dune Strider Boots] have been added to your collection.

Completion Reward:
10 [Crystal Mana Bits] have been added to your collection.

"What Aspect?" Paul asked, assuming the message contents.

"Moon," she replied simply, then conjured it into her hands. The Aspect was like two rough, pocked, softly glowing spheres had been glued together. One was orange and the other blue, like a reflection of the satellites currently shining down on them. "More night theme. Is that bad?" she asked, looking back towards the holy Paladin of Fire and Light.

"It could be worse," he said, and she thought she saw the corner of his mouth twitch slightly. Then his demeanor shifted back as he said, "Most Wayfarers get a few . . . recurring powers that help them survive. Translation and looting are by far the most common."

He gestured towards her glowing book. "Some sort of world guide," he continued listing off, then pointed at the slightly glowing Aspect, "and a way to gain power naturally are also not uncommon but less so than those first two. I thought you might have a way to use those without the normal ritual but after learning about . . . the other Caster you encountered—"

"I can just use them," she said, cutting off the route the conversation was going again. Phoenix didn't want to talk about or even think about Miles ever again. Instead, she refocused on the Aspect in her hand and lifted it slightly higher as she asked, "Should I?"

The former Paladin seemed to ponder for a moment, then stood and collected the spit that she now registered had meat cooking on it. He slid the savory-smelling chunk onto a smooth polished stone plate before handing it over to her, which she took gratefully. She began eating, blowing on it to cool it down once she realized it was hotter than the Emerald Caster had made it seem.

After a few minutes of devouring the delicious bites, she said softly, "Thank you for cooking this for me. I know it's a burden to have to deal with a Mundane body like mine." She glanced up and asked sincerely, "Is there anything I can do to repay you? I . . . I know I'm not powerful yet, but—" She hesitated, searching for the words to express her feelings. "I just . . . I want to be able to do something for you in return."

He met her eyes, and she felt a wave of scrutiny overtake her again. She started to understand that he was somehow using his own Aura to see straight through hers. The now familiar silence hung in the air between them as they both observed each other.

She wondered what she might have said to trigger what she now thought of as a defensive response to ascertain her own intentions when he surprised her by reaching into the bag at his hip and holding out a brightly glowing golden object that looked like a roiling miniature sun.

Phoenix stared at the orb Paul held out and looked between it and him a few times before stating, "That's an Aspect." He simply nodded, and she said in confusion, "I, um . . . I don't understand."

"You wanted to do something for me," he reiterated, to which she nodded, and he clarified, "I want you to bond to this Aspect as well."

Her eyes went wide at the request. "But . . . but why?"

Paul gave a slight huff and said simply, "It will balance out your night."

"But why would you give me something so valuable?" she asked, scrunching up her face in discontent as she added with a frown, "I . . . I haven't done anything to deserve it."

"I never asked you to *earn* it. I asked you to *use* it," he stated, then moved forward to place it on top of her book, which was still floating open in the air next to her. She glanced at the text it generated.

Item: Sun Aspect
A magical aspect of the sun.
Caste: Crystal.
Availability: Rare.
Type: Consumable, ingredient.
Requirements: Less than four unlocked Aspects.
Effect: Unlocks an aspect of one's soul, granting one passive and one cultivating ability.

You are able to absorb the [Sun Aspect].
Do you wish to unlock the Sun aspect of your soul?

Phoenix stared at the item text and then asked without looking away, "Where did you even get this?"

"I looted it in the Reality Rift," he replied simply.

That *did* cause her to look at him. "You have a looting ability, too?"

She saw the corner of his lips twitch as a slight expression of amusement flashed across his face, and he nodded once in affirmation. Then he asked, "Will you bond with it?"

Phoenix looked between the Sun Aspect resting on her book and the Moon Aspect in her hand. Picking up the shimmering golden one with her free hand, she said her thoughts out loud for the man, "Star, Dark, Moon, and Sun. Do you know what kind of Class that will be?"

He gave a shrug. "Something Spell-oriented, most likely. Classes aren't always predictable based on the Aspects alone. Two people with the same combination can end up with different Classes due to the type of person they are or the skills or knowledge they've already obtained."

"How does that work?" the Wayfarer asked curiously.

"One popular example I know of is the Earth, Wind, Water, and Fire combination. This usually results in an Elemental-type Class. The person who had no combat experience, but some knowledge of Mundane magic, became an Elemental Mage. Another who had training in the sword and spear became an Elemental Warrior. Yet another who focused on hand-to-hand combat and was a member of the Cultivator's clergy became an Elemental Monk."

"So, then there's no real guarantee?" Phoenix asked, pondering the information.

"No, but you can get pretty close to whatever you might be aiming for," he clarified.

Then she asked another question that had been nagging at her for a while. "What's 'Mundane magic'?"

Paul gave another huff of slight annoyance, which she assumed was for needing to use so many words to explain what was common knowledge to most of the world's inhabitants. "Magic that anyone, even Mundanes, can do. Rituals, cantrips, and enchantments. It usually takes some time to learn how to do each of those things properly."

"Can you teach me?" she asked, her curiosity piqued.

The stoic blonde looked at her for a long moment in silent contemplation, then nodded slowly. "I know a few easy rituals that should help you survive," he said, then leaned over to grab his bag and pulled out another small pouch, but instead of more tasty food for her to eat, this one contained pure salt.

He walked a few yards away from the fire, gesturing for her to follow. She complied, putting the two Aspects into her collection for the time being. Once the Paladin found a usable clearing, he made sure she was out of the way and grabbed a handful of the salt, creating a simple circle around himself with it.

__"By the divine guidance of the Traveler who wanders the world, show me the path north that I may gain my bearings,"__ Paul said clearly with a feeling of power infused in his words. The circle began to glow a soft teal color before a shimmering line of light appeared, leading from under Paul's leather boots towards the north.

"It's a compass!" Phoenix stated excitedly. "This could have really helped me in the forest."

He simply nodded, held out the bag for her to take, and gestured to another clear spot. "You try."

She took the small bag then remembered something that her book had mentioned about rituals and summoned the glowing tome of information. She had it Spell out the Talent for **[Collector]** and **[Beacon of Hope]** to Paul and asked, "This one says I can use components from my collection, and this one says I can draw diagrams with light. Do I use this instead of the salt?"

Paul nodded. "That's not an uncommon passive ability for mages to get. Aside from making it more convenient, it makes using rituals in combat much more viable. Try it."

It took her a few moments of focus to figure out how to use her finger to draw in the air, leaving a trail of light behind that disappeared with a thought. Once she finished drawing out a circle around her with the soft light, she recited the words that Paul had spoken and was delighted when it began responding.

He then taught her a few more rituals that would hopefully help her survive should she find herself lost and alone in the wilderness again. One to find fresh water. Another to light a small bonfire. Then, a final one to send her a mental alarm that would wake her from sleep should a monster get too close.

Sleep soon called to her, but she wanted to do one more thing before letting it claim her. She sat at the tent opening and reconjured the Sun Aspect from her collection as Paul watched her with his usual stoicism.

After a calming breath, she triggered using the Aspect and felt her blood begin to boil as the mini sun of molten plasma seemed to melt into her. She ground her teeth at the pain but couldn't hold out against it as the searing heat burned through her very soul.

When she awoke the next morning, her book flew in front of her again to explain what had happened.

> *You have unlocked the Sun aspect of your soul.*
> [Sun Aspect] has bonded to your **Strength** attribute, increasing the Caste of your **Strength** to Crystal 1.
> *You have unlocked the Aura passive ability: Radiant Sunlight.*
> *You have unlocked the cultivating ability: Dawn Rises.*

She slowly sat up, not remembering having gotten into the bedroll properly, and clambered out of the tent to find the grass wet with morning dew as she looked around for her companion.

Phoenix almost panicked for a moment when she didn't see Paul near the doused campfire and wondered if he had cut his losses. The Wayfarer was more relieved than she thought she should be when she finally spotted the golden Paladin near the portal opening to the Reality Rift.

As she began to walk towards him, wondering what he was up to, light began to glow not just from the ground but all around him and the Rift. Brilliant sigils moved through the air in a mesmerizing pattern that caused her to stop and watch in awe at the magic being performed before her. A loud thrumming filled the surrounding meadow which she felt more than she heard.

The magic began to appear like runic chains wrapping around the portal before she felt a sudden shockwave of power come from the man at its center. The sigils tightened around the portal, causing it to almost appear like it was cracking before it seemed to shatter, and another blast of wind swept across her. The whirlwind caused her to shield her face and knocked her down to land on her backside.

When she opened her eyes again and looked up, she was met with golden eyes staring down at her and a tan hand outstretched, which she took to help herself stand. As she readjusted her dress, she asked a bit incredulously, "You're a Ritualist?"

He tilted his head slightly in acknowledgment, and she glared in annoyance as she pointed out, "I thought you said you only knew a few easy rituals."

Paul gave her another slightly amused look as he nodded once more and said, "I do." Then he gestured back towards the now completely smooth stone boulder where a Reality Rift had once been and stated, "*That* was not easy."

CHAPTER TWELVE

Crystal Caster

So, you're sure this won't turn me into some sort of space werewolf or something?" Phoenix asked as she held up the Moon Aspect while taking another bite of the sweet fruit Paul had given her for breakfast. The juicy orb was a bright red and was the same as she had earlier, with a single heavy pit at its center that was a glossy black. Paul had informed her it was called a ruebean, and it was delicious.

The older man paused to give her a raised eyebrow before shaking his head and continuing to break down the tent. "No Wolf Aspect, so it's highly unlikely."

"Wait, werewolves are actually a thing?" the Wayfarer asked incredulously.

Paul nodded. "There are many species in the world, and some Aspects have a chance to make variants through transfiguration. Werewolves are considered a transfigured species. Same as vampires, zombies, machina, and many more."

"What's the difference between a transfigured species and a regular one?"

"Made versus born. It's similar to the difference between monsters and avals."

Phoenix scrunched her face in confusion. "What's an aval?"

"Naturally born magical creatures. Like an animal, but they have a Caste level of magic," he answered, then stood as he finished packing up the camp. Instead of pushing them to leave, he came to sit next to her and asked, "Can your book show ability information?"

She nodded and summoned the book to float in front of them. She took another bite of ruebean and said, "What do you want to see?"

Paul seemed to study the book for a bit longer before he said, "I can feel the new layer to your Aura. May I see it?"

Phoenix hesitated for a moment, unsure if she should trust the man despite his help so far. Miles had also tried to help her at first. Maybe Paul simply had more patience than the Magi and was trying to get more information before luring her to his dungeon.

The warrior seemed to read her face and said bluntly, "I don't need to see it if I wanted to harm you."

She understood his point, but it didn't help comfort her. What it did do was remind her that this man was much stronger, and his knowing about her powers wouldn't make her worse off at this point. Plus, she was curious to confirm what she felt intuitively inside her.

Passive Ability: Radiant Sunlight
Type: Aura (magical, light)
Current Caste: Crystal 1
Crystal Effect: Allies within your Aura gain a **[Sun Shell]**. Reconstructing a destroyed **[Sun Shell]** can be done after a short duration and costs a moderate amount of mana.

- Sun Shell (boon, construct, magical, light): A shield that blocks the next incoming physical attack with a chance to knock back and inflict **[Blind]** on the attacker.
- Blind (bane, magical, light): Hinders vision for a short duration.

When she had awoken earlier, Phoenix had suppressed the Magical shield almost subconsciously as she had been suppressing her little **[Starlight Companion]** and the blurring effect of her Dark Aura. Like flipping a mental switch, she made all three reappear with a thought.

Paul stared at the effects thoughtfully, lifting a hand closer to the shield and moving it around to test it out. He even gave his own **[Starlight Companion]** that had appeared over his shoulder an experimental squish.

The new **[Sun Shell]** was like a bubble that surrounded each of them and glittered with gold sparkles in the morning sunlight before fading to become completely transparent. When Phoenix raised an arm to touch it, the edge was just out of reach, and when she tried to move closer, she could sense it move in response, keeping her in its center.

Paul realized what she was trying to do and instead moved closer to her, causing their bubbles to overlap, flickering back into being seen, and as they both reached out to touch the other's shell, their hands passed effortlessly through. The Paladin confused her by saying, "Well, that should be proof enough."

"Proof of what?" she inquired.

"That we're not enemies," he replied simply.

"How does that work?"

"If I tried to harm you, your shield would have been more like a closed window than an open one. It would have tried to protect you from me." Then he gave a slight smirk as he added slightly ominously, "Not that it would have succeeded."

"How does it know if you're trying to hurt me, though? Maybe it's just because you weren't attacking."

The ex-Paladin shrugged. "That's partially true. It's you that determines if I'm an enemy or not. If we were sparring, and you knew I would try to harm you, it would have reacted. Since we're not, though, you must trust me on some level at the moment. Most of the time, your perception about whether others are considered an ally or enemy is a subconscious decision." He paused contemplatively, then added, "I would show you that my Aura would consider you an ally as well, but that would require me to poison you first. You'll just have to believe that the shell protecting me is going off my own perception of you."

Phoenix nodded in understanding as she mulled over the information. Then she brought up the description of her other new ability. She didn't try to hide the book from Paul as he read next to her.

Ability: Dawn Rises
Type: Spell (magical, life)
Cost: Variable mana.
Cooldown: Variable.
Current Caste: Crystal 1 (0%)
Crystal Effect: Can heal a touched target by activating for Low, Moderate, High, or Severe mana cost. The amount healed and respective cooldown time increase with cost.

"It's a healing Spell like that potion, right?" she asked with a bit of excitement. She had always prayed for the ability to be healed, and now she would be able to give others the gift she had always been denied.

Paul's expression softened as he said, "Yes. That's something I was hoping you would get. Some Light and Life to balance the Dark and Death that threatens to surround you."

"Death?" the Wayfarer asked a bit pensively. "What do you mean?"

He frowned slightly, and his mask of stoicism seemed to retake its place on his features. He explained, "You've been here barely over a week and have already slain monsters. It seems to be a path you are destined to walk, like most Wayfarers."

Then Paul gestured to the Moon Aspect that was sitting in her lap. "If you bond with that, you'll become a Crystal Caster. You'll gain even more attention."

"Are Casters really that rare? I was told that the Aspects were expensive, but there are still a lot of people who have them, right?"

He shrugged. "There are enough that it's not strange to meet one, but you won't just be another Caster. You'll be both a Caster and a Wayfarer. I've never heard of a Wayfarer who went on to live a quiet and peaceful life, and they are easily discovered through their Auras."

Phoenix pondered that and couldn't contradict it based on her experience so far. She thought maybe she could be different but realized that would most likely mean not using her powers to help people, and that wasn't what she wanted. She wanted to show people that she could be useful, that she could help them.

She lifted up the Aspect once more to gaze into its odd coloration and asked, "If I become a Crystal Caster, I'll be able to save people who were like me, right? People who are sick or helpless?"

The golden Paladin watched her with a curious expression for a few heartbeats before nodding in acknowledgment. She took a deep breath and steeled her resolve as she triggered absorbing the Aspect.

It seemed to shatter suddenly as the tiny shards began to slowly orbit her hand. The pieces glittered orange and blue in the light and almost looked like a swarm of little moons as they swirled around her arm, migrating up it and around her entire body before startling her by embedding themselves into her flesh. She cried out from both surprise and pain as pinpricks of coldness quickly grew to suffuse her body, and she shivered.

Meanwhile, Paul continued reading her book as he moved to give her some space.

You have unlocked the Moon aspect of your soul.
[Moon Aspect] has bonded to your **Mind** attribute, increasing the Caste of your **Mind** to Crystal 1.
You have unlocked the Perception passive ability: Moonlit Eyes.
You have unlocked the cultivating ability: Lunar Dream.

Then she cried out louder as the cold seemed to battle a raging inferno that began from her core and burst outward in a flash of white-hot light. When she cracked her eyes open, she could clearly see Paul kneeling in front of her with concern in his gold eyes as he watched over her transformation into a Caster.

It was only then that she realized she had fallen to her hands and knees from the shock to her system, noticing white flames licking at her skin, which seemed unharmed despite the pain she felt coursing through her. The flames appeared to be burning away at her without actually leaving any wounds or scarring. Her body instead seemed to heal and toughen, leaving strong and unblemished pale skin behind.

Between the waves of pain, she managed to croak, "What's happening?"

Paul grimaced slightly but tried to reassure her, "It's normal. The magic is burning away impurities and refining the mana within your body. The pain should subside soon. I should have warned you."

Another wave of pain washed over her as she felt her Aura suddenly expand again like it had before, and she recognized a fourth layer getting added to it. It confused her, but she didn't have time to dwell on it—she gave another cry of pain as the pure white flames seemed to engulf her entirely.

When she could think clearly again, Phoenix carefully sat up from the fetal position she had apparently curled into at some point. Paul was already beside her, speaking softly. "Careful. It can take a bit to adjust to a new tier. You're a lot tougher now but we still don't want you accidentally hurting yourself."

"It worked?" she asked, still not completely cognizant.

He gave her that slightly amused look but nodded. "Yes. Congratulations on becoming a Crystal Caster."

After a few more minutes of trying to gain her bearings, he held out a small milky white stone for her that she recognized as a Crystal Mana Bit. Then the ex-Paladin commanded, "Eat it."

She didn't argue, still feeling too out of sorts to protest, and carefully placed the Bit in her mouth. To her surprise, it seemed to melt like a chocolate drop she had gotten from her best friend one time.

Phoenix shook the memory of Jin from her head and focused on the invigorating feeling she was suddenly filled with. It was like a shot of adrenaline mixed with the sensation of having a satisfying meal. It tasted extremely sweet, though, like some sort of sickly syrup that coated her tongue before melting into it. She didn't completely hate it, but she could understand why Paul or anyone else might.

Once she seemed a bit better, Paul prompted, "You gained another Aura from your Class, it looks like." Then he gave her the first real smile she had seen from the man as he gestured towards the book that was still faithfully floating nearby. "It's a pretty promising one."

She lifted an arm to reach out towards her **[Guide Book]**. It responded to her will by coming closer for her to pull into her lap to read over what all had happened for herself.

You have unlocked the core Aspects of your soul.
You have unlocked the Class Aspect: Celestial Astromancer.
[Celestial Astromancer] has bonded to your **Magic** attribute, increasing the Caste of your **Magic** to Crystal 1.
You have unlocked the Aura passive ability: Astral Oasis.
You have unlocked the cultivating ability: Ruler of Relativity.
You have become Crystal Caste.
You have gained the ability to sustain yourself using sources of concentrated mana.
You can now use Crystal Caste Spirit Gems to unlock an additional Class ability per Aspect.

She looked up at Paul, who was carefully watching her as she asked, "Class abilities?"

He nodded. "Yes. You get one per Aspect you bond with, plus the Class Aspect itself. What those abilities end up becoming will be based on a combination of factors but most prominently on your Class, which Aspect the gem bonds to, and what type of Spirit Gem you choose to use."

"I see," she said, though the Wayfarer didn't think she would fully understand until she actually experienced it for herself. For now, she settled on checking out her most recent ability additions, starting with her two new passives.

Passive Ability: Moonlit Eyes
Type: Perception (magical, light)
Current Caste: Crystal 1
Crystal Effect: The level of light does not hinder your sight.

Passive Ability: Astral Oasis
Type: Aura (magical, arcane)
Current Caste: Crystal 1
Crystal Effect: Allies within your Aura have increased regeneration to mana and abilities cost less mana.

"Did I just become a mana battery?" she asked incredulously. It was her Shadow Priest character all over again.

A smile tugged at the corner of Paul's mouth again as he evaded the question. "Getting your Perception ability is good fortune. I was a little concerned you might get a fifth Aura instead, which would not have been ideal."

The Wayfarer gave him a questioning look. "I thought having multiple Auras was a good thing, aside from just being rare."

The ex-Paladin nodded. "It is, but not having enhanced perceptions would have been a great disadvantage," he explained, then stood and walked closer. "Let me carry you again. We can move while we talk more."

She hesitated a moment, thinking that there wouldn't be much talking going on with her barely able to open her eyes, let alone her mouth, at his speed. However, she didn't want to inconvenience him further by slowing down his traveling more than she already had with how often she had passed out.

At her nod and dismissal of her book, he picked her up once more and began jogging while explaining. "While not everyone might want a Familiar or an Execute ability for their powerset," he started saying, and she was surprised that she could actually make out his words over the rush of the wind whipping past them, "everyone wants their Aura and Perception passive. Being without those additional senses makes it incredibly difficult to advance your Caste and survive when fighting against others who have them."

Phoenix continued listening while half-distracted by the scenery flying past them, which she was actually able to make out a bit better now. She wondered if the change was thanks to her new and improved senses.

Everything seemed more vibrant, more magical, more *alive*. Then she realized that it wasn't that everything else had suddenly evolved; it was she who had evolved. The thought made her smile, and she fell into a comfortable silence. She simply relaxed and drank in the magic and beauty of the world passing by.

CHAPTER THIRTEEN

Call For a Hero

Phoenix stretched as they stopped for the evening. Paul hadn't deigned to fill in the silence with conversation, which she hadn't minded after such an eventful week and the flood of information she was still mentally working through.

The landscape hadn't changed much as they made their way across the grasslands that had become hilly once more, finally stopping once they had reached the river that Paul had told her to find if something had happened in the Reality Rift.

While Paul began setting up the camp once more for the night, she found a large log of driftwood that she was surprised she could move. The thing must have weighed almost a hundred pounds, but it didn't even make her sweat to move it near where their fire pit would be.

With a hesitant glance towards Paul, she finally made up her mind to forgo modesty at the moment so that she might have some when they reached a town. Trying to make herself small and unassuming, she removed her dress and conjured the new Sewing Kit she had gained from her quest in an attempt to mend the mostly shredded fabric.

Phoenix was grateful that her mother had taken the time to teach her the skill when she had gained a temporary interest in embroidery in an attempt to fill some of her time. She pulled out the little kit that had a variety of needles in multiple sizes, colored thread, a thimble, and other miscellaneous sewing tools. She picked out a green thread that almost matched the dark green of her dress and began the tedious work of mending the tears back together as best she could.

As she worked, she moved her book over in front of her, and Paul surprised her by sitting right next to her to read it as well. He had finished the tasks quickly and already had more meat and some vegetables she didn't recognize roasting over the small fire.

Instead of pulling up the description for her abilities first, she asked the book for information about the new items she had received and could feel in her collection. She silently hoped the new boots would go well with her dress. While she had never been huge about following fashion trends like some of the girls her age, she did like pretty things and hoped her clothing reflected that.

Item: Dune Strider Boots
Boots made from the hide of a duneworm.
Caste: Crystal.
Availability: Uncommon.
Type: Apparel, boots.
Requirements: Crystal Caste.
Effects:
- Improved ability to walk on sand.
- Keeps the wearer from overheating.

"Well, these would have been nice *before* going into that pocket hellscape," she muttered, but was happy to have the boots anyway. She was pleased to find they were a neutral cream color that matched the undergarments she was currently wearing. She excitedly replaced her torn leather sandals and attempted to conjure them directly onto her feet instead, like she had managed to do with her dress in her naked panic. It seemed fairly intuitive to her will, and the warm boots were a welcome addition.

Phoenix then focused on something else in her inventory that had appeared after the battle in the desert and willed that description to display next.

Item: Soul Cage
A cage for the soul that increases power in exchange for control.
Caste: Crystal.
Availability: Epic.
Type: Tool, ingredient.
Requirements: Crystal Caste or lower.
Effects:
- Implanting this into a body inhabited by a soul or Monster Seed gives the implanter control over them.
- Greatly improves the innate power of the implanted body.

"Give this to me," Paul's voice growled from beside her. The vehemence with which he spoke gave her pause as her brow raised in surprise at him.

He was kind enough to explain instead of simply demanding again. "I'm going to deliver it to the government in Tulimeir for study and safekeeping. It is a vile, dangerous item that should not be in your possession."

She nodded and quickly materialized it in the air in front of him. It looked like a creepy hand with spindly black claws for fingers, which bent inward to create a cage around whatever it held. Before gravity took effect, Paul's Emerald Caste reflexes easily snatched it out of the air, and it quickly disappeared into his dimensional bag.

Phoenix went quiet then, unsure of what to do or say with the tension that still hung in the air after the ex-Paladin's zealous reaction. He watched her carefully for a moment, and then she felt a pressure against her Aura again.

The feeling was much clearer to her now, with her Aura's quadrupled Strength making her all the more aware of what affected it. It felt like oil and water moving around each other as his much more powerful Aura seemed to prod hers. She imagined the feeling to be similar to the police patting somebody down in search of contraband.

"Is that sensation your Aura trying to analyze mine?" she blurted out, feeling more curious than offended at that moment.

His eyes widened in surprise, but he answered with blunt honesty, "Yes," then followed up with, "Most untrained Crystal Casters or Mundanes wouldn't be able to recognize it for what it is, only feeling a slight discomfort, but your Aura is exceptionally powerful for your Caste."

Phoenix nodded, then asked even more hesitantly, "What are you hoping to find?"

Their eyes locked again as he stated simply, "Truth and answers."

"Well," she said hesitantly, "maybe we can find those together? Perhaps . . . maybe you could, um, teach me more about . . . well, everything?"

Paul hesitated to answer, uncertainty crossing his features for the first time since they had met. When he opened his mouth to reply, she shook her head, cutting off his response. "Never mind. Forget I asked," she said in a rush. She had forgotten that the Adventurer was a busy man with his own life and mission, and his plans included pawning her off on someone else, not taking her in like a stray puppy. "You shouldn't need to bother yourself even more with me."

Then, to distract from the awkwardness, she pulled up the description of one of her new abilities. She could feel it within her, begging to be used, but she had held back, wanting to read it before trying.

Ability: Lunar Dream
Type: Spell (construct, magical, illusion)
Cost: Variable mana.

> **Cooldown:** None.
> **Current Caste:** Crystal 1 (0%)
> **Crystal Effect:** Construct an illusory model. Cost varies based on scale and duration. The illusion is semitransparent and intangible.

"Are illusions useful in combat?" she asked, curiously looking up at the Paladin, who moved to turn the spit more after reading the information himself.

"Depending on the circumstance. They can help confuse or distract the enemy. Protect your allies by taking hits that would have been meant for others. There are a wide variety of applications, and each ability will have its own uses," Paul said, then tilted his head towards the text on the book. "This one seems versatile and will likely become much stronger as you cultivate it."

"Cultivate? What do you mean by that?" the Wayfarer inquired while she returned part of her attention back to mending the dress in her lap.

"You don't really need to worry about that yet. Once you increase in Caste again, you can cultivate and upgrade your abilities further with Spirit Gems of the appropriate level," he explained before sitting back down next to her and prompting, "What was the other ability?"

> **Ability:** Ruler of Relativity
> **Type:** Utility (magical, covenant)
> **Cost:** Variable mana.
> **Cooldown:** None.
> **Current Caste:** Crystal 1 (0%)
> **Crystal Effect:** Change the gravitational relationship between you and a target within sight with mana cost dependent on the distance, speed, size, and Caste difference from the target.

"Interesting," was all he had to say before thoughtfully scratching his bearded cheek.

Phoenix frowned slightly at the book after reading the description. Paul seemed to notice her change in expression and said as if trying to reassure her, "It's a good power."

She glanced back at him and queried, "Is it? It seems to focus on melee combat again . . . won't this pull enemies closer or push them away?"

The Wayfarer hesitated as though ashamed to admit her weakness. "I'm just not good at fighting. My week in the woods made that pretty clear. I'm not sure that I'll be cut out for battling up close and personal, but my powers seem to be assuming that's what's going to happen. First a dagger and now this." She gestured towards the floating book. "I thought I would be a support Mage with my Auras or something else on the back lines, not a warrior."

"You can be both," he said softly, pulling the vegetables out of the fire and onto a plate.

She gave a tiny scoff. "Is that possible? It's not like I can be both up front and in back at the same time; my portal doesn't work quite like that."

Paul seemed to hesitate before admitting, "Your Class and Aspects seem to be a bit of a mixture of capabilities and roles." He paused, as though not wanting to say more, before giving a sigh and adding, "It's probably the reason a lot of people actually avoid such an esoteric set."

She narrowed her eyes at him as she paused her sewing and stated, "You knew that before you offered me that Sun Aspect, didn't you?"

The Adventurer didn't waver as he clarified while roasting the still-cooking meat, "It doesn't mean it can't be powerful . . . just that it can be unpredictable in what kind of abilities you end up with. A lot of it is going to depend on the Spirit Gems you choose and the kind of person you become. I can say I've never heard of your exact Class before, though, so I'm not sure where exactly you'll end up. However, I believe it will be anything but average."

Phoenix nodded. "That's okay, I guess . . . I'm used to never being average." She looked down at the ground between her feet and said with a self-deprecating chuckle, "Honestly, I'm lucky to reach 'below average' standards from the 'completely useless' that I normally fall under."

"You're not useless, young one," Paul firmly said as he carved off some of the roast to add to the plate of vegetables, "you have incredible Natural Talents and rather rare abilities. You survived alone for over a week in a monster-infested mountain range."

Phoenix tried to interrupt him to explain that she would have soon died from starvation without his rescue, without mentioning that she *hadn't* survived, but he simply stalled her with a raised hand.

He moved to sit next to her again and continued, "Then you agreed to follow me into a Reality Rift to encounter unknown danger with the intent of becoming stronger." He lowered his hand and rested it on her shoulder, meeting her gaze. "That is not how I would describe someone who is useless."

"Indeed not," a voice full of power said. It was unlike any sound Phoenix had ever experienced so far, and a crushing Aura filled the area, making it almost difficult for her to breathe with the strength of it.

They both spun to face the newcomer behind them, and Paul immediately dropped to his knees, the plate of food forgotten on the log, and he bowed his head in supplication towards the figure.

Phoenix's reaction, on the other hand, even took her by surprise as she whirled around to stand with a black dagger in her hand as though another evil rabbit were about to pounce. Her half-mended dress tumbled to the ground next to the kneeling Paladin as she prepared to defend them both in only her underwear and boots.

A laugh filled the area that caused a shudder of immense power to wash over her. It belonged to what looked like a man dressed in white leather armor with black underclothes and a sword at his side. He had bright pink hair that matched his cloak and glinting metallic rune tattoos in a variety of colors on his exposed cream-colored skin. The fact that he must have been at least fifteen feet tall and slightly glowing was what confirmed that he was definitely *not* human.

Next to him was another of the tall, glowing beings, but this one was feminine and dressed in white cloth that barely seemed to cover her more intimate areas and stood out against her dark umber skin. Her wavy blonde hair flowed freely down her back and seemed to sway as though a gentle breeze surrounded her. The woman impressed her with how graceful, confident, and free she seemed to be. Both of them were the most beautiful beings Phoenix had ever seen, and both had their amused looks locked onto *her*.

Her Aura trembled under their scrutiny, and she felt transfixed by their presence. It was only Paul's voice filling the silence that brought her attention back to her immediate surroundings. "Forgive this child, my Lord and Lady. She does not know of you and means no offense."

The way he said "Lord and Lady" made her feel like he wasn't referring to them as though they were nobles, and her eyes widened as she realized what they must be. Despite all the books, games, movies, and worldly lore surrounding their existence, Phoenix had never thought that she would ever lay eyes on an actual god. When the Magi or Paul had mentioned them, she assumed they were more . . . well, *uninvolved* with mortals, like in her old world.

Magic apparently changed those rules, however, and she dismissed her dagger with a thought. She mimicked the ex-Paladin in an awkward kneel as she spoke in the politest way that she learned from many books involving nobility of the fictional variety. "Forgive me. I can only assume now that you are deities of this world."

"Indeed. I am Hero," the first god replied, still grinning slightly.

"I am Rebel," the goddess added with a smile of her own.

Phoenix stood straight once more and replied, "I'm, um, honored by your presence but . . ." She hesitated for a moment, still shivering under the weight of their gazes and Auras. "But what is the purpose of said presence?"

There was no hint of movement, but when Phoenix next blinked, her eyes were staring into Hero's brilliant blue eyes. He had shrunk down to human size and had bent in front of her. The god was so close that she would have been able to feel his breath on her cheeks if he had been breathing at all. His proximity to her was overwhelming, to say the least. It felt like her very soul was being scorched by the sunlight emanating from him.

"Stand, child, and read," he commanded as he gave a reassuring smile, and this time, she saw the movement as he deliberately reached out next to her and touched the now blank open page of her **[Guide Book]** still floating faithfully in the air at her side. A mixture of shimmering rainbow script flowed across the pages, and when it finished, Hero was no longer in front of her but back by Rebel's side. She carefully stood and glanced at the new message that had been seared onto the page.

New Quest: Divine Call for a Hero
The deities Hero and Rebel have requested your aid to save a nation.
Objective: Accept the divine quest with an Oathbond.
Reward: Permanently increased quality of quest rewards.

Objective: Gain Hero's and Rebel's Mark of Favor.
Reward: Adventuring Pack and Divine Title.

Objective: Retrieve the three legendary royal artifacts of the Tyrandian monarchy.
Reward: Unknown.

Objective: Find the lost heir of the Tyrandian monarchy.
Reward: Unknown.

Objective: Defeat the current Tyrandian Regent and place the rightful heir upon the throne.
Reward: Unknown.

Bonus Objective: Do not cause a civil war within Tyrand.
Reward: Unknown.

Phoenix stared at the message, then back towards the pair of deities, then back to the message. She had questions, *lots* of questions. The one that managed to make it through the jumble of thoughts came out in a whisper: "Why me?"

"Why not you?" Rebel's clear voice rang out like a bell.

"I'm nobody . . . I—" Tears threatened to form in her eyes as all the reasons she was absolutely *not* worthy of something like this flashed through her mind. "I'm not powerful. I just became a Caster this morning. I've never done anything deserving of this . . . *responsibility.*"

Her voice became heated as her fear over future failure gave way to anger over her past uselessness. "I can't save an entire nation! I couldn't even save my own mom or any of my friends!" Her shoulders sank at the admission of weakness as she stated weakly, "I—I'm no hero."

"You believe I do not know who would make a worthy hero?" The god's voice pressed down upon her, and she felt herself bowing again at the sheer force of Hero's power. It was like the world itself was threatening to crush her soul with the pair of immeasurably powerful beings so focused on her.

The Wayfarer could barely catch her breath enough to gasp out, "No, of course, you can . . . I just . . . I . . ." She didn't know what to say. She was at a loss for words to explain just how wrong all of this was.

"Phoenix." The soft feminine voice came from so close that Phoenix looked up from the [**Guide Book**] to find that a now human-sized Rebel was only inches from her.

The Wayfarer tried to straighten her posture as much as possible while the goddess smiled softly at her and continued, "You are free to reject our quest. You are free to choose the path you walk in this world." The goddess gestured to Paul who was still kneeling face down towards the ground in silence. "You are free to choose who you follow." Then she met Phoenix's soft green eyes with brighter emerald ones that seemed to glow in the waning light. "You are free to choose who you try to save."

There was a heavy pause in the air as Phoenix processed her words. If she chose to reject the quest . . . did that mean she was also choosing *not* to save all of those people?

Hero then stood next to Rebel, and Phoenix wanted nothing more than to crumple to the ground in that instance from the spiritual pressure of their proximity. He asked, "Will you choose the path of seeking freedom for others? Will you choose the path of a hero?" His voice reverberated through her, and he asked with finality, "Will you choose to accept our quest and Mark of Favor?"

Phoenix stared at the two deities, her uncertainty melting away as his words reminded her of the choices she had already made since arriving here, the path she had already chosen to attempt walking, and with a trembling voice she whispered, "I will."

"You must give us your Oath," Hero stated, "bond your words with your mana. Swear upon your magic."

"My Lord, she doesn't understand—" Paul began from beside her, but a pulse of the god's power made him fall silent once more.

Rebel glanced down at the ex-Paladin with amusement as she said, "The young Wayfarer is smart enough to abstract the meaning. She will honor her word or suffer her betrayal."

Phoenix scrunched her face with slight anxiety about messing up, but the gods didn't seem to worry about that. She glanced over at Paul, who didn't argue further, then said to the pair of deities, "I swear on my magic that I accept this quest and will attempt to complete it as best I know how."

She felt something ripple through the mana suffusing her body and realized that she had most likely made some kind of unbreakable vow that she would dearly regret not following through on. At the same time, she felt a slight twinge around her right wrist and chanced a look down to find a rainbow of runes etched around it like a tattooed bracelet. She was surprised that she could understand the six runes that each read as whole words: Oath, Bond, Quest, Hero, Rebel, Limitless.

Then, slowly, Hero and Rebel both lifted a hand that overlapped with each other and touched the center of her chest where her bra wasn't covering. It felt like a blade had pierced straight through her heart, and Phoenix could feel something searing not only her flesh but her soul as well. The pain caused her to finally fall to her knees, no longer able to withstand the restrained power of the gods, and she collapsed to the ground unconscious.

§

When he sensed the Wayfarer collapse to the ground, Paul moved for the first time since taking his kneeling position as he checked to make sure she was still alive. The pair of gods had returned to their original position a few yards away and Rebel spoke to him now, "I know your intentions to be pure and honorable, Paul Wayland, and I hope you keep to them."

"Forgive my ignorance, Divine ones, but I don't understand why you would place such a request on a mere *child* with only a fraction of power to accomplish this goal. Why would you ask this?" the former Paladin dared to question.

He glanced up to see Hero look fondly down upon the both of them as the god mercifully replied, "It's not always about the goal, Paul Wayland. It's about how she gets there and who might stand against her or beside her."

"We know you have little faith left to place in us deities," Rebel interjected. "Perhaps you should place your faith in her instead," the goddess suggested, gesturing to the young woman now sleeping in his arms.

"Perhaps you will find a more fulfilling purpose in guiding others down a worthy path," Hero advised, then gave a slight smirk and added, "House Wayland is known for cultivating some of the best heroes, after all."

Then they were gone, and the former Paladin was left to tend to an unconscious teenager . . . again.

CHAPTER FOURTEEN

Walk and Train

Phoenix rubbed at the spot on her chest where the god and goddess had come into physical contact with her. There was no longer any pain, but the memory was still creating phantoms in her mind. She was beginning to hate waking up without the memory of actually attempting to sleep.

When she exited the tent this time, she was startled to not recognize her surroundings. The grassy hillocks were gone, replaced by flatter steppe plains with some sparse plant life that reminded her of tumbleweeds she would see in movies of the Old West. The sound of running water seemed distant, and she noticed Paul a few yards away, surveying the landscape from the edge where the ground suddenly stopped. Whether he was looking out for potential threats or just enjoying the view, she wasn't quite sure.

She groggily made her way over to him, stumbling a few times, and asked, "How long was I out?"

"Two days," he said gruffly. He pointed towards the small campfire nearby that he had made with a large flat boulder and commanded, "Eat."

"At least that explains why I feel like utter garbage," she stated grumpily, then walked over to the plate of food awaiting on the boulder and took its place. As she sat on the stone, she didn't even bother to ask what any of the food was this time before placing it into her mouth.

The meat was slightly tough with a smokey flavor, and the fruit looked like pale blue grapes that seemed to gush with liquid as she popped one into her mouth. She instantly felt better and found herself craving more. This caused her to eye the food warily as she decided to ask, "What is this, and why do I like it so much?"

Paul watched her with an amused look as he explained, "I found some manarins on the way and decided to roast some of the doudrisk I killed when we first met. Both of those are Crystal Caste ingredients, meaning the mana in them is enough to sustain your new Caste level without needing to supplement with Bits."

"What about you?" she asked as she took another tentative bite of the magical food.

He grimaced slightly, then lifted another green-colored stone up for her to see before popping it into his mouth. She couldn't help laughing at the silent answer and popped another of the berries into her own mouth.

Paul then made his way over to the fire and placed himself next to her to share the boulder seat with her as he prompted, "Your book."

She barely even thought about the guide before it appeared in front of her, as though eager to inform. Together, they read through the messages that came after the gods' quest.

Quest: Divine Call for a Hero
Objective Complete: Accepted the divine quest with an Oathbond.
Objective Reward:
The quality of your quest rewards has been permanently enhanced.

Objective Complete: Gained Hero's and Rebel's Soul Mark.
Objective Reward:
[Adventuring Pack] has been added to your collection.
Divine Title has been granted.

Additional objectives still remain.

New Divine Title: Chosen One
Your Aura has been altered by divine entities: Hero and Rebel. The alterations have enhanced the strength of your Aura, increasing its range and resistance to effects from higher Castes. Your soul has been marked as one who has been chosen by the deities of Makera.

"What in the abyss?" Phoenix whispered to herself as she rubbed at the spot on her chest again. The gods had marked her soul? She wasn't sure how she felt about that. She did know, however, that she felt *extremely* uncomfortable with the Title of "Chosen One." She still couldn't fathom why they would choose *her*. There were probably hundreds of thousands of people on this planet who were better suited for this task than she was.

Her introspection was interrupted by Paul's resolute voice. "I will teach you how to control your Aura."

Phoenix looked up at the stoic warrior. "Really?"

He nodded before adding, "And fight."

Her eyes widened, and she couldn't help but sputter, "B-but why?"

They stared at each other for a long moment before he responded, "Because you need it, and I can do it."

Paul then gestured to the spot she was rubbing on her chest. "You have a Soul Mark there now. I noticed when dressing you to travel," he explained and reached into the bag at his belt, pulling out her Sewing Kit and handing it over to her.

She didn't even need to touch it as it vanished into her collection. They both seemed startled by that, and Phoenix realized that her Aura encompassed both Paul and her, as well as the surrounding area. "Sorry. I, um . . . I didn't mean to do that. My Aura just reacted to my thoughts."

"We'll work on learning to retract it first since that's usually the more difficult thing to do," he gruffly said as he reached into his bag again. "Auras naturally seek to expand, but you should try to keep it restrained when around others and only unleash it during combat." Then he held out a small mirror for her. At her questioning look, he gestured with it at her chest once more.

The Wayfarer hesitantly took the mirror with her free hand while balancing her plate of food on her lap and lowered the collar of her dress enough to see the new mark. It was a five-pointed star with feathered wings outstretched behind it. The lines were a dark black, but the interior seemed to shimmer with swirling rainbow colors, similar to the text the divine quest had displayed and the marks around her wrist. She guessed that, as far as sudden and unplanned tattoos went, this wasn't so bad.

"Does this 'Soul Mark' actually do anything?" she asked, curiously tracing a finger over it.

Paul shrugged slightly. "Not in an active sense. It simply lets others know that you are Chosen by Hero and Rebel as one who has gained their favor should they gaze upon it."

Phoenix handed the mirror back to her new trainer. "So if I keep it covered, then people won't realize I have it?"

He gave her a curious look but tilted his head in confirmation as he tucked the mirror back into his bag.

"So, when do we start training?" she asked, excitement beginning to creep up in her.

"Right away," the warrior stated, then ran a hand through his golden hair in an uncharacteristic display of anxiety. "However, you being an Aurabreaker might make training more complicated. I only know of one other even remotely in our part of the world, and I'm not sure they'd be willing to help train another."

Paul sighed and shook his head as though clearing away the worry to reclaim his composure. "Aside from your multiple Auras, are there any other Talents I should know about?"

She hesitated, thinking about her **[Waypoint]** ability and how the Magi had become so possessive of her with its revelation. She wasn't sure how this former holy Paladin would respond. Would he want to possess her as well? Turn her into a weapon for this Alliance of Adventurers? Purge her from the world as some sort of undead abomination variant?

Her uncertainty was what held her back from divulging it, but she knew he could tell if she lied. "Not any that I'm comfortable with sharing," she said quietly. This time, she could *definitely* feel his Aura as it invaded her own, searching for her secrets. She glared a bit at him and muttered, "Rude."

He dipped his head in acknowledgment but didn't apologize. "You are an enigma, young one." Paul then crossed his rather muscular arms and said with a hint of exasperation, "I've never seen someone with so much potential that thinks so little of their self."

"Potential?" she asked, looking at him. It felt like he was reiterating the hope she had been going to sleep with since arriving here, at least when she wasn't just passing out from pain, and it made her think of Morgan's words before sending her here.

"Of course. Everyone has potential," he stated, looking back out towards the horizon. "You just seem to have an impressive start. A Wayfarer Aurabreaker, who has already bested foes, if only barely, and been handpicked by the gods? And that's all in less than a fortnight." Then he gave a slight smirk. "With the right training, you might even make a great Adventurer."

The pair fell into silence. Phoenix was uncomfortable with the positive assessment of her flailing her way through events by sheer luck. She decided that maybe she could open up a bit more about why she disagreed, though. "I'm not so sure. My whole life so far has been people telling me my future only held inevitable death. Too sick to live much longer. Too weak to offer assistance. Too isolated to truly understand what living was really like. Will coming here, becoming an Adventurer, really change all of that?"

"It sounds like you've been given a rare opportunity," Paul said as he softened his stance. He watched her contemplatively, assessing her like he seemed prone to do. "You're so young," he whispered almost mournfully.

She glanced towards him. "Not that young. I just turned eighteen, which is an adult where I come from. Though I admit I don't really feel like an adult yet," Phoenix said, returning Paul's assessing gaze with one of her own. He only looked to be in his early thirties, maybe, so she returned his question. "How old are you?"

He gave a low chuckle and revealed, "I'm 64."

Phoenix gawked at the man standing before her. It sounded impossible, and her brain had to adjust mentally to reconcile what she saw with what he said. "H-how?" she barely managed to blurt out.

His smirk grew as he answered unhelpfully, "Magic."

Before she could say or ask anything more, Paul moved towards the tent to start breaking it down again, saying simply, "Come. We will walk and train."

Paul turned out to be a brutal and unrelenting trainer. He refused to pause the continual barrage of his Aura, poking and prodding her own into the bare minimum of acceptability for being around people. It took a while for her to learn to read Paul's Aura with her own in order to attempt to emulate what he was doing with his.

To her senses, she could feel him expand and retract his Aura as if he were breathing, and he showed no outward indication of what he was doing. It flowed around him and around her, mingling with hers yet remaining separate. Oil and water, she was reminded.

She could feel him pull it inwards till it seemed to meld with his skin, as if they were the same thing, and the power she felt from it was reduced to a bare trickle. She tried pulling on her own Aura, but it felt like a solid wall refusing to budge.

"I don't get it," Phoenix complained as she sat down on the side of the rough path they were following up north along the river. She was exhausted from the mental exertion more than the walking despite having been traveling for hours now.

"I've pushed and pulled, but it's not listening!" she grumbled, then looked up into the assessing gold eyes. "Do I need to increase my Strength or something? I saw that listed as an attribute thing . . ."

Paul gave a slightly annoyed huff and explained, "Those are physical. Your Aura is spiritual. Strength will affect how hard you hit, how much you can lift, and your own body's density."

As if to demonstrate, he proceeded to pick her up and continued walking down the road, cutting off her protests as he continued his lecture, "Agility affects how fast you can move, how flexible you are, how precise you can strike, and how well you can balance."

He seemed to take advantage of the time she played the role of delivery package as he increased his pace to that jog which threatened to steal her breath away. Which was fine as she also played the role of the listening student. "Fortitude determines your health, endurance, resistance to both magic and the elements. While Mind is directly tied to your mental acuity, memory and multitasking capabilities, reaction times, etcetera." He jumped over a boulder blocking the path and Phoenix almost screamed from the sudden shift as her grip tightened on his shirt.

"Those attributes are what your Aspects bind to, pulling a part of your soul to fuse, enhance, and reinforce the physical. Usually, an Aspect will bind to whichever unbound attribute suits them best," he said carefully, as though unsure if she was understanding everything.

"What about Magic? Wouldn't Star have fit that better than Fortitude?" She asked to indicate that she was indeed following along.

He shook his head and explained, "Magic is *always* bound to the Class Aspect. It seems to act as an unlocking mechanism of sorts but there is still a lot of debate and research being done on this."

"Well, what does that attribute do?"

"It determines the depth of your mana well and the power of your magic-based abilities," he said succinctly.

"Aren't all abilities magic?"

The corners of his mouth twitched slightly as he answered simply, "Some more than others."

"So, what affects my Aura?" she asked with a frustrated scrunch of her nose.

Paul slowed down then and set her back on her feet as he replied, "Your willpower. It's not a physical attribute but a representation of the strength of your soul. It is all of you. Unfortunately, I'm not familiar enough with Aurabreakers to help explain how that differs from mine. It's something you'll have to practice and discover for yourself."

She kicked at a rock in annoyance before nodding reluctantly and following him across the rocky riverside once more as the barrage of Aura prodding began anew.

CHAPTER FIFTEEN

How Long

It was another hour before Phoenix finally had a breakthrough when she realized her four Auras that had always felt layered were exactly that. She had to will them all in concert, and she had been focused on the outermost one instead. Once she focused on the innermost one and got it to retract inward easily, she managed to get each layer to follow.

They all behaved like wild animals, though, refusing to stay held back and struggling to break free from her hold while wanting to encompass everything around her. Paul assured her that was normal, and, like a wild animal, it would take patience and perseverance to tame them.

The Adventuring Pack she had received was a relief to have despite being full of mostly Mundane items. There was a simple backpack to contain everything, which didn't matter *that* much considering her collection held everything better, but it was nice to have just in case.

The padded bedroll was a welcome addition, so she didn't feel bad about stealing Paul's every night. There was a glowstone that provided light, but she had her [Starlight Companion] for that. A small campfire cooking kit that was basically foldable metal poles that could be used to set over a fire and hold meat on a spit. That also came with a plate, bowl, cup, and spork. There was also a coil of thin hemp rope that she was certain would come in handy one day.

She grinned at the very Earth-like silver lighter that was also included and came with a note.

Scholar said you would appreciate this. It uses mana for fuel. I hope it helps in your adventure.

Your most faithful patron,
Hero

Unfortunately, there was no magic device included that might help her better control her Aura.

It was another two days when she finally managed to hold it back while speaking, which was fortunate timing as they finally reached civilization. It was the small village that Paul had told her to find should anything have happened to him back in the Reality Rift, which was next to the river they had been following north.

As they wandered through the tiny collection of buildings, the streets were bustling with activity, and everyone was hurrying about. The people here seemed human, with the same tan complexion as Paul but with noticeably darker brown hair, and she wondered if his blonde was actually natural or had been changed to match his holy "Paladin of Light" motif.

Phoenix noticed an odd incongruity with the busy people staring at them; in particular, with the way they stared at Paul. There seemed to be a mix of fear, hate, awe, and respect. It was confusing to her. The shopkeepers would serve Paul with nervous deference while shooting glares at him when he wasn't looking in their direction. They barely paid her waif-like self any attention. At six-foot-one, Paul towered over her five-foot-six self as she trailed along in his shadow.

The first thing Paul did was take her to the only tailor in the area and purchase a set of proper traveling clothes for her, including a heavy, fur-lined coat. When she asked, he explained that where they were heading was going to be much colder. She wasn't really pleased with having to wear pants, but she admitted that they were more practical for traveling through the wilderness. It wasn't like she was against women wearing pants; *she* just didn't like them, much preferring the freedom that flowing skirts offered.

As they were leaving, she paused, having caught her reflection in a large mirror for the first time since becoming a Wayfarer. Her face looked slightly more feminine than she remembered, her chest only a bit larger, and the curves of her hips were more pronounced, causing her waist to be higher than she recalled. She still felt a bit shorter than she would like to be, but her proportions were a huge improvement, in her opinion.

The one thing she absolutely hated, though, was the absence of her long red hair, which had been replaced by a red fuzz in the two weeks since it was rudely stripped from her.

She glared as she rubbed the prickly hairs with a hand and only stopped when Paul's rough baritone startled her by asking, "What is upsetting you?"

Phoenix dropped her hand to her side as she looked up at the larger man. She realized that she had lost the little control she had over her Aura while she was lost in her anger and quickly pulled it back in line with what he had taught her. She stared back at her reflection for another moment before shaking her head. "It's silly . . ."

"Tell me," he commanded.

She sighed. "I just . . . Well, becoming a Wayfarer caused all my hair to . . . burn off?" she explained, gesturing up to her head as she stared at the floor and admitted, "It took years to grow my hair as long as it was and . . . well, it was one of the few things about myself that I actually *liked*."

He glanced at her reflection as well with a contemplative look before turning with another command: "Follow."

Phoenix was mentally reprimanding herself for sounding like a petulant child complaining about not having the toy they wanted. There were so many other things to concern herself over, and the length of her hair shouldn't have been one of them. She just hoped that Paul's opinion of her hadn't declined because of it. She wasn't sure why exactly, but she found that she valued his opinion and wanted to make the man not regret the time he had spent with her so far, not only in saving her but also in training her.

She followed behind the warrior, dutifully silent and trying to focus more on keeping her layered Aura tightly restrained against her skin as he led her into another small shop. The pungent smell of dried plants assaulted her nose, and she looked around to find that they were in some sort of apothecary.

Herbs and vials covered every surface, and Phoenix assumed that they were here to restock on healing potions. She did owe Paul a couple of them, after all. She was surprised when Paul gestured for her to come up to the counter after exchanging a few words that she didn't catch with the shop clerk.

The older woman looked from the Emerald Caster to her, and the elderly face softened into a gentle smile. The clerk responded, "Yes, I have just the thing to help. You're lucky you arrived when you did. This week, the last of us here in town are heading to Vallinsarvi for the blood moon. Let me take her into the back room for a bit."

Phoenix was a bit alarmed by the statement, but Paul gently nudged her to follow after the woman, so she complied. The clerk led her into the back room, which was surprisingly sterile compared to the clutter of the shop. The woman patted the seat of a wooden stool in an obvious gesture for her to sit and pulled out what appeared to be a dark wooden comb.

With increasing anxiety, Phoenix sat on the stool, wondering what in the world was going on, when the woman instructed her, "Alright, dear, it might feel a bit odd, but do your best not to move while I work." Then the woman chuckled and added, "We don't want hair growing where it's unwanted, after all."

"What?" Phoenix asked in surprise.

"I'm only teasing, dear. I can remove anything you don't like with a different tool, but it would be more of a hassle. Now, that gentleman out front said 'long,' but exactly how long do you want it?"

Phoenix was a bit stunned as she pieced together what was supposedly happening, but she answered a moment later, "To the small of my back. That was how I wore it before." The older woman nodded and then carefully went to work, running the teeth of the comb along her scalp and following the faint hairline.

A half hour later, she couldn't wipe the smile from her face as she stared at the mirror, now reflecting her long, beautiful curls of warm burgundy hair. It had a healthy shine, and Phoenix hugged the temporary barber tightly as thanks for her wonderful work.

When she returned to the front of the store, Phoenix also wrapped her arms around Paul, to his uncomfortable surprise. After a moment, he simply patted the top of her head and gently extricated himself from her grip.

Paul did buy more potions then, followed by leading her back out of the town. Phoenix wanted to complain about not getting to sleep in a proper bed that night, but she held her tongue. He had already done much for her by not only clothing her but also returning something she thought would have taken years to get back. She felt sacrificing a night in a bed was a small price to pay in return.

Seeing the crowded streets with new information made her ask her stoic guide, "What's a blood moon, and why are all these people going to Val—Valin—"

"Vallinsarvi. It is one of the region's fortress cities about a fortnight's walk northeast, by Mundane speeds," he explained. "A blood moon is an event that occurs about once every fifteen years. You've seen the orange moon. That's Krafti, and its color shifts over the years as it slowly soaks up mana. Once it turns a bloodred color, it purges that mana. Pouring it out onto the world and causing a massive spike in the world's ambient magic. As a result, more monsters spawn, and they are often stronger than usual.

"When the blood moon ends, usually after about four weeks, the color returns to a pale yellow. Visku, the blue moon, doesn't absorb mana like Krafti, but it does let off a constant trickle—"

"Which is why nights are more dangerous," she interjected.

"Yes," he confirmed before adding thoughtfully, "it is said there used to be a third moon, a green one called Hugrekki, which is now more of an asteroid belt around our planet's center. I don't think there's anyone alive today who might have seen it as a solid moon."

"So, people relocate to this fortress town for a month because of so many monsters spawning all at once?" Phoenix tried summarizing.

Paul nodded in affirmation again. "Yes. It's easier to protect the people behind those reinforced magical walls and rebuild afterward than trying to protect huge swaths of territory. The AOA usually helps coordinate all of this with the local government, and they've always emphasized lives over property."

"That's encouraging. I would hope most people would prioritize that way."

Paul grimaced as he said bitterly, "You'd be surprised by how many people care more about their Bits than their neighbors. From my experience, the more Bits they have, the more they fear losing any of it."

"Actually, that sounds a lot like the world I'm from when you put it like that," Phoenix admitted softly.

Once the small village was out of sight, Paul began his Aura training again while they walked. He had them stop earlier than usual to make camp and had her stand across from him with the setting sun still illuminating the rocky terrain.

"We're going to start combat training in the evenings. We'll be arriving in a region that has monsters more suitable to your Caste soon, and I want you to get some experience fighting them," the Adventurer began. "We have a blood moon approaching and should be doing what we can to assist. Getting some monster kills under your belt will also be helpful if you try to join the AOA."

"Do you think I should? Join them, that is. What about this divine quest I have?" she asked dubiously.

"Everyone helps during a blood moon," he stated firmly. "You're not strong enough to start that quest anyway. If the gods wanted you to hurry off on it, they would have stipulated a time limit."

"How do you know there's not one?" she asked. She had assumed there wasn't one, since her quest hadn't said otherwise, but also believed she couldn't just put it off forever.

Paul surprised her by gesturing towards her right wrist, which she obligingly lifted. He took hold of it while pointing at each rune with his other hand as he explained, "Aside from your book, this is an Oathbond. Indicated by the first two runes."

He pointed at each, then pressed on the one she translated as "Quest" and continued, saying, "This one indicates the 'what' of the vow. A mission, a promise, an item, a target, an abstinence, etcetera.

"The next indicates who the Oath was made to." His finger swept across the symbols for Hero and Rebel before stopping once more on the final shimmery rune.

"This last one shows the time frame, whether it's hours, days, years, or forever." His eyes met hers as he asked, "What does it say to your eyes?"

"Limitless," she answered.

He nodded in return and gave a soft smile. "I'll admit I was curious if your translation ability could read this ancient language. Most of us just learn to recognize the rune as meaning infinite."

His smile vanished as he continued to the blank space of her wrist next to the time limit and said, "Now, the thing that worries me is the lack of a rune here."

"What should be there?"

"The punishment," he said solemnly, and she felt a slight chill run up her spine. "The consequence of breaking your Oath should normally be spelled out here so that you know what might happen should you fail."

"Does no rune mean no punishment?" she asked hopefully but could already sense the sinking feeling in the pit of her stomach.

The Paladin shook his head. "No. If there was no consequence, then the rune for 'Nothing' would be here. The lack of the rune means the ones the Oath was made to"—he tapped the runes for Hero and Rebel again—"get to decide the moment the Oath is broken. It's also not necessarily a conscious choice on their part, but I'm not sure that will be the case with a god."

He paused a moment, contemplating, before dropping her hand and saying, "You should try to keep your Oath hidden. You don't know who out there might want an Oathbonded of Hero or Rebel to fail."

Before she could ask anything more, he took a step back and squared his shoulders. He turned slightly away from her and said, "Now, I'm going to show you a meditation technique that focuses on smooth actions and timing your breathing. I want you to copy it."

With that, she tried her best to follow his surprisingly graceful movements long into the night, both of them unencumbered by the darkness surrounding them.

CHAPTER SIXTEEN

Get Used to It

So aside from poking around for deception and being able to tell I'm a Wayfarer, what else does my Aura reveal?" Phoenix asked as she pulled her new cloak tighter around her. It was starting to get colder during the day now as they kept traveling northeast towards Vallinsarvi. They had entered more forest now, filled with tall evergreen trees, and the wind liked to travel down the road with them.

Paul continued training her Aura technique, getting her used to the feeling of controlling it and resisting his attempts to suppress it. He had to go easy on her since he was so ridiculously stronger than her, and she often found herself feeling like a toddler who was winning at arm wrestling—meaning it was only because he let her.

"Aside from basic information like species and Caste, most Casters will be able to sense whatever abilities any Aura power grants it, but the trick to feeling emotions like deception is a more advanced thing that you likely won't run into unless you find yourself surrounded by others of much higher Caste often," he explained as they walked. "The only other thing most people with Aura senses might be able to perceive is your Titles."

"You mean people will just *know* I'm some 'Chosen One' just because our Auras touch?" she asked, slightly horrified by that idea. She suddenly felt much more motivated to keep it restrained at all times.

He chuckled. "Not quite like that. Similar to the emotions, it usually takes skill to truly discern the effects of Titles, and it's really more of a . . . *flavor*. Most will just sense a heroic and rebellious nature in your Aura at the moment. With just a hint of divinity like many of the clergy have as well."

"Do you have any Titles?" she asked, curious to learn more about her new trainer and guide.

"I have many. Not all are Divine like yours, but the gods will often grant Titles to their disciples."

That made her feel a bit better about the idea of someone poking around her Aura. "So I won't stand out as much then?"

Paul raised a brow at her. "Being a Wayfarer already makes you stand out, young one, not to mention your other rare abilities. If anonymity is your goal, I suggest dedicating yourself to the Hermit once you've completed the quest you've already bound yourself to."

He gave a heavy sigh and surprised her by admitting, "Sometimes I wish I had been smart enough to choose that path for myself."

"Why is that?"

The former Paladin didn't reply at first, seeming lost in thought. When the silence stretched on long enough that she worried that she had somehow angered him, he said, "I've made many choices I've come to regret over the decades I've already lived. Sometimes I wonder if I had just gone off to live peacefully in the mountains somewhere if things would have turned out better."

"Not for me," she found herself replying, "I'd be lost and probably would have starved to death." She glanced up at his frowning face. "You mentioned saving others before. I'm sure they'd feel the same."

Paul gave her a soft smile before saying, "That's the only thing keeping me from running off now. Trying to make up for those mistakes by helping where I can."

Phoenix returned his smile before trying again to gather more information. "So, what Titles do you have?"

"Many from my time as a Paladin and Adventurer," he answered, "I've traveled the continent and gotten a Title for that feat alone."

"You got a Title just from traveling?"

"Yes. I have the [**Traveler of Pyrin**] Title by visiting every nation on this continent and seeing each cardinal coast. It's not necessarily a difficult Title to achieve, yet many never do." He glanced down at her for a moment before adding, "Perhaps one day I can help you achieve it as well."

She liked that idea. Despite their short time together, she had found herself strangely enjoying having the stoic warrior as a traveling companion. He had a subtle sense of humor and had been patient with teaching her despite his relentlessness with it. He never made her feel dumb for not knowing something and would try to explain clearly, even if it was a bit grumbly.

Lost in her thoughts, Paul startled her by stopping in the middle of the dirt road they were following as he looked off to the side ahead of them with sudden alertness.

"What's wrong?"

"Wrong isn't the right word," he replied, then gave her a smirk. "I think I just found a monster for you."

"What kind of monster?" she asked, suddenly tense at the idea of another killer rabbit trying to bite her head off. "It's not a devil bunny, right?"

"I don't count forest critters that a Mundane grandmother could handle," he retorted and chuckled at the affronted look she gave him.

"It had *really* sharp teeth!"

"Then you definitely won't like this one," he replied, then seemed to vanish in a rush of wind.

When the Emerald Caster returned, he was holding onto what looked like a large wooden branch with a few smaller branches coming off it, covered in pine needles—but it was shivering in his grasp.

It wasn't until he set it down that she realized it was indeed a monster as multiple fang-filled mouths opened along its body, and it used those branching limbs to scuttle along the ground away from the overpowered Paladin and towards her instead.

Phoenix stumbled backward and almost tripped over her own feet before Paul barked at her, "Dagger!"

She conjured it to her hand but felt herself reacting too slowly. As it lunged at her, she raised her arms and tried to cover her face.

When she didn't feel the sting of those sharp teeth sinking into her, she opened her eyes to find the monster struggling in midair while it was being held in a firm fist by a glaring Adventurer.

"Is this why you got hurt in the Reality Rift?" he asked. "You just let it hit you?"

"No," she retorted, lowering her arms and returning his glare, "you just surprised me. I didn't think you'd just toss a random monster at me! At least I knew they might show up in the Rift!"

Paul gave a sigh and pinched the bridge of his nose as he said, "I thought your trek through the mountains before would have meant you already learned this lesson, but I think I may have inadvertently made you think otherwise." Then he stared her in the eyes as he said very deliberately, "Monsters are *everywhere* in this world, young one. Whether you see them or not, you should *always* be prepared to fight them."

"But I thought they only came out at night?"

"Most do, but not all," he explained. "Some rest and lurk in the shadows, waiting for unsuspecting prey. Others hide in plain sight." He shook the tree-branch-monster he held. "This Stickler, for instance, will find a tree to blend into near the road and drop down on travelers that pass by."

She looked at the monster in horror, realizing it probably would have killed her if Paul hadn't sensed it. He took a step forward while twisting to move the monster further from her and commanded, "Show me how you're holding that."

Phoenix winced at the command, knowing full well that she was likely terrible, and he confirmed it a moment later. "Your thumb is in the wrong position for that kind of cross guard," he said. "Turn it slightly so it goes along the blade instead of against the guard. You can have more control when you thrust like that. If you need to give it more strength, reverse the hold and attack downward with your thumb against the pommel so it doesn't slip as much."

She tried to adjust her hold on it based on his instructions while trying to ignore the squirming monster only a few feet away that Paul seemed entirely unconcerned about.

When she finally had an acceptable hold on it, he asked, "Are you alright to try again?"

"Are you just going to let it run at me again?"

"You need to get accustomed to reading their movements. I'm not planning to stand by your side all the time to hold the monster for you while you stab it," he replied with a flat look.

Phoenix rolled her eyes at him, and he raised an eyebrow at her. She noticed the twitch at the corner of his mouth, though.

He tried to hold back a smile and asked, "Did you just roll your eyes at me?"

"Maybe," she dodged, refusing to meet his golden gaze.

"Did you lie earlier, and are actually five?"

"I'm eighteen!"

"I'm not sure I believe you anymore. Most eighteen-year-olds I've met were much more respectful to those of higher Caste and accustomed to taking care of themselves."

She flushed in embarrassment at that, suddenly feeling awkward about the differences between her and others he was pointing out. Bitterly, she muttered, "It's not my fault I didn't grow up like other kids. I don't know how to take care of myself when I've never been able to."

After only a moment, she heard him say softly, "I apologize. I didn't mean to bring up the past like that." She looked up to see gentle golden eyes and a frown emphasized by his trimmed beard. His frown turned up into a small smile when he added, "I guess it's up to me now to rectify that."

"What do you mean?"

"Finish defeating this monster, and then we can talk some more. Fill in those knowledge gaps of yours between monsters and training," he said as he took a few steps back and lifted the wriggling branch-monster again. "Are you ready?"

She took a deep breath, centering herself, and nodded.

It went terribly.

Phoenix managed to kill it without Paul needing to intervene again as she used that downward thrust to repeatedly stab it to death, but got many, *many* cuts for her troubles.

As they sat on the side of the road while Paul helped remove the prickly needles embedded in her arms, she muttered, "I suck at this."

"Everyone does at first," he replied, tossing another needle off to the side before it quickly turned to ash now that it was free from her. "It takes practice and dedication. Nobody is born a warrior; they forge themselves into one."

"I'm sure there are people with a Talent for it, though," she said. "Actually, I bet there are people with a literal Natural Talent for fighting, isn't there?"

He chuckled. "Yes, but that doesn't mean they are automatically masters at it. There is always room for improvement. Just because one might have power doesn't mean they instantly know how best to wield that power. It's why cultivating our Caste is such a long journey that many never reach the end of. I, for one, doubt there is even an end to reach."

Then the Paladin lifted her arm up and said, "Now try healing this with your **[Dawn Rises]** ability."

She thought about doing so, then paused and asked, "Which version? There's multiple . . . What do you call the words spoken for an ability here? Chants? Verbal component?"

"Incantations," he answered with a smirk, "I was wondering if you would even ask about that little nuance."

"Why does that one and my **[Lunar Dream]** ability have an incantation, but the others don't? And why is it different for each version of my heal?"

"The length of an incantation usually corresponds to how much time is required to focus and fully activate the ability. Those two have incantations mainly because they are Spells. Your portal, dagger, and gravity ability were all listed as Utilities, correct?"

She nodded, deep in thought, as she conjured her **[Guide Book]** to read over them again. "Yeah, it's listed under their 'Type.' Are there a lot of different types of abilities?"

"Not too many," he replied with a shrug. Lowering her arm, he explained, "There are ten main types that most get categorized into. About triple that in additional modifiers that you might see."

"Modifiers?" she asked, and he held up a hand to stall her.

"First, heal yourself with the little version, then I'll show you one of my abilities to help explain."

Phoenix nodded and began to recite the words, feeling the power suffusing her voice as the magic took form. *"See the dawn."*

As she healed her arm, Paul pressed a hand to her book and closed his eyes for a moment. When he took his hand away, he merely said, "I'm glad this works similar to an Identification Orb." Then he nudged the book towards her so that she could read the single ability he had made appear.

> **Passive Ability:** Penetrating Sight
> **Type:** Perception (magical, covenant, light)
> **Current Caste:** Emerald 9
> **Crystal Effect:** The level of light does not hinder your sight.
> **Sapphire Effect:** You can see the types of magic a creature or item is attuned to.
> **Emerald Effect:** The longer you focus your sight on a target, the easier it becomes to overcome their resistances and analyze their Aura. Looking away resets this effect.

"Your Perception ability is like mine?" she asked, surprisingly pleased by that fact.

"For now," he replied with a nod. "Yours might be different at higher Castes. While some passives specifically might repeat fairly consistently across different people, there's always a chance they become slightly different. It really depends on a lot of other factors, and passives usually have a tendency to take on traits of the other abilities they are bound to."

He shook his head as he adjusted to work on her other arm and added dismissively, "I wouldn't worry too much about that for now, though. We need to get you walking before you run, and that starts with simply understanding the main differences between abilities."

She nodded in understanding and said, "So Spells require an incantation . . . and mana, I assume?"

"Usually, but sometimes health," he explained. "Special Attacks are what I often use, and those more often require stamina, but some use mana as well. It really depends on the nature of it in that case. The other main types you'll see quite often are Boons and Banes, which are really the same thing, just the former has a positive effect while the latter has negative ones."

"I have one of those. My **[Night Blade]** inflicts the **[Mana Siphon]** Bane," she recalled and focused on bringing up just the Bane itself to show him.

> **Status Effect:** Mana Siphon
> **Type:** Bane (drain, magical, arcane, stacking)
> **Effect:** Drains a low amount of mana over time.

"That's a pretty standard type of Bane." He pointed at the text that appeared in parentheses next to the main Type. "These are what I was referring to when I said 'modifiers.' They each refer to a piece that contributes to what it is or how it works. Most are self-explanatory, like that 'Stacking' addendum. It means you can have more than one instance on the same target for compounded effect."

"And I assume the drain just means stealing the mana from them?"

"In this case, yes, but sometimes it will refer to an ability that drains one non-mana resource for another. Mana is considered the default cost for most abilities, so things like healing Spells or stamina rejuvenation won't be considered Drains. Mana, health, and stamina are all a type of resource, and some abilities might trade health or stamina for mana. You're basically draining yourself at that point."

Phoenix hummed in thought as she mulled over the information, then asked, "So why does this say 'magical'? Aren't all abilities magic?"

"Magic, yes, but *Magical* is referring to the three categories of magic. Which are Elemental, Magical, and Divine."

"Then Arcane is?"

"A subtype of Magical magic."

"This is starting to get confusing . . ."

Paul chuckled. "The Order of Magic has long been hard at work in their pursuit of categorizing and labeling all the different types of magic and abilities out there. I don't expect you to learn it all in a single day."

She gave a huff of annoyance and was about to ask more when she froze at the sight of a white flake falling in front of her face. Her head snapped upward, and she almost hurt herself more as she practically ripped her arm from Paul's grasp to stand and stare at the gray sky above them.

Phoenix whispered, not wanting to be wrong and just imagining, "Is it snowing?"

The Paladin stood up beside her and grinned as he asked, "Have you never seen snow before?"

More flakes fell on her face, and she blinked away her tears. Quietly, she admitted, "In pictures and rarely outside my window. I was never allowed to go outside and touch it, though."

Phoenix shivered slightly and dabbed a finger on one of the droplets on her cheek. She smiled up at him. "I never thought I'd ever get to experience snow like this."

He chuckled again. "Well, get used to it because snow is the default weather in Tulim."

CHAPTER SEVENTEEN

Tundra Training

New Quest: Tundra Training
Time to test your mettle.
Objective: Defeat ten Ice-Attuned Crystal Caste monsters.
Reward: Rare Crystal Caste cloak.

"Oh, c-come on!" Phoenix said through chattering teeth as she read the message her book offered up. "It's f-freezing . . . I c-can barely f-feel my hands, let alone s-stab s-something with them!"

It had been another week of traveling, Aura training, and learning to meditate "properly" through the wintry forest, and the snow that had entranced Phoenix at first now chilled her to her core despite being bundled in a heavy fur coat. Her boots kept her from getting too hot, but they didn't do anything to keep her from getting cold in the magic-infused storm they found themselves in.

Her protector had announced that they were now in a Moderate Rate High Crystal Caste biome, and, on average, the monsters that were spawning should be something she could handle. However, he would still be making sure she wouldn't get poorly matched or overwhelmed.

Paul chuckled after reading the book over her shoulder. "Time to fight, young one," he said as he patted her shoulder and then nudged her towards the small hissing monster a few yards away.

She didn't recall snakes ever being able to withstand such cold temperatures and could only assume its blue scales were infused with some sort of Ice magic. She summoned her dagger with a thought, and a second thought unleashed her Aura from the reigns she was getting more comfortable handling.

Phoenix tried to take a calming breath as the wind whipped against her face, tossing her hair into it haphazardly. She used her free hand to remove it for the hundredth time, reminding herself to find something to tie it back with later, and then she charged.

It went worse than the Stickler.

She managed to kill the Snow Snake that dissolved into white ash as soon as it collapsed to the rocky ground, but it was not without cost. She clutched the dripping puncture wound in her calf as she tried to staunch the bleeding, unaccustomed to such a deep wound. Paul was kneeling beside her in an instant, holding what looked like a thick pad that reminded her of gauze directly over the wound to help halt the bleeding as he chastised her. "Sloppy."

She gritted her teeth to try to keep them from chattering. "I know."

"Heal it," he ordered.

Phoenix didn't argue as she touched her leg above where he held and incanted, "*You will see the dawn of tomorrow*," activating the moderate-cost version of the Spell and feeling the same healing sensation trickle through her calf as when she drank a potion.

Paul wiped away the remaining blood and commanded, "Again," as he pulled her up into a standing position. He moved her closer to another of the snakes that he had been holding back with his own terrifying Aura, freezing it in place with fear alone.

"S-s-seriously?!" she barely managed to shout as Paul retracted his Aura and the snake launched itself at her. She brought forth her dagger once more, dodging and striking as fast as her half-frozen limbs could manage.

As she plunged her dagger into the reptilian eye, and it began to dissolve into more ash on top of her, Paul was next to her in the blink of an eye again, helping her back up to her feet. "Better," he assessed before dashing her hopes once more. "Again."

Five more Snow Snakes and a pair of Frost Foxes later, Paul paused to give her a slightly more in-depth assessment. "You're improving quickly."

"My body s-started to warm up when f-fighting for my life," she said with a bit of sarcasm between heavy breaths. She was attempting to tame her wild curls into a more manageable and restrained braid that went down the side of her head and over her left shoulder. She would be ready for this current hunger game she had been thrown into.

"You still have a long way to go to be at the minimum of AOA standards."

Phoenix only nodded before asking, "M-my book mentioned Spirit Gems could be used t-to unlock Class abilities. Would m-more powers help fill in m-my weaknesses?"

Paul thought for a moment, choosing his words carefully as they walked to the next area where the Emerald Caster had sensed another monster. "They might. You should be able to pass the AOA assessment without them, though. I think you undervalue the power of four Aura abilities. Right now, all four of them can help you last longer in a fight than most others of your Caste. The main hole I see currently is that you're not weaving the combat techniques I've shown you with the powers you've already unlocked."

He paused, then gestured towards what seemed like a fuzzy boulder sitting in the middle of their path. "This fight should make those weaknesses more apparent to you. If you don't *use* your abilities, you won't win."

Then the boulder moved and turned to face them, and Phoenix instantly thought she had finally seen an abominable snow monster. It was almost as tall as the gods when it stood and let out a deafening roar.

Phoenix's wide eyes sought Paul's as she asked incredulously, "*That's* Crystal Caste?!" He only nodded, then took a few steps back so the monster would direct its ire at her. She groaned and conjured her weapon once more.

She had been using her **[Night Blade]** power this whole time, but she realized now that she hadn't turned the effects of her Aura back on, which she quickly remedied. She tried to think of what other combat-oriented things she could do but wasn't sure how useful an illusion would be against the towering beast.

The Astromancer tried anyway, whispering the required incantation under her breath, "***Let dreams become reality.***"

The Tundra Yeti didn't seem to care as it plowed through the semitransparent illusory wall she created between them.

Out of the corner of her eye, she noticed Paul drop his face into his hand in exasperation and couldn't help pausing to think incredulously to herself, *Did he just facepalm at me?!*

That thought cost her dearly, as the monster slammed a massive paw into her, shattering her **[Sun Shell]** in the process like golden glass breaking into palm-sized shards. She could hear the crack of her ribs and the Yeti roared at the inconvenience of being blinded for its trouble.

It was almost instinct when she triggered her **[Ruler of Relativity]** ability to distance herself from the creature. She felt the mana drain from her as she moved, but it stopped as soon as she did. She raised her dagger again, but the Yeti was much faster than expected.

As she reactively took a step back, she slipped on a patch of ice and fell forward onto her face. Before she could catch her breath, a heavy weight slammed into her back.

Phoenix heard it first, as the massive foot of the monster cracked her spine, and then the pain flooded her upper body. She couldn't feel anything below the point of impact, and panic added to the pain. She thought her death would be next, as the monster would completely crush her, but the weight suddenly vanished, and Paul was at her side.

She screamed in agony as he turned her body and tried to get her in a position where she could drink. Tears burned her eyes as they flowed freely, and she could hardly register the worried expression on Paul's face as he shoved the potion into her mouth, not even attempting to have her heal it herself this time.

Phoenix barely managed to down the sweet liquid before the pain claimed the last of her consciousness.

Quest: Tundra Training
Objective Complete: Defeated ten Crystal Caste monsters.
Objective Reward:
[Snow Shroud] has been added to your collection.

Completion Reward:
10 [Crystal Mana Bits] have been added to your collection.

Phoenix frowned at her **[Guide Book]** that was floating above her as she awoke in the tent bed. She knew that she hadn't defeated that Yeti monster, but her quest still seemed to count it. She slowly sat up after verifying she could feel all her limbs.

When she exited the tent, she discovered that Paul had moved them into a cave and that a fire was going to warm up the space. She still pulled her coat on and sat by the fire, trying to warm her hands more.

She moved her book around in front of her to read the description of her new item since it had trailed behind her as she had moved—as it was prone to do. Paul sat next to her, taking his now familiar spot to read alongside her.

Item: Snow Shroud
A versatile cloak made from the fur of a Tundra Yeti.
Caste: Crystal.
Availability: Rare.
Type: Apparel, cloak.
Effects:
- Become harder to detect while in snowy terrain.
- Keeps the wearer from becoming chilled.
- Use a [Mana Bit] to shift the cloak's form into a temporary shelter for 8 hours.

"I feel like I don't deserve this," she admitted quietly as she conjured the cloak into her lap, running her hand against the incredibly soft white fur.

"You fought hard, even if you didn't land the killing blow," her Mentor reassured.

"It broke me . . ." she said in a whisper, "one mistake and I would have died if you hadn't interfered . . ."

"I should have interfered sooner," he stated firmly, "I apologize for my miscalculation. You should never have been injured that severely."

She met his gaze and pointed out, "You won't always be there to watch me."

He shifted a bit uncomfortably and acknowledged, "True, but by that point, you should be able to handle yourself better and be able to properly calculate the risks involved yourself." He gestured at the cloak. "Despite the danger and unknown risk, you never backed down from the challenges. You earned that."

Phoenix nodded, contemplating his words, then threw the cloak around her shoulders and sighed in relief at the instant warmth it provided. She then leaned her head against Paul's arm and whispered, "Thank you."

"Don't thank me just yet," he said with a wry smile. "There's a very angry Rabearus outside this cave who's just waiting for me to leave."

She slowly looked up at him. "Please tell me that you plan to take me with you when you do, instead of leaving me to fight it off," she replied with narrowed eyes.

Paul just shrugged and said, "I think you can take it."

"I just got snapped in two like a twig!" she protested incredulously.

"And now you're all better," the merciless Adventurer pointed out. "This time, I'll even give you more advice," he promised as she crossed her arms and glared.

"Weren't you supposed to do that *before* I broke my spine?"

To his credit, Paul looked down with chagrin and said softly, "Again, I apologize. I'm not used to teaching others, nor do I always remember that you didn't grow up in a world like this one."

He glanced towards the mouth of the cave, where she could barely make out a hulking silhouette. "You have the tools, and I believe you also have the abilities to take out this monster. You were close to utilizing one of your strongest powers last time. If you hadn't slipped, you may have very well found the answer and won."

"You know," she interrupted, "you were all blunt and single-word answers when we first met, and now that you're training me, it's like you're beating around the bush," she observed, raising an eyebrow at him.

He shook his head and gave her a crooked smile. "You're right. I might owe you another apology. I've been trying to train you like my father trained me, but he and I are very different people. You and I also have very different starting points."

Phoenix returned his smile and leaned her head against his arm again as she said, "You're forgiven. Just tell me directly what to try doing, and I'll fight that Rabearbear in the morning."

The ex-Paladin chuckled as he corrected her. "Rabearus. And I guess that's fair enough. Eat some food, then get some sleep, young one."

She complied and, in the morning, felt much better about her chances as Paul explained what he wanted her to focus on.

"While I know it says it's a Utility ability with only the Magical and Covenant modifiers, I want you to try using **[Ruler of Relativity]** as though it had the Movement modifier as well," her Mentor explained as they both ate some breakfast. "Push and pull yourself around the battlefield to control your position and gain the advantage."

The Astromancer nodded. She thought about it and practiced a bit in the cave with the cave wall as her target to get used to the feel of the ability siphoning her mana as she altered the gravitational force between them.

Using it for mobility was tricky in multiple respects. She had to become accustomed to directing her mana with her will to determine the amount of force she was increasing, translating to speed in practical terms. The faster she wanted to move, the more mana she had to pour in.

Once she decided to try it on the Rabearus, which amounted to a pissed-off polar bear monster with three heads, she noticed another issue with her gravity ability that she had to account for.

The increased speed also came with timing issues since the larger of the two of them would be moved slower by the ability. In practice, she barely moved at all when pulling a dagger towards her that was lodged into the creature's flank. Meanwhile, she had practically flown at the large beast when she targeted it instead, while it seemed only to be nudged slightly across the floor.

Phoenix was thrown back by the massive paw of the bear after landing that minor puncture wound and took a moment to glare at the dagger that she had just retrieved. She was frustrated with how inadequate it felt at that moment. She knew now that the short, thin blade would do little against the hulking monster's thick hide.

As the beast turned back towards her, she knew that she needed to fight smarter, not harder. Paul had challenged her to use her gravity ability to take down this monster, and she wasn't about to give up.

Her gaze roamed the hulking mass of fur, looking for weak points, but she didn't see anywhere on the massive body that didn't appear to be protected by muscle or teeth. Except for its eyes . . . but she didn't have a ranged weapon, just a dagger.

If she could get close enough to stab it there, deep enough to strike its brain, then it might be enough to take it down. The only problem was its sword-like claws that would savage her before she could get in reach. Even if she managed to dodge those, she'd be landing in a maw of razor-sharp teeth.

Smarter, not harder, she mentally recited. Then, an idea clicked, and she grinned.

As the monster began to charge at her, she lifted the stiletto in front of her, aiming it carefully at the monster's eye, braced herself against the wall, then poured her mana into triggering her [**Ruler of Relativity**] on the blade, this time revers-ing the pull. The dagger shot out like an arrow and buried itself deep in the mid-dle head's eye socket before lodging itself into its skull.

The Rabearus seemed to stutter in its charge and roared in anguish with its remaining two heads. She reconjured her dagger before it could charge again and sent the blade flying towards another healthy eye.

When her aim proved true and another head went limp, she gave a whoop and couldn't help tossing a fist in the air in her excitement. The beast wasn't giv-ing up, though, and charged at her once more in what seemed to be a last-ditch effort to bite off her head.

That time, her newly conjured dagger went straight into its gaping maw, and the monster's momentum carried it forward as it stumbled to the floor. It quickly began dissolving into white ash as it was automatically looted into her collection.

"Good," Paul said with a nod, causing Phoenix to smile at the approval despite her exhaustion from using so much mana during the fight. While conjuring the [**Night Blade**] in the first place took a moderate amount, making her dagger move that quickly away from her took almost as much. The relentless trainer then ges-tured to the cave opening. "Next one is not far."

He then pulled a well-made, gold-embellished dagger from his belt and raised it up for her to take. "Here. Try using two next time."

The Wayfarer gave a small groan then dutifully took the proffered knife and followed along behind him.

CHAPTER EIGHTEEN

Eat, Sleep, and Train

They arrived in the fortress city of Vallinsarvi the following night and Phoenix was grateful she would finally be able to sleep in an actual bed. It felt like they had done nothing but eat, sleep, and train. Phoenix wanted to actually *rest* for a change. Maybe even have a nice warm bath.

Before that could happen, Paul needed to first head to the city's center and talk to the baroness and local AOA commander. Apparently, the presence of an Emerald Caster in this area could set them on edge.

There were tons of people crowding about the streets, which she assumed was in preparation to hunker down for the coming blood moon. As she followed closely, she noticed most of the people she saw were humanoid but not *quite* human.

Some had shimmery, metallic-looking tattoos of various colors all over their exposed warm brown skin, and others had glowing ember eyes with dark, ashen skin that seemed to have markings made of lava peeking through their fur clothing. The fiery type had long, tapered ears like elves, while the other looked much more human.

They were all various shades of dark tones in both skin and hair, from rich mahogany to ashen grays to dark onyx, causing her pale alabaster skin and red hair to stand out in contrast. Even Paul stood out with his lighter tan skin and golden-blonde hair.

Phoenix gently tugged on her Mentor's sleeve and asked him quietly, "What kind of people are they?"

He paused for a moment, then shook his head in an apology. "Sorry. I forgot to warn you earlier, but they are such a common species that it slipped my mind that you might not have them in your world."

"We only have humans as far as I know," she informed him.

"Well, the shorter ones with the metallic rune markings are the runeforged. They naturally excel at magic Spells and crafting," he explained, tilting his head towards a group that was wielding wands to move belongings into one of the buildings.

"The taller, fiery ones are the cinderen, usually attuned to the Earth and Fire Elements," he continued, gesturing towards a group talking in front of a wall filled with informational flyers.

The little tidbit sparked another question she had meant to ask earlier. "How many Elements are there? You only mentioned the three categories before."

He seemed to contemplate for a moment, and she wondered if he was mentally counting them, but the Adventurer said in his teaching tone, "That seems like a simple question at first but context might change the meaning of the word 'element' in this case. We would use that specifically when talking about the Elemental kind, but I think you're asking about all of the subtypes, correct?"

She nodded, and he continued to explain.

"To answer your original question, there are ten Elements: Earth, Fire, Water, Wind, Corrosion, Gem, Ice, Lightning, Metal, and Plant. Most people are familiar with these, as they make up most of the physical world. They are also the most common types of magic or attunement. There are ten more Magical subtypes and three Divine ones."

Phoenix scrunched her nose, "I remember 'Ice-Attuned' being a requirement for my training quest. Does that just mean they can use that type of Elemental magic?"

"No, it means they are *infused* with that type of magic. An attunement is part of their very being. You have a handful of different magic types that your abilities leverage, but you're only attuned to Dimension magic as far as I can see with my Perception ability."

"Huh," she replied thoughtfully, "is that from my **[Aetheric Transmigrator]** Talent?"

"Probably. Many people are born with some kind of attunement or disposition, but plenty more gain them through Aspects."

"So, all this different typing is just how people have decided to categorize the different magic and abilities, right? It's not like the gods or someone randomly came up with this system?"

"That's correct. Though the Scholar has helped navigate and formalize a lot of it. Most people don't care about the nuances of how we label magic but there are people out there who make it their whole career."

"Sounds like most peoples' attitude towards science in my world," she mumbled to herself. "So what are the ten Magical subtypes?"

"Light and Dark, which behave slightly different from their more natural counterparts," he explained as they continued weaving through the crowds. "Life and Death, sometimes referred to as Healing and Disease, depending on the culture. There's Illusion, Song, and Blood," he listed off, sidestepping a runeforged couple herding a gaggle of excited children. "Your portal and storage Talent fall under Dimension. Covenant is like contracts or creature summoning; really, anything that has to do with bonds between things, like your gravity ability. And the last one some consider a kind of 'catch-all,' but it's just Arcane. Raw, unflavored mana."

He paused in front of one of the central buildings. "Wait here while I announce us and find a room for the night."

She nodded and waited patiently against the building, trying to ignore some of the odd looks she was receiving from the crowds moving past.

Her mind wandered back to her abilities and the different types that Paul had talked about. She wondered if she could find a library or something to learn more about what those other ability modifiers he mentioned before meant.

It wasn't too long before her thoughts were interrupted by a small runeforged child tugging on her skirt. Once they had her attention, they asked, "Are you a human too?"

Phoenix stared at the child for a long moment, glancing around to see if there was a guardian nearby before saying softly, "I used to be."

"Not many humans around these parts until the blood moon," the kid seemed to quote, puffing their chest slightly as though playing at being older. Then they asked, "If you're not a human anymore, what did you become?"

Before she could answer, Paul's voice spoke from beside them. "She became a Caster."

The child seemed to shrink slightly in the larger man's presence, but they grinned up at her. "That's awesome! Are you going to be an Adventurer?"

She smiled back down at them. "I'm going to try."

"Genki!" A feminine voice called over the noise of the crowd.

The young runeforged face blanched slightly as they hurriedly said, "Gotta go! Bye! Good luck becoming an Adventurer!"

"I see you made a friend," Paul said to her with that slightly amused look in his eyes and a reluctant tug at the corner of his mouth.

She rolled her eyes at him. "Kids are easier to be friends with."

He chuckled in response. "The innocent usually are." He then gestured for her to follow him again. "This way. We'll get some rest, then I want to take you to some other fortress towns before we go to the capital."

Phoenix nodded, pushing herself off the wall, and followed behind the Emerald Caster.

§

The inn room they shared was simple yet well kept. Paul felt more relaxed after locking the door behind them and casting a ritual, which would ward the room from both prying eyes and ears, and sound an alarm that would wake him should the room be entered.

The young woman watched him curiously as he spread the salt around the outer walls and incanted words that burned the material up as fuel, leaving little evidence behind. Her curiosity and wonder over things that seemed like mundane chores to him were making him reevaluate everything with a new perspective. It was a refreshing change from the monotonous gloom his life seemed to have become lately.

Paul tried to relax further by sitting on one of the small beds that were positioned across the room from each other. It groaned under his weight and dangerously creaked as he adjusted his position to rest his back against the wall with his legs outstretched.

Phoenix stared at his bed wide-eyed before nervously glancing down at hers and asking, "Are these going to collapse on me while I sleep?"

He couldn't help the chuckle as he was once again reminded of her lack of what most would consider common knowledge. "No, they're simply made from Mundane materials that can't normally support the additional weight of a high-tier Caster. You will be fine."

She gave him a dubious look as she eyed him up and down as if measuring him before muttering, "I know muscle weighs more than fat, but still . . ."

It was his turn to roll his eyes and shake his head. "As your Caste increases and magic replaces body parts, it also condenses. This will make you much denser and harder to hurt. The side effect of that is additional weight. Most lower Caste zones only produce lower Caste materials; thus, the furniture is usually only rated for that zone. This is another reason why higher-tier Casters tend to congregate and live in higher Caste cities. It's built for them."

She hummed in thought before readjusting further onto her bed. "Sounds like Caste segregation is pretty common in the world?"

He gave a shrug. "It can be. In a lot of ways, it makes things easier. Aside from the surroundings, Caste influences a lot of one's daily life without one really noticing. Working relations, family hierarchy, one's love life, and life expectancy. Caste is power, and when there's an imbalance in power, it tends to have unforeseen consequences."

"Like what?"

"Well, family hierarchy is usually an easy one to showcase," he said as he tried to paint an example for her. "Imagine a monarchy where the reigning monarch, for whatever reason, is having trouble progressing beyond Sapphire Caste. Their oldest child, however, has already reached Emerald and wants the throne for themselves. Without even needing to murder their parent, the child could simply argue that they are better suited to rule because they are more powerful."

"Huh," she replied with a thoughtful look on her face, "I guess that does make things awkward."

"Now, imagine that the monarch's second-born child managed to reach Ruby. You have a three-way contention for the crown simply because of Caste imbalance."

"So, what happens to the crown?"

He raised an eyebrow at her before saying with deliberation, "The one with the most will and power rules. That's why it's called the Rule of Caste."

As she fell silent, Paul left her to her thoughts and pulled out his journal. He had been writing everything down that had happened to him lately without actually mentioning anything about the odd Wayfarer's divine quest in case anyone managed to get ahold of it. He was fairly certain his little sister, Pati, would attempt to read it as soon as he was finished writing and had placed it on the shelf in his room back home.

The thought of seeing his room again filled him with an odd mixture of emotions that he hadn't quite reconciled yet. It had been so long since he had been home after all, and he hadn't expected to return yet after such a disastrous parting.

"Is something wrong?" Phoenix asked, and he glanced over to see the redhead sitting on the edge of her own bed, watching him curiously.

She had such an odd accent, but he still enjoyed listening to it, even though she continually expected him to return the gesture and participate in one of his least favorite activities: conversation. It wasn't so terrible with her, though, which surprised him.

Paul was irritable at the best of times when forced into social settings, but for some reason, this strange girl settled him. Perhaps it was simply because she knew absolutely nothing about him and held no preconceived ideas about who he was or how he should behave.

His whole life had felt like a series of events inevitably leading to him failing to meet expectations, yet this fragile-looking girl saw him as an indomitable savior. He wondered if that was something he could truly be for her.

"I was just thinking about what awaits me in Tulimeir," he finally answered. "It's been almost six years since I last visited my home there."

"Your home?" she asked, scrunching her nose like an adorable child. "You're originally from there?"

"Yes," he replied simply with a nod, not wanting to reveal much more than that. Instead, he tried to divert. "The tundra is only Crystal Caste outside of a blood moon. Most Casters that are combat-focused can't progress their abilities beyond Sapphire there. So, I travel a lot."

"Why can't they progress?"

"Cultivating abilities requires adequate challenges along with proper meditation to reflect on those experiences. Once you ascend to the next tier, the lower one becomes almost laughably easy to overcome one-on-one. While it's not impossible for a Crystal to overcome a Sapphire, for instance, it would likely require a group effort or a very advantageous matchup. It's why parties of Casters will often be formed to take on higher Caste monsters."

He set his pen down on his journal as he leaned back against the wall more and explained, "A well-balanced party of four to six Adventurers in the higher range of their Caste should be able to take on anything in the lower range of the Caste above them. It would likely be very challenging, but rewarding once victory is obtained."

Paul pointed at her with the pen for emphasis as he added, "That doesn't mean you should take victory for granted just because others might be there to help you. As you learned earlier, one wrong move can Spell disaster and very sudden death."

She nodded but glanced away from him to look out the window at the darkening sky. "I'm not really afraid of dying. I think I'm more worried about failing to meet their standards. Do I have to be in a party to be an Adventurer?"

He wasn't sure how to respond to her lack of concern over death. The little she had revealed about her sickly upbringing and not having anyone left to care for was difficult for him to empathize with. However, he did understand her concerns about not feeling like she was good enough. He had often felt that way, with every failure hammering that feeling into his soul.

Paul refused to let those inadequacies show, focusing instead on her question. "No. A party is not a requirement for membership, but it can be for certain missions. You won't get sent to fight a Sapphire without an adequate party to support you."

Silence fell for a long while as Phoenix stretched and seemed to try to make herself more comfortable on her own bed. He found her little [**Starlight Companion**] construct to be an excellent reading light as the sun finished setting, and she read pieces of her [**Guide Book**] again while he wrote in his journal.

It was comfortable.

"*Wayland has grown fond of the Little Miss,*" a feminine monotone voice said quietly within his mind.

"*She's not entirely unagreeable,*" he silently admitted in response. Then he reluctantly added, "*I'm not sure I'm doing a very good job teaching her, though.*"

"*Wayland is doing fine,*" the familiar voice assured. "*Wayland should claim the Little Miss as his Protégé and make being a Mentor official.*"

His surprise at the suggestion made him pause his writing again, and he glanced over at the young woman. Was that what he had become to her? A Mentor? Was he actually capable and worthy of such a position?

"*Wayland is overthinking it again.*"

He gave an annoyed huff. "*That's not a decision made lightly in the spur of the moment, Bela.*"

"That is why This One is suggesting it before we arrive in Tulimeir. It will make everything easier for us."

"It will cause more questions and speculation," he retorted, resuming his writing so the Wayfarer nearby wouldn't think to ask more questions about his behavior.

"Little Miss is an Aurabreaker Wayfarer, Chosen by gods, and Wayland is Wayland. There will already be many questions and much speculation as soon as both of you walk through the city gates."

"What do you mean by 'Wayland is Wayland'? What's that supposed to mean?"

"Has Wayland forgotten who he is? Forgotten what people already call him?"

Paul grimaced at the way she phrased the question, understanding what she was getting at, and he gave a mental sigh as he answered, *"Right, I'm Lord Wayland, the Blade of Pure Wrath."*

CHAPTER NINETEEN

Tulimeir

H ere is good," Paul informed her as they stood off to the side outside of the large city gates before leaving Vallinsarvi.

Phoenix had been disappointed that she wouldn't get to bathe yet, the grime from traveling and fighting starting to get irritating, but she had greatly enjoyed sleeping on an actual mattress instead of a thin bedroll on top of cold hard stone.

"Good for?" she prompted, unsure why he had stopped where he had.

"Memorize this location to make sure your aural imprint settles, and you can teleport back here later. We will want to take advantage of that particularly rare ability by marking places all across the tundra as we travel, especially the fortress towns like this one," he explained, readjusting the large pack on his shoulder.

"Why don't we just portal back to the inn room we were in? I can remember that easily enough and it would be warmer than outside the gates."

"There are enchantments built into the walls that prevent portals from entering. While you could portal out of the city or from one side to the other within the walls, crossing it from the outside is blocked by the magic. Until you become a much higher Caste or unlock some ability that strengthens your portal to overcome this interference, you won't be able to portal inside."

She grumbled as she looked around the area to memorize it better. "That sounds super inconvenient."

"It's for everyone's safety," he replied, and his grave tone made her pause to look at him. "Imagine if an enemy nation could simply portal in an army of Casters to annihilate everyone."

She gave an involuntary shudder. "I didn't think about enemies like that," she admitted, then raised a brow at him. "Is this nation at war? Am I going to have to worry about some kind of Caster draft?"

"Besides the interdimensional invaders I mentioned earlier trying to destroy our planet?" he asked with an amused look.

Phoenix rolled her eyes. "Yes, aside from them. Am I going to have to worry about neighboring kingdoms sending actual *people* to attack as well?"

Paul shook his head. "Currently, we aren't officially at war with anyone else, though there have been tensions with the small nation of Berg Sirens in the northern sea, last I heard."

"Sirens?" she repeated in surprise, "Like singing, half-human, half-fish merfolk?"

"They are often Song-Attuned, yes, and live in or near the water. There are various subspecies of Sirens, but they are Vauva, like us."

"Vauva?"

"That's what we call the different species that can become Casters. It's simply a collective term for humans, runeforged, cinderen, voxen, sirens, draconids, faeforged, etcetera. There are dozens of different species that fall under the term, but the one thing that connects them all is the ability to absorb Aspects and cultivate their Caste through hard work."

"I thought everyone could do that? Why not just call them 'people'?"

Paul chuckled but shook his head. "Because that would imply that other *very intelligent* species were not people. Being a Vauva is not what defines personhood."

"Oh," she replied, deflating slightly. "Well, what are the others? I'm used to humans being considered the default for being a person."

"We collectively call the others the Vanhin. Those include much older species like the Fae or Dragons."

"Dragons?" she repeated, her eyes going wide in excitement. "Like actual dragons?! Fire breathing, flying, giant reptiles?"

Paul laughed again at her exuberance. "Not all breathe Fire magic specifically, but that does sound like a fairly accurate description. Just don't let them hear you call them that. Their arrogance is even worse than the draconids that came from them."

"You've met some?"

He nodded. "I've met many different types of beings in my travels. Dragons are not the oddest or even the rarest I've come across."

Phoenix felt her smile slightly slip as she pictured meeting a real dragon someday, and she found herself admitting to her stoic companion, "My mom and best friend loved dragons. They used to geek out over them all the time. It made Jin feel more like family when we would talk about them together. About how different books would portray them differently and our favorite versions . . . I wish they could have met one with me."

"Is this 'Jin' the best friend?" Paul asked, and she glanced up to find his golden eyes looking at her softly.

She nodded. "Yeah. She died a couple of years ago from sickness."

"And your mother?" he asked quietly. "You mentioned not having anyone left."

Phoenix hugged herself as she confirmed for him, "Yeah. She died in an accident. That was like half a year ago already, so I've had time to get over both of them."

"I don't think grief works like that," Paul said, surprising her as he moved closer, "I lost my mother in a monster attack almost seven years ago, and I still find myself mourning her at times."

"You do?" she found herself asking. The tightness around her shoulders relaxed at the realization that he wouldn't scold her or tell her to toughen up as some of the nurses had, though most were understanding.

She had been forced to meet with a grief counselor, but she hadn't gotten along with them when she heard them continually refer to her as a boy with "mommy issues"—as though that explained everything about her identity and grief-stricken turmoil.

"Of course," her Mentor replied as he placed a comforting hand on her shoulder, "she was there for the majority of my life. Even when I was often away traveling, I could always look forward to seeing her when I returned.

"Aside from losing her presence, I've lost that hope she gave me as well. It's not just the people we miss but the time we would have been able to spend with them. That kind of grief takes a long time to fade and might never go away."

Phoenix nodded but became hesitant as she asked, "Does it make me a bad person not to think about them all the time? Like, does not wanting to go back to my world mean I don't care about them anymore?"

"They aren't there anymore, young one," he said with a shake of his head. "While we might grieve for eternity, it won't bring them back, and it doesn't do us good to dwell on their loss."

She glanced up when he seemed to tense before looking away as he confided, "I'm often reminded that they wouldn't want to see us wallow in self-pity. I think if we want to honor their memory, the best way to do so will be to live an honorable life that reflects the positive lessons they taught us."

The Wayfarer rubbed her eyes before the tears could fall as she managed to say, "Thanks, Paul."

"For what?"

"Not making me feel like a terrible friend and daughter because I kept living without them," she muttered.

The Paladin smiled warmly and surprised her by saying, "Thank you, Phoenix."

"For what?"

"Not making me feel like a terrible friend and son because I didn't realize before this moment that I could keep living too."

* * *

It was another fortnight of traveling, with her often being carried to save time and their constant battling between training sessions before they approached Tulimeir.

They had visited two other fortress towns and multiple landmarks across the icy tundra as the orange moon became darker, and Paul estimated that it would take only another few weeks before the blood moon triggered its flood.

Paul was judicious in picking the monsters that he let Phoenix battle and simply obliterated anything he deemed too dangerous. It was a trial-by-fire type of training where pain was the largest motivator for improvement.

However, her Mentor had improved his teaching methods as well. He gave her suggestions about what to look for to determine how to approach an enemy and went over her mistakes in more detail afterward with recommendations on what to do differently.

Phoenix felt much more comfortable with the battles now that her cloak prevented her from freezing to death and having been through dozens of monster fights. She never refused any of the commands her Mentor gave her, trying her best to heed the advice and improve herself. With each passing day and each challenge overcome, her abilities increased.

Now, in the distance, there was what looked like a band of gray metal, which Phoenix was told were the walls of the capital. She trudged along behind Paul as they walked northwest along the rocky road towards the city from the last fortress town they had left behind. She wasn't physically tired, but the mental exhaustion of continuous travel and battles was wearing her down, and she just wanted a long hot bath before sleeping for a week.

"So, Blomsterang is the monarch nation that oversees Tulim, which is the name of the duchy that encompasses the tundra. Blomstra is the monarchy's capital city, while Tulimeir is the name of the capital of the duchy," she reiterated.

"Correct," Paul answered without looking back.

"Then there's Vallinsarvi in the forest to the south where we first stayed the night, Linnake was across the northern tip of the gorge to the west, and Suoja was the one near the south end of the mountains to the east, which all act as fortress cities during the blood moon," she continued, trying her best to remember all these different geographical names that she was certain she'd forget.

"That's right," her Mentor responded.

"And the Alliance of Adventurers works with the duke and barons to coordinate Casters under each during the blood moon to protect these four cities?"

"Yes," Paul confirmed, then added, "normally, the AOA works completely independently. The locals submit requests or monster sightings that become missions that individual Adventurers or parties can choose to accept."

"But during the blood moon, the AOA directly assigns the missions instead and the local government backs that authority?"

"Everyone helps during a blood moon," he repeated, then clarified further. "Aside from being easier to coordinate forces and it being the right thing to do, it's a small concession for each side to make every fifteen years to help support the service the AOA provides and the finances the government provides between each blood moon. Nobody is forced to be an Adventurer or a Caster here, after all."

"They still get paid for the missions they do, though, right?" she double-checked.

"The reward is usually posted with each mission, and depending on the outcome, there may be additional rewards. Such as the encountered monster being more dangerous than initially reported or exceptional performance and decision-making for unexpected complications."

"So, it's a job," she concluded, "a very dangerous freelance job to fight monsters."

He chuckled. "That's one way to look at it, and I won't deny that many do."

"You know," she said playfully, "I never really thought I would ever get a job, what with how often it was implied that I should have been dead already, but I admit that, even in my *wildest* dreams, a professional monster hunter never made the list of potential first jobs."

Paul let out a genuine laugh, loud and breath-stealing, that she hadn't heard before. It startled her at first but made her join in a breath later as they continued towards the capital ahead.

When they finally reached the walls, Phoenix was in utter awe of the sheer size of it. The massive metal structure was roughly a hundred feet tall and had huge cannon-like weapons on top that were aiming at various angles as though ready to react to any threat at a moment's notice. She wasn't positive from this close, but it also looked like some kind of pale smoke was rising from the top as well, which was quickly dissipating into the cold air.

She knew from Paul's earlier explanation that the walls were angled and pivoted at points to form a huge eight-pointed star, with the prongs in the cardinal directions being larger than the ordinal ones between to completely encompass the city that was surrounded by miles of flat rocky ice except on the north side, opposite of where they stood, where it abutted the ocean.

Currently, they stood at the connection point between the main southern prong and the smaller southwestern section, where there was a small line leading into the entrance at the base. The guards seemed thorough in checking everyone for potential threats or directing them to certain locations as the line slowly progressed.

Phoenix was immensely grateful now for Paul's insistence on saving their last bottle of the Golden Shower Potion for right before reaching the city, as she had become a ragged mess of blood, dirt, and snow slush. He, however, had remained immaculately clean.

As it became their turn, Paul showed the guard a small card seemingly carved from green marble with writing engraved on it that Phoenix couldn't read from that distance. He explained that Phoenix was with him and planning to join the AOA. Then, they were given directions to the office that Paul would need to report to and that she would need to fill out paperwork for.

While passing through the insanely dense walls, she could have sworn she felt and heard a slight hum coming from somewhere, but it was so faint she wasn't entirely sure that she wasn't just imagining things in her anxiety over the crowds.

As soon as they exited the long tunnel leading through the colossal wall and into the southern section, which she was informed was the International District, they were intercepted by a short, stocky, and bald man covered in shiny rune markings of various shades of blue that stood in stark contrast to his dark midnight skin. He was wearing priestly robes that Phoenix couldn't place as she didn't know the symbols for the different clergies yet.

The man bowed to them once Paul came to a stop in front of him, and the stranger greeted her Mentor respectfully, "Lord Wayland, we welcome you back home. It has been too long."

Paul gave a huff of annoyance as he crossed his arms. "What does your lady want with me, Priest?"

The stranger straightened and glanced at Phoenix before saying, "She merely wishes to assist in your task of guiding the young Adventurer-to-be here. I will lead her to my lady's temple while you see to your own duties, and then I will return her to you."

The former Paladin's eyes narrowed at the man, and his stance became rigid as he shifted slightly to place himself further between her and the priest. His hostile stance was making her nervous.

Paul lowered his voice and asked in a dangerous tone, "Your lady would interfere with the wishes of her siblings?"

"Not interfere; assist, like I said," the man quickly reiterated, obviously not wanting to anger the Emerald Caster. "I assure you, Lord Wayland, that we share the same goal in this matter."

"That is doubtful," he replied curtly, then turned to look at Phoenix. "This man is a priest of the goddess Scholar. While I'm not certain of her intentions, she may have some answers for you."

Phoenix nodded in understanding, the book symbol on the stranger's robes making more sense now, and she stepped forward to follow the priest. He smiled at her and bowed once more to Paul before leading her down the road that led to the east through the crowded city.

CHAPTER TWENTY

Tomes of the Scholar

Tulimeir felt like a huge industrial metropolis pulled straight out of some kind of steampunk storybook with tall glass buildings crammed together to try and accommodate the limited horizontal space of the walled-in fortress city.

Despite the dreary cold, steel-framed skyscrapers, and damp cobblestone streets, the city was alive with colors. Bright banners and signs marked storefronts, and lights shone merrily through the plethora of color-tinted windows. Most outer walls seemed to be made of stained glass rather than stone or metal.

Phoenix thought she might get whiplash as she tried to look at everything at once. Aside from the dazzling colors among the steam that seemed to coat the streets, the smells were an overwhelming assault that she had been ill-prepared for.

Scents that she had no basis for comparison both enticed her in one direction while causing her to recoil from another. It swirled and mixed into a dangerous concoction of fragrance that she was slightly worried might make her ill. The biggest offenders for the various smells were the street vendors peddling food she had never heard of—except the one selling sandwiches, but most of the ingredients she saw looked completely foreign to her.

The next overwhelming factor was the sounds. Everyone was talking everywhere as they crowded the streets, calling out requests for the vendors and haggling over prices. Parents scolded children who strayed too far, and a variety of animals that were either pets, strays, or Familiars roamed around her in a vibrant cacophony. She was only grateful that there didn't seem to be any vehicles adding to it.

The crowds caused a spike in her anxiety as she tried to follow the priest through the bustle, but he never seemed to outpace her. Phoenix noticed more than one curious glance her way, taking in her pale human appearance. She tried to calm her nerves at the unwanted attention by focusing on retracting her Aura as much as possible. Would some random person attempt to snatch her like that Magi had?

"Um, excuse me," she began, hoping to get a bit more information out of her newest guide, "you seemed to know who I am, but what do I call you?"

"My apologies, Miss Fraser," the runeforged said as he glanced over his shoulder at her, "I am Lester Ravone, a priest of the Scholar."

"*The* Scholar?" she reiterated, indicating her curiosity.

"Yes, the goddess of learning, knowledge, and all that is known," he clarified. "My Lady has known of you since your arrival in our world and has shared every thought you have had since."

That idea was a bit disconcerting to her, but she tried not to dwell on it as they seemed to be coming to another major fork in the road. They had been following the road east across the southern prong of the star-shaped city for a while and had eventually come to another tunnel gate leading into the smaller southeastern section. They were forced to slow down by the people congesting the thoroughfare to get past as the crowds going in both directions squeezed through the narrow passage.

Once they managed to escape the oppressive tunnel through the defensive wall, Phoenix was surprised by the change of scenery. If she hadn't known better, she would have wondered if they had stepped through a portal.

The area was much more open here, with buildings allowing more of a buffer between each other. These buildings were no longer the towering steel and glass structures that the rest of the city seemed to encapsulate. Instead, they were an eclectic assortment of themed towers.

The crowds of people going in and out of them, many dressed in priestly robes, and the voices rising above the din, proselytizing to whoever might listen, were clue enough to have her understand that they had reached the Temple District.

Her guide led her to a lone pagoda-looking structure that stood out for its many curving roofs. Even though there was more space around the buildings here, they still tended to go vertical, with the height seeming to indicate their importance. This Temple of the Scholar was one of the taller ones.

The Wayfarer could sense the gazes of the crowd on her as she entered the temple, especially coming from the other followers that bore the same garb as the priest of the Scholar. Phoenix felt her cheeks burn and her heart pound in her chest with every step. She was starting to regret going with the stranger who was leading her into a potential den of sycophants.

The interior mostly felt like a library, with rows and rows of books crammed into the area. After going up many floors via a glass elevator lift and down a hallway, Lester finally stopped in front of a pair of large doors. As he opened one side, he didn't enter but gestured for her to go instead. She complied, and as she entered the inner cloister, she felt an odd tingling sensation as though an Aura encompassed the space.

Her attention was arrested by the adorable little girl standing in the center of the room. The child was dressed in the local garb of leather and fur, but rather than a runeforged or cinderen like the rest of the city, she looked like one of the tan humans from the very first town Phoenix had visited, albeit slightly glowing.

Before the Astromancer could comprehend the presence of the strange girl who looked about the size of a ten-year-old, the girl turned to look at her, and the small face lit up with delight as she gave a squeal and rushed towards her excitedly.

"Phoenix! I'm so glad you've finally arrived! It feels like I've been waiting for *ages* to actually be able to talk to you!" the child said in a rush, bouncing on her toes and seeming to try to do her best not to touch her.

It wasn't until Phoenix registered the power of the Aura coming off the young girl that she recognized it as Divine like the other deities she had met. She inquired hesitantly, "You're Scholar?"

The girl giggled, "Who else? Silly Wayfarer. Now, onto more important questions that I've been *dying* to ask you: What exactly is the internet, and how does it work?"

Phoenix's mind almost short-circuited at the unexpected question, and she actually had to shake her head to focus on an answer as her mind raced through her memories surrounding the concept of the internet. "Oh. Um. That is . . . complex."

"Oh, you're right," the goddess said with slight awe before getting an annoyed look on her face. "You don't even know the actual details. What a shame," she added with a sigh.

"Wait, you know everything I know, so why bother asking?"

The child goddess seemed to almost pout as she crossed her arms. "Most people assume I know everything that everyone knows already," she started explaining. "Usually that's true, but Wayfarers prove the assumption is false. I know every thought within my influence, which is the whole planet, before you ask," the goddess tacked on with a raised hand, forestalling the question Phoenix had indeed been about to voice.

"Wayfarers are from outside my influence. So, when they arrive on the planet, it's not like I get to download their memories. They have to actively think about something for me to know it as well. That's how *I* learn.

"So, while you've had thoughts about some things that *use* the internet, I wanted details about the internet itself," the goddess explained while turning away. She walked towards a desk that held stacks of paper. "You helped quite a bit, really, but not enough for me to impart the knowledge to my followers or have Mentor start teaching everyone about it."

Before Phoenix could voice her suggestion, Scholar responded to the thought. "You're right, but it's not like I can just summon a network engineer out of thin air. Even *I* am limited to this reality."

She took another breath to speak but was interrupted again by the munchkin deity.

"Yes, I do enjoy freaking people out by answering their thoughts. Now, ask your questions, and yes, I'll allow you to voice them this time."

Phoenix was caught off guard once more by the rapid shift in the conversation, and she said warily, "You were the one who requested my presence. I assumed that meant you were the one with all the questions."

The goddess giggled again, her soft brown hair swaying gently around her face. "Oh, I have many more questions. I usually do when Wayfarers arrive on my world."

"Wait, there are more here?" Phoenix interjected.

Scholar shrugged as she replied, "Sure. Just a handful at the moment, but there have been plenty over the millennia. Now again, ask me your question."

Phoenix realized then that she did have questions for the deity and found herself asking, "Why me?"

The goddess shook her head. "Rebel already answered that."

She frowned at the glowing girl. "Rebel sidestepped it. Answering a question with another question isn't an answer; it's misdirection."

"Misdirection can be its own answer. Perhaps you are not meant to know the answer. Next question," the small girl commanded with a wave of her tiny hand.

The redhead wondered why everyone she met seemed to like giving her orders, but she just sighed and complied anyway. "How do I complete my quest?"

"Better," Scholar chuckled, "but you're not ready for that answer yet. Come back to me when you're at *least* Sapphire Caste."

Phoenix held back a groan of frustration before she thought of another question. "Who was the Night Witch, Morgan?"

The goddess's amused smile was replaced with annoyance as she said, "Someone who keeps butting her nose into my world's affairs for her own agenda." Her expression softened as she added, "Though I have her to thank for the majority of Wayfarers that end up here and the knowledge they bring, so it's difficult to complain too much. It's unlikely you'll ever see her again, though, since she seems keen on remaining distant from her . . . *potentials*."

Phoenix wasn't sure if she should press for more information but instead closed her eyes, trying to clear her thoughts with a steadying breath, then asked, "Why did you bring me here?"

Scholar smiled brightly at her. "There we go," she said happily, then lifted her hands, now holding a stack of books that Phoenix knew hadn't been there a second before. "I have some knowledge to aid you in your new life here."

Phoenix couldn't stop the question from escaping her lips. "Why?"

The goddess just smiled wider. "Because I want to," was all the answer given as the girl gestured to the books with a nod of her head. "You won't be able to find these particular versions here in Tulimeir, and I believe you will be here for quite a while."

"What are they?"

The girl gave a wide grin and said almost teasingly, "*These* are called Knowledge Tomes in this world, but from what I've gleaned from your thoughts about video games and stories, you might know them better as 'Skill Books' or 'Jade Slips.'"

Phoenix fell silent for a long moment before trailing her eyes down to the precious treasure held before her. She almost didn't want to jinx it as she clarified, "They transfer knowledge to the user instantly?"

Scholar nodded eagerly. "I helped another Wayfarer create them *ages* ago. All you have to do is read the activation sentence on the first page to very quickly absorb the information."

"And you're just giving them to me?"

The deity continued smiling and said, "I'll grant you the books and my Mark of Favor as well. I do wish for you to succeed in this world, and the tomes containing the foundations of magic will help you do so."

Then her **[Guide Book]** appeared between her and the deity to dutifully perform its task.

New Quest: Tomes of the Scholar
The deity Scholar has offered you a set of magic Knowledge Tomes that make up the series [Magic of Makera] *along with their divine mark.*
Objective: Gain Scholar's Mark of Favor and use the magic Knowledge Tomes.
Reward: Rare ritual material pack.

The goddess smiled at the book and said, "I have to admit, I love the form of this particular Talent you have. Your love of books is admirable."

She wasn't sure why, but what the deity had said made her blush slightly at the compliment. Phoenix took the proffered stack of books, careful not to touch the deity, put them into her collection, and then gave a simple "thank you."

The feeling of embarrassment and gratitude quickly disappeared, though, as the goddess caught her by surprise and wrapped tiny arms around her in a tight hug.

Phoenix was even more alarmed by the intense burning sensation coming from the Soul Mark on her chest as the mini-goddess clung to her. The sharp stab of pain quickly passed as the deity reluctantly released her. Scholar hadn't made contact for long, but Phoenix was instantly gasping for air, and a sheen of sweat coated her brow.

Then the goddess clapped her hands and informed her happily, "Now, I need you to keep following Lester around a little longer. Some of my other siblings also have items for you."

"Wait, what?" Phoenix asked with slight alarm, still trying to recover from whatever the goddess had done to her. The fatigue she was already feeling from standing so close to the divine being was making her want to climb into the nearest bed and just sleep, and the contact had only made it that much worse. She couldn't imagine having to do this even more.

"No more questions today. Go now."

As if to punctuate her dismissal, the door behind her opened once more, causing Phoenix to twist to see that her priestly guide had returned. When she turned to look back at the goddess, there was nobody else in the room with her. She sighed and turned to follow the priest to—supposedly—the next temple and divine encounter.

CHAPTER TWENTY-ONE

Why Do You Fight

Dazien rolled his amethyst eyes at his reflection in the mirror as his partner voiced concerns about their timeline, and he tried to reassure the man. "I've told you already, Uriel. I won't be late to meet you at the AOA because I'm going to nail this exam and be in and out with the next tome in hand with plenty of time to get there."

"It's across town, Daze," the taller cinderen said, unconvinced, while Dazien continued to eye the man through the mirror that he was still using to adjust his clothing. "You have to go through at least two gates, and you know how crowded it's become with the blood moon refugees."

He waved a dismissive hand at the pacing man. "Yes, yes, and again, I'll have plenty of time to get through those ridiculous traffic jams," Dazien reassured him as he ran a hand through the metallic purple hair that matched the shade of his eyes and gem-like nails. Eventually, he gave in and used the brush on the locks that fell to the nape of his neck. "Besides, if it's really backed up, I'll just hop on the Silverline," he added as an afterthought, tucking stray hairs behind tapered ears that were about half the length of his partner's.

"That's even more money out of our pockets," Uriel said flatly, "I know how you get when our funds get low."

"I'll only do it as a last resort," he promised, "I still have a few rides on my pass in case of emergencies. Which this would count as, right?"

"It's the last day to register for the final trials," his friend stressed.

Dazien turned and walked the few steps to intercept Uriel's path, grabbing the man's shoulders and using a pet name that he spoke with fondness. "Senesh, have I *ever* failed to get any paperwork done before?"

Uriel blushed, his cheeks glowing slightly from the molten blood flowing through him, and lowered his ember gaze in acquiescence. "No . . ."

"Then trust that I will be there," he said with a grin. "You will get there earlier while I meet with Warrior, and then I will be there in time to finish signing the forms in person with you. So, stop worrying and trust me."

The cinderen simply nodded and said, "Yes, King."

"Good. So, are we going to Belladonna's tonight to celebrate?"

Uriel gave him a slight smirk. "Isn't it a bit early to plan the celebration when we haven't accomplished it yet?"

Dazien clicked his tongue, shaking his head in feigned disappointment. "There you go with that pessimism again. You just promised to trust me, remember?"

The darker man gave a slight huff that he interpreted as a chuckle. He smiled and continued, "Belladonna's, and I'm splurging on a bottle of manarin wine for us."

"That's a bit much, isn't it?" Uriel protested weakly. "We still need to finish buying a few things for the trials."

"One glass for tonight, and the rest for when we pass the trials and become Adventurers," he clarified, flashing his most charming smile, which seemed to be enough to elicit a small smile from his friend.

"Wonderful," Dazien stated, signaling an end to the brief dispute, and hugged his partner tightly. "I'll see you at the AOA building later then," he added before releasing the cinderen and making his way from their small apartment in the International District of Tulimeir, which was fairly close to his destination of the Temple District to the east.

Despite his words to Uriel, the young Caster also shared his companion's worries about being able to finish buying all their gear, pay the rent, and still celebrate with a nice meal. His hopes rested with their own skills.

They had both been training hard for years to join the AOA, and they had finally managed to scrape up the funds to adequately gear up for the trials and obtain the necessary permission forms. Once they joined up and could more regularly accept missions, their money problems would be solved, and he would be one step closer to his goals.

He arrived quickly at the familiar temple that was almost a third home to him and made his way up to the inner cloister, where he would be meeting the deity of combat. He still wasn't entirely sure what Warrior saw in him that would cause the god to personally oversee his training but could only assume that the deity believed in him and his goals as well.

Dazien moved swiftly and smoothly through the forms of his combat techniques for the Stance of the Sword Sovereign, with his conjured sword acting as his partner during the demonstration.

He had been training with the god, Warrior, for almost five years now and was ready for the final volume of his techniques. It was easy to maintain his focus in the familiar space, the soft canvas flooring a reassuring presence to his careful steps and deliberate movements as he almost soared across the training mats.

Warrior's eyes never left his body as he twisted, lunged, and pivoted through the various techniques. He knew that the god was analyzing every flaw to determine his mastery over it. He was flawless, though, and he knew it. The hours spent perfecting the maneuvers made them second nature and as easy as breathing to him.

Even the sound of the door opening unexpectedly wasn't enough to break him out of the flow of his movements as he performed the deadly dance. Then he ended it with a complex flourish, his breathing only slightly heavy and his soul brimming with the feeling of triumph.

§

Phoenix was led to another pagoda-like tower, but this one had sounds of combat coming from the lower floors. As she entered closely behind her guide, she saw the largest variety and amount of weaponry she had ever seen lining the walls and being wielded by the disciples. She wondered if she was about to meet the God of War himself and suddenly felt very nervous.

Again, she was led to the uppermost floor and taken to an inner room, and like before, the deity was already there. The god looked like one of the cinderen, with an ashy complexion and irises glowing like warm embers. He was dressed in simple leather armor, but his immense Aura flooded the room despite being restrained.

This god wasn't alone, however, as he was watching another person. It was a young man who was probably one of the most handsome she had ever seen, even in pictures.

His warm brown skin was darker than Paul's, and his hair was the color of dark, sparkling amethysts. The stranger was performing what Phoenix thought was some sort of kata while wielding a beautifully embellished sword with a golden hilt and blade seemingly carved from diamond.

She stayed back by the door that had closed behind her, not wanting to interrupt the pair. The young man's graceful movements were a wonder to behold.

He seemed to flow like water, and his lithe muscles could easily be made out under the form-fitting silver clothing that clung to his body like shimmery spandex. Phoenix felt entranced by the beautiful yet deadly display as the sword flashed through the air.

When the movement halted after a particularly impressive flourish, the deity spoke. "Good. You should be ready for the next tome now. Monk Nemor will have it for you downstairs."

The young man unconjured his weapon in an afterimage of golden sparkles and bowed slightly to the god, saying respectfully with the same accent Paul had,

"Thank you, my Lord Warrior. Your guidance has been of the highest honor." Then he turned to the door and began to leave.

As she watched him, he met her gaze, and she was startled to see that his eyes matched the shimmering amethyst of his hair. He was both shiny and dashing, and his movements spoke of assured confidence.

When he got closer, he gave her a charming smile and winked, causing her face to flush in embarrassment. "Your turn," he playfully said as he walked past her and out of the room, leaving her alone with the god that she wasn't even sure how to address.

"Come, child," the god commanded as he gestured to the center of the room, which reminded Phoenix of a martial arts dojo. She took hesitant steps forward until she was just a couple of yards away.

He looked her up and down slowly, giving her that same assessing gaze that Paul often gave her. The kind of gaze that looked for her strengths, weaknesses, and secrets. She had no doubt that this deity saw much more than Paul did, and she thought Paul saw a lot.

"I am Warrior," the god finally said. "Do you know why you are here?"

Phoenix gave a small shrug. "Scholar said that her siblings wanted to give me stuff as well." Then a stray thought crossed her mind, and she asked with a bit of confusion, "You're a god, though, didn't you see her tell me that?"

The deity looked annoyed as he explained, "I could not see you in her sanctuary no more than she can see you here in mine. Unlike me, though, she will know what will occur here as soon as you leave this place and your mind goes over the event. Such is the goddess of learning."

He walked a bit closer to her then, his Aura becoming stifling. "We're not here to discuss my *sister*, however. We're here to talk about you. Paul Wayland has been training you in combat to help prepare you for your quest."

Phoenix nodded. "Yes, he's taught me a lot already. I didn't arrive in this world with any practical experience in . . . well, anything really."

Warrior nodded knowingly. "While I might not have access to your thoughts like Scholar does, I can observe public spaces at my leisure, and I have heard all of your previous conversations." Then he gestured to the side of the room where a small table sat next to racks of various weapons. On top of the table was another stack of books, but it was taller than the stack Scholar had given her.

She cautiously walked over to the pile as Warrior said, "I want you to take them. Use them. Practice them. My temple's doors will always be open for you to seek any assistance or challenge, but Paul Wayland should be a suitable enough trainer."

Before she took the books, she paused and asked, "Scholar didn't really answer before, but why are you giving these to me? I know that Hero and Rebel—for reasons I *cannot* fathom—chose me to save a nation, one that I don't even know the location of, but why are you and her getting involved?"

The deity stared at her for a moment, reminding her once more of the way Paul behaved, and she briefly wondered if it was just a "stoic warrior" thing.

"Things have become unbalanced," the god answered slowly. "We are not only about to be besieged by the worst blood moon this world has ever witnessed, but we are at war. At war with an entire civilization from beyond this reality.

"Even if we triumph in this war, the balance of powers will still be skewed. We may need to be focused on our current problems, but we must also be prepared for the events that will follow. This is merely another small part of an attempt to regain balance."

It was the most information she had managed to get out of a deity so far, but it didn't seem to answer much. She realized, however, that this wasn't just some random charity. Each of these divine beings had agendas of their own and apparently decided that she would be a part of them.

She simply nodded as though she understood, but before she could add the stack of books to her collection, the god surprised her with a question.

"Why do you fight, child?"

Phoenix blinked, frozen in place and uncertain of what he intended. Why did she fight for her life? Why did she fight monsters? So, she asked, "What do you mean?"

He gestured to the array of weapons surrounding the room. "Why do you pick up a weapon and fight? There are others who might fight for you, like Paul Wayland would have. Other paths you could walk to find purpose. Farmers provide food, scholars provide knowledge and insight, and architects provide shelter and defenses. Warriors, though . . . they are the ones that fight. Why do you choose to fight as a warrior does?"

She thought about his words for a long while, trying her best to explain her thoughts to the god standing before her. "I grew up as a burden to everyone around me. You already know I was sick for most of my life, that I was sheltered and tended to by others. My mother died in an accident long before I arrived here. Before that, many of my friends in the hospital died of their sicknesses . . . I was helpless to do anything about it.

"Here, though, monsters roam. Even if I heal or feed people, the monsters will still attack and devour them. If you've been watching me long enough, you'll have seen them come after me. They've bruised and broken me. They even killed me."

"So, you seek revenge?"

She shook her head. "I just don't want to be that helpless child anymore. I don't want more people to die around me because there wasn't anyone strong enough to save them nearby."

"So, you seek control? Sovereignty over your fate?"

She paused, contemplating what she thought was odd wording. Slowly, she shook her head. "No . . . I don't wish to control anything or anyone—except maybe myself. I don't seek to be a queen of fate like you make it sound.

"I just . . . I don't want to be chained down by my weaknesses. I don't want to be weighed by the guilt of failure when I could have been stronger . . . when I could have saved others. I don't just want power for power's sake, but to be strong enough that I won't be a victim again and can save those I need to, just like how Rebel said I could choose."

Phoenix stared at Warrior and stated with finality, "I choose to fight for myself and to help protect the people around me from any danger that may threaten our lives."

New Quest: Ways of the Warrior
The deity Warrior has offered you a set of martial Knowledge Tomes that make up the series [Weapon Wielding Warrior: The Six Sacred Stances] *along with their divine mark.*
Objective: Gain Warrior's Mark of Favor and use the six martial Knowledge Tomes.
Reward: Rare Crystal Caste gloves.

The Astromancer read the quest her book offered, then bowed respectfully to the god in the same manner that she had seen the young man do earlier. "Thank you, Warrior."

She picked up the books to claim them, and as they vanished into her collection, she blinked, and the god stood only an arm's length away. Before she could even react to his close proximity, his hand touched *through* her clothing onto the still-aching Soul Mark on her chest.

The Wayfarer fell to her knees this time as the moment passed, and a breath later, the god was back in his original position across the room from her. She was gasping for air again. Her body trembled from the surge of pain and power that had swept through her despite having lasted less than a second.

As Phoenix glanced up at the god, he simply smiled, nodded, and then vanished. She was grateful that the Aura went with him. Though the room was still suffused with it, the Aura wasn't nearly as overwhelming without the deity's presence.

She didn't stand right away, though, taking a few precious moments to steady herself before she would need to go to her next destination.

CHAPTER TWENTY-TWO

Finding the Path

The priest of the Scholar arrived once more to help Phoenix to her feet and guide her to yet *another* temple. This one was more curved and reminiscent of the Taj Mahal, with intricate carvings of fantastical places engraved into the marble exterior. She paused at the front door that would most likely lead her to yet another divine being and glanced at Lester with pleading eyes.

He chuckled and patted her shoulder consolingly. "Last one," he reassured her, then opened the door and nudged her inside.

"Welcome, wanderer."

Phoenix was greeted by a dark-skinned woman with emerald hair, dressed in a dark green cloak with a nautical compass star emblazoned over the left side of the chest and what seemed like simple traveling clothes underneath. The woman had long tapered ears similar to the cinderen, but she was noticeably missing the other species' indicators of fiery eyes and lava-like markings, so it was obvious that she was something different.

"I am Kyleen Lastrand, a Priestess of the Traveler. It's an honor to meet you in person," the new stranger said with a relaxed smile.

"Priestess Lastrand is originally from the elven nation of Serenydi to the east of Tulim," Lester interjected as if in answer to her silent musings.

The elf smiled and nodded in affirmation. "Indeed. I have traveled far and wide, and my journey has brought me here to guide you to my deity and offer my assistance should you accept their favor."

Phoenix winced slightly. "So Traveler wants to get all handsy, too?"

Kyleen laughed brightly. "I'll leave that for the Traveler to explain. Follow me, please."

As the priestess turned to lead the way, Phoenix gave Lester one last look. He nodded reassuringly, and she reluctantly followed after her newest guide.

The first floor of this particular temple tower seemed like a war room, with framed maps covering every wall and three-dimensional models of various places splayed out across large tables. If she ever wanted to plan a journey to *anywhere*, this was the place she would want to stop by first.

She knew that, eventually, she would need to plan exactly that in order to accomplish her divine task. However, based on what both Paul and Scholar had told her earlier, she wouldn't need to worry about doing that for quite a while since they were preparing to bunker down for the impending blood moon, and she was focused on getting stronger.

The thought that had been brewing in the back of her mind finally formed a question, and she voiced it to the priestess, wondering what information the elf might be privy to. "Warrior mentioned that this blood moon would be the worst one in history, why does he think that?"

Kyleen seemed to hesitate but continued walking and answered, "I would not dare to presume the reasoning of a god, especially one that does not whisper to me, but it has become increasingly known around the world that one of our own has Fallen by betraying us to assist the invading Soul Reapers."

"One of our own?" she repeated in question.

"A god that's represented within the Delegation of Radiance. The Purifier, god of cleansing, has called upon his followers to assist the Soul Reapers in not only destroying our Reality Rifts," the priestess explained cautiously, "but also in performing forbidden rituals. They hope to extend the length of the blood moon in an effort to both thin out resisting forces and cause more deaths."

"That's horrible," Phoenix whispered back. Then she paused a moment before adding awkwardly, "Paul said he was a former Paladin of the Purifier . . ."

Kyleen nodded. "Yes, he was quite the talk of the city a few years back when his journey brought him home and his path forked," the elf said, then glanced back at her before continuing. "I'm not sure if it's my place to explain that particular situation."

"I would rather not say something careless to him, especially if we're going to have to fight his former church," Phoenix pointed out, hoping not to have to make her Mentor uncomfortable by asking him these questions directly. However, she had a feeling that she would want the story from him either way, so she amended her request. "Actually, never mind. You're right. I should hear it from him and get his side of the story first. I owe him that much."

The priestess nodded in understanding and returned to the story. "Anyways, the rituals that managed to go off have basically caused Krafti to . . . Are you familiar with how our moons behave?" the elf questioned, and Phoenix reminded herself that Kyleen wasn't a priestess of Scholar.

She nodded in return, and the woman continued. "Well, it basically seems to have substantially increased its maximum mana threshold and absorption. This, in turn, seems to be causing the event to arrive about a year later than normal, and it's building up an even more massive amount of mana that will take longer to expunge. In effect, instead of a single month of blood moon levels of monster spawns, experts are estimating about ten months."

Phoenix blanched. "*Ten months* of people being crammed together in the city as the world outside gets destroyed by monsters?"

"It is an understatement to say it will be a difficult journey for everyone," the priestess said forlornly, then gave her a sad smile. "It will take everyone's effort to find the path to victory."

Phoenix had barely noticed the other floors they passed by on their way up the tower as she worried about the upcoming struggles the whole world would be facing soon. When they arrived at the top floor, she almost cried at the sight of another glowing deity that she was sure would cause her more pain in the end.

Her curiosity was slightly piqued, though, as she couldn't tell if this one was a god or a goddess. Perhaps it was the lithe features of the elven species they portrayed, with teal instead of green hair like the priestess, but there weren't any strong sex characteristics on display for her to assume with. She tried to steel her nerves as Kyleen gestured for her to continue on. Phoenix cautiously walked forward, stopping a few yards away to give a respectful bow.

The deity smiled gently and said in an androgynous voice, "Welcome, young wanderer. You have journeyed far to arrive here. Not many traverse the cosmos before arriving within my awareness."

"Not all of it was by choice," she shyly admitted. "I am grateful for the experience, though," she added and paused, distracted by the view she suddenly noticed. The temple walls were missing on this uppermost floor, being open to the air, and a chill breeze grazed across her skin, ruffling her hair.

Phoenix shivered slightly as the tickle of the light wind across her flesh caused goosebumps. She took in the view of the Temple District from above with its colorful collection of towers and was in awe at the sight she'd never even seen in pictures before. The three she had visited were some of the tallest, but one stood taller still. A grand, golden castle tower that seemed topped with a crown glimmered in the dull daylight, and even from this distance, she could see giant gemstones embedded into the elegant engravings covering its exterior.

She wondered which god exactly it belonged to and figured that, if she had to gamble, her bet would be on the god of money or monarchs, maybe both.

"I believe you know why I had my disciple bring you to me," the Traveler said with a look of amusement, interrupting her introspection.

"Ah, yes," Phoenix replied with terrible eloquence. "Well, kinda? Scholar and Warrior gave me skill—I mean, Knowledge Tomes—to help in my quest for Hero and Rebel."

The genderless deity smiled once more and stated, "Yes, I requested your presence to also offer my favor and fix a fault within you."

Phoenix's face scrunched up in confusion, frustration, and a bit of offense. She knew that she had *many* faults, but she wanted to fix them herself now, not have some divine entity tinker around with how she was.

Laughter interrupted her internal monologue. "Do not make such a face, young wanderer. It is not a personal failing of yours," the deity assured. Then they appeared again only a foot from her, and she reflexively placed both her hands over her Soul Mark, fearing the pain and fatigue.

More laughter filled the room at her reaction, and Traveler spoke reassuringly. "I see my siblings have caused you a bit of trauma there. Conjure your [**Guide Book**]," they commanded. Like it had a mind of its own, the book appeared without her prompting as though it was happy to assist the deity.

Traveler lifted a hand to touch the open pages.

"Wait!" Phoenix shouted as she reached out and snagged the book, pulling the open pages close to her chest. "Please," she begged the slightly surprised deity, "please . . . not another quest. I—I don't think I could handle more responsibility . . . I'm already pretty overwhelmed right now."

Even more laughter came from the Traveler's lips as they responded, "My dear wanderer, do not fret so much. I only wish to improve upon it, that it may help guide you better in your travels."

New Quest: Path of the Traveler
The deity Traveler has offered to alter your Talent and grant their divine mark.
Objective: Gain Traveler's Mark of Favor and upgrade your [**Guide Book**].
Reward: Uncommon maps.

The Wayfarer gave a weary sigh at the words scrawled upon the pages in front of her and silently nodded her consent. Then, the deity reached forward and placed their hand on the book, causing it to glow for a moment.

Your Natural Talent, [**Guide Book**], *has been updated.*
[**Guide Book**] *can now display maps and images.*

Phoenix glanced up into the deity's face, glad that it wasn't another quest, but her heart sank a moment later when Traveler gave her a mischievous smirk, and their hand passed through the book to set a single finger upon the center of her chest.

Quest: Path of the Traveler
Objective Complete: Gained Traveler's Soul Mark and upgraded your [**Guide Book**].
Objective Reward:
[Maps of Tulim] has been added to your collection.

> **Completion Reward:**
> 20 [Crystal Mana Bits] have been added to your collection.

To her credit, she didn't fall this time. Phoenix wondered if she was strangely getting accustomed to the overwhelming pain of a knife slicing through her heart and piercing her soul. While she didn't collapse, every muscle in her body was trembling fiercely, and she felt as though she was paralyzed in place.

"I will not keep you from your rest any longer. Safe travels, Chosen One," Traveler said in a slight tease before vanishing.

Kyleen returned to her side, slipping an arm around her waist and lifting her arm over the elf's slim shoulders in an effort to help her move.

"No more gods, right?" Phoenix blearily asked.

The priestess gave her a pitiful smile and nodded. "No more gods. At least for today. Let's get you back downstairs to Priest Ravone and back to your Mentor."

"How do you know Paul's my Mentor?" she asked, trying to distract herself from the residual pain.

"As a priestess, my deity has a direct connection to me. They impart information as they deem necessary through whispers in my mind. I just received my own quest to return you to him."

"Isn't that kinda cheating? Why doesn't everyone just become a follower of Scholar so they can know everything?" she inquired, half-contemplating doing that herself.

Kyleen laughed. "Many followers of Scholar hope to do exactly that. But even she is limited in what information she can dole out. Plus, it costs the gods a bit of their Aetherius whenever they directly act in the world, so they don't do things without reason."

"Aetherius?"

"Simply a name we use for the power they gain and spend. It's more concise than using ambiguous terms like 'divinity' or 'power' even though that's what it amounts to."

"Are they the kind of gods that are worship-powered?"

"Something like that," the priestess admitted. "People generate Aetherius by their actions and devotion to them, and in return, the gods can use that Aetherius to grant blessings, Titles, or powers, spawn specific Aspects or Spirit Gems, perform miracles, and ideally help make the world a bit better."

"So, they need people to act as their agents?"

"For most things, yes. What you witnessed when meeting each of them was a magically constructed projection. Even maintaining something like that costs them a trickle of Aetherius, though the cost is less in certain places like their sanctuaries."

"Huh," Phoenix grunted, "that's an interesting little tidbit. Does that mean if the gods do visit you in, let's say, a random meadow in the middle of nowhere, then they must really think you're worth it?"

The priestess laughed once more. "You *are* worth it, Phoenix Fraser."

"I sure hope you're right. Otherwise, I'm starting to think Hero and Rebel made a crappy choice on who to waste their Aetherius on."

"It's not a waste," Kyleen said resolutely, "it put you on the path here."

CHAPTER TWENTY-THREE

The House of Wayland

Paul watched Lester lead Phoenix away for a few moments, not liking the feeling that was settling in his gut, but he wasn't about to start picking fights with even more gods. With an annoyed huff, he turned back towards his own path, taking the left road that followed the western wall of the International District until he reached the first gate leading into the southwestern section of the city, which was designated as the Martial District.

Most of the city's Defenders were trained here, and they were often used as congregation points for missions of various organizations. The Alliance of Adventurer's Tulim branch was located here, closer to the central gate of the inner wall. This was where he made his way to first.

As he moved through the tunnel leading into the Martial District, the crowd seemed to shrink back from his presence, making him able to move quickly through. He wasn't sure if Phoenix had noticed the people subconsciously shying away from his power when she was following behind him during their travels, but if she had, then she had chosen to remain silent about it, which he preferred in general.

Paul hadn't found himself speaking so much in years, not since pleading his case to the Delegation of Radiance when he denounced his god and separated himself from the Purifier. He had been cast out of his home shortly after that debacle and hadn't been back since . . . until today.

Before he'd confront his family, however, he had paperwork to fill out. Paperwork that asked almost as many questions as his new student . . . *almost*.

He couldn't blame Phoenix for seeking answers since he'd likely be stuck doing the same if he had been dumped into a completely new reality. It had made him wish for his old party, though. Miriam would have been much better at handling and comforting the young woman. Gods, even Jerem would have likely been better than he was.

As he entered the AOA building, he felt a shudder of Auras as the Adventurers currently occupying the hall all turned their gazes towards him, the only Emerald Caster among them, and he knew he was likely the highest level one in the city. He didn't let their attention phase him as he moved purposefully towards the desk that was for turning in mission reports.

Paul handed over a small folder and requested an Unexpected Encounters Addendum form as well as the ones for registering new potential Adventurers for the next trials.

"You're lucky you arrived today," the clerk responded as she handed over the forms, "the deadline is this evening, and they've announced it will be the final one until the blood moon has concluded."

He simply nodded with a curt "Thank you" and took the forms. As he turned to go and request a temporary office space, his path was interrupted by a woman he hadn't seen in almost seven years.

"Glad to see you're still alive and have come home in time," the runeforged woman said, brushing back her long hair, currently styled into a plethora of small braids. She smiled and teased, "There was a betting pool going around if you would actually show or not."

The corner of his mouth involuntarily twitched as he observed the smaller Caster and ignored the obvious bait. "Agatha. Congratulations on your promotion."

"Thank you. It still feels a bit odd to go by Director Trayvious now. You've missed quite a bit in your self-exile," she said, prodding again and waved for him to follow her towards the platform lift at the edge of the room. "I'm just glad you at least answered the blood moon summons."

Paul gave an annoyed huff as he muttered, "Hard to simply ignore the orders coming from not just my family but the AOA Central Leadership, the Tulim AOA Director, and even the Queen of Blomsterang."

Agatha raised an eyebrow at him as she pressed a rune on the wall, activating the glass lift, and asked curiously, "You got a missive from the queen? What did it say?"

He gave her a pointed look. "Exactly what you'd expect: 'We're too short-staffed,' 'As a former local,' 'Go protect it or else.'"

The director laughed. "Well, if she wanted to make her lack of love for our little duchy known, then sending *you* is a pretty clear message."

Paul shook his head and followed her out once the lift stopped at the top floor. The high-rise had a beautiful view over the Martial District, with the gathering yard close by, which was currently filled with Adventurers attempting to organize themselves before heading out on their respective missions.

It was one of the very few places in the entire city that had so much open space, and he wasn't sure how much longer that would last to handle the natural population growth of the city. As he walked up to the windows that made up the entirety of the outer wall, he discovered that from this height, he could almost make out the picture that the stone mosaic of the paved ground depicted: a crossed sword and wand over a blue feather centered on a shield.

"Why did you bring me here, Agatha?" he asked quietly, not looking away from the crowds.

"We needed a stronger Emerald Caster that was a dedicated combatant," she began explaining as she took her seat at the large desk near the center of the space.

"No, *here* specifically," Paul clarified as he turned to look at her. "In this office, with all the witnesses seeing us enter?"

"I can't just catch up with an old friend?" the runeforged asked with feigned innocence. Paul gave her a flat look, and she instantly caved. "Okay. I just wanted to discuss your duties within the AOA while you're here."

"You'd trust me with anything more than guard duty?" he questioned, crossing his arms over his chest.

"Please, Paul, you know I'm not the religious type," she scoffed. "I don't care that you were excommunicated and Fell from the Purifier's grace. What I care about is whether you're going to agree to take orders from me, or be a pain in my neck."

"Is that what this is about?" he asked and gave a slight smirk as the tension left his body. "You think I'd go against you just because you haven't hit Emerald yet?"

She stilled, giving him a meaningful look. "You and I both understand the Rule of Caste. People will naturally look to you over me for orders. If you decide to try and overrule—"

"I won't, Agatha," he interjected. "I have enough trouble on my plate already and you know I don't enjoy political games," he assured her as he walked over and sat across from her in a sturdy chair. "I wouldn't mind some . . . *help* with arranging certain things, however, and request you be respectful of other duties I have within the city."

The director gave a sigh of relief and noticeably relaxed as she nodded, adding, "That actually brings me to my next topic." Then she opened one of the desk drawers and pulled out a small marble stamp with a rune engraved on the end that he recognized as she held it up to him.

He almost went slack-jawed at the silent inquiry and verified, "You want *me* to be an Emissary?"

"You've dealt with nobles before—"

"I just said I don't enjoy political games!"

"Are you going to be honoring your father's request or not?"

Paul fell silent, glowering for a long moment before saying, "I haven't discussed it with Patricia yet."

Her eyes narrowed at him as she asked, "Are you *Lord* Wayland or not?"

He let out another annoyed huff and admitted, "For now. However, that doesn't mean I want to be the one stuck with all the political missions."

"Of course not, milord," she said with a victorious grin, "but this will allow me to give you the really important ones that I can't trust anyone else to do."

With a soft groan, Paul shuffled and pulled the green marble card from his belt pouch before sliding it across the desk. Agatha touched the stamp to the top of it, causing both to glow for a moment as the rune became etched on his AOA license.

She didn't return his card immediately, though, as she swapped out another stamp from the desk and showed it to him. "Can I add this one too?"

Paul's expression hardened at the sight of the rune and he replied darkly, "No."

"Now, Paul, I think with your track record and connections, you would make a decent Delegate as—"

"I'm a Fallen Paladin, Agatha. If you try to make me a Delegate Adventurer, the temples might see that as being hostile on your part," he stated flatly.

"I thought they raised you back up when the Purifier Fell too, and his clergy were removed from the Delegation of Radiance."

"No. Now, I'm just a Fallen Paladin to a Fallen God. I would have to rededicate to a different deity that would be willing to raise me to Paladin again. No matter which way you look at it, I am the *last* Adventurer you want handling temple missions," he insisted.

The runeforged seemed to wilt slightly, as she put the stamp back in her drawer. "Fiiine. Let me know if you decide to do the whole rededication thing, though."

"I'm not thrilled about the idea of being betrayed by another god, so let's go ahead and just assume that will *not* be happening."

"In that case, will you try to convince your sister to join us?" the director asked with a grin.

"You know Patricia never listens to me. If she turned you down, then my words won't change her mind," he said, leaning back slightly and appreciating the shift away from the topic of deities.

"Well, I would appreciate your words anyway," she said, mirroring his movements. "Now, what do you want my help with?"

Paul hesitated, debating how much information to divulge to this woman who used to be a friendly acquaintance, but he couldn't truly be sure of her stances on things after being apart for so long.

She had managed to climb the ranks and establish her place at the top of this branch of the AOA, even as a Sapphire Caster, but he wasn't positive if that showed more skill or cunning. Perhaps both were required.

"I met a young woman during my last mission," he began, choosing his words carefully. "A Wayfarer. I want to make sure the Order of Magic and anyone else backs off of her."

Agatha straightened a bit at the news and asked, "You convinced her to join us instead?"

He nodded. "She was already attacked by one of the Magi. I've been training her to better defend herself."

"When did she arrive in this world? Will she need Aspects? Most don't arrive with them. We could probably schedule her for the first trials after the blood moon and get her set up with some sort of temporary position," she fired off while opening another drawer as though looking for something to get all of the processes started at once.

"About a month ago now, and no. We were able to procure some on our own," he explained and pulled out the application for new Adventurers he had received earlier. "I was about to give the AOA the details on her current capabilities since her Class, Celestial Astromancer, is unheard of as far as I know, and hopefully get her in with this next trial."

Agatha stared at the slip of paper for a long moment before finally clarifying. "A few weeks of training after becoming Crystal Caste, and *you*, the Blade of Pure Wrath, believe she is ready for the trials leading into a blood moon?"

Paul nodded when her eyes met his. She let out a tiny gasp as she seemed to realize something and asked him, "Are you claiming her as Protégé?"

He kept her gaze, finally making up his mind as he declared, "Yes, I am."

Paul stood at the gate to his family home. It was one of the few buildings in the city that had a small garden easement around it and was the tallest on this particular block within the northwestern quadrant of the inner city. The sigil of a rose wrapped around a sword was emblazoned proudly on the front door, and he hesitated at the sight of it.

The weight of wearing that sigil seemed to settle upon him once more as he gently pushed the gate open and slowly walked up to it. It had been six years since he had set foot on this particular doorstep, and it still felt too early for him to return . . . too early for him to forgive.

"*Not knocking will not make the door open,*" a mechanical voice spoke in his mind.

"*I know, Bela.*" He mentally sighed. "*Just don't distract me while I try to face my family again. You know how they get when I don't respond to them because I'm focused on talking to you.*"

The monotonous voice returned his sigh as the higher, feminine pitch replied, "*As Wayland commands.*"

Before he could work up the resolve to knock or try the key he had buried in his pack, the door swung open, and a runeforged woman slammed into him, hugging him tightly.

"You came back!" She almost sobbed. "I told them you would. I knew you wouldn't abandon this duty."

He relaxed slightly, and a soft smile tugged at his mouth as he said, "Hello, Pati."

"Don't 'hello Pati' me!" the woman snapped, pushing away from him. Her expression became sterner despite the clear relief and tears of happiness on display as she swiftly moved on to scolding him. "You never once answered any of my questions in the last six years!"

"I see you got my letters, at least," he said, sidestepping the accusation.

"No, you're not getting out of it this time," she said and took his hand, dragging him into their towering family home. "We are going to have a proper catch-up, and you are going to give me straight answers!"

He couldn't stop the chuckle as he asked, "Is that any way to treat your older brother?"

"Oh? Is that what you are?" she snapped back. "And here I thought I had become an only child, left behind to care for an entire noble House and ailing father."

"I thought you wanted to become the Head?" he asked, trying not to let his hurt at the reprimand show. It was always like this between him and his younger sister. She would be outrageous and try to control the flow of conversation, and he would do his best to frustrate her. If, after all this time apart, they had easily fallen back into this pattern, he had the feeling that everything might actually turn out okay between him and his estranged family.

"That's beside the point." The smaller woman dismissively waved as she led him towards her personal study. "Now, are you going to agree to become the Head, or am I going to have to take it off your hands?"

"Isn't that what you want?" Paul asked with a hint of confusion. "I thought you might have wanted to throw me out despite anything our father might have decided on his deathbed."

Patricia laughed loudly. "Gods, no. Haven't you heard, brother? There's a nasty blood moon coming and alien invaders raining from the sky. The House of Wayland needs to put its strongest asset at the helm."

Paul shook his head. "Pati, I'm a Fallen Paladin—"

"Who only fell because he stood up to the evil he saw his now Fallen god propagating and warned the world of what was to come. It's not your fault they didn't listen, and now you have returned to help defend our city from their mistake. You are redeemed in the eyes of the public," the younger noble said.

He almost laughed at the absurdity of the idea she was trying to paint for him. "You can't be serious? You know I don't do politics."

"You won't have to," she promised, grasping his hands in hers to show her sincerity. "Let me manage everything while you become the figurehead we need, the strength we can lean on. Show up and smile—I know that's hard, but we can work on it—and let me handle all the backroom stuff you despise. I know you can play the game—"

"Just because I *can* play it doesn't mean I want to do so for the rest of my life!" he interrupted angrily.

"Just for the blood moon, Paul. I'm close to Emerald. I know this moon will push me into the next Caste," she argued before softening her stance. She pleaded, "Please . . . be our symbol of undeniable strength during this. We need you—*I* need you—to get through this."

Paul ran a hand through his golden hair as he paused their walk through the last hallway before they would reach her study. The wooden panels along the bottom of the walls separating the white marble of the floors and upper walls were a familiar sight that was both comforting and unnerving with the memories they were steeped in.

His mind raced at the repercussions of actually becoming the Lord of House Wayland. He found his thoughts drifting to Phoenix and the struggles she would face once news of her existence spread. Paul had already made the choice to claim her as his official Protégé in an effort to help shield her. Increasing his own social standing would also increase the strength of that shield and make it easier for him to add more.

Instead of answering right away, he went ahead into Patricia's study and made his way to the liquor cabinet he knew would be fully stocked. When the ex-Paladin found what he was looking for, he pulled out the bottle and a glass and poured himself a drink.

His sister smiled brightly at him. "Does the drinking mean you accept my proposal?"

He gave an annoyed huff and downed the glowing pink liquid in the short glass. Then he poured another before firmly stating, "I have conditions." At her raised brow, he continued, "There's a woman I want you to help me shield . . . *politically.*"

Patricia gave him a dubious look. "Brother, I know you like to dally now and then, but you always shut down my suggestions at finding a marriage partner." Then his sister gasped. "Is she expecting?"

Paul gave a pained sigh and stared up at the ceiling, contemplating about asking the gods for patience. He eventually leveled a look at her and announced, "She's my Protégé," then took another long swig from his glass.

CHAPTER TWENTY-FOUR

A Little Light Reading

Paul's eyes narrowed at the pair of disciples half-carrying his new Protégé towards him. Phoenix looked ragged and shaken, and he was already unhappy with the events that had happened since they entered Tulimeir.

"Little Miss looks like they mana-drained her." The familiar voice sounded in his mind again, and he mentally hushed the comment.

He almost growled at the clergy as he asked, "What happened to her?"

The disciples blanched at the Emerald Caste Aura that pressed upon them, an obvious threat should he not like the answer. Lester spoke up first. "My Lady Scholar, Warrior, and Traveler simply granted the child some boons to aid in her tasks."

They all looked at the disheveled young woman who appeared to have just run a marathon, and Paul glared at Lester again. Kyleen added hastily, "They may have gotten a bit . . . closer than they usually do with other mortals."

Phoenix glanced up at him and explained, "They all did something to my Soul Mark. I'll explain later. Can we go sleep now?"

Her clear exhaustion made Paul soften his stance, and he dismissed the clergy with a wave of his hand. "Thank you for guiding her," he stated without seeming to mean it, and placed a hand on her shoulder to steer her into the building he had been standing in front of. He had been waiting there, knowing that any messenger of the Scholar would be able to find him.

He originally had hoped to clean her up a bit more before taking her to the Alliance of Adventurers to finish signing forms, but he realized that Phoenix needed to sleep off whatever the gods had done to her, and he wanted the information she held.

The building he took her into was a dormitory for people staying in the fortress city during the blood moon. Normally, it acted as an inexpensive hotel of sorts, but it was currently packed with visitors from the outlying towns and villages.

Paul was lucky enough to manage to get her a decent room on one of the upper floors. It was the closest dorm to his own home, but he wasn't quite ready to take her there yet.

Pati's reaction had been a mixture of excitement, exasperation, and consternation, and he wasn't ready to expose the young Wayfarer to all of the aristocratic nonsense that was his baggage to carry. Not to mention that he wasn't sure how well she would fare with the small horde of children and older relatives that lived there.

First, he wanted to make sure Phoenix was settled in her Role as an Adventurer before introducing her to his own mess. When he opened the door to a small sitting area, her expression visibly brightened, and she practically lunged onto the plush couch.

Paul chuckled at her antics. The young woman had definitely started to rub off on him after weeks of travel and training, and he felt a lot more comfortable around her now. He wasn't ready to open up to her about *everything*—she was just a child, after all—but she had always been honest with him. Even when he tried to pry out her secrets and gave shallow threats, she hadn't even attempted to lie, instead explaining that she would not divulge them, and he respected her for that.

He gently nudged her over so that he could sit on the couch next to her, the position a clear indication that he wanted to read with her. He had been pleased that she had always been willing to share the ability with him. Paul had even contemplated asking to borrow the book to inspect some of his own items but had dismissed the idea, not particularly ready to divulge some of his own secrets.

She groaned at the effort but still sat up and conjured her book in front of them so that he could catch up in reading. After he read the first two new quests explaining the Knowledge Tome and the third explaining the Talent upgrade, he looked at her with amusement. "Well, that explains the state you're in."

Phoenix rolled her eyes at him and sarcastically said, "Ha. Ha." Then, she pulled out the stack of books from Scholar, showed them to Paul, and touched the first one against the guide's pages.

Item: Magic of Makera: Rituals
A magical tome detailing the foundational patterns, theories, and techniques of the Magic of Makera encompassing rituals of the world.
Caste: Crystal.
Availability: Rare.
Type: Consumable, Knowledge Tome.
Requirements: Crystal Caste or higher.
Effect: Imparts basic ritual patterns, theories, and techniques from throughout history.

Paul frowned at the description and spoke up. "This is not the usual Knowledge Tome for ritual magic."

Phoenix looked up at him. "This one is listed as rare. Doesn't that mean it's better?"

He shrugged. "Normally, I would agree, but just because something is harder to find doesn't mean it's inherently better than something that's tried and true."

She seemed to think it over for a moment but instead decided to give in to exhaustion and just shrugged. "While I already know a bit of ritual magic from you, my world didn't have any magical knowledge, as far as I'm aware, so I'm going to use it. Plus, I'll get a reward just for learning new things. It's a win-win."

Before Paul could warn her about the strain, Phoenix opened the tome and read the activation sentence aloud. "The Scholar is a lovely and benevolent goddess that knows exactly how to win the heart of a bibliophile Wayfarer."

The book seemed to behave in much the same way that the Aspects had as it began to break apart in her hand.

"Wait, did she write that knowing I would have to re—" Her question halted as a cloud of inky lettering quickly swarmed over her, embedding itself into her flesh like slivers trying to burrow their way under her skin, and he helplessly watched as she gasped in pain.

Paul grabbed her shoulder to try and keep her steady as he instructed, "Stay awake. It won't work as well if you pass out again."

Phoenix gritted her teeth and nodded. He knew the information was bombarding her mind faster than she would be able to actively process it. He hadn't enjoyed the few times he had used one as well.

When it was finally finished, she took a gasp of air, and he realized he was unsure when she had begun holding her breath. He had absently forgotten that Crystal Casters still needed to do that mundane function.

After she steadied herself once more, she complained, "I was not expecting a book to *ever* cause me pain." Then she pulled out the next tome and hesitantly touched it to her **[Guide Book]**.

It read almost exactly the same as the first tome but was for cantrips instead of rituals.

"This one also seems slightly different than normal, too," Paul said as he glanced at her. "Are you sure you're up to another one? You should probably rest." He was starting to worry that whatever the gods had done to her might have compromised her judgment and was pushing her to act hastily.

Phoenix grimaced. "I'd rather get all the pain over with at once. I'm hoping to sleep for the next week at this rate," she admitted. "What exactly is cantrip magic? I've heard the term before, both here and in my original world, so I'm not exactly certain what it actually is."

He gave a slight grimace and sourly said, "I'm actually rather . . . *lackluster* with cantrips. Rituals I've become a practiced hand with, but I've always been pretty shoddy with the other types of Mundane magic, as well as crafting in general."

She raised an eyebrow at him, and he explained further. "Cantrips are basic Spells that require a medium. This is usually a wand, or sometimes a staff, made from a magical material. Even Mundanes can use these to channel and amplify the little magic they have in order to perform certain tasks. Repairing a broken cup, healing a minor scrape, watering a small garden, lighting a hearth," he listed off, "little things that help accomplish simple tasks."

"That sounds awesome," she surprised him by saying.

"They're useful," he agreed, "but they won't help fight monsters or accomplish grander or more complex tasks."

"Well, being more useful is my current goal," she quipped, clutching the book in her hand. "Try to keep me awake." She groaned slightly before activating the tome by dryly reading aloud, "Wayfarers all love the goddess Scholar and her magnificent brilliance that guides them in a strange new world."

Paul tried not to laugh as he kept his grip on her shoulder, taking in another swarm of magic letters before he could have advised her otherwise. He shook his head at the brash impulsivity of it. He only hoped she would remain conscious long enough for him to give her the potion he pulled out of the small dimensional pouch on his belt.

He was surprised at her resilience as the information finished inserting itself into her mind. Then he handed her the potion before she could grab the next book and commanded, "Drink." It was a green liquid that he knew she wouldn't recognize, and he answered her unspoken question. "Stamina potion."

Paul had gauged correctly early on that as long as the young woman understood the logic behind a request, she seemed more willing to comply if he requested her to do something as a command. He could sense in her Aura that she didn't particularly care for the controlling nature of the orders, but he could also tell from her demeanor that she disliked social confrontation. If he took control, she would allow it rather than argue.

It made things easier for him, and he had exploited it. It wasn't like he was trying to harm her; in fact, his commands were usually for the exact opposite reason, so he felt no guilt at guiding the Adventurer-in-training with this method. He also suspected it was helping ground her in this new world. Giving her something solid to lean on when everything around her was just like Scholar described: strange and new.

When she finished the potion, she looked markedly better, and she pulled out the next tome that was labeled for Artifice.

"Artifice is like crafting magic items, right?" she asked him.

He nodded and explained, "It's considered a subdivision of enchanting. It's just more involved since various enchantments are applied throughout the crafting process of the item instead of added on after the fact. It generally results in a stronger magical item since the desired effects were considered from the item's conception."

Paul glanced at the final tome still sitting in the young Wayfarer's lap and tilted his head towards that. "I assume that one is enchantments and would recommend using that one first so the information isn't as disjointed when settling in your mind."

She obligingly lifted the tome and touched it to her **[Guide Book]** to display the details, which were also fairly similar to all the others.

"So, what's the difference between rituals and enchantments?" she inquired.

"The short answer is permanence," he replied bluntly before continuing. "You remember the ritual you saw me doing earlier to close that Reality Rift?"

"Yeah." She nodded. "It was quite the light show."

"Well, that ritual is a one-time effect that requires a fairly high up-front cost and has a limited duration."

"Wait, you didn't just destroy the portal?"

"I *closed* the portal. Destroying it would have taken much greater effort and likely result in accomplishing the Soul Reaper's goal of mass destruction to the surrounding lands," he said with a shake of his head. "Not to mention channeling that much power would likely kill me in the process."

"So how long is it closed for?" she asked hesitantly.

"About a year? Give or take a few weeks," Paul estimated with a shrug. "The point is that it wasn't an enchantment. Those are more permanent. Depending on a number of factors, they'll likely require upkeep. Either through the ambient mana available or supplements from Casters or Bits."

"Oh, like how my cloak can use a Mana Bit to turn into a shelter for eight hours?" Phoenix pointed out.

"That's a perfect example," he agreed. "There's also usually a lot more preparation required for enchanting. With permanence comes planning."

The Astromancer nodded along, then flipped open the cover of the tome of enchantments and read aloud again, "'If a grumpy Paladin is ever mean to a Wayfarer, then Scholar will be sure to smite the Paladin and give the Wayfarer many hugs.'"

Paul shook his head at the ridiculous activation sentence the goddess had written but recognized the subtle threat. By taking Phoenix on as his Protégé, he would have the gods to answer to should some terrible end befall her.

Phoenix held her head in her hands with a groan once the book was finished. Even a stamina potion wouldn't help all of the mental fatigue that she had built up, and Paul knew he would need to stop her from trying to use the martial ones before getting some proper sleep.

"Is Wayland trying to melt the Little Miss's mind? This One has never contemplated this method to do so with before." The mechanical voice in the back of his mind spoke up in warning, which he simply acknowledged with an acquiescing thought.

"Just one more, then some sleep, alright?" he suggested, placing his hand back on her shoulder as Phoenix nodded wearily.

She grimaced at the last sentence written in the book of Artifice, then begrudgingly repeated, "'Wayfarers are often Chosen by the divine for reasons unknown, but there is always a core belief: hope that they will change the world for the better.'"

Phoenix could barely keep her eyes open after the tome was finished disintegrating into her, but she tried to read the new message her **[Guide Book]** was displaying for them.

Quest: Books of the Scholar
Objective Complete: Gained Scholar's Soul Mark and used the magic Knowledge Tomes.
Objective Reward:
[Ritual Materials of Makera] has been added to your collection.

Completion Reward:
20 [Crystal Mana Bits] have been added to your collection.

The Astromancer seemed to perk up at the message. "Nice, this should help me practice, right?"

He chuckled and nodded the affirmative, sharing a bit of her excitement in gaining new starter items. He had grown accustomed to his looting power decades ago, and it had been a surprisingly enjoyable time to experience it all again vicariously through his new Protégé.

"Can we try some now? I have so many new ideas," she asked, her exhaustion seemingly forgotten.

Paul chuckled, then reassured her, "Not today. Sleep." She started to protest, but he held up a hand and said firmly, "Sleep. No more tomes. Just rest. Then I'll join you tomorrow with more stamina potions for the other tomes."

Phoenix pouted but nodded. He helped her stand and make her way to the bedroom to sleep in an actual bed. He made sure to lock the dorm as he left to return to his own home for rest and hopefully avoid more of Pati's interrogation.

CHAPTER TWENTY-FIVE

Weapon Wielding Warrior

Paul wasn't surprised to find that Phoenix had slept for the rest of the evening, through the night, and well into the next day before he woke her up with a gentle nudge.

Once he saw she was awake, he left the room to await her in the small dining area and started pulling plates of food out of the dimensional storage basket he had brought along. He chuckled when she almost squealed in delight when she noticed he had bought them some actual food to eat, and she eagerly sat across from him to devour the meal.

They talked a bit about what had happened while they were apart yesterday as they enjoyed the spread of breakfast food, which was mostly Phoenix explaining everything that had happened between her and the three deities in much more detail than just the quest log.

"Did it change?" Paul asked once Phoenix paused to take another bite of eggs. At her questioning look, he gestured to her sternum. "The Soul Mark."

"Oh," she said after swallowing her food. The Wayfarer pulled the collar of her shirt down far enough to display it. The mark had gained more details, adding an open book inside the bottom half of the star, with a dagger that looked very much like her **[Night Blade]** floating above the book with the tip pointed down towards the pages. On the left page was what appeared to be a nautical compass.

He nodded. "As I suspected, they added their own marks of favor to it." He then took another bite of his food.

"So . . ." Phoenix started hesitantly. "What did you do after completing your mission at the Alliance of Adventurers? Did you get a new one? Do you also have a room in this dormitory for the blood moon? Or . . ." She paused, seemingly worried about the answer before asking, "Or are you going to be leaving?"

The question hung in the air for a long moment as Paul finished chewing and asked, "Do you want me to leave?"

"No!" Phoenix said hastily before flushing in embarrassment and saying in a calmer voice, "Sorry . . . No. I would prefer it if you would stay and keep training me, if that's possible. Warrior said you would be a suitable trainer."

Paul paused and sat back contemplatively at that. "Did he now?" He hadn't expected any deity to want a Fallen Paladin anywhere near one of their Chosen.

She nodded. "Yes. He said I could go to the temple for guidance if I needed to, but that I could keep training with you." Phoenix hesitated again, seeming nervous, but went ahead and asked, "So . . . will you stay with me?"

He simply nodded briefly and continued eating his meal, adding a bit more to the conversation between bites. "I will be here in Tulimeir until the blood moon is over. I have duties here that require my presence in particular, and I'm one of the few Emerald Casters who will be defending the city."

"I've been meaning to ask . . ." Once more, she hesitated until Paul gestured for her to continue. "You don't have to answer me, obviously, but the priest earlier . . . He called you *'Lord'* Wayland."

Paul gave a huff of annoyance. He had been unsure if she had caught that little detail from the day before. "Yes. I'm a member of one of the noble Houses of Tulim. That is part of my other duties and one of the main reasons I'm even here in the city right now."

"You, um . . . you don't seem happy about that."

It wasn't exactly a question, but he recognized that she was seeking answers that he had been withholding thus far. He sighed but looked at her, assessing just how much he wanted to let her into his life.

Paul knew that he would need to explain things eventually, especially since he was claiming her as his Protégé, and she needed to know what all that would entail, but it meant that he wasn't lying when he said he would continue training her. She didn't need to know all the details right away.

"I've been away from my House for a long time," he began, tailoring his response to be understandable but not reveal more than he felt comfortable. He knew she would inevitably find out more about him by just being here in the city, but he didn't want to burden her with more information than she was ready to handle.

If he was honest with himself, he also didn't want her to leave because his politics scared her off.

That internal revelation surprised him. He had always been more of a solitary person by nature, but overall, he had enjoyed her companionship over the last few weeks. She didn't mind the silence that he enjoyed. She was curious but respectful of boundaries, and though he could sense her desire for answers, she had never really pushed him to reveal more. It had made him grow hesitant to explain some of the more relevant things about him that might cause her to shun him the way everyone else had.

"I haven't been on the best of terms with my family, and recent events made my relationship with the other members of my House . . . *tenuous*," he continued. "However, about three months ago, my father died, and the family requested my return."

"I'm sorry," Phoenix said instantly, shame and sorrow washing over her Aura, "I know you mentioned losing your mom years ago, but I didn't realize your dad also died so recently. You must be grieving more than I am. Was it also from a monster attack?"

Paul shook his head. "It was just his time, and some of my family believe he simply gave up after losing my mother. He may have been Emerald, but he lived to be five hundred and sixty-eight, which is beyond average for his Caste."

Phoenix gawked at him and blurted out, "What's the average?!"

"About five hundred for most Emerald Casters, so he beat it by a bit," he said with a slight smile. He had briefly touched on age before, but he wasn't sure Phoenix was quite ready for the "centuries" talk.

"*This One agrees,*" the familiar voice piped up, responding to his inner thoughts. "*Little Miss is much too young to confirm the existence of immortal Obsidian Casters, so This One would avoid that if Wayland can.*"

The Wayfarer decided for him, though, when she asked, "What's the average for the other Castes?"

Not wanting to lie, he explained, "It varies a little between species, but Crystals can usually reach one hundred and twenty-five. For Sapphires, two hundred and fifty. Then Ruby Casters are estimated to last a millennium, but I believe the current oldest living Ruby is around seven hundred."

"You said you're already sixty-four and also Emerald Caste. Were you the baby of the family?"

He chuckled. "The oldest, actually. My father was stubborn about settling down and only had children once he inherited the position of family Head."

"Are *you* going to live to be five centuries old?" she asked incredulously.

"Many Adventurers don't see that many years," he admitted softly, "it's a dangerous line of work."

At her sorrowful expression, he offered a reassuring smile. "I don't plan on taking too many risks any time soon, though. We'll ride out this blood moon in this low-Caste biome and stay relatively safe. I'm more powerful than anything that will spawn on the tundra."

Phoenix nodded, then inquired hesitantly, "How do Casters die from old age? You have healing magic here."

Paul nodded and expounded, "Ruby Casters and below still grow old, and eventually, the healing magic just stops healing. The body expires, and the soul moves on. My father went peacefully, at least. I heard the memorial was nice."

"Why did the family have you return, if not for the memorial?" she asked with confusion.

He grimaced, realizing his own slip too late, and decided he might as well divulge further as he said with a sigh, "To take over the House. That is why I was addressed as 'Lord' instead of 'Noble.' With my father's passing, I am now the Head of House Wayland."

Silence fell once more as Phoenix processed, and Paul waited to observe her reaction. She seemed to be struggling with the information, and he wondered if he might have made yet another mistake.

"Thank you for telling me," she finally said before pausing again, then nervously offered, "I . . . I just want to make it clear that I'm trying to trust you, Paul. You've saved my life more times than I can count by now, and you've not only been protecting me but teaching me how to protect myself. I appreciate any trust you give in return, but I don't expect it, and I'll do my best to not betray it."

He nodded at her, feeling a bit uncomfortable with the admission, but met her respect with his own. "Thank you for not pushing, and you don't need to concern yourself with my affairs. I have agreed to continue training you when I am able. If I am no longer able to, I will make that clear. While we're being a bit more . . . trusting with one another, though . . ." He continued after another moment of deliberation, "You should probably just be aware that while I was filling out the paperwork you needed to join the AOA, I officially recognized you as my Protégé."

"What does that mean?"

"It means I'm your Mentor and have vouched for you. I'll be kept in the loop of your activities within the AOA and have some say in certain situations, like turning down or accepting missions on your behalf and filling out the paperwork we need to get you signed up for the trials," he explained carefully.

"That sounds like a lot of control you'll have to make decisions for me," she said dubiously.

He gave a slight nod in acquiescence. "It may seem like it at first, but you can always denounce my recognition. Nobody can force someone to be their Protégé or Mentor."

"So, what's the benefit, aside from not having to deal with the paperwork myself?"

"Protection, advancement, and opportunities," he stated succinctly.

"What do you mean?"

"It's not uncommon for new Adventurers to have a Mentor. Somebody who helps guide them through the system until they're seasoned enough to handle themselves, especially in the higher Caste zones.

"You gain protection in that I can accompany you on lower Caste missions without too much fuss, and you will likely be shielded from any kind of hazing behavior since they'll be risking upsetting me. Advancement comes with the fact that I can accept higher Caste missions on your behalf. This can help demonstrate your capabilities might be beyond what the current expectation is and open doors to other more lucrative or specialized missions for you.

"This goes hand in hand with the opportunity to stand out as an exceptional Adventurer and gain even more chances to push yourself forward or gain access to more resources that will support your career as an Adventurer."

He fell silent once more, letting her absorb the information, and after some consideration, he added, "I will also not betray your trust. I know you have revealed many of your secrets to me, and I have kept them and will continue to do so. My hope is that, by doing all this, it will further protect those secrets and buy you more time to grow stronger."

Phoenix smiled softly. "Thank you, Paul."

The corners of his mouth twitched, and he returned her smile. "Thank *you*, Phoenix."

Her smile grew brighter, and they fell back into comfortable silence as they finished their meal.

§

Phoenix had a lot to process while they ate breakfast at what must have already been lunchtime. She was grateful for the honest conversation, however, and hoped it meant that she finally had a real ally she might be able to depend on in this overwhelming world.

Once their meal was done, they resumed their seats on the couch from the evening before. Phoenix pulled out the stack of martial Knowledge Tomes that Warrior had given her and showed them to Paul while placing the first one on her **[Guide Book]**.

Item: *Weapon Wielding Warrior: The Six Sacred Stances*, Silent Stealth
A magical tome detailing the foundational techniques of the Weapon Wielding Warrior encompassing movement and dagger forms.
Caste: Crystal.
Availability: Legendary.
Type: Consumable, Knowledge Tome.
Requirements: Use of the Absorption Ritual.
Effect: Imparts techniques of the Silent Stealth Sacred Stance.

"This should be useful since all I use is a dagger at the moment," Phoenix commented then looked up at her Mentor. "Ready to make sure I don't faint?"

He nodded and placed a hand on her shoulder. She opened the book and read, "The Silent Stealth Techniques will silence your steps, smooth your movements, and enhance your dagger strikes with deadly precision."

She clenched her teeth again as she absorbed the knowledge that would make her more rogue-like and was glad that she didn't feel as exhausted as she had the day before. Getting altered with even a tiny wisp of the gods' power had taken a lot out of her. She guessed that the only reason she likely wasn't still trying to sleep it off was because the latest changes were more like tweaking the original design already put in place. Or perhaps she was just gaining a bit of tolerance to the effects.

When the magic lettering completely disappeared into her, the Wayfarer immediately noticed how poor her posture was and just how inefficient her movements were as she subconsciously adjusted them. She hadn't realized just how important those slight changes were in how she would fight until the book had informed her otherwise.

Phoenix held off on taking a stamina potion and opened the next tome. "The Powerful Piercing Techniques will enhance the agility of your spear thrusts and power of your double-edged sword strikes."

Her mind was filled with brand new concepts—how to fight enemies with a much longer weapon, and the differences in her shallow dagger slashes and punctures compared to the devastation a spear could inflict *through* a body.

She rested for only a moment before reassuring Paul, "I think I can do one more; then I'll need the potion."

"You don't need to push yourself," he pointed out, then added, "Normally, I wouldn't recommend using so many Knowledge Tomes in such a short amount of time. It's usually better to wait between uses so the information has time to settle properly and not become a jumbled mess."

"Should I stop then? Why didn't you say anything last night?" she whined slightly.

He gave her a slight smirk. "I'm not sure you would have listened. You seemed a bit . . . out of sorts."

She rolled her eyes, but he continued. "But I think these will be okay because they were designed as a set. They were meant to be absorbed in quick succession so that the information will build upon one another when settling."

Phoenix nodded in understanding and picked up the third tome. "The Swift Slashing Techniques will enhance the speed of your single-edged sword slashes and the accuracy of your chain strikes."

The Wayfarer was panting now, and Paul silently passed her the slightly glowing and bitter green potion. The relief from the magic was instantaneous, and she paused to marvel once more at the magical effects that made her feel as if she had just awoken again from a restful sleep.

Three down and three more to go, so she didn't waste time as she read aloud, "The Controlled Cleaving Techniques will enhance the control of your axe strikes and strength of your great sword cleaves."

Phoenix shuddered at the images her imagination was conjuring up of decapitation and severed limbs. These were brutal techniques that most enemies would never walk away from should they hit their target.

"'The Blunt Bashing Techniques will enhance the might of your mace pummels, the drive of your staff craft, and the tenacity of your shield bashes,'" she repeated and was surprised that shields were being included as a weapon. She had never known whether to categorize them as offensive weapons or defensive armor since they would sometimes behave as both, but she was happy with their inclusion as the maneuvers filled her mind.

She took a deep, steadying breath as she held up the final tome. "Last one," she said offhandedly, then flipped open the cover and recited, "The Balanced Body Techniques will enhance the rigor of your hand-to-hand combat skill and imbue various meditation techniques that encompass the whole of the Weapon Wielding Warrior."

Quest: Ways of the Warrior
Objective Complete: Gained Warrior's Soul Mark and used the martial Knowledge Tomes.
Objective Reward:
[Gloves of Gripping] have been added to your collection.

Completion Reward:
20 [Crystal Mana Bits] have been added to your collection.

Phoenix was exhausted once more from the marathon of tomes she had just powered her way through, and she gratefully accepted the second stamina potion Paul offered. Despite her mental fatigue, however, she was itching to try out all the new techniques and maneuvers swimming around in her head. Before she would drag Paul to a nearby training area, though, she was going to check out her newest reward.

She pulled out the pair of silky silver gloves and looked over the information.

Item: Gloves of Gripping
Gloves that increase your holding skills.
Caste: Crystal.
Availability: Rare.
Type: Apparel, gloves.

> **Requirements:** Crystal Caste or higher.
> **Effects:**
> - The wearer cannot be disarmed through Mundane effects.
> - For an ongoing low mana cost, the wearer can grip flat surfaces.

"Ooo, are these spidey gloves?" Phoenix asked, perking up at the idea of climbing up walls and crawling across the ceiling. She dismissed the latter idea, though, unless she got some matching shoes to go with . . . or made them with her new Artifice skills. She almost jumped up to start the new project right away, but Paul's movements distracted her from the tangent goal.

Paul stood and, in a rare sign of affection that surprised her, patted the top of her head as he said, "I have to attend to my duties now. Rest up. We'll be meeting up with someone from the AOA to train this afternoon."

He handed over a silver pile of cloth and added, "Wear this when I come to get you. Then tomorrow morning, you'll need to make your way to the AOA to finish signing any other papers and get your pass for the trials that should be ready by then."

Paul absently scratched his chin as he added, "Normally, I would have you train much longer, but with the blood moon imminent, the local branch has halted trials after this next one. However, I believe you'll do fine, especially with these Knowledge Tomes giving you quite the boost in fighting skill."

"How soon is the next trial?" she asked nervously.

"Five days. We'll use that time to get you more comfortable with the new techniques and help solidify their teachings," he reassured her, then took his leave for the morning.

With only a few hours to herself, Phoenix decided to finally take that warm bath she had been wanting for weeks now in the small room attached to the single bedroom of her dorm. She didn't get fancy with it but vowed to find someplace in this huge city that sold bubbly soaps and candles so she could make it a cozy haven in which to relax.

She had long desired to experience a bath like that after seeing pictures and wellness influencers raving about them. The hospital hadn't been well suited for that, but she vaguely remembered getting to experience a bubble bath as a child and wanted that again. For now, she settled on simple hot water that made her tense muscles melt before taking a nap in her new bed again.

CHAPTER TWENTY-SIX

Practice

Phoenix followed closely behind Paul, both of them dressed in the standard training garb of the AOA. She recalled the young warrior from the previous day had worn it as well. It looked like a tight, long-sleeved cycling uniform made from silvery, spandex-like material called "sliksilk," which clung to her form and was hard to grasp, causing things to slide across the material rather than catching and tearing it.

While Paul's very fit and muscular form filled out the outfit, she felt . . . gangly beside him. Her thin frame didn't make her feel like she had much to show off, and she kept her hair free to provide slightly more coverage.

As they walked down the hall, Paul paused in front of her, almost causing her to collide with his back. She looked around him to see why, only to have her jaw drop as a small black kitten was impossibly dragging what looked like a dead body that had been mauled into a bloody mess. The critter was pulling its victim by the collar down the hall towards them before turning into one of the side rooms.

She glanced up at Paul and asked, "Um . . . did the kitten just murder an Adventurer?"

He just chuckled and shook his head as he continued down the hall and into the training room at the end of it. She had glanced through the doorway the dead body had vanished into as they passed but hadn't seen the victim. She was still unnerved while following the streaks of blood down the hall to the scene of the crime.

The training room reminded her a lot of the arena she had met Warrior in, with its canvas mat flooring and various weapons on racks against the walls. Paul had walked over to one of those racks and was currently inspecting some of the blunt practice swords while she scanned the room for any signs of the murderer.

She knew this was where that Adventurer had been killed based on the red stains all over the floor, but she didn't see any obvious weapons covered in it as well. The Wayfarer was a little disturbed by the stains, which seemed to slowly vanish into the mat. She walked towards the larger puddle near the center and bent down to make sure she wasn't imagining things.

"It's enchanted," Paul said over her shoulder, and she involuntarily jumped at the sudden sound. He looked amused as he explained, "Self-cleaning and self-repair enchantments. Less cleanup between matches."

"But it's eating the evidence!" she said in alarm.

"Evidence?"

"Yes! The clues needed to catch the—" She cut herself off as her eyes landed on the small black kitten sitting in the doorway and staring at her with large emerald eyes.

"You must be the sparring partner I requested?" Paul inquired.

Phoenix did a double take to clarify that he was indeed speaking towards the furry suspect, who actually seemed to give a subdued nod of its tiny head. Then she questioned in a worried, hushed tone, "Paul . . . Are you talking to the cat? And did it *understand*?"

He just chuckled at her. "You really need to work on those Aura senses more, young one."

She scrunched her nose at the slight scolding and hesitantly expanded her Aura to brush against the kitten's own. Blinking in surprise, she glanced back up to confirm with her Mentor. "Sapphire Caste?" Her eyes narrowed at it slightly. "Doesn't feel like other Casters though . . . Is it a . . . what did you call them? Avals? The animals with Castes," she said, trying to describe it.

Paul shook his head slightly. "Yes and no. It might take much more practice and experience, but I can tell she's a transfigured Caster. Guessing that she's an aval or Vanhin would be expected, though. It's good for you to get exposed to the difference." Then he looked back to ask the cat, "What's your name, Adventurer?"

"Bliss," a quiet voice stated simply from the doorway.

Phoenix's eyes locked on the tiny creature once more, and she whispered to her Mentor, "Did the cat just speak words, or is my translation ability more powerful than I thought?"

Paul chuckled again. "Not a cat. A Caster," he reiterated, then gestured towards the small feline. "Remember how I mentioned transfigured Casters when you asked about werewolves?"

She nodded, and he continued, "Well, this one's a Chimera. Or perhaps a Shifter?"

He directed that last question towards the Caster cat, and the small creature gave another nod. This time, she saw it open its fang-filled maw and say, "Chimera," then, to her horror, it lifted a bloody paw and began licking the remaining gore off the pad.

Her horror was further exacerbated by her traitorous Mentor adding, "Bliss is who the AOA sent to be your sparring partner today."

"You want me to *fight* the murder-cat?!" she exclaimed, finally straightening and taking a few steps back from the tiny beast that might be fooling everyone else with its adorable looks, but she *saw* what happened to its victims.

This time, Paul did laugh aloud as he gestured for the kitten fiend to enter the arena. "Yes, actually," he managed to say after quickly calming himself. "I want you to get used to fighting something smarter than most monsters," he explained.

Bliss padded forward on silent feet and onto the arena mat as the soft voice questioned, "More human . . . Or less?"

Paul seemed to contemplate the question a moment before asking, "Can you do something a bit more her size and on two feet? We're going to start off with simple hand-to-hand combat, so nothing too exotic, if possible."

The kitten tilted its head once more in confirmation, and Phoenix wasn't sure if she wanted to fan-girl about magic or run away in fear as the Chimera pushed off the floor with its front paws, which quickly grew with the rest of its body until the creature was now her size but still had the same black fur all over, with emerald eyes watching her carefully. Her attention was caught by the long tail flicking back and forth behind the killer-cat-beast, and she wondered if the creature was excited for its next meal.

A small part of her was internally squealing at seeing an anthropomorphic panther furry in the flesh, but at the same time, it was terrifying to think she might end up like that bloody corpse the cat had dragged out earlier.

"Excellent. Thank you, Bliss," Paul said, politely interrupting her musings. The grumpy Adventurer had never been this polite with *her* before. "Now if you don't mind, just a quick spar with fists and feet. No claws or teeth . . . for now," he added, and Phoenix eyed him warily at the implication that he would eventually let Bliss try to maul her to death.

Bliss remained silent after another nod but let her fingers show compliance as she stretched the massive hand paws. However, no claws were extended like Phoenix would have expected. Perhaps the threat of an Emerald Caster in the room was enough to protect her from the same fate as that other lone Adventurer. The Chimera seemed to at least be following commands from him well.

Paul seemed to observe the form as he mentioned, "This will work nicely. Looks similar to a felion."

"I think my ritual tome mentioned that species," Phoenix replied. "It didn't describe them, though; they were just listed as a requirement. Are they all cat-people?"

He nodded in response, then eyed Bliss and clarified, "Yes, but they normally wear clothes over the fur. Now, square up."

As they took their positions, Paul began lecturing Phoenix. "The trials will consist of various tests that you must pass in order to prove your suitability as an Adventurer: survival, independence, teamwork, judgment, and potential.

"Right now, we're going to focus on the independence part. We need you to turn those new techniques you learned from mental notes into physical reactions. We want them to become second nature, but that takes practice. Now start."

Phoenix could see the palm fly towards her chest, but she was caught off guard by the sudden command and threat that she was slow to react to, so she stumbled back a few steps. She didn't wait for the murder-furry to attack again after that, as she quickly took the stance that had been seared directly into her mind and matched the following series of quick jabs Bliss levied upon her.

The motions felt natural, but Paul was right; she was slow, and her muscles were unused to following the commands her mind was trying to give them. It caused her to stutter and second-guess herself, which resulted in more strikes landing on her than not. Despite garnering more bruises with each passing moment, Paul didn't call for them to stop or slow.

"Unfortunately, practice takes time. Time we are extremely limited on," he continued explaining as she continued stumbling through the fight. "Only four days between now and the tests means we have to push you harder than what's normally acceptable," he firmly said. The Emerald Caster seemed to anticipate their movements and was always able to stay just outside the path of their battle as Phoenix stumbled around.

Phoenix had almost missed the furry black foot swinging towards her thigh, but she managed to move out of its path. However, this caused the flow of her movements to break from what the form wanted, and she stumbled while trying to get back into position. Her distraction cost her another fist to her torso that caused her to wince, and she reactively pushed Bliss away with her [**Ruler of Relativity**] ability.

She was further surprised by her mana draining faster than she'd anticipated for the higher Caste target. She'd have to remember to be careful of that in the future lest she instantly drain herself on accident.

Phoenix heard the sound of canvas tearing as she flew backward and saw massive, bone-white claws dig into the mat from the beast's large feet. They even sported reverse knee joints that could likely send the large cat hurtling forward to close the little distance she gained in an instant. If those curved daggers came out of the Chimera's hands . . . Well, the state of the corpse made perfect sense now.

"No powers!" Paul snapped, causing both of them to freeze for a moment at the flare of Aura pressing down upon theirs. "You're supposed to be practicing your martial techniques first," he reminded them. "Continue."

The foot claws retracted as Bliss launched herself forward simultaneously at the Emerald Caster's order, and it was just as Phoenix had imagined, with those powerful legs closing the distance within the span of a breath. She tried to keep up, realizing that Bliss was matching her speed so long as she didn't get distracted or make a mistake.

"You should be able to accomplish survival easily enough since you already proved it to me by lasting more than a week alone in the forest before you were even a Caster," he stated as he continued to observe their match.

As Phoenix was slowly acclimating to the rhythm of matching strikes with blocks, she began to incorporate her own offensive strikes into counterattacks. Bliss seemed to respond to the change not just by blocking but by adding in her own twist of feints and parries that sent Phoenix's fists and feet flying or hitting nothing but air and causing her to stumble. Every stumble was met with light punishment in the form of a controlled jab or kick, and Phoenix was very aware that the murder-cat was playing with its food.

"Teamwork will be difficult for us to practice, but if you keep your mouth shut and your ears open, I think you'll be okay in this respect. Keeping your head down and following orders, like you did when we were in that Reality Rift, will get you through for now, at least when you're uncertain about things. If you do know the answer to something, however, be sure to voice it. Potential is not something we can really train for, but I've seen enough that any good assessor should be able to see what I saw," he added almost as an afterthought.

It was enough to slightly distract her from the battle at hand as she asked, "What did you see?"

She was quickly punished for her distraction by a quick sweep of her legs. Suddenly, she was out of breath, staring at the ceiling, and trying to process how she ended up there. A panther's face entered her field of view, looking down at her, and Phoenix wondered if she was imagining the pity mixed with amusement in those slitted emerald eyes.

The disapproval in the gold eyes that looked down on her next was definitely not a hallucination, though, as Paul said, "We might need to shift our focus to Judgment instead."

Phoenix let out a pained groan and managed a weak "Ha. Ha," before taking her Mentor's outstretched hand and standing up once more.

"You laugh, but they're going to judge you for how you judge situations," Paul pointed out as he released her and took a step back. "You need to learn how to quickly assess a situation and respond appropriately. Whether that means choosing which monsters to confront yourself or talking when you should be fighting."

"How exactly am I going to learn battle tactics in less than four days?" Phoenix asked with exasperation.

Her Mentor then gave her a rare smirk as he answered with a hint of snark she had only heard once before. "Practice."

She groaned and was going to argue but was cut off by his next command of "Continue," and found herself fighting the flurry of fur that was methodically pushing her harder and harder and dealing out fluffy punishment.

After a half hour of this torture, Paul would have them pause and have Phoenix drink a stamina potion, which caused her to grumble about the cheating panther-person not even looking slightly winded. Then he would make her heal any bruises and have Bliss begin the onslaught anew. It became a vicious cycle of practice until knowledge became action, and action became reaction.

She wasn't sure at first if there was enough time for her to become even halfway decent in time for the trials, but after a half dozen cycles, she noticed the vast improvement she was making as she took less punishment and landed more strikes of her own.

Eventually, they moved on to daggers versus claws. It became a bit more familiar for her to fight like this after having spent over a week in the tundra with Paul practicing this style. She internally cringed at the memories, however, since she *knew* now how terrible her form had been.

Bliss, on the other hand, seemed to be unfazed by her blade strikes, and she reluctantly admitted that the transfigured Adventurer was a good sparring partner. The Chimera had the skill to match her own level and not just pummel her into the mat. This helped guide her growth by not going too easy on her either. Bliss pushed her when she needed it and backed off if she seemed to be straining beyond her current limits.

Phoenix knew she had to push past those limits, though, and Bliss seemed up to the task as the Wayfarer refused to back down. They continued clashing on the mat that was slowly becoming covered in sweat and blood that was continually cleaned up after them by the built-in enchantments.

It wasn't until long after the sun had gone down that Paul finally called a halt to the session and offered a small pouch to her sparring partner. "This was excellent, Bliss. If you wouldn't mind meeting here again tomorrow, I would love to see how Phoenix fares against your other, more exotic forms."

Bliss took the proffered bag and curiously peeked inside, and Phoenix had to suppress a giggle at the thought of curious cats when, in a very catlike motion, the Chimera tilted her head to the side for a few moments as though processing something. Then the Sapphire Caster nodded in the affirmative and asked, "Time?"

"Does noon work?" he inquired. "I have some things to address, and Phoenix has to stop by the AOA for her trial pass."

The panther-woman simply nodded once more and shifted back into the kitten form Phoenix had first seen faster than she could actually process. She had a brief spell of confusion as she wondered where the bag had vanished. That question died in her throat, however, as the murder-kitten pounced, using her like a ladder, before plopping over her shoulder.

Phoenix's terror at thinking the demon-cat was finally going to eat her was quickly replaced by worry that the kitten was melting as it languidly sprawled over her. She had no idea what was happening until the rumbling started. Phoenix looked incredulously at Paul and whispered in horror, "Did she just *fall asleep* on me?!"

Paul's golden eyes sparkled with amusement as he simply confirmed, "It appears so."

"What do I do now?" she asked in growing panic.

"Well, I'm not your father. I'm not going to say 'no' to taking stray pets home," he pointed out, not able to keep the corners of his mouth from curling upward.

"She's not a *pet*," Phoenix argued in a hushed tone, afraid to wake the bone-less fiend. "She's a *murder-cat*."

Her Mentor laughed again, not seeming to care about waking the furry scarf, as he clarified, "That other Adventurer was fine. Bliss took them towards the clinic where new Healers train. Do you really think I would just let her take away a dead body without asking questions?"

Phoenix frowned for a long moment, replaying the scene in her mind before mumbling, "No . . ."

He surprised her again by ruffling her hair and teasing her. "We'll really focus more on the judgment part tomorrow."

She swatted his hand away before following him out of the building and back to her dorm room, where they parted ways. Bliss remained asleep the whole way, and as Phoenix carefully maneuvered the critter onto the foot of her bed, the kitten looked . . . well, blissfully unaware.

CHAPTER TWENTY-SEVEN

Special Pretentiousness Requirements

Phoenix was grateful for Traveler's upgrade as she continued to reference the map of Tulimeir in her book. She quickly realized from the aerial overview it provided that the entire city had been meticulously planned out from its inception, with the only possible room for growth being vertical.

The upside of this for her was that it was fairly straightforward to navigate through once she understood the layout. Heading from her dorm back to the AOA building had been a matter of following the main street outside her building north to the first gate from the inner city, going through that into the western storage and logistics district, then south through the next gate leading into the Martial District, then continued southeast on the same road till she arrived at the towering skyscraper.

People all around her seemed busy with various tasks and steadily moved in and out of the slightly intimidating building. Inside was a wide hall that reminded her of reception areas in fancy offices that she saw on TV but with multiple desks lining the area, and she thought perhaps it was more like a bank.

Above each receiving area were various signs indicating the general purpose. There were two "Mission Receiving" areas, one for Crystal and the other for Sapphire Casters, and the two "Mission Delivery" desks were also divided by Caste. There was one labeled "Mission Requests," and another marked as "Licensing." Then there was "Inquiries," and the last one, labeled "Disbursement."

She made her way over to the line for Inquiries and patiently waited, ignoring some of the curious glances sent her way and trying her best not to fidget under their gazes. The Wayfarer knew she'd probably be curious as well if someone looked as different as she did here. When it was her turn, she walked up and prompted, "I'm here to pick up my trial pass?"

"Third floor. Take a right for two halls, then left for another two halls, then a right, and third door on the right," the young clerk said in a bored tone. They gestured to a lift area in the back right corner before calling out, "Next!"

"Ah, that was right, left, um—"

"Next!" they called out again, and Phoenix got the hint, moving out of the way to head to the platform that the clerk had pointed out.

The platform systems here weren't the quietest mechanisms, she discovered, pressing a rune that her ability translated as "three." Phoenix had gotten a steampunk vibe from the city with the addition of a heavy fondness for stained glass, and this elevator was no exception. The floor itself was a round slab of metal, but she could see the gears against the wall turn and could hear the tiny hiss of valves releasing steam to send the platform upward, while the curved sapphire-tinted glass doors secured her within.

It was fairly fast, with the magic increasing and modulating its propulsion, and the lift let her out quickly. She immediately turned right to walk down the hall, not wanting to let more time pass for her to forget. There weren't nearly as many people on this floor, and there was almost an eerie dissonance between the reception area and here. The literal floor was the same dark gray marble that she assumed must be on every floor.

She passed two hallways, then turned left. Doors were spread at intervals, but she had no idea what the rooms were used for. Another two hallways later, she couldn't remember what the clerk had said. It was two hallways, right? Or was it three? No three doors down then right. Or was it left?

Phoenix turned left, then passed another two identical hallways with the same paneled walls of bleached wood. The wood stood out to her as she hadn't actually seen much of it in the city, which she assumed was due to its scarcity on the frozen tundra. She brushed the errant thought away to refocus on directions.

Was it the second glass door? Wait, it was right, left, right, not another left!

The Astromancer started to panic slightly and tried to retrace her steps, only to turn a corner and crash into a dark figure that was solid enough that she repelled slightly. She tripped and stumbled while trying to reorient herself. Luckily, she was saved from falling as the figure's hand reached out to grab her own, quickly halting her momentum and righting her.

"I am *so* sorry!" Phoenix apologized profusely. "I—I'm lost and I just—" She glanced up to see a cinderen man looking down at her with a frown. "I wasn't looking where I was going . . . I'm sorry," she finished, attempting to tuck some of her hair behind her ear.

The stranger was handsome, with strong features, and a little less than a foot taller than her. He had dark ashen skin and fiery orange irises and matching markings typical of a cinderen. Most of his jet-black hair was pulled back into a short, messy ponytail with some loose locks framing his face.

The only other things that stood out about him were the many golden piercings trailing the outside edges of both his pointed ears and a golden metal choker around his neck, engraved with elegant runes, with matching cuffs around his wrists.

The frown never left his lips as he looked her over, and she asked nervously into the silence, "I, um . . . I didn't hurt you or anything, did I?"

The cinderen's brow furrowed, and he shook his head in the negative before asking in a low voice, "Where are you trying to go?"

"I'm trying to get my pass for the upcoming trials," she explained, still taking in his simple black tunic and pants that bunched into even darker black, fur-lined boots. The dark garb made his glowing markings and eyes stand out even more, and it felt like they were the last embers among ashes.

He tilted his head forward and said in a deep bass, "Me too."

Then he moved past her, and after a moment of processing his statement, she quickly spun on her heels and followed after him. She wouldn't deny that her relief was immediate as he guided her through the maze of identical-looking doors until stopping at one that she wouldn't have been able to distinguish from another.

Once they were inside the room, a runeforged clerk glanced over, taking in their appearance, and sneered at her temporary guide as he said, "Mission requests are on the first floor."

She noticed her strange helper's face twist slightly in what she read as annoyance, and she spoke up for the both of them. "We're here to get our trial passes?"

The clerk looked her over with uncertainty and asked, "Name?"

"I'm Phoenix Fraser, and my friend here . . ."

She gestured for the cinderen to speak, and he stated, "Uriel Karislian."

The clerk shot Uriel another disgusted look before ordering, "Wait here."

As the runeforged vanished through a door behind him, Phoenix turned to her newest pretend friend and said, "Well . . . Nice to meet you, Uriel. Are all clerks in Tulimeir jerks, or does the AOA just have its own special pretentiousness requirements for the position?"

He gave her a side eye, and the frown he had been wearing earlier returned as he replied, "I think it's just my presence. Sorry you have to deal with it."

"Nah," she said with a shake of her head, "the guy downstairs was kind of a prick, too. So, um, you're going to be doing the trials with me?"

He nodded, but when he didn't add to the conversation, she continued a bit more awkwardly, wondering if her feeble attempts at friendliness were coming off as annoying to him. "Um, I . . . Thank you," she murmured.

At his raised eyebrow, she elaborated, "For helping me. I really didn't want to have to go back downstairs and get directions again."

The clerk returned then and carefully set two folders between them on the desk. His entire demeanor seemed to have shifted as he bowed politely towards

Phoenix and said, "Miss Fraser, my apologies for any slight towards you and your friend. Not many people were left to retrieve their passes, and I made the poor assumption that you were both lost."

Uriel gave a short scoff, and she agreed with the unspoken sentiment, wondering what had caused the clerk to so quickly become the supplicant professional. The next words he spoke clued her in. "Your Mentor was able to file most forms for you, which qualified for the deadlines, but we still need your signature on some of them. There is also an additional form that was initially missed. We will need that as well, if it's not too much of an inconvenience at this time."

Paul.

She realized it was *Lord* Wayland who was the reason for the polite shift. She gave a tense, fake smile as she replied, "That's fine. Can I fill them out here?"

The clerk nodded. "Of course, miss. I will take you and your friend to one of the private rooms."

She glanced over at Uriel, who only shook his head at the lie he would have to play along with, and she answered nervously, "That would be great, thank you."

When they were left alone in the small room that only held a small round table with a handful of chairs in it, she sat and said, "Sorry about dragging you along." She began looking through the papers and lifted one, asking rhetorically, "Role designation? What is—Oh." Her roaming eyes found the folder that had Uriel's name on it and handed it to him. "Here's yours. I don't want to steal more of your time."

The cinderen carefully plucked the folder from her grasp and turned only to hesitate at the door before looking back at her with those ember-lit eyes. "Role designation is what you plan to do as an Adventurer."

"What?" she asked in obvious confusion. "I thought Adventurers just kill monsters?"

His expression seemed to soften as he shook his head and walked back to sit down in another chair next to her. "Yes, but how do you plan to do that?" he asked.

"Um . . . with magic powers?" she said, completely lost on what he was trying to get at.

She saw the corner of his mouth twitch, and she was reminded of Paul with his aversion to smiling. Uriel shook his head again and said, "Yes, but do you get up close with a weapon? Do you shoot Spells from a distance? Do you heal others who do the killing instead? What is your Role within a group of Adventurers?"

"Oh!" Phoenix exclaimed, the misunderstanding finally clicking into place. "What Roles are there?"

"Well, normally, you indicate your range placement first, so Forward, Midshift, or Backline. Then you fall into one of five broad categories," Uriel explained, then seemed to recite from memory, "Defender, Mage, Healer, Striker, or Supporter.

After that, some will add another specialization, like Banes or shielding. So, what do you do?"

"I, um, yes?" she said, thinking of how she moved all over and could shield and heal and fight. "I have a dagger. I mostly use that to kill monsters."

"So, a Forward Striker. Do you have more bursty attacks or more Bane-based ones?" he asked, pulling the form she had been holding over to help fill it out with her.

"Um, well, my dagger adds a mana drain that was listed as a Bane."

"If that's the only Bane you have, that's not likely worth adding as a specialization. Are your Special Attacks more about unloading high damage at once with longer cooldowns or more steady over-time damage?"

"I, uh, I don't have any Special Attacks?"

He paused and stared at her for a long moment before she rushed to finish explaining, "I have a dagger, a heal, a portal, a Movement ability, a magic shield, a stealth ability, a tiny defending fairy, and I can make little illusions."

Uriel blinked slowly, processing her words, then circled two of the words listed on the form and slid it back towards her silently.

Phoenix stared at the two words and nodded in agreement with a sigh. "Midshift Supporter is probably best."

"I wish you all the luck in the trials," he added softly and with much sobriety.

She grimaced and muttered, "Thanks."

CHAPTER TWENTY-EIGHT

For Adventure

Phoenix had spent the last four days locked away with Paul and Bliss, training as if her life depended on it. While she felt much more comfortable with her skills now, she was incredibly nervous about putting them to the test. If she failed these trials, it would not only reflect poorly on her new Mentor, but she wouldn't be able to take them again until the blood moon finished, which was still rumored to last for almost a year.

She continued racing down the street, trying her best to follow the signs and even using her book to try to map the way, but she kept getting turned around among the towering buildings of these less-traveled streets. Instead, she kept finding herself *not* at the designated location to meet up for the trials.

Paul had gone over the details with her *extensively* about what to expect and where she needed to put her focus, all while she had been fending off the chimeric sparring partner. Bliss would shift her form into various amalgamations of what Phoenix recognized as similar to an owl, panther, and giant anaconda. The latter was the most terrifying to her, but thankfully, Paul had deemed most of *those* abilities to be "above-Caste" for her current skills. However, she *did* get more healing practice with that one.

Needless to say, she hadn't always been able to catch everything Paul was lecturing her over while trying not to get eaten. She caught a lot, but it was just enough to make her feel woefully underprepared for being judged as an elite monster fighter. Her last hope was that with the impending blood moon, the assessor would be more lenient in their grading in order to get more Defenders for the city at such a critical time.

First, however, she needed to actually *find* the group of trial participants and hopefully not get left behind or marked down for being late. She picked up her pace, even attempting to use her Utility-turned-Movement ability, **[Ruler of Relativity]**, to empower her steps.

She stumbled a bit at first while trying to get the timing right to push from the ground, but her Crystal Caste Mind and Agility helped her get the hang of it quickly enough. She just hoped it would be enough to get her there before she missed any vital information.

> **New Quest:** For Adventure
> *Are you up to the challenges of this new path?*
> **Objective:** Pass the trials to join the Alliance of Adventurers.
> **Reward:** Epic cultivating magical trinket.

Phoenix shooed her book away hastily as she arrived at her destination. She was relieved at the sight of a large group of people, mostly around her age, milling about a large stone platform. It was located between the southern wall of the western district and the towering buildings all around it, which she had learned were mostly used for mass storage of resources that kept the city alive.

"Alright, people, listen up!" a Sapphire Caste runeforged man who she assumed was the assessor yelled out to the group of would-be Adventurers. Phoenix had just barely made it there in time.

There were sixteen of them taking the trials, and she noticed almost all of the others waiting with her were runeforged and cinderen, like most of the city's population. However, she did notice *one* other participant standing out just as much as she did.

It was the young man she had seen with Warrior. His dark purple hair glinted like stained metal in the little bits of rare sunlight peeking through the dense clouds. Phoenix wanted to approach him—maybe learn more about his relationship with the god—but the others surrounding the beautiful stranger made her hesitant.

The amethyst warrior seemed to have an entourage of other young people listening and laughing with him. His relaxed yet almost regal bearing seemed to somehow put others at ease despite the trials ahead of them.

"Smithson! Stop your chattering and listen!" the assessor yelled at the chuckling group.

"Of course, Mister Trayvious. I meant no disrespect. We are all just excited to finally become Adventurers," the young warrior replied gracefully with a very slight bow.

"We'll see," the assessor replied, then gestured towards all of them to address the whole group. "You all know a blood moon is imminent, and this is the final trial until it passes. Make no mistake that this is the *most* dangerous time to become a freshly licensed Adventurer, as you won't be given the luxury of getting the experience of normal missions. It's your life on the line, and you will be *fatally* disappointed should you not perform *above* the usual standards," Trayvious explained to the group with a heavy warning.

Any hope of leniency Phoenix had was killed with those words. Apparently, in a shocking turn of events, the Alliance of Adventurers seemed to actually care about the survival of their members and potential recruits. She had gotten that vibe from Paul when he spoke of the organization, but the few official functionaries she had met so far reminded her that it *was* an organization. One with a bottom line. It was nice to see that Paul's positive picture was proving to be more accurate in actual practice and out in the field, if not in the administration of it.

"For the first trial, we'll be going as a group to do a few missions out by the gorge to the west. Remember, unexpected encounters are likely, especially if we go into the night. If I deem anything too dangerous, you *will* follow my orders to retreat, or you will be disqualified from *ever* joining the AOA. Do I make myself clear?"

"Yes, sir!" the group said in response, which she managed to mumble along with in time.

"Very good," the assessor said, then glanced down at a stone tablet in his hands that was slightly glowing from the magic infused into it. He appeared to read some of the information before calling out, "Fraser!"

Phoenix froze, uncertain of what she could have possibly done to get singled out, but the runeforged called out again, "Phoenix Fraser?!"

"Y-yes? I'm here," she squeaked from the back of the group, which parted to let everyone see her. She felt extremely uncomfortable with all the attention focused on her.

"I've been informed that you have a portal ability that can take us to Linnake?" Trayvious inquired.

"Ah. Y-yes, my Mentor took me to a bunch of places across Tulim to learn them for portaling." She glanced around at the group before saying, "I can take one Sapphire Caster or about ten Crystal Casters every five minutes. It's not *exact*, depending on various magic levels of the people going through . . ." She trailed off when she realized these people probably didn't care about the nuances of her ability.

He nodded in understanding. "That's fine. Portals are extremely rare, so having one at all is helpful. Cutting our travel time to fifteen minutes instead of a week will help us get this over with *much* sooner."

Phoenix briefly wondered if this was part of Paul's plan, having her focus on leveling her portal ability as they went from monster to monster, despite him not being able to go through it. He even had her test it out in the later towns by portaling other people to other forts she had been to, which was what helped her gauge how many she could get through. She thought it was just for performing logistic missions that he had mentioned, but perhaps he wanted to give her a foot up in the trials, too.

"Alright, keep together, everyone. I'll be going first to make sure the area is secure, then the rest will follow, with Miss Fraser arriving last," the assessor commanded and gestured to the clear area behind him.

Phoenix conjured her circular portal floating slightly above the ground. She had always enjoyed the magical sight of the silver ring surrounding a star-filled night sky, and she felt that adventures waited just on the other side, and in this instance, that was exactly what was awaiting them.

Trayvious nodded at her in approval, then stepped through the portal, which vanished behind him as the magic was fully consumed by his higher Caste. Phoenix felt awkward again as she sensed people murmur and glance in her direction periodically as they waited for the cooldown of her ability to finish. She looked away from the others, finding her boots and gloves to be *extremely* interesting at the moment and not wanting to draw more attention to herself.

Once she felt her power was ready again, she conjured the next portal, with ten of the would-be Adventurers making their way through before it vanished again. Only five of them remained now, and one of them made their way over to her with a casual stride, followed by a cinderen man trailing behind like a shadow.

She was surprised to recognize the shadow from their run-in at the AOA, and Uriel seemed just as indifferent to the world as she first remembered. She hadn't expected these two men to be connected in some way after meeting them in completely separate ways.

"Hello. Phoenix was it?" the beautiful stranger that the assessor had called Smithson asked her politely.

She nodded, remaining silent, unsure of what the warrior wanted.

"I'm Dazien, but my friends just call me Daze or King, and this is Uriel," the amethyst-colored man said brightly.

She turned to her former pretend friend, only to be met with that same frown that was borderline a scowl, but he still politely nodded to her in greeting. Both of the young men were dressed in simple traveling gear that was mostly black with gray fur. Uriel was also carrying a large backpack slung over his equally large shoulders.

Phoenix bowed to the pair in greeting as she said softly, "We've met before."

"That's right. I saw you at Warrior's temple, didn't I?" he asked as though he had just now recalled the encounter, and his gem-like eyes seemed to sparkle with amusement. It made her not believe for a second that he had forgotten their run-in before approaching her.

"Yes, and we met when getting our trial passes," she added, gesturing towards the taller cinderen, who was about half a head taller than his companion.

That caused Dazien to raise his brow in surprise as he gave Uriel a side eye. "Is that so?" he questioned rhetorically, then the young warrior gave her a charming smile and said reassuringly, "Well, I just came over to thank you for saving us the travel time. A portal ability is quite special. Are you more of a group Supporter?"

She gave a nervous shrug and explained, "I, um . . . I haven't unlocked all of my abilities yet, so I'm not really sure where I'll end up when it comes to group roles, but Uriel suggested I go with Midshift Supporter."

Dazien raised an eyebrow again, giving another *look* at his friend before asking her, "You don't know what your Class will lean towards? Was it unknown or something?"

Phoenix nodded her head. "Um, well, I haven't really asked around, but my Mentor had never heard of it before."

"Ah. I guess we'll get to see what you're capable of in a bit then," he said cheerfully before turning to leave.

"Um, what roles do you two fill?" she asked in a rush. The warrior turned back to look at her, and she quickly added, "If you don't mind my asking, that is."

Dazien gave an amused chuckle and stuck a thumb back towards his companion. "Uriel here is a Backline Mage and all about area attacks while I protect him, among other things."

She had only been slightly distracted by the flash of crystalline nails on his hand when he spoke, the same color as his eyes, "I see," she said softly. Then she succumbed to her curiosity and managed to ask the charismatic man awkwardly, "Um, I hope this isn't rude, but I don't recognize your species . . ."

As she trailed off, he gave her another surprised look followed by a soft chuckle. "While I admit we are quite rare, it's odd that you've never heard of a gemite before at your age."

She recognized the name as one of the species in this world which the tome of rituals referred to for certain requirements, but the book hadn't gone so far as to describe them, much like the other species it had listed in places as required participants or targets. The ritual she recalled about gemites was specifically for changing a Mundane one's "gem color properties," and she now had a better reference for what that actually meant.

Phoenix quickly gave a vague excuse, not wanting to chance a kidnapping again, and she briefly wondered if gemites had a similar problem with being so rare and shiny looking. "I never really got out much. Most of what I've learned of the wide world I've discovered in like the last month and a half." Then she felt her ability become ready once more. "Time for us to go," she said to the pair and conjured the last portal, letting the rest go through as she followed behind.

CHAPTER TWENTY-NINE

A Little Domineering

The wind whipped around wildly as the group stood at the top of what seemed like a massive crack in the earth, not far from the outcropping of rock that the group had gathered on. Phoenix had managed to portal all of them right outside the gates to Linnake, one of Tulim's fortress towns that was located on the northern coast, west of Tulimeir, and high upon a cliff overlooking what Phoenix thought of as the arctic ocean.

The city was well-guarded from most dangers with its high altitude and cliffs to the north and east. The eastern cliffs fell into the massive gorge that ran south from the coast, which was their true destination. So, after about an hour of walking south along the ravine's edge, their assessor had finally brought them to a halt after referencing his tablet once more.

"Alright, people! We've gotten reports of some Crystal Caste fliers making their way from near here to terrorize the fort we left, which is eating up their mana battery supply for the wall's defenses. The report of numbers has been inconsistent, so stay vigilant," Trayvious informed them before walking to the edge and peering down into the icy ravine. After a moment of observation, he asked, "Malik, thoughts on how to approach?"

A young cinderen spoke up. "We could send a scout down to find the location of their nest. Do we know what type of fliers?"

"Colpteras, according to the reports," he replied as though unwilling to put much stock in the information. "They only attacked during the nights when there were snowstorms, so the visual confirmation is as unreliable as their numbers. We will sometimes have scouting pre-missions to make it more reliable, but things can always change. Remember this, everyone: Mission information is a best guess, do not put blind faith in it, or you will most likely die."

Phoenix conjured her **[Guide Book]** and willed the information for Colpteras to appear. At Paul's suggestion, she purchased what she fondly referred to as the

Tulim Monster Manual, which was basically an encyclopedia for every known monster encountered on the tundra. Getting the book and basically feeding the information to her guide ability while it sat in her collection made for easier referencing, rather than having to lug the giant textbook out and actually *hold* it. She absolutely loved that her book could access her collection like that.

When she read over the information and the attached picture, it seemed like a large white bat that used echolocation to navigate and had some Ice powers, but was fairly weak to physical attacks. She frowned, something about the description bugging her, as she thought about what Trayvious had described.

"What is it?" a pleasant whisper said into her ear, and she jumped in surprise at the purple-haired man who had somehow appeared next to her without her noticing. Dazien smiled impishly at her reaction, then gestured to the glowing book. "You seemed upset at it."

"Oh, um . . ." She wasn't sure if she should speak out of place, unsure if her reasoning was sound, but the young warrior just smiled reassuringly. "Well . . . the information here describes Colpteras as blind creatures that rely on echolocation . . ." The gemite nodded to indicate that he was following along. "It just doesn't sound like the type of monster that would attack during what I assume would be an obnoxiously loud blizzard."

"That's a good point. What do you think it could be?" he asked, curiously leaning closer to her book to read the description himself.

Phoenix shrugged. "I'm not sure. I haven't exactly read through all of the known monsters yet," she said, slightly gesturing to the book. "Do you know what other white creatures there are with bat wings and Ice powers? For all *I* know, it could be an Ice Harpy."

Dazien frowned. "I don't think the magical rating of this region could result in an Ice Harpy spawning, but this is gearing up to be a rather extreme blood moon if what I hear around town is to be believed. Maybe a young one? I'm not sure if there are variants of harpies below Emerald that can appear. A drake of some kind would be more likely."

Phoenix stared at him with wide eyes before asking incredulously, "Wait, harpies are real here too?"

It was his turn to look surprised as he asked, "What do you mean by 'real here'?"

"Smithson!" Trayvious's voice interrupted their whispered conversation, and they both turned to see everyone staring at them. She flushed red with embarrassment while her visitor gave a grin and casually rocked back on the heels of his heavy boots. "Would you like to share your thoughts with the rest of us?"

"Of course, Mister Trayvious," he said confidently and gestured at Phoenix. "Miss Fraser here just pointed out that the Colpteras would likely have trouble moving in a storm, so we're probably looking at some sort of drake or maybe wyvern instead," he explained without hesitation.

Trayvious glanced at Phoenix with an assessing gaze before nodding and replying, "Very good. How would you suggest we combat them, Mister Smithson? Send a scout like Mister Malik suggested?"

Dazien looked contemplative as he responded, "That could work, but it would be dangerous for the scout if it were stronger than initially thought. Going as a group might give us the strength advantage, but if it has ranged attacks, it could be disadvantageous if we were grouped together. Do we have anyone here who could scout and return to us quickly? We could set up a formation here to lure the beasts into."

"Bait into a kill box?" Phoenix asked curiously, then shut her mouth as the attention turned back to her.

Dazien grinned at her and nodded. "Exactly."

The warrior looked back at the others, continuing, "We send a runner down there to get their attention and lead them back into our waiting arms. I can even handle communication so the scout can inform us immediately of what they encounter, and we can be better prepared for their arrival."

Trayvious nodded again, then looked to the rest of them. "Any other suggestions?" When nobody spoke up, he continued, "Very well. Who here is both capable and willing to play the scout?"

A cinderen girl with ash gray hair who had been part of Dazien's earlier entourage spoke up. "I have stealth capabilities for scouting, but I don't think I could outrun a flying monster which sounds like we would need in order to be bait."

Phoenix thought about the task as though it were another of Paul's training challenges and, with a silent internal groan, slowly raised her hand.

"Miss Fraser? Was there something else you wanted to add?" Trayvious asked with a raised brow.

"I, um . . . I might be able to outrun it. I have some movement-enhancing ability, and I might even be able to get the monster to go through my portal. Or at least use it to get back here safely."

"Very well. Do you need assistance in the descent?" he asked, gesturing towards the sheer edge of the cliff.

She nodded, and another candidate stepped forward. "I can assist with that. One of my Wind abilities can allow someone to fall slowly. If she's planning to portal back up anyways, it should work for the plan."

"Good. All of you should come to me to get a Sense Stone, then you all have ten minutes to organize your 'kill box' and discuss what to do once the monsters arrive," he said to the group. Then he addressed Dazien again. "Smithson, why don't you go ahead and use that communication ability you mentioned? How many can you include in it?"

"Thirty, sir," he replied promptly.

"Alright, that covers everyone. Get us connected, then move forward with making your plans."

Phoenix was startled when shimmery golden lettering appeared floating in the air in front of her.

> *You have received an invitation to become a* [**Subject**] *of Dazien Smithson.*
> *Do you accept?*

She glanced up warily at the gemite with a raised eyebrow and asked, "Subject?"

He grinned and said unashamedly, "My powerset might be a *little* domineering at times, but when one is destined for greatness, such as myself, you can only gracefully accept the burdens of leadership."

Phoenix rolled her eyes at the exaggerated pomp and glanced back at the words before asking, "This isn't some kind of magic contract that permanently binds me to you, right?"

The new leader laughed aloud. It was a lovely sound, and Phoenix wanted to hear it more, but he replied, "No, no, it's just my communication ability," then flashed her another impish smile. "If you want to be bound by me, we'll need to have dinner first," he added with a playful wink.

Her face almost turned as red as her hair at the flirtation, and Dazien laughed again as he returned to his group of friends to discuss their upcoming strategy.

Phoenix quickly accepted the communication invite and walked up to Trayvious to receive her Sense Stone. She asked about how it functioned, which got some odd looks from the others near her before she joined the rest of the group to listen to their plan.

The Sense Stone looked like a diamond prism that had an odd matte texture while still shifting colors in the sunlight, with large runes carved on the top half and much smaller runes crammed together on the bottom half.

When she tossed it into the air as instructed, it circled around her as though taking her measurements and then floated directly above her head like a little *Sims* crystal marker, and she briefly wondered yet again if she was just another player in the game of this world. Were the gods basically game admins? Overpowered moderators with access to all the cheat commands?

She was brought back to the present after they all decided on a formation and location to set up their ambush site. Phoenix and the other candidate with a Wind Aspect walked to the edge of the gorge, where the runeforged cast a Spell on her and said, "Alright, you can just jump down now. Once you land, the Boon will end, though, so make sure you're at the bottom and don't land on the edge or something. I guess if that happens, you can always portal back up, and we can try again, especially if you don't find them right away."

Phoenix nodded in understanding and steeled her nerves, swallowing down her anxiety as she leaped off the cliff. She was immediately relieved when she didn't plummet to the ground, gently floating down as the wind blew around her. It seemed like she could aim where she wanted to land rather naturally, and she wondered if this power would eventually level up and allow full-fledged flight.

The sides of the ravine were sheer rock covered in ice and snow, and the bottom was much the same. Little plant life seemed to grow naturally in these frozen wastelands, and Phoenix found herself wondering, not for the first time, why anyone would build cities out here.

As she landed at the bottom, she quickly conjured her dagger, as well as the second one Paul gave her that she had been using from her collection and surveyed her surroundings. Her white fur cloak and blurring shadows from her Dark Aura helped her blend into the surrounding snow despite the Sense Stone floating above and the [Starlight Companion] hovering over her shoulder.

When no immediate threat appeared, she started walking down the gorge, heading south while looking for caves in the cliffside that could serve as potential nests. After a solid ten minutes of walking, she tried something that she only just started practicing with her Mentor yesterday. She expanded her Aura in a specific direction to get it to go farther away than normal, trying to sense the monsters.

Paul had told her that the range she was able to produce was impressive for her Caste, even if she still didn't feel fully in control of it. Projecting it outward, though, was much easier than trying to reign it in, and she soon felt what she was looking for.

Unfortunately for her, it seemed like the monsters also noticed the brush of her Aura as a shriek echoed through the icy gorge.

Then she saw the wings.

Giant white leather stretched out a few yards from its sinewy body, lifting it up into the sky. Closely followed by another. And another.

Her book had to actually move in front of her face since she couldn't take her eyes off the creatures.

<table>
<tr><td>

New Quest: Mission: Frosty Fliers
You have been tasked with defeating the monsters for the mission.
Objective: Defeat the three Frost Wyrmlings.
Reward: Rare Crystal Caste wand.

</td></tr>
</table>

Oooh! A wand! Yes!

The back of her mind distracted her slightly with the thought, but she shook her head and refocused on the threats making their way towards her.

They looked a bit like pale white snakes with frills around their head, which, of course, was basically just a gaping mouth full of razor-sharp teeth that wanted nothing more than to eat her at that moment. The biggest difference from a snake, however, was the two hind legs and large wings for arms.

"Phoenix?! What was that sound? Did you find them? What is it?" Dazien's voice sounded in her mind.

She thought back frantically as she turned on her heels to run, *"Frost Wyrmlings! Three of them. Pretty sure I got their attention!"*

Another shriek rang out behind her, and she glanced back, immediately regretting her decision to volunteer as bait. They were *fast*. Much faster than she had anticipated.

The Astromancer conjured the **[Sun Shell]** from her **[Radiant Sunlight]** Aura just in time for her little **[Starlight Companion]** to nudge a giant shard of ice to land dangerously close to her but not hit the shield or get in her path as she put on another burst of speed in a panic. The mana drained much quicker to fling her across the ground towards the large boulder jutting out from the gorge floor ahead of her that she had targeted.

"Looks like they shoot Ice bolts!" Phoenix shouted through the voice chat as she kept running, trying to make sure the monsters were close enough that she wouldn't lose them before getting her portal open. She was glad that Paul had suggested adjusting the size of her portal ring while she had been trying to level it up since there was no way the beasts would fit through the normal size she made.

"They can also boost their speed for a short time, so make sure they don't get too close," another voice that she recognized as Uriel said over the chat. She assumed that information was gained from a book similar to the manual she had bought, and the Wayfarer was glad that she wasn't the only one who had thought of bringing one.

Phoenix glanced back again to try and discern how big she would need to make the portal and to gauge their proximity, but she was disturbed by how quickly they closed the distance. As they got to within a few yards behind her, she yelled over the chat network, *"Incoming!"* as she opened the portal large enough for a small plane and jumped through.

She felt her **[Sun Shell]** shatter as one of the Wyrmlings closed its maw around her on the other side. The effects of the shell caused it to throw its head back from the shock of being temporarily blinded instead of finishing chomping down on her.

The Wayfarer stumbled a few feet, slightly disoriented by the shield breaking. *"Phoenix, you need to get out of the strike zone!"* Dazien's voice yelled out, and she triggered her **[Ruler of Relativity]** again to push herself away from the giant monster that was attempting to take another bite out of her. She flew forward at a dangerous speed, having shoved a ton of mana into it in another surge of panic, and could feel the barrage of attacks landing behind her, pummeling the wyrmling into the rocky ground.

The force of the attacks and the suddenness of her reaction caused her to stumble and roll across the snow-covered rocks, not quite making it to the defensive line the other candidates had set up around her portal. Another shriek filled the air—the second wyrmling came flying through the portal at frightening speed and moved to devour her as she lay alone and unguarded on the ground.

But she wasn't alone, nor was she unguarded, as she glanced up to see Dazien standing between her and the monster. He was holding a shield and wearing armor that she didn't remember him having before, along with wielding the gleaming diamond sword she recalled from their first encounter.

Her Aura was still projecting outward, and she noticed the Defender's form blur slightly as a sparkling shell of light enveloped the newcomer, as well as a new pink **[Starlight Companion]** floating behind his shoulder, ready to offer aid.

She assumed the warrior must have triggered some ability when he planted his feet firmly, and the monster slammed into his shield while he didn't budge an inch. Then, the sparkling sword moved faster and faster as Dazien attacked with it and sliced into the monster's face. It screamed in even more pain than the initial impact had caused it to.

Then the amethyst tank shouted at the beast as it reared back, "***You have forsaken my rule and thus forfeit your freedom!***"

What looked like a rune-etched steel cage sprang into existence around the Wyrmling. Without a moment's hesitation, Dazien turned and helped her up. "Can you run?" he asked her. With a nod, she took his outstretched hand as they ran back to the line of other would-be Adventurers.

More explosions rang out behind them as they reached the other applicants, and Phoenix turned to watch in amazement as the monsters were pummeled with a variety of magical and ranged attacks.

She noticed Uriel standing off to the side on his own, chanting something under his breath before fire rained from the sky onto what remained of the creatures, turning them into scorching piles of seared flesh. She briefly wondered if she would ever get a Spell that could deal damage on that kind of scale.

"Is he a Fire Mage?" Phoenix asked Dazien as she nodded towards his lone companion.

The young warrior glanced back and said reluctantly, "Something like that," before turning to look her over once more. "Are you hurt?"

She shook her head. "No, my Sun Aura protected me, and the snow softened a bit of my fall. What about you? That thing slammed straight into you." She looked him up and down, taking in the full regalia of armor, sword, and shield and asked bluntly, "Are you some kind of knight?"

The Defender scoffed and said cheekily, "My lady, I am no mere knight. I am a Warrior King." Dazien gave that same playful wink again and then performed a courtly bow before turning to see to his friend.

Phoenix noticed Uriel putting back on the gold choker she had first noticed on him and briefly wondered why he had taken it off, but her thoughts were interrupted as her book floated in front of her.

Quest: Frosty Fliers
Objective Complete: Defeated the three Frost Wyrmlings.
Objective Reward:
[Wand of the Snow Queen] has been added to your collection.

Completion Reward:
10 [Crystal Mana Bits] have been added to your collection.

She grinned and eagerly asked the book for more information about the new treasure. This time, it even showed her a little picture of the item: an elegant blue crystalline shaft with swirls of white running through it and a large sapphire gem affixed to one end.

Item: Wand of the Snow Queen
A wand imbued with an affinity for ice.
Caste: Crystal.
Availability: Rare.
Type: Tool, wand.
Effects:
* Can be used as a medium for cantrips.
* Can be used as a medium for Ice Spells, which will result in increased effects.
* Can cool Mundane objects with which it comes in direct contact.

Well, she didn't have any Ice powers, but it was nice to finally have a wand for all the Mundane magic she had learned from the tome Scholar had gifted her. She was mainly hoping to help tidy up her living space, which she abhorred having to clean. It might have seemed like a silly Spell to desire, but the time she saved on cleaning left her with time to do more important things . . . like finding a good book to read.

"What's that?" Dazien's voice asked from next to her, and she jumped in surprise again, reflexively closing the book and causing it to disappear in a shower of sparkling silver light.

"Nothing!" she reflexively answered, then added hastily, trying to wave off the question, "Just one of my abilities."

She was saved from needing to answer his next question when Trayvious called out to them, "Alright, everyone, let's get moving. Good job on the teamwork. We still have some more missions to cover, and I need to get more individual assessments."

As the monsters suddenly began disintegrating into white ash behind him, he glanced back at the group, who looked just as startled as he was, and asked, "I'm guessing one of you has a looting ability of some sort?"

Phoenix slowly raised her hand, looking at the ground in embarrassment.

CHAPTER THIRTY

One Against Many

Paul sat in his father's study, which now belonged to him. He was going through a stack of tedious paperwork, trying to sort out all the responsibilities and messes that his new inheritance had dropped on top of him. He was not particularly happy with his father naming him as heir, and that Patricia had actually agreed with the choice despite his politically savvy sister being far more suitable for the role.

The Emerald Caster knew *why* his father had chosen him. It wasn't because he was the firstborn or the oldest son or any of that nonsense that some noble Houses adhered to. No, it was simply because of his strength. He was one of the few in the family who took the adventuring path, the pressure for excellence being extreme since any who did usually became well renowned and expected to represent their House. He was also on the cusp of Ruby Caste, which would officially make him the strongest Wayland in over six centuries.

His House was not a large one like it had once been, but it was *very* respected. He had almost destroyed that respect with his connection to the Purifier and Fall from grace, but the fact that he had broken his ties with the Fallen god *before* the entire clergy had been denounced went a long way in protecting his family's reputation. Still, the looks and rumors that surrounded him personally were an annoyance.

A knock on the door interrupted his thoughts, and he automatically replied, "Enter."

The head steward, Roger, entered and bowed respectfully. "My lord, I have gotten the information you sought about Wayfarers and came across some particularly interesting news from out of Blomstra."

"Oh?" Paul prompted, leaning back in his chair to focus on the man who, like him, was one of the minority of humans in the city.

"Yes, my lord," he handed over a folder of papers for Paul to look through as he summarized, "Apparently, there was a Wayfarer landing site discovered in the Blue Ridge Mountains about a month ago."

"Two months," the former Paladin offhandedly replied as he skimmed through the information, now certain that this was where Phoenix had arrived. The location and timing were just too aligned not to be.

"I'm sorry, sir?" the steward asked with slight confusion.

"I'm sure the Order of Magic dragged their feet on reporting in. I'm confident that my little apprentice was the one who caused it," he explained while continuing to read through the papers.

"*We should send an assassin to clean up that mess,*" the monotonous voice suggested in his mind. "*We don't want them trying to take the Little Miss again.*"

He paused, reading over a particular section, and asked Roger, "What unfortunate accident held them up?"

"Ah, yes, it appears that one of the Crystal Magi, the Noble Miles Milligan, had an unfortunate encounter with a Porcutor. He didn't survive."

"Unfortunate," Paul repeated dryly, not looking up from the folder nor sounding at all sorry for the loss of the man whose name he recalled from Phoenix's tale.

He mentally pointed out to his inner companion, "*See, no assassin needed. Problem solved,*" and he could have sworn he felt her grumble in response.

Roger paused as he continued reading the papers, then inquired hesitantly, "Should I inform the OOM of the current state of their lone Wayfarer that is missing from the landing site?"

Paul looked up at the steward, his gold eyes staring daggers as he said in a low warning, "You will not speak of my Protégé's origins to anyone. She is under my protection now and has chosen to walk a path separate from the Magi. Any information regarding her should be held in the *strictest* of confidence. Do I make myself clear, Roger?"

The steward bowed in deference. "Of course, my lord."

"You are dismissed," Paul said with a wave and turned back to the papers.

After the door shut behind the man, he let out a heavy sigh. He wasn't certain why he had reacted that way. Over the month and a half that he had spent with the young woman, he realized that he had become attached and protective of her.

Perhaps it was because he felt compelled to heed Hero's suggestion. Maybe it was just his innate sense of duty returning to him that had pushed him to become an Adventurer and then a Paladin in the first place. Perhaps, since he found her, he felt responsible for her. Or maybe it was just that he enjoyed having a meaningful role in someone else's life as a Mentor and companion.

It could have been all of these things or none of them, but what he did know was that, after the many weeks of traveling and training together, he felt a connection to her and wanted to see her grow and succeed at the impossible task that had been laid out before her.

Paul ran a hand through his hair in exasperation. He was too old to feel confused by his own emotions like this. He could admit to himself that he had felt completely lost at first after betraying the Purifier when he refused to carry out the god's demands. The strength and assurance he had gotten from walking the pure path of righteousness had been harshly ripped from him, and he felt like a drowning man grasping at any rope of redemption that was tossed towards him.

To that end, he had been fighting off the Purifier's Renseres ever since discovering their twisted designs and getting thrown out of the clergy. He was even forced to leave his House after he and his father argued about his disgrace and defiance against the Delegation of Radiance. When it was his words against a god's, standing before the delegation consisting of representatives for every clergy that worshiped one of the "good" ones, it wasn't a surprise that he was branded Fallen.

When the Purifier's plans became public, however, and the forbidden rituals were completed all across the world—leading to the current fiasco with the impending blood moon and the arrival of the Soul Reapers in their reality—Paul had been vindicated. His words from years before proved that he had been the truthful herald of a deceitful god.

Then the DOR suddenly changed their tune, and it was the Purifier branded as Fallen, but his disgrace remained in their devout eyes. Until he found another patron, he wouldn't regain his Title as a Paladin.

Paul hadn't cared nor had the time to bother with any of that. He had barely come up for air in the last couple of years after the Soul Reapers arrived as he hunted them down. However, the upcoming blood moon, his father's death, and Phoenix's sudden appearance had halted all that.

He had planned to turn in his mission, hand over control of the family House to his sister, and then leave again to wherever the war took him. Petition the crown to allow him to take missions where he would be of more use. Not stay in this backwater city that wouldn't see much of the invasion.

Even if the Soul Reapers' forces did show up here in one of their spaceships that the AOA had gotten reports of, they would most likely be Crystal or Sapphire Caste due to the low magical rating of the area being unable to support the magical vessels.

At the peak of Emerald, Paul felt wasted here.

However, Phoenix was here now, and he had resources he could call upon from his House that he wouldn't have elsewhere. So, his plans adapted, and he decided to stay; to ride out the blood moon and try to make sure his new Protégé lived through it.

"Wayland had grown dedicated again," the familiar voice observed in his mind. *"Will Wayland be as zealous in this task as he was with hunting the undead?"*

"Aren't I in all of my tasks?" he replied with a bemused smirk. *"Zeal is one of my Aspects, after all. It would be a disservice to Phoenix if I didn't give her my best."*

"This One just hopes that Wayland doesn't see the Little Miss more as a mission than a companion. Wayland needs friends again."

Paul frowned at that, recalling what happened to the last group of people he thought of as friends. *"Perhaps it's better if I don't grow too attached."*

"This One believes Wayland is stronger when he fights for friends rather than for just a mission. Wayland needs to be strong to protect the Little Miss."

He gave a heavy sigh and reluctantly nodded. *"I know. Even as the strongest on the tundra, I don't feel like it's going to be enough for her and all the attention she'll garner."*

§

"Is that an airship?" Phoenix asked the small group she had gotten pulled into, staring up at the sky to try and make out the distant figure that had caught her attention. It looked like an old wooden pirate ship sailing through the air far, *far* away in the distance.

"You've never seen a flying vessel before?" one of the group members asked with a laugh. "Have you been living in a cave your whole life?"

Phoenix flushed in embarrassment and looked at the ground. She hadn't been thrilled about Dazien insisting she walk with him and Uriel, along with the rest of his entourage, who turned out to be mostly fawning admirers. Apparently, Dazien had a way with others that drew them towards him like moths to a flame, and his apparent relationship with the god, Warrior, was well-known. Perhaps he really was some kind of nobility?

She again felt the urge to ask him about his divine connection but held her tongue just in case it caused the others to laugh at her ignorance again. Nobody was addressing him as lord, sire, or highness, though, so she doubted his claims of kingliness. Still, even without being a noble, he had the grace and confidence she would have expected from one.

"Come now, Franz," Dazien said to the boy who had scoffed at her. "You know that those ships can't come to cities like ours. Without the magic to support it, it's easy to never see one if you never travel to a place that can."

Franz rolled his eyes. "Still, we can see them way out here on clear days like today. She'd have to be blind, had never left the city, or be one of the unluckiest people to walk the tundra."

"Probably that last one," Phoenix muttered.

Dazien laughed as he replied, "Unlucky? You helped us best three Frost Wyrmlings."

"I did almost get eaten," she pointed out.

"Well, then you were *lucky* to have me there to shield you," he grinned. Then he called out to the assessor leading the group, "Whose turn is it next? There's only a few of us left to solo something."

Trayvious gestured to a large furry boulder ahead of them and yelled back, "Karislian, you're up!"

Uriel stepped past them, making his way to the front of the group to challenge the creature in their path. At the sight of the monster, Phoenix flinched and subconsciously moved behind Dazien, who gave her a questioning look over his shoulder and silently asked her over the mental chat, *"What are you doing back there?"*

Phoenix felt the fear and panic rising in her at the sight of the Tundra Yeti. *"I, uh."* She swallowed as though it might help calm her anxiety. *"I've fought one of those before . . . It, um . . . it did not go well."*

"Did you win?"

She shook her head in the negative, staring at the ground in silent terror.

He glanced back to his friend, who was standing a few yards in front of the group now and was removing the collar from around his neck. Then Dazien stepped to the side and put a hand around her shoulders, saying in a reassuring whisper, *"It was probably just a bad matchup for your powers then."* He gently lifted her chin up with his other hand. *"Watch how Uriel handles it."*

"May the seed I sow bloom in beautiful chaos," the darker man said into his hands before pulling one back and tossing something at the sitting creature that apparently hadn't noticed them yet.

She couldn't tell what the tiny thing was, but as soon as it landed on the monster, it burst apart in a series of cacophonous explosions that alighted upon it. The Yeti roared in pain and anger, standing to search for its attacker.

Uriel was already casting his next Spell, though, as he incanted in a tone that caused a shiver to run down her spine, **"A touch of frost and your death follows."**

The monster started to gain patches of ice across its body and suddenly seemed to notice the cinderen. As it slowly stumbled towards their direction, Phoenix was about to call out for him not to let it get too close and break him the way it had her.

Dazien's arm around her shoulders pulled her back as he said, "Just watch."

When the Yeti was still a half dozen yards away from the Mage, Uriel finished chanting another Spell. **"Be the bearer of the all-consuming plague."** The monster seemed to halt its stumbling approach as though it was struck by an invisible force.

There didn't seem to be an immediate effect aside from the creature stopping, but the monster roared again with a renewed sense of fury as she saw dark patches start to appear on its fur. The apparent disease slowly began growing and rotting away at its flesh as the confused creature tried to pull the patches that were hurting it away rather than attack the source of the malignant Bane.

Uriel continued his onslaught of Spells. ***"Succumb to the might of the tyrannical winds."***

They could all feel the blast of air that shot down from the sky and forced the monster to be slammed into the dirt.

"Your days have come to an end," the Mage said with cold finality, and a dark void surrounded the Yeti, hiding it from view.

After about ten seconds that felt like an eternity of agonizing howls, the sounds abruptly ended along with the void, and the Tundra Yeti was gone, utterly annihilated.

Phoenix stared, slack-jawed at the display of overwhelming power that just destroyed a monster that almost killed her a few weeks ago. She was amazed that there was someone so talented among her fellow Crystal Casters. Then she felt very small and inadequate as the Mage turned back to the group, refastening his gold choker.

Uriel silently nodded to Trayvious before returning to his usual place behind Dazien.

"Good work, Senesh. That monster won't be hurting anyone now," the amethyst warrior said to his companion as he patted the broad shoulder in congratulations.

Phoenix looked from the Mage to the spot the Yeti had been and then back to Uriel before saying in utter confusion at the difference in their power, *"How?"*

Dazien grinned. "Like I said, it's all about the matchup. He's good at dealing a *lot* of damage over time to monsters, and you're good at running awa—Er . . . at being mobile," he corrected before adding, "and other things that you have yet to reveal to us, I'm sure."

Phoenix rolled her eyes at him and turned to follow the rest of the group that trailed after their assessor.

After another half hour of walking, they paused again.

"Fraser, your turn."

Phoenix's heart jumped into her throat as Trayvious called her name. She walked forward to join the Sapphire Caster at the crest of a small hill and followed his gaze down to a pack of what appeared to be five monstrous variants of white wolves tearing into their latest kill, which she couldn't recognize as anything other than a bloody mess.

The Wayfarer glanced back at the instructor and asked with alarm, "All of them?"

He nodded and said, "If you don't believe you're up to the challenge, then you can, of course, decline, and I will ask someone else."

The rest of the group had joined them to look into the small valley to see the pack and began murmuring to themselves.

Dazien spoke up as he took in the threat. "Sir, you can't seriously expect a single Crystal to take on five Snolves alone."

"That is *her* choice to make, Smithson, not yours. Now wait quietly," he ordered before turning back to Phoenix. "Well, Miss Fraser?"

Her book suddenly appeared in front of her, causing her, Trayvious, and Dazien to look down at the message.

New Quest: One Against Many
You have been tasked with defeating the monsters in the valley.
Objective: Defeat the five Snolves.
Reward: Rare Crystal Caste bracelet.

She waved away the book, ignoring the looks the two men gave her as she glanced down at the pack once more in consideration. Paul had been diligent in putting her through her paces over the last month, having her take on a variety of monsters so she could determine which tactics worked best in different situations. He had made her fight groups before, but they were either much smaller creatures or fewer than this. It would be a challenge, but one that she would face.

"I'll try it, sir," she said with a sound of resolve that she felt didn't quite fit with the flips her stomach was doing.

He nodded and said, "If it gets too dicey, just portal back up here, alright?"

Phoenix returned his nod and, without another word, conjured her [**Night Blade**] in one hand and the golden dagger Paul had given her in the other. She made her way down the hilltop towards the unaware monsters as she kept her [**Sun Shell**] and [**Starlight Companion**] dismissed and tried to go for a stealthier approach.

Her cloak, combined with her [**Embrace of Shadows**] Aura, blurred her from the beasts' notice and let her get fairly close before she lunged forward, triggering her [**Ruler of Relativity**] to pull herself towards the closest Snolf.

The Snolves were about the same size as her, and they moved towards each other at roughly the same speed. As they collided, she plunged both of the daggers into the beast. It yelped at the sudden attack, and she pushed off the creature as she flipped backward to land on the packed snow. That was a move she had learned from her martial tomes and spent the last few days ingraining into her muscle memory. Then she aimed for the next monster already charging towards her.

She triggered [**Ruler of Relativity**] again, pushing her [**Night Blade**] to fly from her hand and bury itself into the creature's throat. Before that Snolf fell to the ground, Phoenix reactivated her Sun and Star Auras, causing a bubble of light to momentarily surround her and the little fairy blob to reappear right as two more of the monsters lunged at her.

The [**Sun Shell**] shattered as the beasts collided with it, and both were thrown off course, howling at the blinding pain. She dashed at the opportunity, reconjuring her [**Night Blade**] and triggering her gravity ability once more to rend one of the blinded beasts with her daggers and gain back some of her mana from the [**Mana Siphon**] Bane her dagger delivered.

Phoenix grunted in pain as the last Snolf to engage managed to tackle her from behind and make her fall onto the ground. She felt claws tear into her back, and she used her ability once more to get the monster away from her, causing the Snolf to fly straight up into the air while she was crushed against the packed snow.

She rolled to the side and stood once more, clutching her daggers and gritting her teeth against the pain before starting to move again.

Phoenix slid under the uncut but blinded Snolf and pushed her Dark stiletto upward. Her gravity-empowered magic sent it flying straight up through the Snolf's neck, where it buried itself in the monster's brain, killing it instantly.

Then she continued to use her ability to pull herself across the snow towards the trees, sliding near the other blinded Snolf that was injured but still alive, and tore her daggers across its underside as she passed.

The monster she had caught in the throat earlier had died from its wound, but the first one she had stabbed wasn't dead, though it was limping pretty badly. The last Snolf made its death apparent when it finally crashed back into the rocky earth with a very wet crunch.

With only one enemy left, and feeling dangerously low on mana, she physically pushed herself up to stand once more and ran towards the limping Snolf, not trusting her aim or mana supply at that distance. When the Snolf angrily lunged at her, she shoved her dagger straight into its open maw.

CHAPTER THIRTY-ONE

A Lot of Interesting Quirks

Dazien stood with his arms crossed as Phoenix slid down the hillside to engage with the pack of Crystal Caste Snolves and found himself intrigued. He had never seen such an assortment of odd powers before, and he couldn't figure out what that mysterious magic book was all about.

"You're interested in her," Uriel's smooth voice said from over his shoulder, and he grinned up at his companion.

"She has a lot of interesting quirks," he admitted before looking back to watch her fight. "When I saw her here, she struck me as the silent wallflower type. Quiet, unassuming, obedient. I thought she might be some kind of mender or group support.

"She doesn't want to put herself forward, but then she pulls off crazy things like baiting Wyrmlings and fighting a pack of Snolves," he exclaimed, gesturing towards the battle taking place below them for emphasis. "That's not something a Healer *or* Supporter normally does!

"Also, when I first came across her, it was when she was meeting with Warrior. How does someone as soft as her catch his attention? Plus, there's something off about her Aura that I can't quite place." He cocked his head to the side and put a hand to his chin, deep in thought.

Uriel shrugged. "You know I can't sense Auras right now."

"I know," he replied with exasperation, "it's hard for me to explain, too, because my Aura senses are rather crap. You know I haven't been able to find a decent trainer for that. Despite Warrior's chiding, I still haven't been able to hone it to his liking."

"She has four Auras," Trayvious said from beside them.

Both of the young men looked at him in surprise.

"It's probably what felt off to you. Her Aura has four layers that reinforce it, making it much stronger than other Crystal Casters that you would be more familiar with," the assessor explained as though giving a lecture.

Dazien nodded in understanding. "So, she's an Aurabreaker. Plus, she mentioned not having all her abilities unlocked."

He glanced back as the young woman's glittery shield broke when two Snolves impacted with it. "She has defensive, stealth, portal, and loot abilities. Plus, whatever that ability is that lets her move things around like that."

"Telekinesis?" Uriel suggested watching her as well.

"Something like that. It doesn't behave like a normal Movement skill since it's affecting the monsters, too."

They both paused as a Snolf flew a few dozen yards straight up into the air, and Dazien chuckled. "They always say it's the quiet ones you need to watch out for." Then he gave his companion a sidelong look and added, "You know . . . you two might have more in common than I originally thought."

Uriel rolled his eyes and asked, "Are you trying to collect the silently chaotic ones?"

Dazien gave him an impish grin. "They are the most fun after all."

As the fighting came to an end, he asked the Mage, "So what do you think? Should we have her join our team?"

"My king would ask his servant for permission?" Uriel asked with a rare smirk.

"A wise king always seeks the counsel of his most trusted advisor, Uriel. I would not have her join if you were not willing to work with her. If she doesn't interest you as well, then we'll just keep searching," he said resolutely.

He observed Uriel watching the girl, who was now painted in so much blood that her hair no longer stood out as it once had. As she slowly trudged back up the hill, looking exhausted, white ash began to fall off of her as she looted the monsters that the blood belonged to.

The cinderen glanced back at him and gestured towards the rest of Dazien's entourage standing a few feet away before speaking silently using his communication ability. "*She's better than the others trying to claim you and doesn't seem to care about my Silencer in the slightest. I won't decline her inclusion.*"

Dazien smiled at the small victory. "Great, we can ask her after the trial results."

"You may want to check with her Mentor first." Trayvious spoke up, surprising the pair once more.

He raised an eyebrow. "Her Mentor? Like an official *Mentor* Mentor? The one she mentioned taking her around to portal locations?"

The assessor nodded. "He has claimed her officially as Protégé and has been training her personally. I doubt he would let her join just any party."

Dazien scoffed. "We are not just *any* party. We have the benefit of a god overseeing my training."

Trayvious quirked a brow and said, "I don't think this man cares much for gods anymore. The Blade of Pure Wrath is not known for his leniency, nor his piety, after what happened with the Purifier."

Both men became a shade paler at his words, and Dazien clarified, "The heir of House Wayland has returned?"

"That's *Lord* Wayland now, and yes. He returned about a week ago." Trayvious nodded towards Phoenix. "With *her*. I would not normally share that knowledge with you, but I thought it prudent to warn you before gaining *that* man's wrath."

The two companions glanced over at the redhead once more as she was casting a healing Spell on herself.

"Of course, she has a heal too," Dazien muttered in resignation before giving a resolute nod. "Still, I will ask her first. Then maybe she can help convince the lord for us. If she is being trained by *him*, then surely she will be a worthy party member."

"And you can discover more of her interesting quirks," Uriel said, seeing straight through Dazien's motivations.

§

As the group of would-be Adventurers was milling about the flat expanse of tundra, the assessor had chosen for them to each display their individual "camping" skills. Phoenix wondered if this was really a requirement to being an Adventurer.

Nevertheless, she got to work, starting with the ritual her Mentor had taught her and had her practice every night they were roaming before they would meditate. She began drawing a magic circle with a finger of starlight around her little area, which would act as a temporary barrier that would alarm her if any monsters got within a few yards of it.

Trayvious wandered over towards her as he slowly made the rounds, observing everyone and asking a few sporadic questions. When he reached her, he studied the ritual circle and asked, "Did Lord Wayland teach you?"

She nodded and elaborated for him, "This and a few other survival rituals. When he found—Um, I mean before we met, I had gotten lost alone in a forest and almost died multiple times."

The assessor gave her a curious look and noted, "Not many people would admit that weakness, especially during an examination like this. Which forest, if I might ask?"

She tilted her head to the side, trying to recall if Paul had mentioned it, then conjured her book instead to look at the map of Tulim. It didn't reach the area she had been in, but she pointed off in the general direction beyond the map's border as she turned it for the runeforged to examine, "It was a mountain range somewhere over here? I don't think Paul ever told me the name."

His eyes widened as he clarified, "Blue Ridge?" She shrugged, and he questioned further, "How long were you lost there for?"

Phoenix grimaced at the memory and reluctantly admitted, "Eight days. I didn't have any powers at first and ran into Paul just after arriving in some grassy hills instead."

He stared at her for a moment before nodding and saying simply, "I see . . . Well, I'm glad you survived the ordeal."

She didn't bother correcting him about the false assumption before he moved along to the next applicant, who was busy setting up a tent, and the Wayfarer turned back to finish her own tasks.

After her alarm was accounted for, she started going about the next step of setting up a campfire, this time pulling out her new wand and trying one of the cantrips she had absorbed. This took much less time than the ritual to get going as she pulled a few branches out of her collection from her time in the Blue Ridge Mountains and whispered, "***Let the Provider's fire light the hearth.***" She smiled as the bundle crackled with slowly growing flames. That was so much easier than her previous attempts.

With the fire now providing warmth, she took her cloak off, set it on the ground in her designated spot, and touched a Mana Bit to the clasp. The Bit seemed to melt into the metal and ripple across the white fur before the cloak shifted its form, seemingly splitting open along the hem and gaining a second layer. Functionally, it had transformed into a furry, single-person tent, just big enough for her to wiggle into and sleep comfortably in.

It had worked well enough while traveling around the tundra with Paul, but she definitely preferred her new bed in her dorm room. She was just glad that the enchantment lasted a whole eight hours, even after she had learned that Crystal Casters only needed about five hours of sleep to feel fully rested.

With her tasks complete, she popped a Crystal Mana Bit into her mouth for an easy dinner, took a seat at the entrance of her little tent, and summoned her book to display the information for her newest reward.

Item: Bracelet of Elemental Conversion
A band designed to convert monsters into components.
Caste: Crystal.
Availability: Rare.
Type: Apparel, bracelet.
Requirements: Crystal Caste or higher.
Effect: Consume a Crystal Caste [Monster Seed] to generate Crystal Caste Elemental Shards of an appropriate type in accordance with the provided Seed.

The accompanying image just looked like a simple silver band with ten small colored stones embedded around it. The listed effect made her even more curious, however, and slightly suspicious of both the item and her looting ability itself. She then pulled up the information for the item she had looted from one of the Snolves directly.

Item: Monster Seed
The remnant Seed of a deceased monster.
Caste: Crystal.
Availability: Uncommon.
Type: Consumable, ingredient.
Requirements: Crystal Caste.
Effects:
- Can be consumed to slightly increase the progression of your lowest Caste ability.
- Can be used as a component for various rituals or enchantments.

She conjured the Seed from her collection to get a better idea of its dimensions and found it to look very similar to a walnut that had been bleached white and was about triple the size. It also was heavier than it looked for a normal seed. She debated whether she should use it or convert it into Elemental Shards so she could examine some of those as well.

"Nice! You got a Monster Seed!" a cinderen said as he approached her casually, tilting his head towards the item resting in her palm. "Those are pretty uncommon. You gonna use it?"

Phoenix took in the man's appearance and admitted softly, "I'm not sure." She then inquired cautiously, "You're Malik, right?"

He smiled and nodded. "Rayk Malik," he confirmed, then added, "my mother likes to buy those in bulk when possible and turn a profit on them. She makes quite the Bits on them out here where they can be harder to come by for the higher Castes."

"Would it be better to sell it then?" she asked.

Rayk laughed and shook his head. "Gods, no. You should use it. I know some Adventurers like to act all self-righteous about it, but as my mother likes to point out, time is money. When it can take years, decades, or even centuries to get to the next Caste for some, every little advantage can be priceless."

"That's quite the sales pitch," Phoenix admitted, studying the Seed a bit further while contemplating. "What about Elemental Shards?"

"Shards? Well, they're—Actually, can I sit for this?" he asked a bit awkwardly. She nodded, and he sat on the ground beside her, nearer to the fire to keep warm. Once he settled, he continued, "Thanks. Now, Shards are pretty useful but generally more common. You have a looting ability, right?"

She was a bit disoriented from the sudden topic shift but nodded again. Malik's smile seemed to grow a little wider and slightly more predatory as he said, "My mother would *love* you. She's always going on about wanting to get someone with a looting power to work for her."

Phoenix shifted awkwardly and tried to redirect the conversation. "Shards are used in rituals and enchantments, too, right?"

"Oh, yeah," he replied with a shrug, "they're definitely used more often than Monster Seeds. This is another reason to just go ahead and use the Seeds rather than wait for some random ritual requirement to call for them. Plus, if *you're* more powerful, it's easier to get more Seeds."

That did make some sort of sense to her. She conjured her new bracelet directly onto her wrist, conveniently hiding her Oathbond underneath the cuff, and held it up for him to look at. "This converts Seeds into Shards. Would it be worth doing?"

The cinderen looked at it curiously and replied thoughtfully, "Perhaps . . . depending on how much you got out of it. Does it do all types of Shards? I only see the ten colors for the Elements on this."

"It only does Elemental ones. Are there Magical and Divine ones, too?" she asked, remembering Paul's lecture about types and subtypes.

Malik laughed. "While technically, yes, I don't think anyone I know has ever seen Divine Shards. They are ridiculously rare since, as I'm sure you know, Shards usually form from the condensation of the ambient magic of an area. You would need a large space brimming with Radiant or Void energy for an extended period of time to generate one."

"What about the third type of Divine magic?" she asked in confusion. She could have sworn Paul had said there were three.

Rayk's expression became confused suddenly, and the smile dropped from his face as he asked, "Are you just messing with me now?" He glanced over at Trayvious, then back to her, and said flatly, "The third would be impossible."

He stood abruptly and dusted the back of his pants off as she stammered out, "I-I'm sorry. I wasn't trying to mess with you or anything. I honestly didn't know. I, um, I didn't get out much until recently, and I'm still learning a lot."

His ember eyes softened slightly at whatever he must have seen in her own as he nodded and said, "Well, if becoming an Adventurer doesn't work out for you . . . or even if it does, you should come visit my mother's shop in Tulimeir. Just ask around for the Mother's Cupboard. It's right near Market Station. Tell them I sent you."

She stared blankly after him as he departed with a backward wave over his shoulder, and she had the errant thought, *Did I just get scouted for a job?*

CHAPTER THIRTY-TWO

Cultivating Our Experiences

Come in," Phoenix called out as a soft knock came from her bedroom door. She was drying and combing her hair as she sat on the edge of her bed, looking out the tinted glass wall that revealed the city below, the lights simulating a sea of stars in the dark night.

She had just finished her hot shower and gotten fresh clothes, having enjoyed the feel of warm water on her tired muscles that the purifying golden potion just couldn't accomplish. She had also been surprised to discover she had some muscle now, which made sense after all the training and gaining Crystal Caste Strength. She had been so exhausted before that she hadn't even noticed it when taking a bath. She was also glad to be back in her own space after the long week of monster hunting for the Adventurer trials.

Paul opened the door, dressed in a nice but casual white shirt and beige pants, and moved to sit next to her on the edge of the bed. He didn't have to say anything for Phoenix to guess why he was there, and she said, "I think I did well, all things considered. I might not be as powerful or focused as some of the others, but I was able to hold my own."

The noble nodded. "I had little doubt."

She rolled her eyes and nudged his arm. "Little is not none."

"Sometimes you hesitate when you should strike. It will take practice for you to overcome that," he observed, and she knew he was right. Bliss had punished her often enough for it while training.

"I guess I'm lucky to have you helping me then," she teased.

"About that . . ." he began, and she froze mid-brush and paled, worried that he might tell her that he changed his mind after all. "I got some information while you were away about the Magi who hurt you."

She shifted uncomfortably, unsure what that had to do with helping her, and waited for him to continue.

"He was killed by a Sapphire Caste monster. He won't be coming after you, and the OOM doesn't know about you." Paul paused, then hesitantly said, "I know I warned you away from them, but they don't *all* have ill intentions, and I should have checked with you first. Did you want to meet with them?"

Phoenix looked at the ground, then up at Paul, trying to gauge what he wanted. He was *very* good at hiding his emotions, though. She took a steadying breath and quietly asked the question she partially feared the answer to, "Why are you asking me this?"

Paul watched her for a moment, then said, "I'm merely giving you the choice of learning more about your arrival in this world. Maybe even find a way back to your own. If you wish to join them, I can introduce you there."

Silence fell for a long while. Then, in barely more than a whisper, Phoenix asked the same question he had asked her not that long ago, "Do you want me to leave?"

He met her eyes and firmly stated, "No."

"Then I won't. My book . . . My *choices* guided me here. I think I'm meant to be here. I can become stronger here. If I go back . . . it would be like choosing to become weak again. To give up my freedom for safety. I don't want to become limited again."

Paul nodded at her words. "If that is what you choose, then you will stay. I just wanted the choice to be one of your own making, not because I made it for you."

She replied sincerely, "Thank you for giving me that choice, but I want to see where this path leads me. Besides, I didn't go through all that training just to give up now."

The corners of his mouth twitched, and he added, "Well, there's plenty of time after the blood moon and your quest to do more research on Wayfarers."

"Speaking of time," she said, pulling out the Monster Seed she had held off on using until she could get advice from her Mentor, "should I use this to help speed up my progress?"

"No," he flatly replied, glaring at the Seed in her hand for a moment. Then, he softened his expression and ran a hand through his hair. This time, she didn't need to prompt him for more information as he explained further, "Sorry, there's nothing necessarily wrong with using Seeds to speed up progress. Many Casters will do that, given the chance and funding.

"The problem is that if you ever want to reach Obsidian Caste, the peak of mortal power, they will hinder your progress and make it impossible. That goes for the non-combatants, too. We increase our Caste normally by properly challenging ourselves. By pushing through our current limits and cultivating our experiences into empowerment."

Paul gave a huff of annoyance as he said, "I should have probably explained it earlier but . . . but I'm not very good at this mentoring thing."

"I think you're doing pretty good," Phoenix offered, nudging him again to try and lighten the mood.

He gave her a small, weary smile and said, "Probably because I haven't taught you that there are people better suited out there."

She smiled and gave him a look of feigned incredulity. "Was that a *joke*? I didn't know you were capable."

Paul chuckled softly, then shifted the topic a bit. "It's part of the reason we meditate too."

"What?" she asked, thrown off by the tangent.

"With Seeds, there is no meditation requirement. You use them, and the Caste increases. Without them, you need to not only properly challenge yourself but also reflect on that challenge. Meditation is what cultivates the experience. That's why I taught you the Steps of Light; it's the meditation technique I know best. Your Knowledge Tomes taught you some different ones that might be more efficient for you to use instead."

She nodded thoughtfully, then lifted the Seed once more. "So, should I turn this into Elemental Shards?"

He gave her a raised eyebrow and asked, "You got more treasure during your trial?"

Phoenix grinned, lifted her bracelet, and touched the Monster Seed to it, letting Paul read the information for the resulting Shards from her [**Guide Book**].

Item: Ice Shard
Condensed ambient Ice magic.
Caste: Crystal.
Availability: Common.
Type: Consumable, ingredient.
Effect: Can be used as a component for various rituals or enchantments.

There were fifty of them now in her inventory, and when she asked Paul if that was a lot, he confirmed that she definitely got her money's worth out of the conversion. Pulling one out of her collection, she found a roughly diamond-shaped pale blue crystal that glowed slightly from within and was about the size of her thumb.

She swapped it out for her other treasure and happily showed the [**Wand of the Snow Queen**] off to Paul next.

"Does this mean the sitting room and kitchen will actually be clean when I stop by next time?" he asked in a teasing reprimand.

"Hey! I never had to clean before. That's what the janitors and nurses did," she retorted. Then she lifted the wand up towards the bathroom before pausing and turning to ask, "Is it evil to use a Spell that invokes the Purifier? What with him being a Fallen god and all?"

The former Paladin shook his head and said with a tired sigh, "No."

"Just checking!" she quickly explained, then incanted, "***By the Purifier's command, bring order to chaos and cleansing to the tainted land.***"

As the cantrip triggered and the items that were strewn about the floor and sink counter moved to order themselves neatly and become pristinely clean, she glanced back at Paul again and added, "It's a bit dramatic for a housekeeping Spell, isn't it?"

Paul gave a wry smile. "No one ever claimed the gods to be humble."

Phoenix found herself bouncing in excitement as the AOA functionary handed her the shiny new license, seemingly carved from white marble, marking her as an official Adventurer. She thanked the cinderen clerk at the licensing desk and rushed outside, away from the crowded interior.

Once outside, she found a rare patch of sunlight to bask in. She sat down in a lotus position against the tinted glass building, and her book appeared in front of her.

Quest: For Adventure
Objective Complete: Passed the trials to join the Alliance of Adventurers.
Objective Reward:
[Flame of Life] has been added to your collection.

Completion Reward:
10 [Crystal Mana Bits] have been added to your collection.

New Title: Adventurer
Your Aura has been slightly modified by your accomplishment. The desire for adventure can be sensed within it. Your Aura has slightly increased effects when affecting a Mundane ally.

The new Adventurer grinned at the message, pleasantly surprised by the unexpected Title. She wondered how many more she might get and if she might ever be able to convince Paul to share the information about all of his other Titles with her.

She adjusted her newly repaired cloak. It had taken a beating over the fortnight of challenges, and she had been forced to take it to a magical tailor before it became destroyed. That last night had been exceptionally cold with the number of holes in the side of her tent, and she made a mental note to buy a backup later in case her cloak got shredded again.

Phoenix debated selling or trading some of her Ice Shards for more variety so she could try some of the other rituals and enchantment recipes she had floating around in her mind. She had been contemplating them for a while and wanted to play with some now that the mad rush of training for the trials could relax a bit. She wasn't sure where to go to trade the Shards, though. Perhaps that shop Rayk Malik had mentioned his mother ran?

She contemplated asking around and going on a little city adventure to find it. She had a couple of hours until she planned on meeting Paul for lunch back at her dorm and then their training session afterward, which would focus more on meditation this time after their earlier conversation.

Phoenix looked up as her sunlight disappeared to find Dazien Smithson grinning down at her before he crouched low to eye level and pointed at the book. "What kind of ability is this?"

She drew it close to her chest protectively, replying quietly, "It's nothing . . . it just gives me some information."

He cocked his head to the side curiously. "Sounds interesting. Which Aspect gave it?"

"Um, none," she admitted awkwardly, "it's a Talent."

"It still would have come from an Aspect, though, since you're human," he pointed out and added as though she was the one insulting him. "I know enough about your species to know about the adaptable talents they're usually born with."

She stood then, shaking her head and muttering, "I'm not human," then shut the book, and it vanished in a shower of starlight.

"Not human?" Dazien asked in confusion, and then his grin widened in realization. "Is *that* what I'm sensing in your Aura? Mister Trayvious thought it was just your Aurabreaker abilities, but I *knew* there was something else odd about it."

Her eyes widened at his words for a moment, and then she looked away. She could feel her face flushing and nose scrunching up as she tried her best not to become upset and managed to say bitterly, "I don't need you to tell me how odd I am."

His smile vanished, and he seemed to try to recover, sounding much more sincere as he said, "No, I didn't mean it like that. It was just something I didn't understand. It was odd to me because of my ignorance, not because of your being. Please, I meant no offense, my lady." He then surprised her by bowing deeply in apology.

Phoenix wasn't exactly sure what it was, but something about his contrite attitude helped her relax. He really did seem sincere and like he wanted to befriend her. He had also tried to help her during the trials, making her feel better about not being as strong as Uriel. Perhaps these two men were more like Paul, and she could trust them to help her.

Her stance softened as she looked from Dazien to the cinderen standing silently behind him. She asked Uriel with a slight tease, "Does he always play the noble?"

The Mage gave her the smallest hint of a smirk and said, "He does."

Dazien straightened to look at his friend in mock hurt. "You wound me, Uriel. I do not *play* at nobility; it's a natural trait."

Phoenix couldn't stop the snort of laughter at his response. This guy was just too much. As they turned back to focus on her, she shrank a bit and stepped to the side slightly. "Well, I have, um . . . things to do . . . so . . ."

"Wait, please," Dazien said, trying to halt her escape. "Uriel and I wanted to discuss some things with you."

She raised an eyebrow at him, then glanced at the Mage pointedly.

"Well, *I* wanted to discuss some things. He just likes to watch," Dazien amended, giving her that same impish grin.

The implication behind those words went completely over her head until Uriel smacked Dazien's shoulder and warned his friend, "You tease her too much, and she won't listen to you further."

"Sorry, sorry," the warrior said, holding his hands up in a defensive gesture as her face turned red. Then, he asked, "Look, do you have time to just talk?"

She looked between the two, unsure of why they had approached her and why their groupies hadn't followed the would-be king. Then she realized that she could actually use their help to speed the selling process up for her, since they were probably more knowledgeable about the city and how selling loot worked. "Actually, if you can help me sell some of my items, then I might have time to talk before lunch with my Mentor."

The sudden stillness that overtook them at her words caused her to become concerned, and she asked, "What? Does that not work for you?"

"No. I mean, that's fine. We just didn't know you had plans with your Mentor today. We wouldn't want to keep Lord Wayland waiting for you," Dazien said hurriedly.

She shrugged like it wasn't a big deal. "I have plans with him almost every day," she explained as she crossed her arms a bit defensively. "He's very diligent in training me." Then she looked at him curiously and asked, "Wait, how do you know who my Mentor is?"

"Ah." Dazien looked a bit awkward. "Mister Trayvious mentioned it as a warning."

"Warning?"

"We can talk about that later." He waved a hand in the air, trying to dismiss the topic. "What are you trying to sell? We don't mind helping you out either way."

Phoenix thought about pushing him more, but he hadn't refused to answer; he just postponed. So, she acquiesced and conjured an Ice Shard into her outstretched palm for him to observe.

"A dimensional storage power?" he asked as he curiously glanced at the Shard.

"Another Natural Talent," she answered, trying to head off the follow-up question.

Amethyst purple eyes looked back up to meet her mossy green ones. "You never did say what species those came from," he pointed out. "Despite my honesty in informing you of my own when you asked me the same."

She shook her curls. "Maybe when we're having that private discussion later," she said to hold him off.

He nodded, slightly frowning. "I know a lady who works as a merchant broker with directing supplies in the inner city," he said, gesturing to the northeast, "I can introduce you to her, and she can help direct you to some of the shops that would be most suitable or who have standing requests for certain things. You might get a better deal from someone specifically requesting more Ice Shards than going to a random shop to sell off everything."

Phoenix nodded. "Well then," she said, slowly giving him a small smirk, "lead the way, Your Majesty."

Dazien smiled brilliantly at her, his eyes sparkling with amusement as he gave an exaggerated bow. "Follow me, my lady."

CHAPTER THIRTY-THREE

I Am Not a Tyrant

An hour later, they had finished talking with Dazien's merchant contact as she offloaded not just the Shards but a large amount of monster materials that she hadn't found a use for yet, including the large stack of demon bunny meat.

The trip had been slightly prolonged, as they were required to fend off other Adventurers and merchants who had stopped to chat and congratulate Dazien on becoming an Adventurer himself, many asking for a sparring session later.

The number of people who not only knew Dazien but seemed to truly wish to befriend him boggled her mind. She quickly learned to follow Uriel's example to handle this: Stay silent and simply nod or shrug to any random question directed towards her.

She absently thought how odd of a group they must make. She and Uriel seemed complete opposites from the outside, with only their silence as a commonality. Both of them trailed after the suave and charming warrior who gracefully handled anyone who approached him with a smile and genuine care.

As they finally made their way to a small café near the Temple District, they were led to one of the private rooms the café was known for, and Phoenix got her first taste of Makera's equivalent of *coffee*. It was nice, warm, and sweeter than she vaguely remembered black coffee on Earth being when she managed to con—er, *convince* a nurse to let her try some. She preferred the slightly sweeter version and added a bit of cream to it from whatever this world's variant of a cow was; she'd have to remember to ask Paul later.

"So," Phoenix began, "did you just want to pry out my secrets?" she asked, breaking the silence that had fallen as they watched the snow fall outside the window. The weather suddenly turned when they were busy shopping, and the sun was now hidden by heavy clouds with white snowflakes that fell softly on the fortressed city.

The Wayfarer turned to meet their gazes as she sat across the small table from them. "Or did you want to get closer to my Mentor through me?" she asked pointedly, having been thinking about Dazien's words and behavior for a while now; that was the only motivation she had come up with. He obviously wanted *something* from her.

Dazien blinked at her for a moment, then looked at Uriel and asked with concern, "Do I come off as a manipulative villain?"

The Mage shrugged. "Mostly when you try to be secretive."

The warrior gave a dramatic sigh. "This is why I normally don't try to be. Honesty really is for the best, especially when I'm obviously a terrible liar."

He shook his head then addressed Phoenix again. "No, Miss Fraser." Then he cocked his head briefly at a thought. "Well, I *would* love to learn more of your secrets, as I've often been told I'm too curious for my own good, but that isn't why I wanted to talk to you. "*We*"—he pointed between Uriel and himself—"want *you* to join our adventuring party."

It was her turn to blink at them. The words didn't quite register at first, and her mouth spoke in utter bewilderment before her brain caught up. "Why?"

"You bring a lot to the table," the gemite began explaining, "plus, I'm sure we haven't seen everything you're capable of yet. You mentioned still needing to unlock more abilities, so your value as a party member will only increase."

His tone was confident, but she was still having trouble understanding as he added, "From a purely tactical perspective, you're a good addition to a standard group, like ours will be."

"What does 'standard group' mean?" she interrupted, unfamiliar with the term or really anything involving adventuring parties. She had been so focused on training to *become* an Adventurer that she hadn't really taken the time to learn more about the organization as a whole.

Dazien paused, giving her a curious look, and clarified, "A group made of at least one of each Role. There are other specialist parties out there that might focus on performing a specific type of mission extremely efficiently, such as scouting teams made up of Supporters.

"I'm officially listed as a Forward Defender, and as I mentioned before, Uriel's a Backline Mage. So, you would be our Supporter." He paused, taking a bite of the fluffy white cake on his plate before adding, "From a group cohesion perspective, though, which is arguably more important, I enjoy your company, and Uriel doesn't completely hate it either."

Phoenix glanced at the silent man for confirmation and raised an eyebrow as she asked with a hint of sarcasm, "Oh, not *completely* hated?"

Uriel gave that small smirk again. "You're acceptable."

She couldn't help smiling back at him with a shake of her head, starting to understand his dry sense of humor. "So, because I don't fall into the category of 'obnoxious groupie that drools over every word His Majesty here utters,' I am worthy of a spot on your team?"

Dazien gave a pained look. "Believe it or not, it's been difficult for me to find party members that I feel I can trust for exactly the reason you're pointing out. I don't want people fawning over me when we're out in the wilds fighting monsters."

He seemed to brush off the melancholy she saw in those eyes and continued with a lighter tone, "But we would both be a benefit to you as well, I believe. I was able to protect you during the encounter with the Wyrmlings," he pointed out and added, "Uriel was also able to defeat a foe that you mentioned having failed at vanquishing. I think we all complement each other quite well."

Phoenix sat back in her seat and took another sip of her coffee, contemplating his words. She was hesitant about joining a party for multiple reasons. Aside from the plethora of secrets surrounding her, from gods and divine quests to her very origins and abilities, Paul had warned that her powerset might not be suitable for the average group. Dazien had made a strong case for her inclusion, however.

She didn't want to dismiss the opportunity out of hand, but she couldn't accept it at that moment. The Protégé gave a small sigh, which caused Dazien to frown slightly, and she said cautiously, "I'll need to talk with Paul first."

"Paul?" Dazien asked in confusion, then it seemed to click. "Ah, you mean Lord Wayland. Right, of course. That was why Mister Trayvious mentioned him to us. He overheard Uriel and I discussing you joining." He gave a hesitant chuckle, admitting a bit sheepishly, "He said we should have asked your Mentor before you."

Phoenix blinked and laughed, surprising the pair. "I'm glad you didn't listen to him. Paul might be my Mentor, but he doesn't own me." She shook her head at the idea. "Like I said, though, he does take training me seriously, and I value his opinion. I'm sure he'll look into both of you and determine if it is a good match or not. I'm starting to suspect he's doing a lot of things behind the scenes when it comes to my adventuring career," she said, muttering that last part, wondering once more exactly *how* Trayvious had so much information on her that she didn't remember being on the forms she filled out.

The Astromancer took another sip of the warm coffee as she watched the snow some more while the others also enjoyed their drinks. She thought a bit more about the team-up and then decided to try showing a little more trust in the pair, offering up her promised information. "I'm a Wayfarer."

Phoenix knew now that it wasn't really that big of a secret since she had quickly found out that her status as one could be easily gleaned from her Aura if people gave it a poke as she could now with the cinderen, runeforged, humans, avals, and, of course, monsters. Her training with Paul had helped her better understand the things she was reading when her Aura brushed against another, and species was the easiest to discern. Obviously, even Dazien knew something was different about her from it, which is why he asked.

Dazien's eyes went wide in surprise, but Uriel looked slightly confused and looked to his partner for answers. "You're from a completely other world?" the warrior asked for clarification.

She nodded. "Paul was the first decent person I met in this world, and he's protected and guided me since. That was a little over two months ago now."

"That explains so much," Dazien said, tilting his head and placing a hand on his chin as he thought aloud. "The unusual assortment of talents, not knowing about Harpies or Sense Stones, never seeing airships, wait . . . if I remember the stories right, most Wayfarers don't arrive with Aspects."

"I didn't," she explained, "my, um, Talents helped me get a couple quickly, and Paul gave me one to complete the set."

"What are they?" he curiously asked.

Phoenix hesitated but knew this question would need to be answered if they were going to be in a party together. She wasn't sure if that was going to happen or not; however, it wasn't like her Class was some grand secret, especially considering the other ones she kept. "Star, Dark, Moon, and Sun, which gave me the Celestial Astromancer Class. Like I told you before, it's not really known, so I'm not quite sure what Role I might actually end up in. Plus, I still have all of my Class abilities to unlock . . ."

Dazien gave a low whistle. "That is quite a lot. You only have two-thirds of your powerset filled."

She slumped in shame, and he grinned at her as he added, "Yet you still became an Adventurer. That is quite impressive." This time, she flushed in embarrassment at the compliment. He continued speaking, trying to put her more at ease. "I still have two Class abilities to unlock myself."

"What are your Aspects? If you don't mind my asking . . ." Phoenix questioned shyly.

Dazien gave her an odd look and said, "You don't need permission to ask a question, Miss Fraser. I am not some tyrant that will have you strung up for the slight of being curious. I would have been hung ages ago if that were the case."

Uriel cleared his throat, and Dazien gave him that same betrayed look of mock hurt, saying defensively to his friend, "I am *not* a tyrant!"

"Bow before me?" Uriel asked the affronted man.

"That is *one* Spell!" he retorted, holding up a single finger for emphasis. "And you know that we don't *choose* the incantation!"

Phoenix giggled at the pair's antics, and they both turned to stare at her. Their gaze made her stop abruptly. "What?" she asked, feeling slightly uncomfortable.

"It's nothing, sorry," Dazien said, shaking his head and then gave a dramatic sigh. "This probably won't help my case for *not* being a tyrant, but it does help it for being a king." The gemite gave her that charming smile that seemed to be his usual go-to and said, "My Aspects are Sword, Noble, Metal, and Potent, for the Warrior King Class."

"Warrior King? You really weren't joking, were you? You're planning to become an actual king?" she asked in amazement at the sheer audacity.

He grinned and stated confidently, "It is the path I have chosen."

She glanced at Uriel and asked, "And are you the King's Mage?"

The cinderen nodded and said simply, "I have chosen to follow him."

Dazien patted Uriel's shoulder. "My most trusted advisor and closest friend for many years."

"And what are your Aspects?" she hesitantly asked the Mage.

The gemite didn't answer for his friend this time, the smile slightly dropping as he looked to his companion, squeezing his shoulder gently in a motion of support.

Uriel gazed at her with his ember-lit eyes, mesmerizing her for a moment as though there were secrets hidden in the flames. He seemed to be assessing her but not in the way Paul, Trayvious, or Warrior had. It was like the Mage was judging not only her trustworthiness but also wondering how she might react or if he even cared about how she did.

Then he said simply, "Fire, Ice, Storm, and Potent for Cataclysm Mage."

Her eyes widened slightly in surprise, and the pair seemed to watch her intently. Then she leaned forward excitedly. "Are you serious? That's awesome!"

They both seemed startled by her reaction, and Uriel asked in surprise, "What?"

"*Cataclysm* powers?! That sounds super powerful! With Fire and Ice? That's very Robert Frost. It's very intimidating, but it explains why you're so talented!" Phoenix said in a rush, thinking back to her video games and books about insanely powerful mages.

Dazien smiled brightly at her. "See Uriel? It's not just me that thinks you're talented!"

"After what he did to that Tundra Yeti?" Phoenix asked in disbelief. "Who would argue that he's not? When I fought that thing, it literally broke me," she admitted with a shudder, then pointed out to the Mage. "You'll be able to save so many people with your power!"

Uriel frowned at that. "I'm not a Healer. My powers are for destruction and nothing more."

Phoenix nodded but pointed out pragmatically, "Sure, but when there's a swarm of monsters invading the city, that's what'll save the Healers and others who can't fight from being killed, right?"

Uriel looked unconvinced but remained silent. Dazien was still grinning widely at her unexpected reaction, and seemed like he was going to ask another question when an alarm started blaring from outside.

CHAPTER THIRTY-FOUR

We Will Use You

Mister Oerwynt,

I am writing to request your presence at the Estate of the Noble House of Wayland in Tulimeir of Tulim in regard to a matter of utmost importance concerning the divine item within your possession. During my travels performing my duty as an Adventurer, I discovered a prime candidate for consideration. It would behoove you to make haste with the item before the imminent Purge of Krafti, when travel will become impeded and—

So, when exactly are you bringing her?"

Paul paused writing the letter on the desk in front of him, which was beginning to feel more like his own. He had slowly been converting the lord's study to be more to his liking, but between meetings, research, paperwork, and training Phoenix, he hadn't made much progress.

The new lord looked up to peer unamused at his younger sister and said flatly, "Not today."

Patricia frowned and rolled her eyes at him. "It's been almost three weeks since you've returned with her, and that is the same answer you have given me every time I've asked."

"And it will continue to be my answer until I believe she's settled enough," he responded, attempting to go back to writing his letter to his old teammate. It was still early in the morning, and he wanted to finish in time to stop by the Pyrin Postal Service Station or find a more direct and expensive form of messenger service before his meeting with Agatha, followed by lunch with Phoenix and more training.

The runeforged sat down in the plush chair across from him without invitation and continued prodding. "You told me she's picking up her Adventuring License today; I'd say she's settled."

Paul didn't look up as he corrected, "Now she has to settle into her new duties as an Adventurer."

She scoffed at him, "Then after that, I'm sure you'll find some other thing she'll need to settle into."

"That's the plan," he said without missing a beat.

"Paauul," she whined as though they were both kids again, then leaned forward to try to get his attention better, "this is your *Protégé* we're talking about here. How do you expect me to properly protect her from the aristocratic vipers if you won't even let me meet her?"

"With your own viper's tongue, Pati," he responded promptly. Then he finally paused, glanced up, and inquired, "Are you trying to tell me it is beyond your capabilities?"

"Please," she said in mock offense, "I've been able to keep them chasing their own tails. Unless she does something outrageously public, there won't be a soul among the nobles who will know she even exists."

"Public spectacles are not really her thing from what I've seen so far," he said before turning back to his letter once more, "she's rather non-confrontational unless attacked first."

"And I might have *known* that if you'd bring her here!" Patricia exclaimed, throwing up her hands in exasperation before rocking back in her chair and muttering sadly, "It's like you're afraid of her meeting your family. Like you're ashamed of us . . ."

Paul stopped his pen strokes and leveled his gaze at her. "That is not true, sister."

"Then help me understand!"

He gave a long sigh and finally set his pen down and matched her posture as he explained, "I've told you she's a Wayfarer. When she landed here, she was powerless, lost, scared, and under constant threat from both monsters and the Magi. I've built rapport with her, but she's having trouble learning to trust the people of this world, with good reason."

"*You* barely trust people," Patricia pointed out.

"I'm learning along with her," he said in all seriousness, and the runeforged sobered as he continued. "We both need time, Pati. Getting thrown to the Snolves without having a single person to confide in is not going to make your job any easier and could easily destroy the relationship I've built with her. That's not something I want to risk right now. So please, show *me* some trust and wait for me to let you know when she's ready."

His sister gave a drawn-out sigh but didn't argue, merely nodding in acquiescence. Paul watched as she leaned forward again and pulled the piece of paper he had been writing on towards her to read over it.

Her face contorted in anger as she asked in disgust, "You're seriously writing to that prick?"

"He has something I need."

"Then send a messenger to collect it. He doesn't need to come here."

He met her eyes and stated bluntly, "I don't trust anyone else."

They stared at each other for a long while, neither blinking nor glancing away. They didn't even breathe as the silent battle of wills filled the space, and neither of them had lungs that required it.

Patricia finally blinked and looked away with an annoyed huff as she tossed the paper back on the desk and promptly stood. "Cheating Emerald, not needing to blink," she complained, then waved towards the letter. "That makes you sound like a pretentious prick as well, you know. He'll never respond to something like that. He might even think it was a trick or trap of some kind and vanish again."

"*Little Flower is correct, Wayland,*" the background voice within his mind added in that constant monotone, "*There is a ninety-four percent chance that Steel Skull will not believe it is Wayland.*"

As Pati turned and left the study, he picked up the piece of paper again and reread it himself. With a huff of annoyance, he crumpled it up, tossed it in the fireplace across the room, and pulled out a fresh sheet.

Jerem,

I'm back in Tulimeir.
I have a Protégé now.
Bring the weapon.

—Paul

Paul found himself once more in the office of the Branch Director of the Alliance of Adventurers and unhappy with the events that were unfolding around him. Agatha Trayvious had requested his presence at a meeting concerning an upcoming mission, but had failed to mention the additional presence of the cinderen man sitting beside him. The two men sat on the other side of the large desk, which Agatha claimed as she looked between the pair, but they were pointedly *not* looking at each other.

"Well, let's dispense with the pleasantries, and I'll just get to the point of why I requested both of you here today," the director said, aimlessly shuffling papers around her desk as an obvious distraction.

The cinderen spoke first. "If this is some sort of power play—"

"No, Duke Tul," Agatha said quickly, cutting off that line of thought, "I am merely abiding by your own request to be informed of and included in discussions regarding any missions that might deploy one of our few Emerald Casters or involve either the Soul Reapers or the Purifier's Renseres."

"You have a mission for me then?" Paul asked as calmly as he could after being ambushed like this.

"You can't possibly be considering sending a Fallen—"

"Please, Your Grace," Agatha interjected once more, "remember, you are here as a courtesy. With the blood moon nigh, we need to put aside our differences and past grudges in order to best serve the people of Tulim."

"Does Wayland want to set Fancy Tul's hair on fire?" the feminine voice said from within his mind, and Paul glanced over at the man he had a rather contentious history with. *"There is not much, so it should not hurt too painfully."*

He tried to hold back the smirk the mental image conjured but replied silently, *"No, Bela. Now be quiet, please."*

Paul's fellow hostage grumbled in discontent at the director's words but fell silent with a curt nod and gestured for her to continue.

"Thank you," she said with a return tilt of the head, her long dark braids falling forward. She pushed them back behind her shoulder as she continued, "We've gotten reports of potential Soul Reaper activity at a Reality Rift near the southeastern edge of the tundra, just across the border with Epa Toivo."

"What is Marquess Surul doing about it?" Duke Tul asked, seemingly deciding to ignore Paul's presence and focus on Agatha's report instead.

"Please, Victor, you and I both know that Surul doesn't do anything himself," Paul said sourly.

"That's *Duke* Tul to you," the cinderen retorted, then continued addressing Agatha. "The Toivoans have protection treaties in place with Kun Nul Lun. Have they dispatched anyone?"

Paul tried his best not to roll his eyes as he also chose to respond to the duke through Agatha. "The king there sits up in his shining, heavily guarded palace in San Gra Lan and only cares about his own people. He won't risk draconid lives to help the Sandstep voxen, despite whatever protection treaty he signed in exchange for better trade."

"The AOA stationed there should still have honored the treaty and posted a mission," Tul said in growing agitation, his grip on the arms of the chair tightening as though trying to keep himself from lunging at Paul.

"They did," Agatha said, obviously not trying very hard to hold back an amused smile. "Nobody responded within the first week. I'm guessing it was due to the same reasons that the king seemed so unmoved. So, they opened it to the entire country and increased the reward, as per procedures. After another week of no suitable parties stepping forward, they have called upon neighboring nations. Which brings us to the problem of not having known about a problem that threatens one of our own border towns until now," she said darkly. "We had a team nearby that happened to be accompanied by one of our Emeralds and dispatched a runner to relay the new mission. Which they accepted with the additional request for reinforcements."

"Which Emerald?" Paul asked curiously. He had already made a point to meet with most of them after arriving back in town to make clear his intentions of assisting with the blood moon and building some rapport. He had a reputation needing repair, after all, which his sister had dutifully reminded him of earlier.

"Talvehtia," the director answered with a slight sigh.

"Talvehtia?" Victor repeated incredulously. "The man can barely take care of a Rune Floof, and you want him running headfirst into a Rift with Soul Reapers?"

"What were the reported enemy Castes and numbers?" Paul questioned, trying to get a clearer picture of the problem.

"No solid numbers, but the reports mention many Sapphire Caste Auras," she read from one of her papers.

"Cages or Casters?" he asked.

"Don't know," Agatha responded with a frown. "It's because of the unknown that reinforcements were requested."

"And you want me to be the reinforcements?" Paul questioned, assuming that was why he was being included in this conversation at all.

She nodded, and the duke scoffed again and muttered, "I'm not sure he's much better than Talvehtia."

"Talvehtia is normally an Emerald Caste Blacksmith, Your Grace," she reminded with the patience of a saint. "He had agreed to go on missions recently just to get some more hunting experience before this blood moon."

"And a disgraced former Paladin is so much better?" the cinderen sneered.

"Yes," she answered bluntly, "Lord Wayland has been a Midshift Striker with the AOA for over four decades. He has successfully completed over five hundred combat missions with experience in both teams and solo situations."

She leaned forward slightly to stare at the duke while she pointed at Paul and said sternly, "Despite your desires, this man is the most powerful Caster in the tundra, and any mission we want to ensure succeeds at all costs will require his inclusion, Your Grace."

Duke Tul stared at her for a long moment before slowly turning to finally look at Paul and asked, "And you accept this position of responsibility?"

That had not been what Paul had expected to come out of the man's mouth, and he raised an eyebrow in silent question.

"If you do, make no mistake, *Lord* Wayland. We will use you. We will despise you. We will fear and envy you. We will wring out every drop of power you can give and then keep squeezing," the low-level Emerald Caste duke said without a hint of humor. "The people of this city mean more to me than any ill reputation you may be dragging around, any threat that might bear down on these walls,

walls that have stood for over five millennia, or any self-righteous agenda you may be trying to enact behind the scenes," Duke Tul continued. "And once this is all over, once the blood moon is done and the Soul Reapers repelled, once the people of the tundra, *my* tundra, are safe and can live without fear of annihilation . . . we might even respect you." Victor finished monologuing and locked eyes with Paul, "Do you accept the *responsibility* of keeping my people safe?"

Paul contemplated the man before him and the responsibilities he had already taken upon himself and slowly nodded, asking the director, "When do I leave?"

"In three days. I want to gather a few other people and then—" Agatha was cut off as an alarm rang in her office, and a small model of the city near her desk showed the Temple District flashing with white light. The smaller woman breathed out. "Shit."

CHAPTER THIRTY-FIVE

Call to Arms

Phoenix followed a step behind the two men who had stood up abruptly and asked, "What's happening?"

"A monster spawning inside the walls," Dazien promptly answered, the joviality from a moment ago now gone. "Near to us, too, if we can hear the alarms. We need to go out and help."

She and Uriel nodded to him in understanding and followed as he led the way out of the café and to where the alarms were indicating. The fortress city had a detection system in place to respond and evacuate people as needed in the event of a monster breach, bypassing their external defenses. It wasn't an extremely common occurrence, but the Moderate spawn rate of the zone made it an inevitability in the city.

Dazien seemed particularly unhappy when they discovered the location of the spawning monster. He frowned at the Monster Seed that was currently floating in the air near the southern entrance to the Temple District.

The location could have been worse. The buildings were sparser here, which meant less potential for structural damage, but there were a *lot* of people out in the open going about their pious duties, worshiping both inside and outside of the temples, which meant collateral damage was going to be likely.

Many of the clergy were helping to direct people away, and other nearby Adventurers had appeared around the Seed, which was currently glowing white and getting brighter with each passing second as they waited for it to bloom.

"Is that the monster?" she asked with uncertainty.

"One in the process of spawning," Dazien clarified for her. "It's rare to witness them in this form, but first, the Seed appears, and then the monster forms around it."

"Can we just stop it? Take or break the Seed?"

"It's not really there yet." Uriel spoke up, surprising her slightly. "It's in a transitional state; basically, a mirage of what the magic is creating. It normally only takes a few minutes for it to fully form and then bloom into a monster," he explained in that soft smooth voice.

Dazien nodded slowly. "We're lucky the blood moon hasn't actually started yet, or the chance for a Sapphire would be higher, and people would likely die. There are too many civilians here to protect all of them from the damage a Sapphire could do before we could take it down."

Phoenix looked at them and asked nervously, "Should we focus on helping the evacuation then?"

The gemite shook his head. "The clergy know the routes to the bunkers better than we do. We can help protect them by distracting the monster. Depending on what it is, we may be useful or unneeded. We won't know until it shows itself." He looked around at the other Adventurers and guards that had gathered. "Phoenix, can you sense what Caste the others are with your Aura?"

She raised an eyebrow and asked in surprise, "You want me to expand my Aura over everyone?"

He met her gaze firmly. "We are about to enter combat with an unknown force that could be stronger than us. At the very least, your Auras can help others who might be better suited to combat it. The others will welcome it rather than see it as rude in this situation."

She nodded and carefully released the restraint she held on her Aura, feeling it expand and wash over the area. The others were a bit startled by the appearance of tiny **[Starlight Companions]** floating next to them in a variety of colors, glittering shells surrounding them, the shadows that blurred their forms, and the less visual effect of increased mana regeneration; however, most turned to look at her with a nod of appreciation. She focused a bit on taking inventory of their Castes and reported, "There are six other Crystals."

Dazien frowned again, and she heard murmuring begin among the gathered city defenders who were forming a loose circle around the bright glow that was now three Seeds. Phoenix blinked and squinted her eyes as she asked, "Um, did those just multiply?"

"Yes . . ." the amethyst warrior answered slowly, "and they don't appear to be done."

As she watched, more Seeds seemed to phase into existence, floating near the first one and glowing with their own white light.

"I wouldn't normally be so worried about a monster spawn if we weren't so close to a blood moon, especially *this* one, but I wasn't expecting something like that to appear so early," the gemite said warily as the numbers continued increasing.

With a breath and a shimmer of golden sparkles, Dazien was suddenly wearing the armor and steel shield she had seen him wear during their trials, and another dazzle of golden lights had him holding his diamond sword as well.

"Swarms are not unheard of outside a blood moon," Uriel calmly pointed out, "the more plentiful the numbers, the less individually powerful. This might be a good thing for us," the cinderen added but moved back from them. He removed the gold band from his neck and experimentally reached out a hand towards his **[Starlight Companion]** and frowned as it shied away from him.

Phoenix had never seen one of the squishy companions do that before, usually allowing their protectee to play with their malleable forms, but her confusion was distracted by finally sensing Uriel's Aura, which she hadn't realized was a blank spot to her senses before since she had been more focused on restraining her Aura around others and not poking around theirs.

His Aura felt like he would destroy the world.

She asked Dazien in a concerned whisper, "Why does he stay away from everyone? And what's with that choker?"

He frowned and explained with a tinge of frustration, though she didn't feel it was directed at her, "They're Chains of Silence, also called Silencers. His Aura causes damage to everything around him, *including* allies, so he uses the Silencers to help keep it restrained. I'm sure you can feel it now."

He was right; she could definitely feel it now that the Silencer wasn't hiding it, and it was cutting away at anything that came in range. Dust and dirt, the snowflakes that fell around them, and everything in the small area near him were slowly being annihilated.

She nodded in confirmation to Dazien, and he finished explaining, "That's why he stands away from everyone when he takes it off to use his abilities. It's simply for their safety. We should focus up, though. It's about to spawn."

It was only a few moments later when thirteen ghost-like creatures began taking shape around the Seeds and became much more solid, but still seemed slightly incorporeal. Phoenix only had a second to read the book that popped up in front of her before dismissing it and preparing to fight.

New Quest: Call to Arms: Temple Threat
Monsters have spawned within the city walls. Help defend the Temple District.
Objective: Help defeat the Wailing Wights.
Reward: Rare Crystal Caste fabric.

If Phoenix had to picture what a banshee mixed with a dementor would look like, these phantoms would have been it. Their formless shapes were made up of semitransparent cloaks that seemed ripped towards the top to create a gaping mouth with crooked shards for teeth. The eyes were brightly glowing circles that appeared under the shadowy cloth. The only solid-looking part of them was the curved claws that made up their whole fingers.

Her heart sank at the sight of them, and she looked at her daggers, suspecting that they would be useless for this ethereal enemy.

Chaos ensued a moment later as the other Casters sprang into action, some moving forward to engage in melee while others began chanting incantations. She was close enough to hear Uriel's words again.

"Wind stings. Ice bites. Snow freezes. The blizzard claims life."

A flurry of freezing ice and snow erupted, centered on where the Seeds had bloomed into monsters. The ghostly creatures let out deafening wails and began to visibly slow as frost appeared on them. Some turned to Uriel in their anger and moved towards their little trio.

Dazien firmly stood in front of Uriel and Phoenix as he asked over his shoulder at her, "Can your telekinesis power pull them in front of me?"

"Telekinesis? I don't—Oh! Uh, maybe? I can try," Phoenix replied as she realized what he wanted. "I'll have to use you as a brace. Can you do that thing that makes you unmovable?"

He nodded, shifting his stance slightly. "It'll eat through a chunk of mana, and I can't move again without canceling it," he warned.

She moved directly behind him and said, "I'll try to be quick then. How many? They *are* all Crystal themselves, and we don't know their level within the Caste."

"Caste and levels don't matter when they're threatening Uriel. Bring any going for him or the civilians," he replied resolutely.

She looked around him and saw two going for Uriel standing behind them and one going for a civilian who hadn't been intercepted by one of the other Casters.

"Three targets, first one incoming," she said as she braced herself against his back and triggered [**Ruler of Relativity**] on the first phantom that was about to take a swipe out of the unguarded Mundane.

Dazien triggered his ability as soon as she felt her power push her against him, and they stopped moving forward as the Wight seemed to be dragged towards them. Phoenix gasped loudly, feeling crushed by the force trying to pull her towards the higher-level monster.

"Are you okay?" the warrior called back to her as the phantom came closer.

"Caste level . . . way stronger," she managed to croak out, "kill it . . . fast."

During her numerous monster fights, Phoenix had come to realize that the terms of Low, Mid, High, and Peak, when referring to the levels within a Caste, actually made a noticeable difference in a creature's power. Low referred to the first three levels, Mid was levels four through six, High the three after that, while Peak referred to the top when a creature was either maxed out for their species or about to ascend to the next Caste.

Paul was at the peak of Emerald, with only a couple of abilities remaining at level nine, according to him, while Phoenix was still low Crystal and would struggle against anything in the higher ranges on her own, which these Wights were proving to be. She wasn't great at sensing the ranges of others yet, but she really hoped her two new companions weren't at the bottom like she was.

Her fear was slightly abated when Dazien raised an arm towards the first monster and incanted, *"Bow before your king!"*

The phantoms only had glowing hollows for eyes, but if Phoenix could have seen the creature, she would have sworn it glared at Dazien before moving in front of him in what could be considered a kneel despite not having legs.

The amethyst warrior swung his sword down on the creature. It caught the blade in one of its ethereal claws as the other claw swiped up to rend him in two. The **[Sun Shell]** shattered, but the claw barely scratched the warrior's armor, and the Wight wailed from the blinding effect of her Aura's shield.

Phoenix had to wait to resummon the effect, but she took advantage of the moment and swung around the Defender to swing her daggers into the cloaked figure. She had not expected them to go *through* the monster, however, and she lost her balance at the dissonance between her actions and the result.

The miscalculation cost her own shield as the monster swiped at her stumbling form instead and shattered her shell into shards of light. But it didn't seem as affected by the blinding Bane this time as its claw proceeded to dig into her back. The reaction made her wonder if Banes had some sort of diminishing returns built in, where they became less effective the more often they triggered on a target.

"I challenge your honor!" Dazien cried out, and the claws halted their movement towards her spine. The monster turned to face the warrior with another sound that reminded her of nails on a chalkboard in movies.

Dazien pulled his sword back and pushed the blade through the center of the monster's chest with a clean thrust. The glittering diamond sword caused the creature to scream loudly before it went silent and almost seemed to explode into white ash.

Phoenix tried to reach her back and muttered, *"You will see the dawn of tomorrow,"* activating the moderate-cost version of the Spell. She stood as the pain subsided and looked between the dust drifting in the air, the amethyst warrior, and her own daggers before asking incredulously, *"How?"*

He lifted the tip of the blade and stated with a raised brow, "Magic sword?"

"Magic dagger!" she exclaimed, lifting her own **[Night Blade]** for him to see.

The would-be king gave a smug smirk and asked, "Yes, but is yours a Divine blade of Radiance capable of affecting incorporeal beings?"

"That is such bull—" Her retort was cut off by the sound of Uriel's own incantation reaching her, reminding her that there were still enemies to fight.

"Let fire rain upon my enemies that they may burn before my will."

Phoenix heard Uriel cast as she took another look around the area to find the next phantom to pull and witnessed flames raining from the sky, intermixing with the blizzard to burn the other Wights still trapped within the area from the valiant efforts of the other fighters.

"Are you ready for the next?" she asked. It was more of a warning than an actual question, as she triggered her gravity ability once more. She grunted in pain as she was pushed against Dazien again, who quickly retriggered the ability he had to keep them in place.

As the next one started jerkily moving towards them, Dazien raised a hand towards the last of the three that would reach Uriel before they would be ready to intercept it and said in a cold voice, *"You have forsaken my rule and thus forfeit your freedom!"*

A rune-etched metal cage surrounded the phantom, halting its movement. Then he shouted, *"To arms!"* and Phoenix felt strength flood her body and realized the battle cry was more than just for motivation as he swung his sword once more at the creature.

This phantom, however, was not being forced to kneel and, instead of fighting her gravitational pull, used it to move forward faster, past his blade. Instead of slamming against his shield, it became even more translucent and went *through* the pair of them.

As Phoenix turned to put her daggers between her and the enemy, she found out she wasn't fast enough for their difference in speed levels. The creature raked its long claws down her front, ripping through her cloak, shirt, and flesh. The force of the blow alone sent her crashing straight into the ground as she gasped for air, feeling the warmth of her body quickly escape her.

She thought she heard Uriel's voice say, *"A touch of frost and your death follows,"* and she glanced up at Dazien as numbness quickly started to creep into her. She barely managed to finish resummoning a **[Sun Shell]** around the warrior—cursing that her heal was still stuck on cooldown—before darkness consumed her senses.

CHAPTER THIRTY-SIX

Could Have Gone Better

Dazien realized his mistake too late as the Wight passed through him. When he turned, Phoenix was already falling to the ground. He lunged over her, causing his **[Stand Your Ground]** ability to cancel its effects, but the stacks of **[Tenacity]** he had built up with it were boosting his Strength attribute quite a bit. He sensed Phoenix's Aura power surrounding him in warm light once more as he thrust his sword forward at the creature, piercing its shoulder instead of its center, as it reacted faster than he had anticipated.

The phantom's counterattack was intercepted by the glittering shell, blinding it for a moment, and he activated his Special Attack, **[Accelerating Strikes]**. Each slice of his sword became faster and faster as he poured his stamina into it. Each of the attacks from his conjured sword added a Bane, which reduced the monster's regeneration.

Frost started appearing on the creature, and Dazien recognized one of Uriel's Ice Spells, which took effect on it and slowed it down. He pushed his stamina to the limit as he chipped away at the higher-level monster and hoped it would be enough.

In a last-ditch effort, the battered phantom moved backward away from the furious warrior and opened its jaw wider than was natural. It let out a reverberating scream that slowly increased in volume as Dark energy gathered in its void of a mouth.

Dazien didn't wait. He adjusted his grip on his sword and hurled it like a spear towards the monster just as it released the ball of Dark energy to fly towards the warrior. As his sword plunged into the Wight's chest, a little blue pixie moved in front of him and deflected the Magical attack.

The Wight began dissolving into white ash, and Dazien turned back to smile at Phoenix and thank her for the tiny Aura companion that had saved him from the attack, only to pale at the sight of her still body staining the snow around her a dark red.

The Warrior King moved to her side and knelt down to check if she was alive. A moment later, he remembered that if her Aura effects were still around, then that meant she was still alive, if only barely. He sucked in a breath as his eyes fell upon the Soul Mark emblazoned on her chest through the tattered remnants of her shirt, and he sensed the Favor of five gods at once. They were not minor gods either, nor ones that he wanted to displease by having led Phoenix to her death. He tore his gaze from the Mark to her wounds, which were bleeding heavily.

"She is Chosen by so many?" Uriel's voice asked in shock from behind him, and he glanced up at his friend, who had moved closer to check on them despite the risk he posed.

"That doesn't matter right now," he said, harsher than he had meant to, the panic threatening to override his control. "She's going to die if we can't find a Healer."

The gemite glanced towards the other Casters, who were still fighting. The Temple of the Mender wasn't close to the south entrance of the district where they were located, and he was afraid moving her would only make it worse.

"I'll have to check my [**Armory**]. Watch over her while I'm in there," he ordered Uriel. Dazien then conjured what looked like a solid gold door encrusted with jewels that came up from the ground, and opened it before disappearing through the portal of light behind it.

§

Uriel bent to try and use Phoenix's cloak to slow down the bleeding, but the amount was worrisome. He didn't waste time refastening his Silencer and hoped his Aura didn't cause even more blood loss.

A loud explosion of light washed over the area as one of the phantoms was crushed in an instant by whatever force had just landed in the center of the phantoms that were still fighting the others.

When Uriel could see again, a man in gleaming white and gold armor was standing up where he had just cratered into the earth. He was holding a massive golden sword glowing with holy light, and the next moment, the man seemed to vanish as the remaining Wights flashed and became white ash without so much as a whimper.

Uriel recognized that armor. He knew who that massive great sword belonged to. The only thing missing from what he remembered of the Paladin was the long, white cape clasped with the sigil of a sun that signified the Purifier.

He barely registered his own movement through the air until he tried to take a breath and could feel the grip around his throat, holding him a few inches above the ground. His hands gripped the golden gauntlet of the district's newest savior, and his apparent foe, as he felt the wrath emanating from this man's Aura pressing down upon him.

"You've broken your promise, Karislian," Lord Wayland spat out at him as he struggled to get enough leverage to speak in his defense. "You swore to remain Silenced."

Dazien came out of the door a moment later, yelling, "Found it!" before freezing at the sight of the Emerald Caster holding him aloft like a disobedient puppy who then glared at the young warrior with those golden eyes that still visited his nightmares from time to time.

To his dismay, Dazien returned that glare with his own defiant one.

"*King, it's Lord Wayland. Don't attack,*" he managed to warn his partner over the mental communication they always maintained with Dazien's [**Noble Subjects**] ability. The last thing Uriel needed was for his partner to jump to his defense and piss off the Emerald Caster that could easily kill them.

He could see Dazien's glare vanish in surprise before he staggered a moment later as the overwhelming Aura narrowed on him as well.

Uriel knew why people called this man the Blade of Pure Wrath, and he had hoped never to run into the former Paladin again. He was sure that not only he and Dazien but all the Casters who had suddenly stopped fighting could feel the presence of the noble lord who could smite them all without uttering a single word.

The silence that had descended upon the area was broken by his companion. "Lord Wayland," Dazien managed to say in a calm and measured voice, visibly steeling himself as he looked towards Phoenix. Uriel wondered how his partner was able to force himself to move towards them. The gemite lifted the vial in his hand as though it might offer him some protection from the wrathful lord and explained. "It's a healing potion . . . Please, release my partner."

Wayland held out his hand for it, and Dazien complied with the silent order. Both of them recognized at the same time that the lord didn't trust either of them near his apprentice. Not that they could blame him at that moment.

Dazien handed over the potion, and he was dropped unceremoniously to the ground while the lord knelt down faster than Uriel's own Crystal Caste Perception could follow.

He quickly staggered to his feet, gulping for breath, and ungracefully retreated behind his partner, who had a better chance of talking the lord into letting them live.

The two companions watched as Wayland braced Phoenix and fed her the potion, as though he had done this a dozen times already, and they both realized at the same time that he probably had. Uriel stared at Phoenix anew, wondering just what kind of harsh training she had gone through under this terrifying man.

As her wounds began closing, they felt the pressure of the Emerald Aura lessen and recede back to a more polite sphere around the Mentor and Protégé, allowing Dazien and Uriel to feel like they could breathe normally once more. They had relaxed, only to tense again as the former Paladin glared up at them and asked in that rough voice that Uriel could still remember from their brief discussions years ago, "Why is she here?"

That was not the question either of them had been expecting to be asked first, but then again, they hadn't expected the Blade of Pure Wrath to be here in the first place.

"I—We were nearby when the alarms went off," Dazien tried to explain, but the words that normally came to him so easily faltered as the much more powerful man stared through the both of them. The older man remained silent, though, waiting for more, so Dazien continued, "We came to check it out and realized there weren't enough protectors in the area as it was spawning—"

"You knew it would be a Swarm?" the lord cut in.

Dazien swallowed and nodded but stood resolutely, "Yes, but we are Adventurers, sir. People needed protection, and we were the closest to respond."

Merciless eyes narrowed at the young warrior, and Uriel was glad they were not leveled at him as the former Paladin asked, "Why was she with you?"

"Ah," Dazien said, shifting uncomfortably, "well, my companion and I were discussing some matters with her after getting the results of our trials."

"And you thought three freshly licensed Crystal Caste Adventurers would be fine with taking on an entire Swarm in the middle of the city?"

Dazien's brow furrowed. "With all due respect, sir, numbers don't matter when lives are at stake."

"You can't save anyone if you're dead," the Wrath Blade growled at the younger warrior. "And your lack of judgment almost killed her," he added, gesturing towards Phoenix, whose wounds had now fully closed, but she remained unconscious. "Does her life mean less than the other lives you thought were at stake?"

"Of course not!" Dazien exclaimed, and Uriel was reminded of a child being scolded. He could see his friend grit his teeth as the Defender also understood that that was exactly what was happening.

His partner continued speaking in their defense, however. "She's not some monster fodder we were willing to throw away. We value her capabilities, which were critical in this fight. Her adaptability and courage in the face of adversity is why we asked her to join our team."

Dazien shut his mouth as Uriel recognized his friend's words were getting away from him again, and they both winced as the Emerald Aura flared out to press down on them again, and the lord of wrath growled, "Absolutely *not*."

Wayland gently lifted Phoenix into his arms before walking off towards the Temple of the Mender without so much as another glance at the two of them.

"That could have gone better," he said dryly after the oppressive Aura vanished.

Dazien crossed his arms and gave him a flat look. "Really now?"

He nodded and asked, "Are you going to give up on recruiting her?"

"Of course not," the Warrior King responded promptly. "She is way too interesting to let an Emerald Caster stop me. Even one that seems like the incarnation of the Purifier with anger management issues."

§

This was turning out to be an exceedingly terrible day for Paul as he carefully carried Phoenix to the Temple of the Mender nearby. He had fed her a potion, but she hadn't awoken, and he wanted to make sure there wasn't some underlying cause for it. Despite being a Paladin, and what most people might assume with his dedication to the Purifier, he wasn't a Healer.

Not a single ability he unlocked could heal damage, and he hadn't expected, nor wanted, any of them to do so when he had chosen his Aspects decades ago. It wasn't until after becoming an Adventurer that he found himself in situations where he regretted that choice. So, he was happy when Phoenix had gotten one, not having to face the same regretful realizations that he had over the years when the potions ran out.

Nobody stopped him as he entered the temple, and one of the priests quickly responded to show him to a private room. The Healer examined the Wayfarer while ordering one of the acolytes to fetch another of their priests.

"Is there something wrong?" Paul asked, wishing he could observe the status of others like most dedicated Healers were capable of.

The priest shook his head and clarified, "There's a Void Bane keeping her weakened and draining her mana. However, we should be able to take care of it. I called for one of our cleansing specialists."

"*This One told Wayland we should have stocked up on cleansing potions while near Blomstra,*" Bela interjected.

Paul relaxed and held back a sigh as he replied telepathically, "*Void Banes are exceedingly rare normally, and I can cure almost everything else with my Aura.*" Then he sat in the chair that was currently empty next to the bed he had laid Phoenix in as he tried his best to wait patiently. He was usually fairly good at the waiting game, but it was difficult in his agitated state after almost losing his Protégé to monsters that out-leveled and outnumbered her. Plus, the sight of *that* particular boy leaning over her broken body . . .

"This One does not believe Little Storm was hurting the Little Miss, Wayland," his mental companion spoke up again. *"And Wayland has been able to protect Little Miss so far. He is no match for us."*

"I can't always be there!" he snapped, and the voice went silent, sensing his anger.

He ran a hand over his face in frustration. How was he going to protect her if he was hundreds of miles away? How could he protect her from becoming friends with boys who were bad influences? How could he protect a whole city, a whole tundra, if he couldn't even keep his own apprentice safe?

He was pulled from his spiraling thoughts as the room was suddenly filled with a Divine Aura, and he jerked his head up to see a motherly-looking runeforged smiling benevolently at him. He dropped to a knee and said in greeting, "Lady Mender."

"Oh, Paul Wayland, there's no need for kneeling when we both know you don't mean it." The goddess chuckled.

He grimaced and slowly rose. "Have you come to mark her as well?"

She let out a hearty laugh that time and shook her head. "That does seem to be the popular trend recently, doesn't it? But no, aside from her not being awake to accept my Favor, I'm not sure enough yet to accept the risk."

"Risk?" he asked in confusion. Surely, every god was aware of her immortality by this point. What risk could there be?

"Never you mind that," she waved off, "let's talk about *you*. Now, you seem to be a bit distressed. Would you like to talk about it?"

Paul glanced around the room and suddenly realized that they were alone, aside from the unconscious Wayfarer. He was slightly alarmed that he hadn't even noticed that the priest had left earlier when he had been lost in his thoughts. It felt like it had been decades since he had been that unaware, as his Emerald Caste Mind attribute usually made multitasking and observing a breeze.

That realization alone was enough for him to nod at the goddess and sit at her indication to do so when she took her own seat. He replayed his worries to her, trying to explain why he was feeling so lost, and she smiled, nodded, and asked for clarification at times.

When he finished and asked for guidance, she sighed and said, "Well, it sounds to me like you're having trouble adjusting to being the parent of a teenager."

Paul stared at her speechlessly for a long while before stating dispassionately, "I'm not her parent."

"Yet here you are with all the same worries," Mender pointed out with an amused smile.

He scowled and looked down at his hands, pondering over everything he had said and how he had possibly misled her when describing his relationship with the Wayfarer. Then he clarified, "I'm her Mentor. Nothing more." After a pause, he added, "But just out of curiosity, what do you normally tell parents who share these worries?"

"Well, that often depends on the parent and child in question, but for you, I would start by suggesting having an open and honest conversation with her. Explain your goals in regard to her, why you have them, and how she can help you achieve them. You might be surprised what treating her more like an adult and companion—rather than a toddler that needs cleaning up after—will do to relieve both your worries and hers."

The goddess stood then and added, "You might want to try that approach with the young men you terrified and degraded earlier today as well. Especially considering they worked hard to protect her and are doing wonders for your Protégé's mood."

Paul grimaced again at the goddess and said dryly, "I'll take it into consideration."

CHAPTER THIRTY-SEVEN

Like an Accident

Dazien remained silent in the small kitchen area as he idly made spiced tea for his partner, who was currently sitting near the small hearth of the single-room apartment they shared. The only furnishings they had managed to get included the armchair and loveseat near the fireplace, with a small table between the two seats and the single two-person bed pushed in the far corner against the tinted one-way glass.

They had spent about an hour dealing with the form the AOA requested from them about the events of that morning, such as which people were involved or if any civilians were injured. That also included picking up payment for the standing "Call to Arms" mission that the city had in place to incentivize and thank Adventurers who responded to emergency internal breaches.

Once that was done, both of them grabbed a meal at the café they had originally left in their haste, thanking the host for understanding their sudden departure and paying for their previous items. They managed to do some training after lunch, but they found themselves tired and distracted as they went through their forms and meditation.

It was nearing sundown when the pair made their way back home, as they both wanted to recover more from the mental exhaustion of the near-death experience with both the Wights and wrathful lord.

The sun was starting to set while Dazien literally waited for water to boil, and he turned to lean against the counter to watch his companion. He finally broke the silence by cautiously asking, "So . . . what are we going to do about Lord Wayland?"

Uriel sent him a dubious glance and said, "You're the one interested in getting his Protégé to join our team."

"Don't give me that. You seemed to be enjoying her company as well this morning, and we knew that her Mentor would be a hurdle in our attempts, but he seemed particularly . . . *aggressive* towards you," the warrior pointed out. "I know you mentioned having a history with him, but you had described Paladin Wayland as being on your side of things." He hesitated, unsure if he should poke old wounds. "That didn't seem to be the case today."

Uriel shrugged indifferently and seemed to shrink in on himself. "It's been eight years. Maybe he changed his mind."

"Perhaps if we could just talk to him in a less *combative* setting. Explain things to him—"

"He's the Blade of Pure Wrath, Daze," Uriel interjected, "not the Saint of Patient Listening."

He rolled his eyes and began to walk over to his companion when the kettle whistled, interrupting his response as he turned back to it and finished pouring it into their individual mugs. Once he handed his partner the relaxing brew, he sat on the loveseat near the chair and asked carefully, "Perhaps we stick to our original plan then and have Phoenix talk to him on our behalf? We can just . . . stay clear of crossing paths?"

Uriel took a drink and shook his head. "It's not going to work, Daze. You saw how he was with her; how he was ready to kill me for her."

They both shuddered at the thought, and the Defender tried to reassure his best friend, "I don't think he would have gone that far. He was probably just—"

His words were cut off by a loud knock at the door, and they almost spilled the tea in their hands at the unexpected visitor. They weren't exactly in the best part of the city, so Dazien carefully and silently set his mug down before slowly making his way to the door. He was about to press the rune on the door that would turn it into a one-way window when a rough voice said, "Open up, kid. We need to talk."

They both froze at that voice. Perhaps the lord of wrath *would* go that far and had come to finish them off.

"Either you open it, Smithson, or I do," said Lord Wayland from the other side of the entrance, and Dazien hurried to comply before he was left having to pay for a new door.

The noble didn't ask to enter as he walked past him and into the single room where Uriel still sat frozen in his seat in a mixture of fear and resignation that Dazien had never seen before, as if the Mage was ready for the death approaching him. Dazien couldn't allow that.

Wayland seemed to surprise Uriel by sitting on the far side of the loveseat instead of just smiting him where he sat. Dazien was simply grateful that he didn't have to follow his partner in death from avenging Uriel if Wayland had attacked.

He looked between the two men, but as neither seemed to want to speak first, he prompted the conversation with, "Lord Wayland, I would like to apologize once more for not protecting your Protégé proper—"

"She's not yours to protect," the Emerald Caster bluntly interrupted.

"Right," he sourly replied, cringing internally over his slight.

He moved towards Uriel and leaned against the arm of the chair in order to offer a physical buffer between his partner and the intimidating lord in their home. "I would like to change that, however," he pressed, ignoring Uriel's attention snapping up to bore into him. "We are young, like Phoenix, but we have worked hard to get where we are, also much like she has, I imagine."

"I already know how hard you've worked, Smithson," the former Paladin interrupted again.

That was when Dazien registered that Wayland had called him by his family name, which he had never given to the man. He remained silent as the Emerald Caster, who shouldn't have known anything about him at all, began detailing his life as though listing off mission highlights.

"Orphaned at the age of four to be raised at the Temple of the Parent. Met this one"—he gestured towards Uriel—"at the age of thirteen when he joined the temple as well. Began training with Warrior's oversight at the age of fifteen. Remained unadopted until aging out of the program at sixteen, and gained the Warrior King Class at the age of seventeen from inherited Aspects left by your parents. Became an Adventurer at the age of nineteen and officially completed your first mission today," he finished, never breaking his golden gaze from the gemite's own amethyst. Then Wayland asked him, in a rare moment of speechlessness for Dazien, "Did I miss anything?"

Dazien shook himself out of his stupor as he cleared his throat and gave a weak smirk. "You forgot that time I convinced another Caster to take us out on the tundra to hunt monsters to better prepare for the trials."

The lord merely raised a brow at his attempt to lighten the mood.

Dazien cleared his throat once more before nodding at the ground and correcting his response. "Yes, Lord Wayland, that's my life summed up." Then he swallowed his fear and looked up again to ask, "Are you going to tell us what everyone else does? Are you going to say that we're either underqualified or too much of a risk and order us to stay away from Phoenix?"

Instead of answering the question, the veteran Adventurer asked one of his own. "What do you plan to do with your party?"

Dazien felt like his heart missed a beat before the words registered. If Wayland was asking that kind of question, then that implied he was actually considering allowing it.

He fought to keep the grin off his face as he answered. "I plan to lead it. That's what my powerset is all about, really. I'm officially a Forward Defender with a leadership support specialization, but I'm sure you already knew that," he pointed out before continuing. "I already have Uriel as a Backline Mage with an area Bane specialization, which you also knew, and I believe Phoenix would be a great addition as a versatile Supporter that can fill any Role we might need more of in any given situation. I'm still looking for a suitable Healer and Striker, but it's been . . ." He paused and glanced at Uriel, who was still staring intently at him as though he had lost his mind for speaking to the Wrath Blade like he was. "*Difficult*," Dazien settled on before continuing with a soft smile towards Wayland. "Not many people are willing to give him or me a chance like you did for Uriel all those years ago."

The lord gazed towards Uriel then, who seemed to wilt even more.

Dazien continued to try to draw attention away from his introverted partner. "You were one of the people who supported the Chains of Silence to give him a chance at a normal life. I'm asking that you give him the chance to be an Adventurer like yourself now. A chance to save others, like you did for him."

Silence fell in the room as the pair of Crystal Casters endured the judgmental gaze of the Blade of Pure Wrath.

When the lord finally responded, he merely asked, "You like to talk a *lot*, don't you?"

Dazien found himself grinning back, despite the subtle slight, as he responded, "Nobody can argue that I didn't try to communicate my thoughts properly." He then gestured a thumb towards Uriel as he added lightly, "Plus, I need to talk enough for the both of us."

The older man gave an annoyed huff and muttered, "I bet Pati would love to have you on board with that silver tongue. Is that how you convinced the AOA and government to allow that amendment for Karislian to remove his Silencers?"

"It took us almost two years to get them to finally agree on the terms of that special dispensation," the gemite said dryly. He then asked hopefully, "Does that mean you'll give us a chance too?"

Wayland sighed and stood as he said, "I'll leave the decision to Phoenix."

Dazien almost jumped for joy at the proclamation, but his celebration was postponed by the Emerald Aura that suddenly held both of their Crystal ones in a vice grip as the Wrath Blade declared coldly, "If you hurt her, though, and I don't mean by not defending her in combat like today, I mean if *either* of you lay a *finger* on her in aggression, you will no longer find yourselves among the living and, be assured, it will look like an accident."

Then Wayland was gone in a rush of wind, letting Dazien and Uriel be able to breathe again as the door slowly shut automatically with the passing of the vengeful Paladin.

§

Phoenix awoke to the familiar sight of her **[Guide Book]** floating above her with a new message.

Quest: Call to Arms: Temple Threat
Objective Complete: Helped defeat the Wailing Wights.
Objective Reward:
[Bolts of Shadeweave] have been added to your collection.

Completion Reward:
10 [Crystal Mana Bits] have been added to your collection.

"It shouldn't count if I didn't defeat them," Phoenix croaked pitifully at the book, angry at herself for once again falling in battle.

"You helped defeat every one of them," Paul's voice said firmly from beside her, and she turned to look at him. He was sitting with his legs crossed in a plush chair, wearing his casual clothes, and seemed to have paused writing in a leather-bound book to watch her intently. "From the reports I got, there would have been casualties if you hadn't been there."

"Would have been? Does that mean there weren't any?" she asked, slowly pushing herself into a seated position, recognizing that she had been moved to her own bedroom at some point.

"Correct," Paul answered, closing his book and slipping it into the pouch at his side. "You performed admirably, but you shouldn't have been there in the first place."

He partially stood, just enough to sit next to her on the edge of the bed, and gestured to her glowing book, softly asking, "Will you tell me your side of the story?" Then his expression hardened slightly. "Starting with those two I found over your savaged body?"

She winced but nodded and moved the book in front of him, going over the events of her day. When she finished her story up to the point where she blacked out, she asked, "Do you know what happened after that?"

"I do," he answered but didn't elaborate. She pouted at his silence, and he gave a sigh, "I was informed of the breach shortly after it had spawned. I arrived soon after you fell, I believe. That's when I met your two . . . *companions*." He said the last word with a grumble.

"They didn't force me to do anything I wouldn't have done on my own, Paul," she said quietly, "and knowing that my powers helped save lives, I wouldn't have changed getting involved. This is why I decided to walk this path; it's what you've been training me for."

"I know," he conceded, "I just don't like how close things got."

"You and I both know you won't always be there to look after me. That's *why* you're training me, right? So that you won't have to babysit all the time," she said, then paused before adding hesitantly, "It sounds like you didn't like Dazien and Uriel . . ."

He scoffed and stated bluntly, "I was not impressed."

"Really? Between Dazien's knightly persona and Uriel's silent stoicism, I thought combined they basically equate to the Crystal version of you."

He rolled his eyes at her, and she laughed. "I'm joking. Honestly, though, I thought we worked well together. I wasn't sure I should try joining a party at all after getting such a random assortment of powers." She tugged at a lock of her red hair nervously. "Actually, I didn't think anybody would *want* me to join them because of the lack of focus. I was surprised that they were even interested in me."

Paul gave another of his annoyed huffs as he said, "You're an Aurabreaker. You could stand there doing nothing and be a benefit that any party would love to drag around." He fell silent for a moment as though not wanting to admit his next words. "You're not just your Auras, though, and they saw that. I'll give that upstart king that much credit, at least."

She grinned slightly. "Maybe you do approve, then."

"I wouldn't go *that* far," he stated dryly.

Phoenix chuckled, and they continued to sit together, just contemplating in comfortable silence for a moment. Then she could feel his Aura searching through hers, like he often did, as he asked, "Do you *want* to join them?"

She met his gaze and softly asked, "You think I'd lie about my feelings?"

"I think we all lie to ourselves sometimes," he pointed out with a small shrug. "Maybe unknowingly, but I don't want you feeling pressured into doing something you're not comfortable with."

"Well," she began, "I think they made good points that our skills complement each other. I also told them that I would heed your advice on the matter. I think they've been honest about their intentions, though." Then she added as almost an afterthought, "Plus, they make me laugh . . . I think I want a bit more of that in my life."

Paul's expression softened, and he withdrew his Aura to a more unobtrusive level. "If you want to be in their party, I won't stop you."

She gave a short laugh. "Oh, I know. I told them as much. Like I said, though, your opinion matters to me. If you think they'd be a terrible fit, then I'll decline."

He shook his head. "You've been asleep for a while," he confessed, "it's almost morning, and I spent the night already looking into them."

"Of course you did," she interjected and added teasingly, "You know, you're starting to act more like an overprotective father than a combat Mentor."

Paul gave another huff. "Even if I hadn't, I got a good look at their Auras, if you could even call them that," he grumbled. "I knew the talkative one spoke truthfully. They seem to value you as a teammate, not a pawn or tool to improve their status."

"So, they pass the dad inspection?" she asked with a sly grin.

He rolled his eyes at her but nodded, then held up a finger. "On one condition." He waited for her full attention, then stated firmly, "They join you in our training sessions."

She laughed and nodded. "Great. I'll let them know, and we can try out a session in the morning. If you're available?"

He nodded and stood, saying simply, "I'll be sure to make time for it. Get some more rest until then."

She was pleasantly surprised by the head pat he gave her as he said farewell before he retreated for the rest of the night. As she heard Paul close the front door, she pulled out the reward from the quest, having forgotten to show it to him during their brief conversation.

It was an odd-looking thing, and she agreed that "trinket" was the only word she could come up with for it.

Item: Flame of Life
A trinket designed to inform others that the attuned Caster is still living.
Caste: Crystal, Cultivating.
Availability: Epic.
Type: Trinket, tracking.
Requirements: Crystal Caste.
Effects:
- Bonding to the item allows it to track the life status of the bonded.
- As the Bonded Caster cultivates their Caste, the trinket increases with it, allowing continuity of tracking.

The object looked like a glass orb about the size of a small plum. It had what seemed like an attached metal stand on one side, and a matching pointed decorative piece on the opposite side. Inside the orb, she could make out a faintly glowing yellow flame burning within it that was obviously magical.

She set it on the nightstand beside her bed and contemplated giving it to Paul. On the one hand, it might give away her secret if something happened to her on a mission. On the other hand, it might help reassure him that she was still alive whenever they were apart, but she wasn't sure that he worried *that* much about her. He did encourage her into monster fighting, after all.

The Wayfarer returned the trinket to her collection and put the item out of her mind until she came up with a better solution. Perhaps some actual restful sleep would help clear her mind on it.

CHAPTER THIRTY-EIGHT

Favor

Phoenix plopped into the plush booth as Dazien groaned, rubbing his ribs, while he also took a seat. They were once more in the café they had originally visited before their fight with the Wights.

Uriel sat next to him, looking equally exhausted, and the Wayfarer sat opposite the two, looking at the menu once more to see what food options there were.

"Your Mentor is a madman," the amethyst warrior complained, "he does know we're still Crystal Caste, right? Does he always beat you until you can't stand?"

Phoenix grinned and shook her head. "No, I usually spar with Bliss. I've never actually seen him slap around another person like that before," she explained, then added thoughtfully, "I wonder if he was just trying to make you give up sooner rather than later."

"Forget that," he rebuked. "After going through all that, I'm not turning back now."

She narrowed her eyes at him. "You're claiming sunk-cost via pain? That's a new one to me," she observed, then directed her next question to Uriel. "Is King Dazien some sort of masochist?"

The Mage shook his head and answered bluntly, "More on the sadist end, I think. Usually involving lots of rope."

"Hey now, how did that spirit of wrath beating us half to death turn into a discussion about my personal proclivities?" the gemite asked, affronted.

Phoenix continued speaking to Uriel as if she didn't hear Dazien. "That checks out. He does have that cage ability, after all, which is kinda like rope."

"Is this how things are going to be?" Dazien asked, not bothering to hide the grin on his face. "You two combining forces to humiliate your king?"

"I have sworn no oaths of fealty, *Your Majesty*," Phoenix replied, then stuck a tongue out at him. Getting thoroughly trounced repeatedly by Paul during hours of training had stripped away many of the personal walls between the three new companions.

The waiter arrived then and took their orders before leaving the private room once more, and Phoenix turned back to Uriel. "I didn't realize you knew the sword as well," she said, gesturing to the weapon leaned against the wall next to them; he'd removed it from his hip to sit comfortably in the booth.

Uriel nodded and pointed a thumb at Dazien. "This one wanted a sparring partner."

"It's a good skill to have when you run out of mana!" the warrior retorted defensively.

"That is a fair point," Phoenix admitted.

"Thank you!" Dazien said, throwing up his hands, then wincing at the gesture to rub his sore ribs again.

She leaned forward to touch his arm before he could protest again and incanted, "**See the dawn,**" triggering her low-cost heal to take the edge off the remaining pain for him.

He relaxed under her touch and gave a softer smile. "Thank you, that's much better."

"It's no big deal. Just ask next time, and I could have remembered to do it sooner. I haven't used it on others, like at all."

"I'll try to remember that," he replied. "I'm just glad you finally agreed with me on something. It's always good to have a backup skill that doesn't require mana to protect yourself should your powers become compromised."

She nodded in agreement, then added, "Plus, it's not like you can really expect the Defender to keep *everything* off you."

Dazien's jaw dropped as he stared in shock at her. Phoenix burst out laughing at the expression, and even Uriel chuckled as the Defender said in exaggerated offense, "You *wound* me . . . truly, I don't know if I can take much more of the pain from the dagger in my back."

"I'm joking," she said between chuckles, "you did great with those Wights. I wouldn't have gotten that last one you caged up before it got to Uriel."

The humor dropped from Dazien's face as he frowned and said seriously, "I wasn't able to protect you, though."

"Hey now, nobody died," she pointed out, trying to cheer him up. "That was the goal, right?"

He nodded, and their conversation paused again when the waiter returned with magical caffeine and pastries. Phoenix took a bite of the warm confectionary and gave an appreciative moan, then said, "I'm surprised they have food like this here. I haven't seen anything growing in this frozen wasteland."

The warrior explained between his own bites, "We have the Cultivator's Citadel to thank for that. It grows most of the city's food using a variety of magic rituals, enchantments, and tools."

"We could have used those on Earth," she said thoughtfully.

Dazien paused his eating as he quietly asked, "Is that the name of your old world?"

She nodded, and he asked with more curiosity, "Was there a problem with getting food there?"

"Magic . . . wasn't really a thing there. At all. A lot of food depended on shipping routes, fair weather, and access. The storms and fires were getting worse every year from pollution. We also didn't have healing magic, so when new viruses would break out that we didn't have cures for . . ." She gave a heavy sigh before continuing. "Well, a lot of people died when that would happen, and food supplies would become disrupted . . . which would cause more people to go hungry. That's not even mentioning the problems of just affording food in some areas. We couldn't just magic away the problems . . ." She trailed off, not wanting to talk about it further and spoil the mood even more.

"I'm sorry. That sounds terrible," Dazien said apologetically. He then asked hesitantly, "Did you leave behind any family?" She shook her head in the negative, and he prompted, "Friends?"

Phoenix just shrugged and didn't expect the next question.

"Lovers?"

She scoffed at the idea. "Yeah, right. Even if I was interested, there was never an opportunity for that for me. Before I arrived in this world, I had been practically bedridden my whole life."

The two men looked at her in surprise, and she gave them a look as though it should have been obvious. "No magic, remember? No god of healing on my planet to cure a building full of sick kids. I just happened to be one of them."

"That's horrible," he replied, looking shocked by the idea.

"It was," she agreed, then smiled softly and added wistfully, "I could never have imagined being somewhere like here, eating cake with a couple of teammates after hours of fighting."

"I'm not sure you could call getting our hides handed to us 'fighting,'" the warrior replied.

Phoenix chuckled, then took another bite of her pastry and sipped the warm coffee. She was just enjoying the moment for a bit as the group fell into a comfortable silence.

"So," Dazien started, and she almost laughed at his insatiable curiosity that was giving her own a run for its money. "No more questions about your old world." He then asked a bit hesitantly, "Can we ask how you got that Soul Mark on your chest?"

She froze as she registered the question, then slowly looked up at the pair, not sure if she should start panicking. "You saw?"

They both nodded, and Uriel explained awkwardly, "Your shirt was kind of destroyed by that attack. When we went to check on you . . . it was kind of hard *not* to notice."

Phoenix set her coffee down, thinking through her response as she looked out the window. Her teammates didn't interrupt her thoughts as they waited patiently, busying themselves with eating and drinking as the snow continued to fall outside.

Finally, she explained delicately, "I was given a divine quest, and the gods felt it their prerogative to mark my soul with their personal stamp of approval. And before you ask, no, I don't want to go into more details about it." She softened slightly and added, "Not right now, at least."

"Fair enough," Dazien acquiesced with a nod. She found herself grateful that he at least seemed to know when to back down from a touchy subject.

Then a thought came to her. "Do you have a Soul Mark? I heard the others talk about how Warrior favors you."

"Ah, well. Not like that," Dazien said a bit awkwardly. "Most people *say* I have Warrior's favor because he has seen to a lot of my training personally, which is *not* common. However, he has not graced me with a mark like that," he said, gesturing to where hers lay hidden beneath her shirt before continuing. "I'm not considered one of the Chosen and Soul Marks signifying that are extremely rare. I've honestly only seen one other before from a single god. To be Chosen by five different deities is simply unheard of."

"Who else did you meet with a mark?" she asked curiously. She was interested in meeting someone else like her.

"Ah," Dazien said, looking down at his plate with awkward resolve, "it's not really my place to say." He looked back up and added pointedly, "Just as I would not say anything about yours to others."

"Oh, right," she said, mentally berating herself and waving the question away. "Of course. I was just curious about someone who might have gone through something similar to me. It's fine, though. I appreciate you keeping my secrets . . . I think I actually trust you more now for *not* telling me."

Silence fell again, threatening to become awkward this time, but Uriel surprised both of them by asking her, "Who is Robert Frost?"

Phoenix grinned at the change of topic. "A poet. He wrote a particularly famous poem that reminds me of you. I'm not sure you would like it, though."

The Mage shrugged and gestured for her to continue, so she did, taking on the slightly singsong voice of recitation. "'Some say the world will end in fire, some say in ice. From what I've tasted of desire, I hold with those who favor fire. But if it had to perish twice, I think I know enough of hate to say that for destruction ice is also great, and would suffice.'"

Dazien shook his head in amusement. "I can see why you would think of Uriel, but it's a rather depressing poem, is it not?"

She shrugged. "I like to think of it in more abstract terms. I mean, in the literal sense, sure, fire and ice can destroy the world, and probably will in the end. But when he equates fire to desire and ice to hate, I think it describes a bit of our nature as people. If we become too extreme in either our apathy or greed, we will destroy ourselves. Though, I think I agree that I'd rather burn from chasing my desires than freeze from a heart full of hate."

They both stared at her for a moment before the amethyst warrior shook his head again with a soft chuckle. "That's a rather philosophical interpretation."

Phoenix shrugged again. "It might not be an accurate one, but I had a lot of time to read and think before monsters and magic kinda took over my life."

"Monsters and magic do that," Uriel said, and the companions laughed at the truth of it.

Phoenix was watching Paul pace around her dorm room while trying to explain that he wasn't abandoning her. It was almost adorable how much he seemed to be fretting over it.

"I should hopefully be back in a week. Two at most," Paul said as he handed her a tiny, five-sided, rune-etched metal rod about the length of her finger. "This will let you into my home should an emergency arise. You *can* stay out of trouble for a few days, yes?"

She rolled her eyes at him and said sarcastically, "Yes, Dad."

He huffed at her. "With your tendencies, I wouldn't be surprised if you died on a mission while I was gone."

"Your confidence in my survival abilities is reassuring as always," she continued, laughing internally at how flustered he seemed to be, completely unlike when they first met. Phoenix wondered if it was a result of becoming closer as a student and Mentor, or if her last near-death experience was actually much closer than she had thought, and he was truly worried about her survival without him there to shove a healing potion into her.

"I'll be fine," she tried to reassure him. "I have my party now, and we're basically just planning to train all week in anticipation of the blood moon. Dazien mentioned that we'll be stationed in Tulimeir rather than an outlying town or out patrolling the tundra, which I suspect you had something to do with," she hinted with a pointed look.

"I might as well take advantage of the benefits my position gives," he replied unapologetically.

"Sounds a bit corrupt for someone so focused on purifying things."

Phoenix realized she made a mistake somehow when he abruptly turned to stare at her; she wasn't quite sure what she had said that seemed to put him on edge. She returned his gaze with confusion and asked, "What?"

"Nothing," he said gruffly after a moment, then added, "it's not corruption. I simply requested that you be kept close to the city to accommodate your training. It's not like I bribed an official to chain you here."

"I guess if you were going to bribe them to do anything, it would be to keep yourself near me?"

Paul shook his head. "No. The Soul Reapers are too much of a threat to go unchecked and unchallenged. If this Rift I'm going to is detonated, it will likely wipe out a few nearby villages, aside from disrupting the overall magical ecosystem of the area. I'm not going because the AOA ordered me to; I'm going because the enemy needs to be stopped."

Phoenix nodded, more subdued by the thought of destruction on that large of a scale. "I'll try my best to stay safe," she replied softly, matching his sincerity.

Then she pulled out the small Flame of Life trinket and lifted it for him to see. "I got this as a quest reward. I, um, that is . . . you can hold onto it if you want to make sure I'm staying safe."

Paul stared at the object in her hand for a moment before meeting her eyes and giving a rare smile. "I would appreciate that."

She nodded and offered it out for him to take, which he obligingly took, then held out his own hand with his palm up.

When she raised a questioning eyebrow, he gave a soft chuckle and took her hand, explaining, "The tip here is to prick your finger with. That will bond it to you so it can track your status."

Phoenix scrunched her nose at the idea but nodded and pushed her finger to the very pointy, decorative-looking piece at the top of it. She watched as the few drops of blood trickled down into it, causing the tiny flame within to turn white and grow, filling the orb, while the pointy bit seemed to melt and vanish into it to no longer prick anything else.

"Thank you, young one. Stay safe while I'm gone," he said, then simply patted her head before leaving the small dorm.

She finished getting herself ready and made her way to the departure area at the western gate. This was the same location where she had arrived for her trials, and it was where she usually spent the first two hours of her day now. The AOA had been eager to create a temporary mission for her to help with the logistics of portaling lower Caste parties to various locations around the tundra.

With portals being a rare high-value commodity, even her Crystal Caste one saw steady use every morning as parties of people departed for the day. Once those were done, she would meet up with her own party for training as the moon got more red-tinged with every passing night.

CHAPTER THIRTY-NINE

Words Are Weapons

Phoenix made her way through the Temple District, vaguely recalling the way Priest Lester had led her before to find the Temple of the Warrior, and only occasionally double-checking the map in her book. Her party had agreed to go there instead to train while Paul was away, and Phoenix found herself curious about how it might differ from the AOA room they had gone to.

As the only-slightly-lost Wayfarer turned a corner, she felt a brief sense of relief when the temple loomed before her once more, then promptly rolled her eyes at the group waiting near the entrance.

Dazien was sitting on top of a low wall with a woman on each side, laughing as he spoke animatedly to the others standing nearby, all dressed in the silvery training gear she had slowly been getting accustomed to. It seemed to be the most popular attire for sparring in, but she wished it did more for the cold.

Uriel leaned against the wall a few feet away from the group. She assumed that was so he wouldn't get entangled with them. Luckily, he was conveniently placed directly between herself and the entourage as she approached from the side of the building. Though she swore the directions she was following on the map should have brought her to the front.

Phoenix cautiously made her way closer, her anxiety increasing with every step as she aimed to hide behind her teammate's much larger form and use him as a social shield.

She overheard one of the cinderen girls with ashy gray hair, whom she vaguely recognized from their trials. This girl, who was currently one of the two sitting directly next to Dazien, said loudly, "Honestly, King, you should join our party. All we need is a good Defender, and with my family's connections, you know we'll get the *best* missions—not limited to being kept in the city and potentially stuck as a Watcher on the wall for days."

The amethyst warrior laughed. "Keeping vigil on the wall is an important duty. It's the city's most important line of defense against the dangers of the tundra."

"Being a Watcher is *boring*," said a runeforged man while leaning against the wall next to the first girl. Phoenix recognized this one as Franz from their assessment, and he continued with a sneer, "It might as well be a *punishment* mission. There's no *adventure* to be had!"

The group laughed in agreement, and Phoenix slowed a bit. She turned on her blurring shadows with her Dark Aura ability and held it tightly around herself to try to remain less noticeable. Phoenix started to feel guilty, wondering if she had hurt her new teammates' careers and reputation simply by joining their party. She would need to have another talk with Paul when he got back about interfering with what missions they could go on, Mentor privileges or not.

The first girl spoke up again, sounding more adamant than before. "Seriously, King. We could go right now and have you added to our party roster."

The pushy behavior of the young woman rankled Phoenix, and she immediately wanted to avoid any kind of interaction with her. Silently, she slipped next to Uriel, removing the shadows once his body acted as the shield instead.

The Mage looked down at her with a raised eyebrow, but she just shook her head and stayed silent beside him. She was grateful that he resumed his watch, content with not asking questions.

Dazien smiled indulgently at the pushy cinderen woman but shook his head. "I am honored by the invitation, Noble Murinah, but I already have my own party that I am quite pleased with so far."

"Is it true that by teaming up with that pale human girl, you were able to get training from the Blade of Pure Wrath himself?" one of the other groupies asked, and Phoenix felt her brow raise in surprise at the moniker she could only assume referred to her Mentor. She immediately wanted to go ask him how he got something that outrageous in the first place.

"I guess that would make sense why you would include someone like her," another runeforged said with a laugh. "I heard that all she was good for is running around."

"Is she like a glorified Siva, portaling you around and carrying your stuff?" one of the cinderen asked, and the group laughed at the mental image. Phoenix felt her cheeks redden in embarrassment.

During her time in the city, she learned of the avals called Sivatherium, or "Siva" for short, which were the common pack animals used around the world, similar to horses or donkeys from Earth. They looked like a mix between a moose and a giraffe, with a long neck and legs, a stumpy tail, and large silver antlers. The creature's fur was mostly white with little silver spots all over it and orbs like quicksilver for eyes.

She had instantly fallen in love with the gentle avals but recognized the insult for what it was. They didn't see her as worth anything more than carrying the bags . . . not a *real* Adventurer.

"Miss Fraser is a valued member of my party," Dazien said, a bit firmer than he normally addressed others. "She has already proven her worth in combat and has talents that I daresay are even greater than my own."

"I doubt that," Murinah said bitterly, "who could compare to someone destined to be a king such as yourself, who is even being trained by a god?"

"Perhaps he meant talents *outside* of adventuring," Franz said with another sneer, then gave a twisted grin. "She does have a sort of *exotic* appeal to her. Tell us, King, is she even paler under her clothes? I bet it would only take you a few words to get her to bow down for you."

The young warrior's expression went dark, but Uriel's voice rose above the chatter and startled everyone present. "Daze!"

The whole group turned to look at the Mage, and she wanted to disappear into the shadows altogether. Uriel surprised her by gripping her hand and pulling her along next to him. To her horror, he walked away from the safety of the half-wall and towards the entrance to the temple, which lay beyond the gathering.

Dazien looked stricken as he seemed to realize that she overheard their conversation, and Uriel paused as he reached the Defender's place perched on the wall. Uriel was tall enough to stare eye-to-eye with him before stating simply, "We'll be waiting inside." Then he continued leading her into the temple.

Uriel didn't say anything else as he led her up a few floors and to a smaller sparring room with a padded floor and an assortment of weapons on one of the walls. She was actually grateful for the silence at that moment, unsure how to react to the gossip. The idea that they thought of her like that made her sick to her stomach.

Her companion walked over to the side and grabbed two practice swords before returning to her, lifting one towards her in a silent invitation.

She stared at it for a long moment before she took it, her awareness feeling distant. The sword in her hand made her idly remember that she had been mostly focused on training with daggers, and she hadn't really tried her other forms yet.

Uriel took his place in the center of the mat and waited patiently. He was already clothed for sparring as the others had been, and she sent her cloak, dress, and boots into her collection, stepping out onto the small arena in just her matching silver training gear she wore underneath. The laughter of the group still rang in her head, and unwanted tears pricked at the corners of her eyes.

The movement of Uriel's sword entering an on-guard position distracted her enough from her thoughts to raise her own wooden sword in response. It wasn't until he tapped his own sword to hers, trying to feel her out, that she actually registered what he wanted.

As her mossy eyes met the ember ones of the cinderen, something inside of her seemed to be released. She swung her sword in a downward arc, which he met with his own horizontal block, and he actually *smiled* at her. Smiled! She had only seen a slight smirk before, but there were teeth showing and everything.

He parried and returned her attack, which she responded to in kind. Slowly, the movements began coming more naturally, as if they had only been waiting for her to call upon them.

They continued trading blows back and forth. As they felt out each other's skill level, the pace increased slowly, becoming faster and more complex as they both began to push themselves.

Her mind was no longer on the petty groupies, the burdens she thought she was bringing to her party, or her Mentor's doubts about her survivability; it was only filled with fighting—with forms, counters, parries, footwork, breathing, thrusting, and slashing. For once, in all her weeks of training, she wasn't thinking about anything other than the moment she was experiencing.

Then Uriel overextended, and she took advantage to pull him off balance. He fell to the mat, and she turned to place the tip of her practice sword at his throat before he could try to get up again. They were both sweating and breathing heavily, but Uriel still smiled at her, and she slowly smiled in return.

Clapping coming from the doorway startled the pair, and Phoenix automatically lifted the sword in the direction of the potential threat.

Dazien halted his clapping and raised his hands defensively before saying with a sheepish grin, "I can understand now why Warrior favors you as his Chosen. That was impressive, my lady."

Phoenix dropped the tip of her sword and replied sourly, "I'm not *your* lady, Dazien." She then reached out an arm to help Uriel up, which he accepted.

The gemite cautiously walked forward, lowering his hands. "Forgive me, Phoenix. I hope you know that what the others were saying was out of line and not reflective of how I see you."

She gave a huff of annoyance and said, "I get it. Really, I do."

Uriel returned to Dazien's side near the room's entrance, and she started walking over to the wall of weapons where the Mage had gotten the swords originally as she continued, venting, "They all want you in their party, and they think I don't deserve to be in it, or something dumb like that. I'm the new kid, so I get the brunt of their angst. You don't have to try to apologize."

Dazien caught her arm to stop her movement and drag her attention to him. "I do, though. You've done nothing to deserve those words."

"You're not the one who said them," she pointed out, pulling her arm out of his grasp. "You can't control what other people say. You can only control your own actions, and right now, your actions have shown me that you'll defend me from monsters with your shield and from your other *friends* with your words."

Phoenix picked up another wooden sword, testing its weight, as she added, "There's nothing more I could ask from you."

The warrior's brow furrowed as he asked in confusion. "Then why does it seem like you're angry with me?"

She paused, contemplating his words. She *was* angry. She wasn't exactly sure when that had happened, and honestly, it felt rather new to her. She had experienced frustration, fear, annoyance, despair, but anger . . . she couldn't exactly remember the last time she felt it. She didn't think she was angry at *him*, though.

"I don't know," she answered softly, then turned away from the Defender and returned back to the center of the mat, wielding a wooden sword in each hand. Then she took a steadying breath, calling to mind the meditation technique her tome had imparted on her, and began to dance.

$

"Daze!"

Uriel's voice had taken Dazien by surprise when he looked up from the group around him on the wall outside of Warrior's temple. His heart sank when he finally noticed Phoenix's presence next to his best friend. Her face was red, and she looked as though she might cry if she glanced his way.

"I'll take her to our usual room to let off some steam," his partner said silently in his mind, the disapproval palpable. *"She doesn't need to listen to your noble* friends *degrade her like that, and frankly, I don't want to listen to it either."*

"You know I don't either," he mentally replied using his ability. He hated it when his different friend groups collided like this, but Franz's words were on a different level than normal and completely unacceptable.

Uriel's eyes flickered to the others in the group before he replied with a simple challenge: *"Prove it."* Then he added out loud for everyone else's sake, "We'll be waiting inside."

His partner's dismissal returned Dazien's attention to the current situation he found himself in, and he remained silent as he watched his party enter the temple. How was he supposed to *prove* that he didn't approve of what was being said? He already said he didn't; wasn't that proof enough?

His thoughts were drawn back to the people around him as one of the girls snickered, "Did you see her face? It was almost as red as her ridiculous curls."

The others chuckled, and Dazien felt conflicted. He thought her hair was interesting. The runeforged had mostly dark hair, worn in braids or shaved close to the scalp, while the cinderen mostly had silken, jet-black hair or ashy, gray coils that seemed to defy gravity. He had seen the occasional human, voxen, or elf in the city, a small minority that usually lived in the International District, and they usually had similar dark locks with the occasional exception.

However, he had never seen hair like hers before. The large, untamable curls changed every time he saw them and seemed to constantly rebel against the braid she tried restraining them in. It wasn't that he disliked the other types of hair; it was just *different* . . . like his own.

He dropped down from the wall, intent on joining his party, but his attention was brought back again to the group when Murinah called out to him, "King, you should just forget those two. You are so far above them. You shouldn't let them chain you down if you really want to be royalty someday."

The other girl on the wall spoke up again. "She couldn't even take a *joke*. How does she expect to stand up to a monster? She looked like she was going to cry."

Franz spoke up again with a smirk. "I don't know. The tears might add to her value in regard to those other *talents* King mentioned. They say it's the quiet ones that are often the craziest in—"

Dazien didn't even register his body moving until his fist collided with the man's jaw and sent him to the ground. The group went silent as he said in a voice that sent a shiver down their spines as his own body trembled with cold fury, "Do *not* speak of my companions like that *ever* again. They are not *objects* for you to measure the value of, nor are their private proclivities for you to judge. Next time I hear disparaging words about them, it won't be my fist that silences you."

Without another look at the others, he turned and stalked into the temple to find his party. He made his way to the room that he and Uriel usually took and had planned to train with Phoenix in. When he finally arrived, he heard the familiar clack of practice swords striking one another on the other side of the door that he very carefully opened so as not to cause a critical distraction.

The Warrior King was stunned by what he saw. Phoenix and Uriel were exchanging blows, moving faster with each strike. He hadn't known that Phoenix could even wield a sword since he had only ever seen her use daggers before. Her long braid kept losing curls as she moved, and he found himself smiling at the wildness of it.

Then he noticed that Uriel was *smiling*. That was odd. He had known the man for seven years and thought he could count on his fingers how often he had seen a genuine smile on that face.

He wondered if he should ask his companion about that later. What about this woman made Uriel smile like that? Then he saw the Mage slip up, and Phoenix took advantage of it. He clapped at the display and was taken aback when she raised her sword at him as though he was to receive the next beating.

Dazien raised his hands, wondering if she hadn't realized it was him. He knew how battle energy could sometimes cloud one's perception, and he tried to give a reassuring smile. "I can understand now why Warrior favors you as his Chosen. That was impressive, my lady."

He was relieved when she dropped her sword but then concerned again at her next words.

"I'm not *your* lady, Dazien."

He winced at that, wondering if she thought that he had been telling others that she was his, especially considering what his now-former-friend had said.

He tried to apologize, but she rebuffed him and walked away towards the weapon racks. He tried to get her full attention, but she brushed him off once more, saying she didn't blame him. However, her attitude and body language seemed to be saying the opposite of her words as she grabbed a second practice sword.

Feeling his frustration rise, he couldn't help asking, "Then why does it seem like you're angry with me?"

She paused and got a far-off look before saying softly, "I don't know."

As she ignored him and went towards the center of the mat, he was about to follow after her when Uriel caught his gaze and shook his head, gesturing to join him off to the side.

Dazien clenched his fists, not wanting to just let things stay like this, but he joined his friend. He was about to ask what the Mage wanted when the movement from the center of the room caught his attention. He felt his jaw drop as he recognized the meditative Dual Sword Dance of the Weapon Wielding Warrior.

He had only seen it performed once before by a visiting Cleric of the Warrior, but the memory had been seared into his mind. Watching Phoenix perform the fluid movements now in front of him had him completely entranced.

The amethyst warrior couldn't tear his gaze away, but he asked his friend quietly, "Did you know she could use the sword?"

"No," the smooth voice responded, "I had thought to teach her some, to get her mind off . . . things."

"Thank you," he said promptly, "I didn't know she was there. I—" He paused, trying to collect his thoughts as his eyes continued following the twirling swords and Phoenix's fiery hair. "You asked me to prove I don't agree with them, so I don't think I'm going to spend more time with them."

He barely registered Uriel looking towards him from the periphery of his vision and continued to explain. "If I can only control my own actions as she said, then I don't want to surround myself with people who think it . . . *funny* to disparage my companions. I understand enough to know that words are weapons in their own right."

Uriel nodded. "Sometimes words aren't enough of a shield or balm." His friend gestured towards Phoenix's dance. "Sometimes actions are required."

"I'm starting to realize that words of support mean little without the actions to back them." He gave a slight grimace. "That's probably why I punched him for his words."

Uriel gave him a surprised look, then smirked and said simply, "Good."

"Do you think she'll forgive me?" Dazien asked, gesturing towards the woman now deep in the meditative trance of the dance.

"You? Yes. Herself? I'm not so sure," his partner responded thoughtfully.

Dazien finally looked away from the dance at that point to meet his friend's gaze in confusion. "Herself? She didn't do anything wrong."

Uriel shrugged. "I don't believe that's how she sees things. I think she and I share this trait as well."

"*You* didn't do anything wrong either," he said adamantly for what must have been the millionth time.

His partner just shrugged once more and didn't speak further on the subject. Instead, Uriel went over to the other side of the mat where he wouldn't interfere with Phoenix and began his own version of sword meditation that Dazien had taught him years ago.

He crossed his arms over his chest as he turned back to continue watching Phoenix, muttering to himself, "Maybe I *am* drawn to the silently chaotic types."

CHAPTER FORTY

A Red Moon Rises

You know, I thought an Adventuring Guild in a magical world would be more like a bulletin board system where people just grab whatever job they wanted to try and then get paid when they return with the monster's head or something," Phoenix began describing as she and her two newest companions sat in a small conference room similar to the one she and Uriel had first filled out forms in after they met. A folder with a small stack of papers sat in the middle of their table as Dazien handled the initial perusal and distribution between them.

"Why do I get sent to the world with all the forms and paperwork involved?" she complained, signing yet another piece of bleached white paper and wondering where they even got the materials for this glossy type.

Dazien chuckled and said, "They say it's to maintain the organization's records of accomplishments to better negotiate deals with the cities they are stationed in, but really, it's to help keep stupid kids like us from trying to bite off more than we can chew."

"Wait, an organization that actually *cares* about its employees?" she asked in mock surprise. "Where I'm from, those were few and far between."

"Nobody likes having to deal with grieving families claiming negligence or foul play on their part," the warrior said solemnly, then looked at her curiously. "And I thought you were too sick to get a job before?"

"Yeah, but people loved sharing their horror stories online," she said with a shrug. "I read about a company who was so brutal about increasing productivity that the employees couldn't even go to the toilet if they wanted to meet their quotas."

The would-be king looked thoughtful for a moment before clarifying, "'Online' was that place everyone could see at the same time through their own personal Knowledge Tablet, right?"

Phoenix nodded as she signed another form. Then, she snapped her head up to stare at the gemite. "Wait, what's a Knowledge Tablet?"

"You've seen them before," Dazien said as he handed a form over to Uriel and added to the silent man. "This one needs you to put down your temporary position and sign next to it, then give it to Phoenix to add hers under yours."

The cinderen nodded, and Dazien turned back to her to continue his previous explanation. "Allan Trayvious had one to read the AOA information about all of us and take notes when we took our trials."

She recalled the runeforged man with intricate braids weaved into a crosshatch pattern close to his scalp and vaguely remembered the glowing stone tablet he had carried around for much of their excursion. "What exactly does it do?"

"Just that. It stores written information in a convenient fashion that can be navigated through runes on the edge and touching motions. They are insanely cost prohibitive though," he added, trying to tone down the excitement visibly growing on her face. "I'm sure the one Mister Trayvious had was loaned by the AOA and likely only one of a handful in the city. I only know of noble Houses and a couple of high-end merchants having them."

Phoenix frowned in disappointment. "Why are they so expensive? Is it hard to make or something?"

"*Very*," he emphasized. "Aside from the skill requirement, which usually needs some kind of crafting-specific passive ability, the materials are also hard to acquire as that particular stone has only been found in a small region far from here."

"Can't they just use a different type of stone?" she asked in confusion, taking the proffered form that Uriel had finished with. "The Artifice I know seems pretty flexible on material requirements."

Dazien sighed as if this much talking and explaining things was taxing even *his* normal limits of conversation, which, in Phoenix's limited experience, was quite high, since the man seemed to know and talk with *everyone* they came across. "You said you learned Artifice crafting from a Knowledge Tome, right?"

When she nodded, he continued, "That was likely composed of the simplest recipes and examples while giving you the more important foundational understanding of *how* to create a magic item. This is great for someone who isn't a dedicated Crafter Caster, which you would *need* to be in order to create something as sophisticated as a Knowledge Tablet or be a century or two old with a lifetime of experience.

"The more general Artifice magic is meant for Mundanes to make simpler everyday items like glowstones or self-cleaning rugs. Maybe even get a bit braver with it and make a fancy friendship bracelet that vibrates when the other person touches theirs to let them know they want to meet up or something."

"Why do you need to be brave to make something like that?" she asked, instantly thinking of making some herself as the pieces to the recipe floated around her mind.

He paused and looked at her seriously. "Because if you get crafting things *wrong*, they have a tendency to explode. Especially the further into the process you get."

Phoenix met his gaze, recognizing the warning. Then, after a moment of thinking about it, she shrugged and said, "Meh, I can heal myself," and signed her name on the form in front of her.

Uriel chuckled, and Dazien shot him a *look* before trying to redirect the conversation. "Let's just finish getting these forms done and go see what missions are available for us in the city. We can also check if they have our assignment for the blood moon after getting these forms into their system."

"System? Like a computer network?" she asked in even more confusion.

"More like a system of administrative functionaries that try to organize everyone as efficiently as possible," he said. "'Computer' is the name of those boxes that can see the 'Online' place, right?"

"Right," she confirmed quickly, waving off the question to ask her own. "So they just have people planning everything and mapping assignments out on, like, paper or wall boards?"

He paused, then added, "Well, they do have a BEL."

"A bell? How does ringing a bell help at all?"

"Not that kind of bell," Dazien replied with a shake of his head and spelled out the word for her. "B.E.L. She's one of the golems made for the city of Tulimeir by the founder of House Teras. They have insanely good memory and organizational skills and even some crafting abilities similar to a Caster. You've actually met one of them already," the gemite added, "the merchant I took you to before was a BEL that simply deals with acquisitions, mostly helping businesses determine efficient supply trades with one another."

"I thought she was a cinderen," Phoenix said in confusion, trying to picture the woman she had only met briefly to offload her loot.

"I would assume that was the goal when the Lady Teras of the time designed them, hoping they wouldn't be off-putting to the people they assist," Dazien postulated with a shrug, and tapped the form in front of her. "Let's focus on signing these so we can get out of here."

"What is this one even for?" she asked, holding up the one she had already finished signing that listed all of their roles.

"It's to declare our temporary party to accept missions with the concept being that we're looking to add additional members or trying out a new team composition and will be following it up later with an official party declaration form," he replied automatically. He then stopped suddenly and stared up at her with wide eyes before asking incredulously, "Wait, you *signed* that without even reading what it was?"

Phoenix slowly looked between him and the form with matching wide eyes. She couldn't understand what his behavior was about, so she asked, "Is it required for us to get missions or payment?"

"Yes, but—"

"Then it doesn't matter if I read it, only that I signed it," she pointed out, "otherwise, none of these other forms matter, right?"

Dazien clenched his teeth as he replied, "Yes, but—"

"Plus, *you* read them. Which means there's probably nothing malicious or anything, right? Unless you're suggesting that I can't trust your intent with something as simple as a non-magical contract?" She paused and gave the form another wary glance before clarifying, "This *isn't* magical, right?"

Dazien groaned and dropped his head into his hands as though hit with a sudden migraine, and Uriel chuckled in quiet amusement.

Phoenix walked alongside Uriel as they followed Dazien through the southern International District of Tulimeir and into one of the taller skyscrapers near the south tip of the walls. The cinderen gave a shake of his head as a smirk tugged at the corners of his mouth.

Phoenix questioned in a whisper to him, "Where is he taking us?"

"It's a surprise," Dazien replied over his shoulder and walked to the double doors. As they passed over the runes engraved on the floor, Phoenix could hear the hiss of steam that she had become increasingly familiar with. The sound was a ubiquitous presence in the city, and the doors opened automatically to let them pass.

"We're pretty far south," she noted with a bit of worry as the warrior led them to a glass lift much like the one at the AOA building that seemed to be the standard form of vertical travel here. "I have to get up early for my portal duties. I don't really want to be out too late, so can we get the food to go?"

"We won't be that late," the gemite assured, touching the rune for the destination floor as more steam hissed quietly. "I still have some rides left on my Quickpass. You can take the Greenline home."

"Greenline?" she asked in confusion as the lift carried them upward.

Dazien raised a brow at her and asked, "Has nobody told you about the Quicksteam? Have you just been walking all over the city?"

"Um, yes? They told me I'm not allowed to just portal around the city unless it's to specific designated areas."

He rubbed at his temples and muttered, "Some Mentor," before explaining. "The Quicksteam is a mass transport system to get around the city quickly. It has different colored routes that people will refer to as 'lines,' Greenline, Silverline, Redline, etcetera." He paused and seemed to change his mind as he said, "You know what? Why don't we just show you later when we take you home? We can get you your own pass and everything."

Phoenix smiled and nodded. "I would like that, thanks." She had never been able to ride in a subway or on a train, and this sounded very similar to that concept.

"To be clear, though, when they said only portal to designated areas, that should include your private dwelling. So, you can just portal home tonight if it gets late. Portals are so rare that I forget that's an option for you. The city rules, however, just don't want portalists popping into the street and messing up traffic or into a business and scaring the patrons."

"Ah, that's a relief. While it's been nice to walk around and see all the new things, sometimes I just want to get home and sleep," she replied with a chuckle.

"For now, it's time for Daze's favorite restaurant," Uriel said as he tilted his head towards the glass door, and the lift slowed as it prepared to stop.

Phoenix was distracted then by the sight of a cozy rooftop restaurant that overlooked the city below and could even see the tundra beyond the walls nearby. Tables of various sizes but mostly on the smaller end were spread around with dark satin-like cloth covering them, and candles in a variety of colors provided a dim light that was supplemented by the stars shining above as the night was beginning. Visku was already shining, and its constant blue light added to the magical atmosphere of the area.

"Ah, Mister Smithson! It is good to see you again. It's been some time since your last visit. I assume your trials went smoothly?" the host asked as he stood at a small podium near the lift when their group walked off the metal platform. He was a human man with a lighter tan complexion, which Paul and most of the other humans she had seen so far had, and warm brown hair swept back neatly.

"Of course, Mister Pratamo," Dazien answered smoothly, seeming to turn up his charm factor. She had started to recognize that he had a habit of doing it when talking with others aside from her and Uriel.

"In fact, we just finished our temporary team sign-up and got our assignments earlier today, which we've come to celebrate, and *this*," the amethyst warrior said as he gestured towards her, "is my newest party member, Phoenix Fraser. Phoenix, I'd like you to meet Hugo Pratamo. He's the owner of this fine establishment, Belladonna."

"A pleasure to meet any friend of Mister Smithson," the host said with a slight bow, hand over his heart, as she had seen others do in greeting. Then he asked, "Are you new to the city?"

She nodded as she mimicked the small bow in return and glanced towards Dazien.

He must have seen the slight panic in her eyes as he answered for her, "She only arrived a couple of months ago, but she impressed me so much during the trials that I just *had* to get her to join my party as its Supporter."

The owner raised his brow in surprise as he said, "High praise indeed," then turned to smile at her. "Well, let me show you to a table. I'm sure Mister Smithson and Mister Karislian can guide you in your menu selections, but we just received a fresh batch of Silverfin Sashin this morning, which I highly recommend."

He led them to a table near the eastern edge of the building, and Phoenix felt her anxiety rise as the gazes of the people already eating and chatting glanced in her direction. When they all sat, Dazien took it upon himself to explain all of the different food options to her as she had trouble recognizing any of them.

"Silverfin Sashin is a rich, fatty type of fish from the warmer waters to the southeast," the gemite explained after having ordered some manarin wine. "I've never tried it before, but I've heard salivating stories about it."

"Huh," she responded absently, trying hard to ignore any stares from the other patrons by glancing over the slick paper. "What's a sansprab?"

"A type of aval common to the Epa Toivo Desert region," Uriel replied promptly. "They have three legs on opposite sides of their rounded body with a hard shell covered in wispy fur."

"So, they're furry crabs?" she asked, trying to smooth down her curls that she thought might be behaving a bit more wild than normal and causing more attention towards her.

"What they are is delicious," responded Dazien with a grin. "I might have that myself, though the Sashin is a rarer opportunity."

He paused, watching her carefully as she tried fixing her green dress to be a bit more presentable, not having expected the fancier setting where people would be observing her. When he didn't continue and a frown formed on his smooth features, she asked, "What? Does it really seem that bad?"

He quirked a brow and inquired, "What do you think seems bad?"

"My outfit . . . and hair . . . and well, everything," she explained, gesturing to herself as though it was obvious.

Uriel joined Dazien with a deepening frown, and the Defender replied, "Phoenix, you look perfect." Then he flushed slightly and added, "Perfectly acceptable for the setting." He glanced around at the other guests and pointed out, "Besides, nobody is looking."

"They keep glancing at me," she said softly, ashamed to have to point it out to the men who had treated her like she wasn't any different from them. "Everywhere I go in this city, people stare. I'm different. I don't look like them and stand out for it."

Dazien's smile softened as he asked, "Is that such a bad thing? Standing out, I mean."

When she looked up to meet his amethyst eyes, he gestured with a hand towards his own dark purple locks with his matching crystalline nails on display as well. She swallowed, remembering that he was like her in how different they were from others. However, he had never seemed bothered by any of the attention, and people didn't seem to be staring at him *all* the time like she felt they were doing to her.

"I don't want to sound dismissive," the gemite continued gently, "but perhaps they're not as concerned with your presence as you believe them to be." He nodded towards the rest of the room. "Just look for yourself."

She actually chanced looking around and found that he was correct; nobody was looking near their table at all. They were laughing and talking, eating delicious food, and drinking intoxicating liquids in a variety of playful colors. Nobody cared about the small group of outsiders at the edge of the roof that they likely assumed were enjoying their own dinner.

Phoenix gave a soft smile and felt herself relax as she whispered, "Thanks, Daze."

Her temporary party leader smiled brightly and gestured back to the menu. "You don't ever need to thank me for stating the truth. Let's just focus on what to eat and get—"

His words cut off as they all felt a wave of mana ripple through the air, and everyone turned to look southeast, where the sensation had seemed to come from. There were audible gasps and people standing up to better gaze in the distance where the other moon was rising.

Phoenix found herself standing as well to watch Krafti slowly show its deep crimson light, washing the land in the color of spilled blood, which Visku's blue couldn't seem to override or even tint into a purple. Everything was turning red, and even she could recognize what was happening as she said in barely more than a whisper, "A red moon rises, blood will be spilled this night . . ."

"While you're not wrong," Dazien replied with his own breathless awe at the signal in the sky marking the start of the blood moon, "let us hope none of it belongs to the people we're meant to protect."

CHAPTER FORTY-ONE

Good Match

Dazien bid Phoenix goodnight and waved as she walked through her portal, which took her straight back to her dorm room. Dinner had been delicious despite the dramatic interruption of the blood moon officially beginning and washing everything in a red light that made his silvery fish a much bloodier tint than it should have been.

Unlike Phoenix's convenient method of returning home, Uriel and he were left to walk through the crimson-lit streets of the International District to their apartment. Despite being late in the night, the streets weren't empty as people hurried to their destinations, some with armor and obviously going to their new stations, while others simply wanted to avoid Krafti's ominous light.

"We're going to be busy for a while now, aren't we?" Uriel asked him quietly as they walked side by side down the street.

He nodded. "They said ten months at least, maybe a year. The estimates are difficult since they've never dealt with something like this before." He glanced up at the scarlet moon. "It feels like the end of the world, even though I know it's not."

"It might be," his pessimistic partner pointed out, "our cities weren't built for this much time, and the Soul Reapers are an entirely foreign threat. The entire world will lose a lot of people."

Dazien frowned. "Probably," he agreed and added, "but we can hope those we care about remain safe and do our best to protect them. Do you want to visit the orphanage again before our first shift tomorrow?"

"They might appreciate seeing their king before we get overwhelmed with missions," Uriel pointed out. "You and Jennica still haven't made up yet."

"I'm not sure anything I say to her will make her forgive me for becoming an Adventurer," Dazien said with a sigh. "Perhaps you'll have a better chance of placating—"

His words cut off as he noticed a woman standing outside of their apartment building, his frown deepening when he realized who it was.

"When did you tell Murinah where we lived?" Uriel silently asked over their mental chat.

"I didn't," he warily replied. *"It's been almost four years since I moved in with you, though. She was bound to find out eventually."*

"I know most people have an unhealthy level of interest in you," his partner said with a frown that matched his own. *"I'm even likely one of them,"* he softly admitted, *"but I don't like how she tries to claim you and pressure you all the time. The way she looks at you like . . ."*

"Like a treasure," Dazien finished for him before greeting the noblewoman aloud with as much casual aloofness as he could muster. "Noble Murinah, fancy meeting you here."

"Hello, King," the cinderen woman greeted in return, "sorry to visit your home like this, but you didn't stop by the Temple of the Warrior or Parent today, and I needed to talk with you."

"Are you sure she doesn't have some kind of tracking Spell on you?" Uriel unhelpfully distracted him with a mental question that he ignored because, frankly, he wasn't sure how this woman kept finding him.

"I was busy filling out the forms for my new party today," he said in an honest explanation, then gestured to the sky. "Perfect timing, all things considered."

She frowned at him. "New party? But I thought you'd be joining me—"

"I respectfully declined that invitation, Noble Murinah," he said firmly, having learned over the years not to let others try to decide things for him nor be submissive in his stances lest they walk all over him. "There is still too far a gap in our respective social standings for me to be comfortable with attaching myself to someone of your station. We've talked about this before."

"I know, but you and I both know that you belong among the nobility. Surely being attached to me in a more official capacity would help others see that and—"

"And assume that I seduced or conned my way into the good graces of a noble House," he pointed out . . . *again*. It was an old excuse he used to keep the clingier nobles off him without being rude or making it obvious that he simply didn't want to be claimed by them. "My stance on this hasn't changed. Besides, I like leading my own party and the members I have chosen."

Murinah glanced towards Uriel, who she rarely paid attention to after he had explained almost six years ago that the Mage was his right-hand man, and she had assumed that meant he was a lowly servant. She had always looked down on the peasantry, and it had always annoyed him, but she had made an exception for him and helped him over the years to learn the ways of the nobility that they couldn't teach him in school.

"And I assume he's your official Mage now?"

"You know he is," he pointed out. "I've been saying that for years."

She got an awkward look on her face before saying with rare hesitancy, "Perhaps . . . I mean, if you're *certain* about leading your own party . . . Maybe I could be your Supporter? You know I'm a stealth specialist and would be a great addition."

"*Wow. Dodged an arrow there,*" Uriel commented again, and Dazien was tempted to close the communication just so he wouldn't accidentally say the wrong thing to the noblewoman in front of them.

"I already have a Supporter," he answered, actually agreeing with Uriel's assessment of having a decent excuse. "You heard the others discussing her the other day in a rather disparaging manner, remember?"

"That strange girl with the portal?" Murinah clarified with a crinkled nose. "Isn't she a bit young for you?"

Dazien laughed at that and couldn't stop his retort. "Then aren't *I* a bit young for *you?*"

She flushed in embarrassment, a soft orange glow emanating from her cheeks—where a cinderen's molten blood betrayed their emotions. "You're almost twenty," she said in her defense. "Five years isn't that much older. Nobody would care in a decade anyways."

He nodded in agreement. "You're right. I'm just pointing out a small flaw in your logic. Phoenix isn't that much younger than I am. Age difference also matters less when talking about *party members*, which *is* what we're talking about, right?"

The glow in her cheeks became subtly brighter as she murmured, "Right. It's not like you would be *interested* in someone like her anyway."

Dazien frowned at that, wondering if she was trying to make fun of Phoenix's appearance like the others had. "What's that supposed to mean?"

"Well, she's like the complete opposite of everyone else you've been with before," she replied with a roll of her fiery red eyes.

Dazien gave a side-eyed glance at his partner, who adamantly refused to return his gaze. Uriel always seemed to dislike when his love life became the topic of conversation. Not much had actually changed in that regard recently, but he had a long history of romantic entanglements that were mostly made up of cinderen and runeforged.

He gave a smirk at the memories she conjured up and replied, "I'm fairly certain most people who know me understand that my tastes vary wildly. That said, Phoenix is just a party member and friend, one that I appreciate for both her skills and personality." He softened as he recalled her earlier anxiety in the restaurant over standing out from the crowd. "Plus, she has a unique perspective that's been hard for me to find in a companion."

"Unique perspective?"

He tugged at a tuft of his hair for emphasis. "Her red curls are as unique here as my amethyst locks," he explained, then gave a warm smile. "She's a good match for me."

§

Saiya Dewsong was clutching her twin sister's paw in her own as they tried to make their way back towards the entrance to the Reality Rift they currently found themselves lost in. The rest of their party had already been torn to shreds by the Sapphire Caste monsters that seemed even stronger than normal for their Caste.

They should never have agreed to separate from the group of Adventurers that had arrived from Tulim. That party had an Emerald Caster at least, despite them being a crafting Class, while their party of Toivoan locals only had a single Sapphire as their party leader, who was now very dead.

"It'll be okay," her sister said over her shoulder, "we can wait outside for reinforcements."

Saiya could sense the fear and anger in Rayna's Aura, a blessing of her own Perception power, and knew that her sister was trying to put on a brave front as she led them through the sweltering jungle that should have been composed of mostly Crystal Caste enemies, given the levels of ambient magic within the Rift.

She didn't think the blood moon that had begun the night before would have affected the interiors of the Reality Rift, but perhaps she had been mistaken about the bleed effect of the Rifts being only one-way.

The voxen yelped as one of her two tails caught on a branch, and her fear made her worry that it was the grasp of a monster catching up to devour her as well. Her Familiar beside her looked over, and she could sense his worry as well. She patted the back of the furry sansprab and said with as much comfort as she could while being half-dragged by Rayna, "I'm okay. We'll be safe soon."

Saiya glanced back up at her twin and asked, "Are you angry at me for not being able to heal the others fast enough?"

Rayna snorted derisively. "No. I'm angry that they were idiots and thought we could fight above-Caste like that. The others refused to listen to your warnings about their strength, and now we're running for our lives in this horribly humid place."

"At least we still have our lives," she murmured and could sense the frustration as her sister turned to look at her again.

"For now. We should be grateful they died fighting in here instead of in the middle of the village where their clan would be at risk for their foolishness." The pugilist placed clawed hands on slim hips, sweat coating the smooth chestnut skin of an exposed midriff as she continued berating the fallen. "We warned them about rash choices resulting in death. Our clan was a prime example of what happens when a leader is foolish and arrogant enough not to think long-term."

Saiya shrunk in on herself a little, her long-furred ears falling to either side of her face, as she said, "Nobody could have predicted that swarm in the middle of the day within the camp."

Rayna almost growled as the anger flared hotter, "No, but our dear leader didn't need to be so *distracted* at the time."

She looked away and simply nodded in agreement. She reached out to hold her sister's paw once more for comfort when a rustle sounded from the trees behind them. Rayna grabbed her to throw her forward and act as her temporary Defender. As the Sapphire Caste Pantula monster came into view, she yelled, "Run!"

Her twin nodded, the fear once more infusing their Auras as the voxen spun and grabbed her paw to pull her along. Her Familiar made the choice not to follow, attempting to buy them time to flee.

"Sandy!" she screamed as the furry crab, about the size of a large dog, raised its front two legs and swelled up to make itself look even bigger. Tears streamed down Saiya's face as one of the spear-like legs of the heavily armored monster came down hard and pierced straight through her Familiar's fuzzy shell, killing it almost instantly.

She closed her eyes tightly, not wanting to watch the monster continue to eat her Familiar and friend as she felt the bond between them snap. Rayna continued leading her, stumbling through the leafy underbrush and the towering trees dripping in vines.

They weren't going to make it.

They were going to die here and finally join the rest of their clan in the great beyond. The realization caused her to trip and fall, her twin crying out and trying to pull her back as their inevitable death finished its meal and was looking at them as dessert.

Then, a beam of bright golden light ripped through the Pantula like it was merely a stuffed animal, leaving a gaping hole through its center, and a man wearing glittering gold and white armor appeared between them and the corpse. His Emerald Caste Aura made it clear that reinforcements had finally arrived to battle the Soul Reapers.

CHAPTER FORTY-TWO

Showtime

It was their third night of keeping watch on the wall, and Phoenix groaned into the mental voice chat, apologizing for what felt like the hundredth time. *"I'm sorry, you guys. I'm going to yell at Paul as soon as he gets back."*

When they had received their assignment for the start of the blood moon, they were given the dreaded wall Watch for three nights, followed by a night off. This would be the repeating rotation they kept until assigned elsewhere as their numbers and threats shifted during the coming months.

The Watch wasn't dreaded due to its danger on the supposed frontline but because of its reputation of boredom, since most monsters would be intercepted by the Wall Response parties long before they ever actually reached the walls. The flat plains of rock and ice surrounding the east, south, and west sides of the city acted as a natural early warning system that parties could respond to without draining the power reserves of the city's wall defenses.

Dazien chuckled from his position a couple dozen yards further down the wall. *"It's not that bad. Gives us plenty of time to talk more about all your fun little secrets."*

Things had gotten more relaxed between the trio as they fell into a comfortable routine together: training in the evening, having a late dinner, and then going on watch, with their shift ending at dawn.

Phoenix groaned into the chat again, rubbing at her temples. *"I think you've squeezed all of them out of me by this point."*

"Not true," Dazien responded and started listing. *"There's still that divine quest, Natural Talents you refuse to divulge details on, your favorite flower—"*

Phoenix laughed. *"Favorite flower?"*

"Sure, we don't know it, so therefore, it's technically *a secret from us,"* he said with a grin that she could barely make out at this distance.

"I don't even know the names of any flowers in this world, let alone my favorite from among them," she said in exasperation. *"I can barely name the food I eat, remember? Is there a Knowledge Tome for just the Makera encyclopedia of stuff?"*

Dazien laughed, and even Uriel's chuckle could be heard through the mental link. *"I'll have to ask around,"* he said. *"Maybe we can stop by the Temple of the Scholar after our shift."*

"Oh, I've been meaning to go there and—What's that?" Phoenix broke off midsentence as she spotted a dark shadow in the red light illuminating the sky over the snow-covered tundra. She pointed east, mainly so the others could gauge the direction.

Dazien's voice answered a moment later, *"Monster swarm. Gods, there are dozens of them flying this way. Some sort of bird monster."*

Phoenix squinted at the dark cloud. *"How can you tell from this distance?"*

"My Perception passive," he answered, then went silent in their party chat as he focused on reporting what he had seen to their commanding officer.

Dazien's communication had the very convenient capability of being able to direct a member's thoughts to a specific person or subset of people. So, while they could talk amongst themselves, they could also include others, like the commander on duty with them, without having to worry about unwanted chatter.

According to the procedures and guidelines they had been given when getting assigned this mission, the monsters were still too far out to raise the alarms and call for one of the Response teams.

A runeforged guard arrived a few moments later and held up some sort of spyglass to view the threat. The woman exchanged some words with Dazien that Phoenix couldn't hear, and then he updated them.

"We're going on low alert. If they keep getting closer without veering off, we'll increase it. They'll send a Response party, but with how high in the sky they are, they're not positive about whether anyone on duty can handle them before they reach us. So, we should probably prepare for combat."

Phoenix nodded and grinned, rubbing her hands together, and began to draw on the ground beneath her. *Finally,* she had enough time to prepare one of the new rituals that had been floating around in her mind before the combat would begin. She was hoping this ritual, from the Knowledge Tome that Scholar had given her, would be perfect for this particular situation.

As she traced out the intricate lines with her trail of light from her [**Beacon of Hope**] Talent, she idly wondered if she could convince both Scholar and Warrior to give her the next set of books sometime. They had all been labeled as the first in the series, after all, and she was curious how many more there might be and if she could put them to use now.

She finished drawing out the ritual diagram but hadn't activated it yet as she turned to see where the monsters were now in their unexpected migration. They were much closer than she had expected, and she briefly thought Dazien's estimate of "dozens" was actually a conservative guess. There must have been over a hundred of the large, eagle-sized birds making their way straight for the city.

"What are you planning?" Dazien said from beside her rather than through the voice chat, and she jumped slightly in surprise.

"Stop doing that," she scolded.

He gave her an impish grin. *"Never.* So, what's all this?" he asked, gesturing to the ritual diagram.

She smiled sweetly. "I guess you're just going to have to wait and see," she quipped, then gestured back to his spot. "Aren't you supposed to be over there to man the cannon thingy when they call for a volley?"

He nodded at the identical device behind her. "As are you."

"I will. I'm just planning to follow it up with this," she said, waving at the glowing ground. Then the alarm began to sound, and Dazien nodded to her.

"Showtime," he said before returning to his spot on the wall.

Her book suddenly appeared before her, blocking her view and being as helpful as ever.

New Quest: Bird Breaker
Flying monsters are attacking the city. Help do your part.
Objective: Help defeat twenty Flaywings.
Reward: Rare Crystal Caste Spirit Gem.

Oh? A Spirit Gem? Yes! That means a new ability, she excitedly thought to herself before releasing her Aura, adding it to the others nearby as they prepared for the monsters to reach the walls. Then she took her position at the magical armament, aiming it at the incoming swarm.

The wall-mounted weapon was a rather heavy ballista-like device that she had to grab the massive handles of and heave into position. She would get one shot, and then it would take a minute to charge back up. Within that time, they were told that they could cast ranged Spells at their discretion but that they needed to be back in place for the next volley. She planned to add to the onslaught during that brief window.

Phoenix could feel the adrenaline rise in her as the Flaywings got closer. When the signal went out, she fired. The concussive force from the sound alone whipped her curls loose from her braid as the cannons on the wall sent out massive blades of ice towards the flock, slicing through many of the monsters that she could now sense were Crystal Caste.

She moved quickly to the center of her prepared ritual diagram and activated it, preparing to cast her **[Lunar Dream]** Spell that she had been practicing like crazy in private to get a better hang of its uses after her embarrassing display with Paul against the Tundra Yeti.

"Let dreams become reality."

As the ritual consumed the materials from her collection to fuel itself, she felt it activate, and the magic started coursing through her, making the area light up. It almost felt like she downed five shots of magical espresso with how much energy she felt buzzing through her.

Then, she formed the illusive construct in her mind and cast it through the ritual to amplify its scale and send it out to perform her commands.

A large bird made of starlight appeared in the air in front of her outside of the walls, inspired by one of her favorite fictional heroes from Earth. It quickly grew to the size of a three-story building, its majestic wings outspread, before it flapped them once and then moved towards the swarm of monsters.

As it looked like it was about to consume a portion of them in its giant beak, it shattered into dozens of smaller versions to fly around the enemy forces and cause as much confusion and chaos as possible.

The small illusions spurred the Flaywings into chasing after, dodging, or colliding with their brethren. This distraction, in turn, caused them to take more damage from the array of area Spells the other Watchers on the wall were casting.

For a moment, Phoenix thought she saw Uriel's **[Rain of Fire]** Spell go off in their midst before she collapsed to her knees. Feeling the majority of her mana drained by the ritual and a massive headache threatening her senses.

She dragged herself over to the cannon again, with only ten seconds to spare, as she aimed and triggered it again as it pulled from the city's mana reserves. She was too spent to add to the next round of individual casts, but she was happy enough with how well her first one had gone and was still going.

Only two more rounds of cannon volleys later, the alarm ended, and Phoenix grinned at her book. She finally felt like she deserved the rewards for completing this quest, unlike the previous one with the Wights.

Quest: Bird Breaker
Objective Complete: Helped defeat twenty Flaywings.
Objective Reward:
[Wing Spirit Gem] has been added to your collection.

Completion Reward:
20 [Crystal Mana Bits] have been added to your collection.

Hidden Objective Complete: Helped defeat all of the Flaywings.
Bonus Reward:
[Crystal Eye] has been added to your collection.

§

Paul carefully observed the gathering of Casters outside the Reality Rift that he had finished purging monsters from. He had been disturbed to find another of those sickly-looking Seeds within it and hoped his seal on the Rift would be enough to keep it contained. At least until he could let the AOA and Ducal Guards know of its compromised status like the last one that he had visited.

He was only half-paying attention to Talvehtia talking to the group, assuring them that their mission had been accomplished and informing them of their planned return to Tulimeir. The other Emerald Caster did a decent job of leading them, all things considered, but the man was definitely better suited for smithing over monster hunting.

His gaze returned to the pair of voxen he had just barely managed to arrive in time to save. That familiar monotone once more gave structure to his scattered thoughts.

"*The Little Lotus and Little Crystal might make good companions for the Little Miss.*"

Paul smirked at her nicknames for the pair whose appearances and Auras spoke fairly plainly about both their powers and personalities. He could easily see their attunements as well with his Perception ability. Both had Song and Illusion, but the Healer also had Water and Life, while the other had Earth and Gem.

He assumed from the crystalline weapons adorning the latter's fists that she was a Striker. However, it was the calming effects of the Healer's Aura that piqued his interest the most, especially considering who was part of his Protégé's party. The matchup was almost *too* perfect, though, and made him hesitant.

"*They're complete strangers, Bela,*" he finally replied, "*we know nothing about them.*"

"*So, Wayland must learn more,*" she pointed out pragmatically and then suggested the thing he almost disliked most. "*Talk to them.*"

Paul grimaced and didn't respond right away. He mulled over the ideas and ways he might approach them without simply terrifying them. Apparently, he didn't need to figure out much himself since the twins decided to approach him first.

"Thank you for saving us, sir," the one whose Aura felt like a peaceful pond under the tremor of grief said to him. "Could we know your name?"

"Paul," he stated simply, not wanting his family name to bias them at all yet. "I'm sorry I couldn't save your Familiar," he offered in condolence.

The young voxen nodded quietly as her mirror image said, "I'm Rayna, and this is my sister Saiya." Then she asked him with a lot less grief and a lot more curiosity, "So you're from Tulim's capital? Is it true everything is made of glass and smoke there?"

"Steam," he corrected. He then asked, despite his better judgment, "Would you like to see it for yourself?"

At that, two sets of foxy ears perked up as the twins looked from him to each other. The gentler one then clarified, "You want us to join you?"

"We're only Crystal Caste still," the bolder one interjected, "we're not gonna be any help to an Emerald—"

"I have a Protégé who is Crystal Caste," he clarified. "Aside from that, you may find a fresh start in Tulimeir."

Saiya glanced back to her sister, who simply shrugged. "Our lives have been basically nothing but a series of fresh starts, so what's another? It's not like there's anything left for us back in Viimeinen. Plus, the AOA branch there is complete garbage."

Paul frowned at that. While most branches were run independently across the globe, they should still adhere to the specific standards set by the Central Leadership based out of Havenshire. He idly wondered if that branch had lost its official membership yet or was due to soon, once an inspector made the rounds.

His thoughts were interrupted as a new Aura entered his senses, and he tensed for a moment before recognizing that it was only a Peak Sapphire Caster. Still, they weren't expecting visitors, and the timing seemed suspicious. Perhaps they missed one of the Soul Reapers?

"We have company," he merely warned the twins before moving to intercept the stranger. He wasn't surprised that it was another voxen since that species, along with humans, dominated the region, but he was surprised at the snow-white fur and silver hair that marked him as definitely *not* one of the locals.

The newcomer was dressed in white Cleric robes and raised a white-furred hand in greeting. He cautiously approached and said with a grin, "Hello there! Just passing through. You wouldn't happen to know if this is indeed the road to Tulimeir, yes?"

Paul's eyes narrowed on the suspicious-looking man, his eyes lingering on the godly insignia stitched onto the breast of his robes in the shape of a pair of silver wings. "What brings a Cleric of the Rebel to this remote part of the world?"

"Ah." The smaller man slowed his approach and gave a nervous chuckle as he asked, "Is it safe to assume that you're part of the nation's authority and won't take kindly to my presence, nor believe anything I might say?"

He refused to give this stranger the benefit of a smile as he crossed his arms over his chest and said, "Depends on what you have to say and if it's a lie. Why don't you start with your name, Cleric?"

The stranger grinned widely. "I'm Everin Starlark, and just following the road towards my destiny."

"*Oh, wonderful,*" the monotone whisper in his mind somehow managed to say sarcastically. "*This Rebel Fox is one of those crazy ones that twist words to hide lies.*"

Paul gave a heavy sigh. "*Let's just get home and worry about gods and their disciples later.*"

CHAPTER FORTY-THREE

Keeping Friends Close

Hey, Cam," Murinah said in her singsong sweetness, "you don't have a portal imprint near the Razorteeth Mountains yet, right?"

Her younger brother shook his head, looking up from the book he was currently reading in his room. "No, why? Do you have a mission out there?"

She nodded and closed the door as she entered. "There's a mission I want, but Ramir said he could only give it to me if I had a full party or a porter to get me back faster."

Cam gave her a look of disgust as he said, "I don't know why you go to that guy. He's got sleaze written all over his face. The guy would probably sell his own mother for enough Bits."

"It's because he likes Bits so much that I go to him," she replied with a roll of her eyes as she sat on the edge of his bed. "I can make sure we get the good missions with a little bit of extra *incentive*."

"I hate that you bribe people like that," the younger cinderen stated, setting his book on the nightstand. "We're the noble House of Ruwena. We shouldn't have to throw money around to gain people's respect and consideration."

"Oh, my naive little brother," she said with a sad shake of her head, the messy bun letting loose a few gray strands, "Anyways, that's not the point of why I'm here."

"I'm not really sure why you're still here," he said in annoyance as he crossed his arms, "I already said I can't portal you there."

"Yes, but I know of someone who *can* and—"

"Then why aren't you bothering them right now instead?"

Murinah glared at her sibling. "I'm getting there, if you wouldn't so rudely interrupt," she scolded. "Anyways, she *can't* stay with me for the mission to portal me back. So, I figured we could get you a new aural imprint over there, and we could give her some friendly 'welcome to the AOA' hazing at the same time."

"Hazing?" Cam asked her, looking slightly concerned.

"Just a little prank to scare her a bit," she explained, "nothing serious or any-thing, but she's been so outcast from the rest of the Adventurers in our Caste that I thought it might help break the ice a little and let her know that she's being treated just like everyone else who's a new recruit, you know?"

He slowly nodded as he agreed. "I know that the hazing is pretty common right after joining. Was she in your trial group or something?"

"Yup! You know how we should be keeping friends close. The poor thing doesn't really have any friends like that, what with not knowing much about our customs and culture at all. She stands out so much with that red hair of hers," Murinah said with pity drenching her voice.

"Oh, I think I've noticed her at the portal grounds before. The one with the silver ring around a portal that looks like the night sky?" Camrin clarified. She nodded, and he seemed to draw more of a conclusion about her. "She seemed pretty quiet and standoffish with everyone now that you mention it."

"See! Let's make her relax a bit. I've got it all planned out, okay?" she said. Her grin widened as her little brother agreed to join her, and yet another piece of her plan slid into place in order to win back her love.

§

"So, I just touch it?" Dazien asked her.

"I think? Paul said it was like using an Identification Orb, whatever that is," Phoenix admitted sheepishly.

"They usually go with Knowledge Tablets to help identify items and people. The fact that your ability is basically a free magical version of those is extremely beneficial. Especially when combined with a looting ability." The Defender gestured towards Uriel. "We've both used those before to see our abilities. You have to will the information into the orb by touching it, then touch the orb to the tablet to display the information."

"I don't have to touch my book; I can just think of what I want," she explained and gestured to the [**Guide Book**], where the description of her portal ability appeared. Her two teammates read as they ate their morning meal in her dorm room after just finishing their eighth round of wall Watch that night.

"That's useful, if for nothing else than to easily see the progress of the ability," Dazien replied, then placed his hand on the book, concentrating on the ability he wanted to view.

Passive Ability: Eagle Eye
Type: Perception
Current Caste: Crystal 5
Crystal Effect: You have greater control over your vision and can focus on details from a great distance.

"Eagle Eye?" Phoenix said in dismay, "I thought you were all about kingly swordness? That sounds like a hunter or sniper skill."

Dazien chuckled. "I'll have you know that eagles are very kingly birds that rule the skies. I also unlocked the Class ability for that Aspect already, so it's much more advanced than the others. It will be one of the first to hit the Crystal Cap."

"Passive abilities increase based on the average level of the other two in their Aspect, right?"

"That's correct," he confirmed, "they're both limited and empowered by them. It's also the main reason they are considered 'passive' even if some might have more active components to them, like conjuring the door to my personal dimensional storage."

"That makes some sense," Phoenix admitted, then turned to Uriel and gestured once more to the book. "Want to try?"

The Mage leaned forward and placed a finger on the page, displaying his own Perception ability for them.

Passive Ability: Scent in the Air
Type: Perception
Current Caste: Crystal 5
Crystal Effect: You have an extremely heightened and more controlled sense of smell.

She raised an eyebrow. "Scent-based? Interesting."

Uriel shrugged. "It has its uses."

Phoenix nodded, chewing the bite of her eggs before asking Dazien, "Can I see that immovable object ability of yours?"

The Defender laughed. "I don't think it's *completely* immovable. I'm pretty sure Lord Wayland could backhand me across the room even with it active," he said wryly but complied with her request.

Ability: Stand Your Ground
Type: Utility (channel, elemental, metal)
Cost: Moderate mana per second.
Cooldown: None.
Current Caste: Crystal 6 (54%)
Crystal Effect: Become rooted in place, greatly increasing your resistance to physical damage, and gain an instance of [**Tenacity**] each second until your next movement.
• Tenacity (boon, elemental, metal, stacking): Increased [**Strength**] and resistance to Elemental damage. Instances are quickly lost when moving.

Phoenix gave a low whistle. "That's an impressive defensive ability."

"Metal Aspects are usually pretty good for Defenders. I'm quite pleased with it," he happily said as he took another bite of food.

Then Phoenix had an idea, and she asked the would-be king, "Hey, can you try touching it, but this time, instead of focusing on a single ability, just think of your whole self?"

He quirked an eyebrow. "What are you hoping to accomplish with that?"

She grinned mischievously. "I want to see your character sheet."

"Character sheet?"

"Just try it, and hopefully, you'll see," she urged. He rolled his eyes before touching the book again and seeming to concentrate on what she had requested.

Name: Dazien Smithson
Species: Gemite (Amethyst)
Caste: Crystal 4

Attributes
Strength (Potent): Crystal 5
Agility (Sword): Crystal 3
Fortitude (Metal): Crystal 6
Mind (Noble): Crystal 6
Magic (Warrior King): Crystal 3

Natural Talents
Treasure Attunement
Drinking Buddy
Earthborn
Shiny
Right of Divinity

Titles
Orphan
Loyal Friend
Warrior Trainee
Slayer
Adventurer

Aspects
Potent
• Eagle Eye (Perception Passive)
• Duelist - Crystal 6 (88%)
• Rallying Cry (Class) - Crystal 5 (23%)

Sword
- Armory (Utility Passive)
- Accelerating Strikes - Crystal 7 (12%)

Metal
- Tribute (Utility Passive)
- Stand Your Ground - Crystal 6 (54%)
- To the Dungeon (Class) - Crystal 6 (5%)

Noble
- Noble Subjects (Utility Passive)
- Lead the Charge - Crystal 7 (60%)
- King's Banner (Class) - Crystal 6 (2%)

Warrior King (Class)
- Monarch's Dominion (Aura Passive)
- Call of Fealty - Crystal 6 (19%)

"Huh," he said after a moment of reading, then sighed in frustration. "I guess there goes all of *my* secrets."

Before Phoenix could start badgering him for every little detail about his own abilities, Dazien shut the book, causing it to disappear in a shower of stardust, and changed the subject. "Seeing my two missing Class abilities highlighted like that, though, reminds me; you got a Spirit Gem earlier, didn't you? You never told us what your new ability is."

She flushed slightly and admitted, "I, um, I haven't used it yet."

"Oh? Do you want us there for the Absorption Ritual or something? You should know it already; it's a pretty basic one," he asked thoughtfully.

"No. I mean, I do know it, but I don't need it," she tried to explain before giving a sigh. "I'm just waiting for Paul to get back so he can be there too."

"Oh!" he exclaimed in surprise before shaking his head. "I should have expected that. Does he require you to check with him first? He seems like the strict type that would want to micromanage like that. I've met a couple of Mentors before who liked to pick everything for their Protégés and control what path they walked."

"No, I just . . . it's just something I kinda promised him I'd talk with him about before doing," she said. "I value his opinion even if you don't."

Dazien shook his head. "Sorry, Phoenix, I didn't mean it like that. It's good to seek your Mentor's advice, and we're lucky to have any Emerald Caster offering assistance in our training, let alone a man with his position and experience."

He smiled gently and added, "We'll wait for the lord's return." Then his grin turned more playful as he asked, "So, that ritual you used earlier to increase the size of your illusion, could we use that on Uriel to increase the area of his Spells?"

She felt her lip pout as she shook her head and glared towards the taunting warrior. "I *wish*. It only boosts the area of non-damaging Illusion abilities. Pretty sure *every* Mage would be using it otherwise."

The two men nodded in agreement, and Dazien asked, "Are we still planning to train before dinner tonight? It's the last night of Watch before we get a night off."

"Yeah, I just have to do my usual portaling stop. You know how they moved my time to the afternoon since we got the night shift, and I'm crashing in bed after you leave. However, it should leave plenty of time," she said offhandedly. "Meet at the temple training room around seven?"

They both nodded and finished eating before retiring to their own apartments for some sleep.

§

Paul was relieved to be back in Tulimeir and to find his Protégé in one piece. However, he was not happy to get scolded by Patricia. She went on a rant at him about how said Protégé went and did exactly what he had said she wouldn't: making a spectacle of herself while defending the city from a monster attack on the walls.

He wouldn't admit to his sister that the ingenuity of using the ability in that manner made him proud in a way that he hadn't experienced before. As she complained about not being able to stamp out the questions and rumors as easily anymore, his brief elation turned to worry.

"Are people trying to look into her?" Paul asked.

"There are definitely questions about the mysterious redhead that guards the wall and portals people around the whole tundra," Patricia complained as she poured herself another drink from his own collection in his study. "You do flashy crap like a giant starlight bird, and there will be people who notice. I even have a Madam Malik who has traced her dorm payments to our House asking about setting up a meeting."

Paul raised a brow. "Isn't that the proprietor of—"

"Mother's Cupboard, yeah," she finished for him and slid into the seat across from his, taking a long sip of the blue liquid in her glass. "It sounds like she wants to offer her a job that would put the AOA's part-time portaling mission to shame."

He scoffed. "She would be wasted there."

Patricia's eyes almost bugged out as she said incredulously, "Well, Paul, I wouldn't know because you refuse to let me meet her and judge her capabilities for myself!"

"I'm actually impressed you held yourself back from arranging an 'accidental' run-in while I was gone," he muttered as he pulled out a green leather-bound journal to begin writing down some thoughts as they conversed. "Have you still been keeping tabs on the party?"

"Of course," the woman said haughtily, "they've been stuck on the wall like you requested. The three of them train and get a meal before their night shift. She does that portaling gig for about an hour before they meet up. I don't think she leaves her dorm for anything else, though . . ."

Paul glanced up to see why his sister trailed off. He didn't like the frown on her face as he prompted, "What is it?"

"She never goes out, Paul. Cooped up in that tiny room all alone . . . There's a whole wonderful magical world out there, and she seems to be hiding from it," she pointed out with obvious concern. "It's like she's afraid of everyone and everything."

"She's a bit like me when it comes to socializing," he explained defensively. "Besides, there's a blood moon going on."

"Exactly," Pati replied. "From what little you've told me, all this girl has experienced so far is monsters and missions and people wanting to use her for their own benefits. I think those two boys are helping, but you should also help her understand what exactly it is we're defending from the evil things she's faced. Show her the wonders of Tulimeir and that its people will call her friend if she lets them."

Paul sat back in his seat, mulling over the advice. He pulled out a small card of paper from one of the drawers on his desk and wrote down two names on it before handing it to his sister.

She took it and read aloud, "'Saiya and Rayna Dewsong.' What is this for?"

"You wanted to be let in on my plans," he started, trying to offer a peace offering in return for both her troubles while he was away and voicing her concerns without fear of him. "They are twin voxen from Epa Toivo who were part of one of the adventuring groups that had been dispatched to the Reality Rift I went to."

"Okay," she said in confusion, "I still don't see what that has to do with us."

"Saiya is a Backline Healer, and Rayna is a Forward Striker. Both are Crystal Casters whose party was decimated in the Rift."

"And you want them to join Phoenix's party," she said, finally catching on. He nodded, and the shrewd politician asked, "What makes you trust them with the position? You said the boys changed your mind with the way they talked about Phoenix and respected her skills over position, but I doubt these voxen have ever met her before."

"That's why I'm telling you about them," he explained with a small smirk. "Check them out and let me know if they'll be a problem. I think the Healer specifically will help balance out the whole group, though. She's very . . . *calming*."

Patricia gave him a skeptical look, then conjured a large flower bud that she slipped the card into before making it vanish once more. "I'll start with the AOA then," she said and stood to leave. "While you start with having an encouraging pep talk with your little Protégé."

Paul nodded. "I was actually planning to make my way over there now," he replied. Standing with her and following his sister out the door.

Their paths diverged as Pati continued west to cross the inner wall before heading south to the AOA building, and he stayed within the inner city and headed south to the dorms where he had set up Phoenix at.

"Wayland does not think Little Flower will treat the twins as pets?" Bela asked once his sister left.

He chuckled and shook his head. *"If she tried, I'm sure that feisty one would punch her for it, higher Caste or not."*

"What about looking into that Rebel Fox?"

"I'll check in on him later myself. Since he went straight to Rebel's Temple after we arrived, there's not much I can do about him until he makes any potential scheme clear."

It was almost five in the afternoon, and he knew his apprentice would be leaving soon to help at the portal grounds. He let himself in the front door of the single-bedroom dorm with his copy of the key, not liking to draw attention to himself in the hallway. He immediately felt his mood lift at the sight of Phoenix sitting at the small kitchen table by the window, drinking coffee and playing with a glowstone in her hand.

She looked up as he entered and smiled brightly. "Paul! You're back!"

He returned her smile and moved closer to sit across from her. "I said I wouldn't be more than two weeks."

"I guess we are almost there, aren't we?" the Wayfarer replied. "I'm not sure I mentioned before how glad I am that you all track time just like in my world. The thirteen-months thing is a bit different but much easier to adjust for than if you had different hours in a day or days in a week. Though it is a bit hard to get used to the different names for the days and months."

Paul chuckled. "I see you've kept learning things in my absence," he noted.

"Hate him all you want, but at least Dazien *likes* to give me answers to all my questions," she teased with a roll of her eyes.

He paused slightly, unsure how best to approach the subject that Pati had urged him to address without revealing that he had his sister essentially spying on her. "About those two," he began, "it seems like you're getting along with them . . ."

She smiled softly and nodded. "Yeah, we all get along pretty good, I think. They've been teaching me a lot, and I think Dazien has taken it upon himself to show me all the different restaurants in the International District." She then added with a laugh, "I'm finally learning the names of all the things I'm eating."

Paul mentally berated himself; he should have thought of doing something like that. Perhaps he could take her to some of the places around the city that were historically significant. She seemed to enjoy stories in general and might like interesting details that places like that offered. Maybe he could show her the gardens on his family roof. Explain all the different plants and flowers . . .

"So, how did your mission go?" she asked, breaking him from his tangent thoughts.

"We won," the Paladin said bluntly, "however, there were some losses before I arrived. I met some people there that I think I'd like you to meet once they've settled here."

"Oh?" she prompted curiously.

"Yeah, I think you might like them. Maybe . . . maybe even add them to your small group of friends," he tried suggesting.

Phoenix frowned. "I'm not sure I would call Dazien and Uriel friends per se. We're a party, so more like co-workers, I guess. He made a point of saying it's temporary as he decides for sure if he wants me on his team or not."

Paul raised an eyebrow and said, "I'm not sure they see it that way."

"I'm not sure if I have time for *friends*, Paul," she pressed, "I have duties, training, patrols, and lots of learning to catch up on." She emphasized the point by holding up the glowstone in her hand. "Did you know you can change the color of these little lights by touching a Shard to them?"

He absently nodded, then said, "You still have time for friends, Phoenix. You just need to open up a little and trust that not everyone is out to use you." He hesitated a moment, almost as uncomfortable with the prospect as she was, and suggested gently, "You can consider me a friend, at least."

She blinked up at him owlishly. "Friends?"

He smiled softly. "We get along, offer support, and want to see the other succeed. Is that not friends?"

"It feels a bit different with you," she said, adjusting in her seat awkwardly. "You're my Mentor, not *just* a friend."

Paul's smile widened as he said, "More than a friend? I guess I can accept that. Now, don't let me hold you up. Think about what I said and make some more friends. Okay, young one?"

She rolled her eyes but matched his smile and said sarcastically, "Okay, *Dad*."

CHAPTER FORTY-FOUR

Fight the Inevitable

Phoenix was waiting for the final people of her scheduled portal assignments when an unexpected pair walked up to her. She tensed and internally groaned when she realized they were who she was waiting on.

It was the pretty cinderen girl with ash gray hair in a messy bun that had been pushing Dazien to join their party instead. Murinah, she thought her name was, as well as another younger cinderen that she didn't know but recognized as one of the other Crystal Casters that offered portaling services. They both strode up purposefully towards her as the woman said with a smile, "Hello, you're Phoenix, right?"

Phoenix nodded and was about to double-check their plans with her when the woman cheerfully continued.

"I'm Noble Murinah Ruwena, and this is my younger brother Camrin. We're here for our scheduled portal?"

Phoenix nodded again, slightly startled by the woman's friendly behavior. She couldn't recall her even glancing in her direction during the trials when Dazien had been taking most of the group's attention.

"We need to go to the mountains in the east. Preferably the northern ridge, if you're capable," Murinah informed her. "Can you help us out?"

She wondered if she had been too quick to judge the woman who smiled happily at her. Maybe she had just been trying to fit in with the group or was trying to act the way she thought Dazien would want her to in order to have him join her party?

Phoenix bowed her head in acknowledgment and reconfirmed, "I have a location in a cave near there. Northern ridge of the Razorteeth Mountains?"

When the older woman nodded, she conjured the portal and stepped back for them to go through.

Murinah gestured to the silver ring and said, "You said it was a cave? Can you go with us and at least help guide us to the entrance and get our bearings?"

Phoenix looked up at her in surprise. "Th-that's not exactly standard procedure . . ."

The noblewoman waved a dismissive hand in the air. "I know, but this is your last portal for the day, correct? The attendant mentioned it when we scheduled. Just a quick hop through, lead us out of the cave, point us in the right direction, and hop back. It should only be for a few minutes, and when we get back in town later, I'll buy you a drink as thanks!"

She hesitated again but didn't want to argue with a fellow Adventurer, and Paul *did* say she should be more open to making new friends . . . she could spare a few minutes to make sure they didn't get lost.

Phoenix nodded in acquiescence, and Murinah happily clapped her hands. "Wonderful! Thank you so much for making this easier for us!"

The pair walked through the portal, and Phoenix followed behind them a step later. She arrived in the small cave where she had fought an angry bear monster. Luckily, the cave was not currently inhabited, and she couldn't hear the weather outside of the entrance, which she knew was around the bend, so it should be a decent day for traveling.

As Murinah turned and smiled in a way that made her feel slightly uncomfortable, Phoenix hastily informed the siblings, "It's right this way to the exit." She gestured down one of the paths and finished explaining, "I won't be able to give you a return portal back to Tulimeir, obviously, but it should be about a two-week walk to the southeast from here. You'll run into the eastern trade road if you just go straight south."

Camrin walked past her and said with a wave of his hand, "Don't worry about that. One of the reasons we scheduled a portal was so I could gain that aural imprint for myself to help you out more during portal duties."

He headed towards the entrance, and Murinah put a hand on Phoenix's shoulder, which caused her to flinch slightly in surprise as she looked back towards the cinderen. The woman leaned closer to her and said sweetly, "Thank you again. You've been *so* helpful."

Then Murinah lifted a fist as though to show her something held within it.

Maybe a tip? Phoenix wondered. She hadn't seen much of the tipping system in this world and found herself curious.

Murinah surprised her, however, when she opened her palm and blew into it at the same time, causing a fine dark powder to whip up into her face. Phoenix began to cough and pushed the smiling woman away from her, taking a few steps back in her panic. Then she felt something hard and cold cinch around her neck, giving an audible click, and she remembered that Camrin was still behind her.

Phoenix conjured her [**Night Blade**] and swung it around towards him as he held something in his hands that was connected by a pair of chains to whatever had gone around her throat. She tried to pull it from his grip but only managed to make him drop one, which swung around behind her from the force.

As she pulled her arm back to thrust the dagger into the man's arm that was holding the other chain, another click sounded, and her attack was interrupted by a manacle snapping around her wrist. In her growing haze, she had forgotten Murinah was now behind her.

"Now, now, little human, don't fight the inevitable," the noblewoman cooed.

She tried to swing her dagger again, the chain silent despite the movement, but her aim was severely off and she stumbled. Murinah ended up catching her and saved her from a mouthful of cave dirt.

"Shhh, there now. We've got a surprise for you later. Sleep now, and you'll see it soon," the cinderen whispered to her. Another click sounded from far away, and her previously free wrist felt heavier but distant.

Phoenix slumped against her assailant as the room started to spin, and the last thing she noticed was her portal flickering out of existence.

§

Camrin caught the unconscious redhead, who began to fall as Murinah pushed the annoyance backward to free herself from the extra weight. Her brother set the limp form down in a position that would allow him to finish restraining her legs and connect her wrists closer together, then pulled the rope from his dimensional bag.

Murinah wiped off her powdered palm carefully with a kerchief before clapping her hands together and giggling. "I can't believe how smoothly that went. What a naive idiot this one is."

Camrin grumbled sourly, "I don't think anyone would expect an attack like that from a fellow Adventurer." He hadn't been exactly fond of Murinah's plan to haze the younger woman, but she had been able to assure him that it was all simply part of scaring her before reassuring their good intentions of friendship. The reminder made her remember that she was still in the middle of her con, and she tried to reassure him until the charade was up.

"That's what made it such a great plan," she explained. "Now, hurry up. That powder won't last long on a Crystal Caster. We need to make sure she can't possibly escape to make her properly panic before revealing the surprise. She'll be so relieved, and we can celebrate the new camaraderie later."

Her brother finished linking the rope between the Silencer manacles on her wrists and ankle cuffs he had tied around her, then complained, not for the first time, "I'm still not sure she'll be so happy about this. Plus, aren't these Silencers a controlled magic item? Couldn't we end up in a lot of trouble for using them?"

"That's why I took this one from Father's *private* stock." She rolled her eyes at him. "And *she* doesn't know they're controlled. Besides, even if she does, it will help show her that we trust her with our secret. Instant friendship!"

Camrin grunted in acknowledgment as he wrapped a long strip of cloth around the pale woman's mouth a few times to keep her silent, then hefted the dead weight over his shoulder. Despite being only fifteen, her brother was still a Crystal Caster already, which made carrying the slight girl an easy feat.

"Let's just get this over with," he grumbled. "What was the mission to scout out for this anyways?"

Murinah led the way out of the cave and moved further north after assessing their location. "Some miners from a nearby facility had sent reports of Miserlings nearby. Of course, nobody likes going after those. We're to scout out their nest, then return to inform the AOA of the actual size of the threat."

"Miserlings?" Camrin said with a disgusted look. "Those things are nasty, Muri. I don't care if they used to be part of Father's research. I don't want to go anywhere near them."

Her expression darkened as she said coldly, "Suck it up, Cam. If you want to be an actual Adventurer someday, then you need to accept that sometimes you'll need to get your hands dirty."

They were silent for the remainder of the walk, and when they reached a small outcropping of rock that overlooked a dip between the ragged edges of the mountain they were currently on, the pair were able to look down on a large nest of bones and rocks where a dozen pitch-black creatures lay asleep in the shadows of the mountain.

The Miserlings had sinewy, hound-like bodies with six gangly legs that ended in a trio of serrated claws. Their long necks extended into a rounded blob of a face with three eyes, four nostril slits, and a wide mouth with matching serrated teeth.

Camrin set the redhead onto the outcropping into a kneeling position between them, and Murinah bent down to give the temporary captive a sharp slap to wake up the thorn in her side.

Phoenix seemed groggy after the sudden smack, change of location, and the after-effects of the poison she had dosed the outsider with. When it seemed like the woman finally registered the tight ropes around her legs and wrist bindings behind her back, the cliché captive tried to struggle out of them.

Murinah grabbed the red curls that seemed to have stolen Dazien's attention and gave the annoying woman the most wicked and maniacal grin she could muster. She whispered quietly into the pale ear, "I just wanted you to know that Miserlings are best known for *playing* with their food. I want you to remember— when you start to feel the pain—that you brought this on yourself. You should *never* have gotten between me and Dazien. He and I are destined for greatness. And you?"

She started to slowly drag Phoenix towards the edge near the monsters, and the redhead's eyes widened as she struggled harder. "You should have stayed in your place, you *worthless* peasant."

Then Murinah shoved the restrained woman off the side of the sheer mountain and into the pile of monsters sleeping below before quickly turning and retreating, grabbing a shocked Camrin by the hand and dragging him along behind her.

"What in the frozen abyss have you done?!" Camrin angrily exclaimed as she pulled him down the path they had come from. "You said we were going to *scare* her, Muri! Not feed her to a pack of monsters! We have to go back and save her!"

"Not unless you want them eating us next, idiot," she retorted, triggering one of her stealth abilities to assist in their retreat.

§

Phoenix's mind was racing as she fell through the air, barely registering the sound of the younger boy yelling in outrage at his sister before she landed hard on the packed snow and rocks, her bound body tumbling further towards the nest. The loud thud and sound of displaced rocks were all the warnings the monsters needed to rise from their slumber and stalk towards the intruder.

She glanced up to get her first sight of the Miserlings and immediately regretted it. They were void creatures of nightmares. Their skin wasn't fur but glistened like it was wet. The three solid white eyes on each of them stared at her, but she wasn't sure if they could even see anything. Their long tongues lashed out as though tasting the air, and she wondered if they could somehow taste or smell the fear permeating through her.

Phoenix tried to stand and make a run for it, but they were on her in an instant, and Murinah's words finally made sense as the serrated claws tore into her, not deep but slowly tearing her flesh. She screamed against the cloth over her mouth, and tears blurred her vision. This only seemed to excite the monsters.

It was not over quickly. True to the psychopath's words, they *played* with her, trying to squeeze out every bit of pain they could as they slowly devoured her.

When Phoenix regained consciousness, she was lying on top of her bed, completely naked, with her **[Guide Book]** floating in the air above her.

You have died.
All equipment has been returned to your collection.
*[**Waypoint**] has guided your soul back to your designated location.*
You have been reconstituted to a state of full integrity.
Twenty-four hours remain until this effect can be triggered again.

Phoenix stared at the message silently as her mind slowly comprehended what had happened. She simply lay there, and for the first time in a long time, she sobbed.

CHAPTER FORTY-FIVE

Who Would Dare

This isn't like her," Dazien muttered, glancing at his pocket watch. "She's never this late to training."

Uriel shrugged as he continued through his sword forms. "Maybe Lord Wayland finally returned."

"Then she would have brought him here to beat us into the mat," he pointed out. Another moment later, he unconjured his sword and announced, "I'm going to go search for her. Maybe something happened in the west district. The alarms there won't reach us here."

His partner halted and sheathed his sword, moving to follow after him without further objection.

As they arrived at the portal grounds, they were confused when one of the attendants informed them that Phoenix had completed all of her scheduled assignments hours ago. They weren't sure where she could have possibly gone and didn't even know who to ask, except perhaps her benefactor.

When they next arrived at the building belonging to House Wayland to ask if perhaps the lord had returned, they were informed that he had reported his mission as complete and had indeed returned to the city that morning but was currently in meetings elsewhere in the city. When the pair asked about Phoenix, they were surprised to learn that she had never been there before.

It was in the middle of when they would normally be eating their dinner when they arrived at her dorm and knocked, with silence as the only response. Dazien looked at his partner and asked, "Any chance you can detect if she's in there before I break in to check things out?"

Uriel nodded slowly, then motioned the warrior back. Dazien complied as his partner removed the Silencer and breathed in deeply through his nose. A moment later, Uriel nodded again before relatching the collar and said, "I can detect her scent, but it also smells a bit like tears are mixed in with some distress. I don't smell fear, though, so I'm not sure we should—"

"Phoenix!" Dazien called out, stepping forward and pounding louder on the door. "Open the door before I force it open!"

"You're going to get the guards called on us," the Mage muttered, glancing down the hall to make sure no prying eyes were upon them.

They heard movement on the other side, and then the door unlocked but only cracked open slightly.

Dazien started asking questions in frustrated concern as he pushed it wider and entered. "*Where* have you been? You were supposed to be training with us hours ago. We have to—" He halted when his gaze fell upon Phoenix. Her face was splotched and tearstained face, and she rubbed at her eyes.

Her simple cream nightgown hugged her form before flaring out around her legs, but it was the combination of her tears and wild red curls falling loose around her face and down her back that arrested his attention. He had never seen her cry before, nor her hair completely unbraided, and the chaos of it left him momentarily mesmerized.

"Are you alright?" Uriel's smooth and gentle voice broke through his distraction as he refocused on the reason for her tears, which she was furiously wiping away. He noted the rainbow runes on her wrist as well, having never seen them before.

When training, she normally covered her wrists with the long sleeves of the sliksilk training outfit, and outside of that, she always wore long sleeves that had a habit of going past her entire hand, not to mention the bracelet he'd seen glint underneath a handful of times. He had thought it was an attempt to cover her paler skin that she seemed so self-conscious about, a sentiment he could fully empathize with, but perhaps it was also to hide the fact that she had an Oathbond.

"It—" Her voice caught, and she took a steadying breath before stating, "It was just a nightmare."

"You were *sleeping*?" Dazien asked incredulously. He had so many more questions now, but his companion's hand on his shoulder stopped him from pressing her for more information.

He forced himself to relax, trying to calm his frustration to focus on what she needed instead, and said as carefully as he could, "We have our Watch on the wall in a half mark. Are you going to be well enough to go?"

She nodded and began walking towards her bedroom to finish getting ready. About ten minutes later, she was wearing a more practical shirt and pants with boots that he hadn't seen her wear before, and was finishing tying the end of her long braid.

"Where's your cloak?" he asked when he registered what was missing from her usual ensemble.

Phoenix just shrugged and said, "It needs the tailor again."

"Seriously?" he asked as he followed her out of the dorm with Uriel close behind. "You really need to get one with a self-repair enchant if it's getting damaged that often. The up-front cost will save you a ton of Bits in the long run."

§

Phoenix was engraving small runes into the palm-sized stone in front of her. She was using the new etching tool she had purchased from a merchant that Dazien had introduced her to after she collected her pay from the AOA for the week. She looked at her **[Guide Book]** floating nearby to reference the diagram she came up with based on her understanding of enchantments before continuing the delicate work.

She had told her teammates she wanted the day to just relax and recuperate once their Watch had finished the night before, and they hadn't pushed her. Their concern became more apparent as her subdued attitude continued during the night, which progressed uneventfully for them, though they had sent out a number of other Response parties to intercept land-bound monsters they had spotted.

After her ordeal at the hands of a jealous psychopath, she came up with a concept for an item she wanted to try making that she thought might help her feel better when leaving her dorm room again.

As for dealing with the trauma of the event . . . she decided to take the old-fashioned route of attempting to bury those memories as deep as she could and never thinking about it again. Which only seemed to work up to the point she tried to sleep, quickly startling awake a few hours later, kicking the blankets and memories of swarming monsters off of her in terror, only to find herself alone in her room, drenched in sweat and breathing heavily.

Phoenix remembered some stories about soldiers who went to war and suffered from PTSD, having flashbacks and nightmares, like what she found herself suddenly experiencing, but she had never known any of them personally and didn't know how people actually went about treating it. Plus, she had been in plenty of monster fights before without having this kind of reaction. Perhaps she just needed some time to put it behind her.

After calming herself down, she forwent sleep to work on her side projects some more. The first one was an altered enchantment diagram she had been thinking about since learning about the alarm system within the city of Tulimeir. The second, which was currently in her hand, was a small stone that would hopefully save her life if she ever got kidnapped again.

The general concept for the device was simple enough: trickle some mana into the signal stone, and that would act as a tracking beacon for the receiver stone, and the different markings around the edge would light up in the direction of the signal.

It was an emergency SOS flare for her to use in case the maniac siblings tried to kidnap her again. That way, they could be caught in the act, and she would have some actual proof that wouldn't reveal her ability to resurrect herself and get her stuck in a Magi's lab somewhere.

She had debated multiple times over the course of the morning about confiding in Paul about her **[Waypoint]** ability, but she was leaning towards keeping her silence. She didn't want to burden the few people in her life with even more problems when they already put up with her weaknesses. She also didn't want to be seen as a victim who couldn't protect herself. She was an Adventurer! If she couldn't overcome this new fear she was struggling with, how could she be trusted to protect others?

No, she would show that she could handle the situation herself. Prepare better with a device of her own creation. Prove that she was tough enough to handle any monster that she came across and not let her fear dictate her actions. She would show everyone the evil inside Murinah Ruwena.

She had been naive again, letting down her guard just like she had with Miles. Phoenix had thought herself safe with other Adventurers, but they had shown her how unreliable that belief was. If she couldn't trust the AOA to weed out the psychopaths, then how did she know who among them to trust? How could she work with other parties based on their membership alone? Could she even really trust her own teammates? She had only known them for a little over a month, after all.

Phoenix realized that she didn't really know anything about them outside of their roles within the party, the time they trained together, and the assortment of foods the pair enjoyed. That either made her a terribly trusting simpleton or a terrible friend. Both were things she needed to change, the latter even more so if she didn't want to cause Paul to worry even more.

She scrunched her face as her hand slipped *again*, and she grabbed some more slate putty to fix her mistake before continuing to engrave. Phoenix hadn't noticed the passing of time until the sound of a throat clearing startled her. She flinched violently, half rising out of her chair and turning to see what new threat had snuck up on her.

Paul watched her in surprise and frowned at her reaction.

She let out a breath and visibly relaxed as she registered his presence, sighing heavily. "Don't sneak up on me like that," she complained wearily and slumped back into the chair at the small dining table she had been working at, placing a hand on her forehead to try and steady her racing mind.

"I didn't realize you were so deep in thought there," he said as he took a seat across from her. He watched her harried appearance for a moment before asking, "Have you been up all night?"

She gave a half-shrug. "I slept a couple hours earlier," she replied and tapped the stone she had been working on. "Mind focused on finishing this." Paul nodded in understanding, still giving her an assessing gaze, and she asked a few moments later with a bit of annoyance, "*What?*"

He frowned at her again. She felt the familiar brush of his Aura against hers, and visibly flinched. Phoenix stood up once more to step away from him and pulled her own Aura in tightly, trying to make it as solid and unreadable as possible while saying through clenched teeth, "Not tonight, Paul."

"What happened?" he asked sternly, not moving from his seat, but he pulled back his Aura, hopefully recognizing the unusual discomfort it was causing her.

"Nothing," she automatically said as she rubbed at her arms for comfort and warmth. At his flat look, she explained, "Just nightmares. I'll be fine."

"Nightmares?" he questioned, crossing his arms over his chest.

"Yes, nightmares. Have you never had a nightmare before?" she snapped back.

He quirked an eyebrow at her, and she groaned, then rubbed her face with both her hands as she retook her seat, giving in to her exhaustion. "I'm sorry, Paul . . . Can you just blame my tired brain and forget tonight is happening? I'm not really in the best place right now."

Her Mentor nodded slowly, then leaned forward, resting his arms on the table, before pulling the large, rolled-up scroll that she had discarded on the table earlier towards him to read. After examining it for a few moments, he asked. "Is this the city's Monster Spawn Alert enchantment?"

She simply tilted her head in confirmation.

He inquired further, "This is different though, larger and . . . relayed?"

"I was trying to think of a way to expand it to the outlying towns when I discovered that the communication between the smaller villages and fort towns are . . . well, basically nonexistent compared to what I'm used to in my old world," she tried to explain to him, gesturing to the scroll. "It's more of a theory, though, since I have no idea how to test it out on such a large scale."

Paul thoughtfully hummed as he studied it more and asked, "Can I hold onto this?"

"Sure. It won't do me much good," she said with a dismissive wave.

He then rolled up the scroll, sliding it into the dimensional bag at his hip, and leaned forward again to grab the receiving stone to look over it. "This looks like a tracking device of some kind?"

She nodded and lifted the signal stone she was still working on, appreciating the change of topic. "I'm trying to link it to an activatable signal rather than the normal passive trigger some animal collars have to find lost pets. I'm also trying to add in pieces from the alarm ritual you taught me so they'll both inform the holder while only tracking when activated."

Paul placed the receiving stone down with a nod and said, "I can leave then and let you get some rest today. You don't really seem to be up to talking about other things and are focused on this."

Phoenix's hand moved without thought as it clutched at his long white sleeve. "No, please." Her voice was barely a whisper, but he seemed to have understood as he paused. "Don't leave me alone."

She realized that the last thing she wanted at the moment was to be left alone once more for her memories and fears to consume her. It also made her realize that Paul had become the only person she felt *safe* with. That realization alone made her change her mind. If she couldn't trust *Paul,* then she really was completely alone in a strange world.

He nodded, placing his free hand over hers in a comforting gesture. Then he made her smile slightly by trying to change the topic once more and get her mind away from whatever seemed to be bothering her. "Is now a bad time to ask why the Flame of Life you gave me was flickering yesterday afternoon?" His words only served to reinforce the decision to confide in her Mentor and friend.

Phoenix gave him a wry look. "Are you really watching it all the time like some kind of stalker?"

He grimaced and muttered, "Not *all* the time. I just make sure to check it every now and then to make sure it doesn't go out randomly."

"You make it sound like I'm just going to suddenly keel over with a stiff breeze," she complained.

Paul gave her a teasing grin that she rarely got to see. "With how many potions I've had to force-feed you? I'm lucky you survived without me."

She chuckled, shaking her head, but couldn't really argue the point.

Then he continued inquiring. "I've never seen a Flame of Life flicker like that before. I didn't even know it was possible or what it might mean. Did you get into a fight but manage to heal yourself?"

Phoenix slowly shook her head once more, then conjured her book into her lap but didn't hand it over right away. She asked nervously, "You, um . . . you can keep another secret of mine, right? You haven't dragged me off to your lair or anything yet for being a Wayfarer . . ."

Paul gave an awkward chuckle as he noted, "That Magi really gave you a bad impression of the people in this world, didn't he?"

She nodded solemnly, and her Mentor seemed to still at her serious tone. She felt another hesitant brush of his Aura against hers, but it wasn't pushing to read her; it was asking permission to *understand* her.

Phoenix gathered her resolve and let him in. Allowing him to read her fear and frustration as she handed over the book with her most secret Talent on display.

> **Natural Talent:** Waypoint
> When suffering lethal damage, instead of crossing the Veil, your soul will be transported to the last place you designated as your Waypoint. Your body will be reconstituted there, regaining a state of full integrity. This effect can only be triggered once every twenty-four hours.

As his face darkened at the description, she added cautiously, "The Flame probably flickered because I *did die* yesterday, at least for a little while." Then, she displayed the revival message she got when waking.

He sat there for a long moment, reading and rereading the ability and message before asking his next question. "How did you die?"

Phoenix gave a short laugh that almost sounded like a sob as she asked wryly, "The first time? Or the most recent?"

The Wrath Blade looked up at her sharply and changed his question. "How many times have you died?"

"Twice," she said, gently stroking her braid as a distraction. "The first time I was cornered by a Shanther and fell off a cliff. That's when I revived and met Miles. He made it *quite* clear that this Talent made me extremely valuable," she continued explaining. "Then yesterday, I was tricked, incapacitated, and . . . *fed* to a pack of Miserlings."

The Emerald Aura became a suffocating presence then. Even she could sense the anger permeating it due to the mental image she was sure her words were conjuring if he was familiar with the creatures.

It relaxed a moment later as he pulled the Aura back into himself, likely realizing the effect it was having on her, and he commanded, "Tell me who tricked you."

Hesitantly, she asked, "Are . . . What are you going to do to them?"

Paul stared at her wide-eyed as he asked in disbelief, "You would try to *protect* your killer?"

"No, I just . . . I don't want you killing them out of anger or revenge . . . I don't want anyone dying because of me," she said falteringly.

His golden eyes went wider, then narrowed as he growled, "Phoenix, they *murdered* you. And in one of the most disturbing ways I could have imagined. I am familiar with how Miserlings hunt. If you didn't have this *impossible* ability, you wouldn't be here, and I would currently be mourning."

Phoenix looked towards him, surprised at the strong emotions he was channeling even with his Aura retracted.

Her Mentor almost appeared to beg her as he said, "Tell me who would *dare* to have ripped you from my life."

"Murinah Ruwena and her brother, Camrin." Then a faint memory replayed in her mind, and she added, "Though the brother sounded upset? I'm not sure he was in on it."

His eyes closed, rubbing at his temple as he said, "House Ruwena. Being a noble might make things messier, but she *will* pay for what she's done."

She couldn't stop herself from inquiring, "How are you going to do that?" His eyes were cold as he gazed at her, and she clarified, "I mean, how will anyone believe I was killed when I'm clearly not dead?"

Paul's expression softened as he said, "You leave that to me and don't worry about them anymore. I'll probably have to dig around for some other things to pin on her and talk with some of my contacts. Besides, we don't want anyone else finding out about your **[Waypoint]** ability," he added. She raised an eyebrow, and he explained as he gestured to the large window making up the wall beside them, "That Magi was right. There are a lot of people out there that would claim you to either study this Talent or use you as an expendable tool for suicide missions."

The Emerald Caster frowned and admitted, "I may be strong here in Tulim, but if word got outside of the city, there are many I could not protect you from. I may be close, but I'm not Ruby yet, whereas most of the global leaders are."

Phoenix nodded at the logic. She had been nervous because she didn't want to be experimented on, but she hadn't considered people trying to take advantage of the power like Paul had suggested with missions that would *definitely* kill her. She resolved to keep her silence about it. Now that she at least had Paul to confide in, the weight she had been feeling slowly crushing her had lightened considerably.

Paul leaned forward in his chair and placed a hand on top of hers in an uncommon display of affection. "Phoenix, I wish you had trusted me sooner, but I don't blame you for not saying anything after that Magi had betrayed you." His hand squeezed hers as he said decisively, "I don't want you to feel like you need to hide things from me. I will *never* hurt or betray you. You are my Protégé, and I will protect and support you as such."

She wiped the tears from her eyes with her free hand and nodded, saying in a broken voice, "Thank you, Paul."

CHAPTER FORTY-SIX

Monsters in Our Minds

Once his Protégé seemed to have calmed down, he relocated them from the dining area to the sitting room. As Paul focused on making some tea that should help relax the young woman rather than more magic-infused coffee, he tried to change to a lighter topic they hadn't had a chance to discuss yet. "I heard there was some excitement on the wall while I was gone."

Phoenix nodded, and when she didn't elaborate, he prompted, "You constructed a giant bird made of stars? I didn't think your ability would do something on the scale that was described to me."

"I used one of the rituals in Scholar's Knowledge Tome," she explained softly.

When she didn't speak further, he gestured towards her book that was still floating nearby. "Anything new for me to read from that? No new items? I would have thought defeating all those monsters would have been lucrative."

As he walked over with the cup of tea, she shook herself and seemed to try to dispel her exhaustion. When her attention finally returned to the present, she took the cup and gave a tentative sip, her nose wrinkling slightly.

Once he sat beside her on the sofa, an item appeared in her free hand with the appearance of a large pear-cut gem about the width of his thumb that had been hollowed out and filled to the brim with variously colored feathers.

Phoenix took another deep breath and said with a bit more energy, "The Wing Spirit Gem. I was waiting for you to return before using it."

Item: Wing Spirit Gem
A magical gem containing the spiritual concept of wings made manifest.
Caste: Crystal.
Availability: Rare.
Type: Consumable, ingredient.
Requirements: Crystal Caste with less than five unlocked Class abilities.

> **Effect:** Unlocks a random Class ability weighted towards a suitable Aspect.
>
> *You are able to absorb the* [Wing Spirit Gem].
> *Do you wish to unlock a Class ability infused with the Wing concept?*

He chuckled at her. "You don't have to wait for my permission. Honestly, there are only a few Spirit Gems you really need to watch out for. Things like Death or Void, apocalypse or cataclysm, corruption or discord, or the ones named after Fallen gods. Unless you have a particular concern, you seem to know what to look out for."

Phoenix gave him a crooked grin. "I know, it's just that I like having you confirm it," she said, then sighed and held up the gem to peer into it herself. "So. Wings. Flying ability?"

Paul gave her an amused look and shrugged. "Potentially, but it could be any number of abilities that are wing-themed." Then he paused and asked, "Are you sure you're up to this right now? You should probably get some more sleep."

Red curls bounced as she shook her head in the negative. "Maybe in a bit. Let's just see what this ends up being." Then she triggered absorbing the gem, and it seemed to crack slightly before shattering into a myriad of feathers, swarming into her. He found her hand suddenly on his sleeve, tightening in a death grip, and he knew the uncomfortable feeling was invading her senses.

He worried that the swarm of pain might be triggering new nightmares that he now had to worry about accidentally reminding her of. He knew how Miserlings normally spawned in packs and would torture their prey for a long time before devouring them.

Paul remembered putting a poor Caster out of their misery long ago when he came upon them too late and without a Healer. It was one of those times he had desperately wished he had a healing ability. Killing them quickly had been the only mercy he could grant.

The idea that Phoenix had suffered through that and would *remember* that horror forever made his blood boil with rage.

He wrapped an arm around her to try and steady her against his larger frame, and she seemed to breathe easier as the moment quickly passed. Her book floated closer again to offer up the new ability description.

Her jaw dropped as they both read it over, and she asked incredulously, "Is that . . . Is that really what I think it is?"

> **Class Ability:** Wings of the Cosmos
> **Type:** Familiar (ritual, summon, magical, covenant, dimension)
> **Cost:** Severe mana and stamina.

> **Cooldown:** None.
> **Current Caste:** Crystal 1 (0%)
> **Crystal Effect:** Summon a [**Cosmic Phoenix**] to serve as a Familiar.

Paul grinned at her. "Congratulations. You got your Familiar ability."

She stood up quickly, catching him by surprise as she asked in a rush, "Now. Can we summon it now? Please?"

He laughed at the sudden excitement that seemed to overtake her, and he was relieved to see her apathy and sorrow dissipate. "Do you have the materials? Some Familiars take some pretty specific or hard-to-find components," he warned, gently tapping the oddly-not-quite-diamond-shaped metal plate in the center of his forehead, deciding to show her a bit more trust on his own part. "Orebela here took a boatload of Light Shards at Crystal."

Phoenix stared at the little golden third-eye guard that most people assumed was some sort of magic item augment and asked in utter shock, "*That's* a Familiar?!"

Paul nodded and said, "She doesn't really like being apart from me. Mostly, she increases my Magical resistance, damage, and senses, but she has a few other tricks."

"*This One can meet Little Miss now?*" the familiar monotone voice echoed in his mind.

"Perhaps I'll introduce her properly to you later," he clarified for the both of them. "Now, what does your Familiar's ritual take? You should simply know from the power itself."

He knew it would be similar to the feeling of remembering something from a Knowledge Tome, and she recited, "One hundred Light Shards, one hundred Dark Shards, and two hundred Crystal Mana Bits."

Then she winced at the cost and admitted, "I don't have those types of Shards. The local monsters have been mostly giving Water, Ice, and Earth-typed Shards when I loot them, aside from the usual monster parts, or when I turn their Seeds into Shards. I got a few Void Shards from those Wights, which should sell really well, but I've been holding onto them in case I think of a good crafting use. I guess I'll have to stop by the market again."

"Perhaps you should get some sleep first?" he suggested again. Then, to further support his position, he pointed to the line on the book where the ability's cost was listed. "This is going to take a lot out of you, and I'm pretty sure you don't want to pass out as soon as you get to meet your newest companion."

She looked like she wanted to argue but slumped and nodded, then asked hesitantly, "Will you, um . . . will you stay here? Please?" He raised an eyebrow, and she admitted meekly, "I just . . . I really don't want to be alone right now."

With a final assessing gaze, he nodded in acquiescence.

* * *

A few hours later, Paul was sitting in a plush chair, silently writing in his journal next to Phoenix, who was sound asleep in her bed. He had tried his best to use his Aura to soothe her nightmares, as her rigid defenses were less resistant to his presence once she fell unconscious. He was impressed with the improvement she had made since it was harder for him to read her now than when they first met, but it was like reading an open book when she slept.

His Aura was also not the most soothing, and he was well aware of that. He found himself wondering what he could possibly do to help the sudden night terrors she was experiencing. In all the time he had known her, she rarely had nightmares, despite knowing she had been through enough battles with monsters to warrant them.

He had never met someone who had survived their frenzy like Phoenix had. Though, he guessed she hadn't survived it.

Despite having the brief thought earlier, now a whole new slew of worries plagued his mind as he sat in silence and contemplated the ramifications of going through horrible deaths and having to live with those memories. Perhaps he should go back to the Temple of the Mender and seek guidance once more. Surely, they had someone much more qualified than he was to help someone dealing with severe trauma like this.

His attention was drawn to the front door in the next room when he got the sense of a weak Aura on the other side of it, followed by a soft knock at the door.

Paul quietly moved to open the door to a startled, purple-haired gemite with matching eyes that went wide upon recognizing him.

The young man stammered, "L-Lord Wayland. I . . . I was unaware you would be here."

Dazien hesitated, then awkwardly asked, "Should I come back another time?"

Paul just opened the door a bit more and walked over to one of the chairs in the small sitting area by the hearth. Then he gestured to one of the other seats and gave a simple order: "Sit."

The younger warrior hesitated another moment before straightening with resolve and stepping inside, shutting the door behind him, and taking the seat opposite the Emerald Caster. The gemite seemed uncomfortable with the sudden situation but went ahead and asked, "Is Miss Fraser not in?"

"She's still sleeping," he stated simply, his assessing gaze falling on the Defender now.

The would-be king raised an eyebrow at him as though wanting to inquire exactly why *he* was here if she was sleeping, but Paul cut off that inaccurate line of thinking. "I arrived here this afternoon to find a sleep-deprived tinkerer jumping at every little movement." He gestured to the mess still on the table over by the window. "She unlocked a Familiar power, and I was able to convince her to sleep before attempting to summon it."

"*Little King seems guilty*," Orebela's voice echoed his own observations. "*Perhaps something else happened that Little Miss did not speak of?*"

His golden eyes locked on amethyst ones as he pressed his Aura on the young man, asking, "Now, what exactly did you do to her while I was gone?"

Dazien's eyes went wide at the accusation. "Me?! Sir, why would you believe I did something to her?" Then those eyes narrowed into a glare. "Despite what many people seem to think of gemites in this city, I would never try to take advantage of her. To even suggest—"

"Because you are here without your shadow," he interjected simply, not wanting the kid to get the wrong idea and think he was some kind of anti-gemite bigot. "And you feel guilty."

The young warrior muttered under his breath, "Bloody Aura senses." Then he straightened slightly and clarified, "I am here alone mainly because Uriel has a recurring appointment every other Blosol with Priest Jacob, as you should well know. I was concerned about Phoenix because she was acting very oddly last night. I don't think my guilt has anything to do with that, however."

Dazien then explained what had happened the previous day, with Phoenix coming back to her dorm to sleep and having nightmares after her portal duties, then not seeming entirely coherent and acting much more subdued than even when they had first met. He finished by asking Paul, "Did she tell you anything?"

"*You trust Little King?*" Orebela questioned. "*He talks a lot.*"

Paul knew his Familiar was right, and even if he was starting to trust the young man, he wasn't about to divulge this particular secret. So, he shook his head and lied. "Just nightmares. Until she decides to open up, you'll just have to wait. I suggest *not* pushing her," he warned, assuming that was exactly what the upstart sovereign had planned. "She seemed rather . . . volatile when I tried. You should let her come to you when she trusts you enough."

Dazien frowned at his words but nodded in understanding, slumping in his chair slightly. "I'm not sure what to do," the kid admitted, surprising Paul with the unexpected vulnerability on display. "I'm supposed to be leading this party, and I'm not sure how to help one of its members. How can I expect them to trust and follow when I'm uncertain of the course to take?"

Paul leaned back in his chair, thinking for a moment before saying, "Nobody leads alone. Find certainty in the knowledge that those who choose to follow you will not only trust in what you think is best but will support you when you slip." He crossed his arms over his chest. "If you want to help Phoenix since she's the one currently slipping, you need to let her know that she's not alone in whatever challenge she faces. Whether it's from the monsters out there"—he gestured to the window then tapped at his temple—"or the monsters in here."

Dazien grimaced at him and agreed. "I'm well aware that the monsters in our minds can sometimes be a greater threat than the ones we face on the battlefield. My partner has been a shining example of that fact."

Paul tilted his head in acknowledgment. "Yes, he would know all about that, wouldn't he?" he said rhetorically. He then leaned back and asked curiously, "And how did you manage to help him?"

"Well, it helped to know that he was devoted to following me," Dazien pointed out with a smirk.

"Yes, but before that," he clarified, "how did you get him to devote himself to you in the first place?"

The young leader contemplated for a moment before saying, "I just . . . I don't know. I was just there for him. Defended him. Told him that no matter what he might believe he deserved, I would always be there."

Paul gave a slight smile. "I think you have your answer then. Now, since you're here and obviously have the time, why don't you tell me a bit more about your history and interactions with the other nobles in the city?"

"The other nobles?" Dazien repeated in confusion, then gave a wry smirk. "Trying to play the game of politics, Lord Wayland? You didn't strike me as the type."

"Let's just say I have a new reason to be concerned about what some of the other Houses are up to," he said, sidestepping the question. "You're probably more up-to-date on the current status of things since you seem rather popular with the younger scions. Are there any that you would consider . . . more self-centered than most people?"

Dazien gave him a dubious look. "I feel like this is somehow a trick question."

He chuckled, feeling a bit better about the party Phoenix had chosen, and clarified, "I guess what I'm really curious about are which ones you think might resort to dirtier tactics that one might need to literally watch their back for."

"Ah, well . . . I will admit there are a few," the Defender said, shifting in his seat.

Paul grinned. "Tell me everything about them."

CHAPTER FORTY-SEVEN

Phoenix

Phoenix followed after Paul, having finished securing the necessary materials for her Familiar ritual. Her excitement for the new companion had helped banish the memories that had been plaguing her sleep, and she found it easier to put it behind her as she looked forward to what was ahead instead.

Paul had taken her to the Market District in the northeast quadrant of the inner city to get the Shards she was missing, but also surprised her by simply spending time together looking at various shops. While she wasn't a *huge* fan of shopping, mainly because of the crowds and forced socialness, she did enjoy learning. Getting to ask Paul what everything was gave her tons of new information to think about, and it did wonders to help get her mind off her nightmares.

Being back in a skirt with her hair freed from its braid also helped her mood. She wasn't planning to fight anything today with her Mentor at her side, so she felt comfortable donning the long, emerald winter dress and silvery, fur-lined boots and gloves that Paul had encouraged her to buy at a cute little boutique. He offered to buy them for her, but she refused, not liking the idea of anyone spending money on her when she was *finally* capable of doing that herself.

The only enchantments on them were for maintenance, and she was enjoying the idea they reaffirmed: that today was for *not* fighting things.

It was because there was no training planned that she was surprised to find Dazien and Uriel waiting outside of the building her Mentor was leading her to. "What are you two doing here?" she asked the pair.

Dazien grinned brightly at her. "Lord Wayland informed us that you unlocked a Familiar ability and told us you'd be performing the ritual here. We wanted to be by your side for support, of course."

"We can leave if you'd rather do this alone." Uriel spoke up, his ember eyes watching her with concern. "No hard feelings or anything. This is for you, after all."

Phoenix blinked at them for far too long before saying with awkward nervousness, "Um, thank you, but you can stay, I think." She wasn't quite sure how to react to the display of camaraderie, so instead, she turned to Paul and asked, "Where are we?"

He pulled out a tiny metal rod that was identical to the one he had given her before he had left a week ago and placed it into a small hole in the door frame. "My home," the older warrior said simply and led the trio inside.

It was very minimalistic inside, with lots of white and silver embellishments, except for the green plants that seemed to be growing on every surface and in each corner. Paul stood out in contrast with his golden coloring, and she instantly thought he looked like the sun feeding the outstretched leaves.

Instead of leading them to an upper floor of the tall building, he surprised Phoenix by taking an elevator down, below the ground, and suddenly she was wondering how much of the city she had never known lay underneath the tightly packed metropolis.

"So, what exactly are we summoning today?" Dazien asked as they rode the glass lift downward.

She summoned her book for them to show the ability that had bonded to her Star Aspect.

Uriel let out a snort of laughter while Dazien glanced up at her with an impish grin and sparkles in his gem-like eyes as he clarified, "Seriously?"

"What? It's going to be amazing!" she argued, thinking of the mythical birds of legend. Perhaps she had been mistaken, and they were basically magic chickens in this world?

Her temporary leader's retort was cut off by the lift doors opening, and the lord of the House led them to a permanent ritual chamber. Phoenix contemplated visiting more often just to take advantage of these kinds of accommodations as the large room spread out before them, lit by glowstones embedded in the ceiling. Then she wondered why Paul had never brought her here before. Did he not want her here?

She shook her head at her thoughts. No, if Paul had tried to bring her here right away, she would have probably freaked out, thinking he was trying to kidnap her like that Magi. Despite having just revealed her most kidnap-worthy secret, her Mentor had given her a key to this home over a week ago. However, she hadn't seen a reason to come by without him here, and he had mentioned using it for emergencies.

Now, though, perhaps it was him trying to show that he finally trusted her? That he wanted her in his life more? She pushed those thoughts aside and focused on her work, using a finger of light to draw out the most elaborate ritual diagram she had ever done before.

Paul, Dazien, and Uriel stood along the back wall watching her work, and the Defender couldn't stop grinning as he asked, "Seriously, does no one else find it amusing that *Phoenix* is about to summon a *phoenix*?!"

The other two men just rolled their eyes at Dazien, and understanding the joke, Phoenix snorted a laugh like Uriel had. "I would find it more hilarious if you managed to summon an actual king," she quipped.

He grinned back at her. "It would be kind of pointless to summon myself."

Once everything looked good, she stood on the edge of the diagram, took a deep, calming breath, and looked to her companions. "Ready?"

The three men all nodded, and she lifted her arms in front of her with her palms facing the center of the circle. Then, she began the long incantation.

"From the ashes of the first star, I call you. Until the final nova, I command you. You are the beginning and the end. You are the first and last breath of the universe. Our bond heralds the genesis of a new dawn. Come forward, that we may burn brightly across the cosmos."

As Phoenix spoke, she felt her mana get drawn out of her and into the circle as the diagram grew brighter and brighter. When she finished speaking, the multicolored light of the ritual pulsed and swirled to the center of the circle. It formed a small silvery star that slowly grew larger and floated down to the floor before seeming to solidify and shift into a sphere of swirling dark blues and purples that reminded her of the sheet of night her portal would display.

Phoenix dropped to a knee as the remaining mana and stamina were siphoned from her, and the colors stopped shifting. The sphere suddenly began to crack, and she realized it was an egg.

A few moments later, the shell split in two and dissolved into silvery stardust around a ball of blue and purple feathers with silver speckles.

She couldn't help but crawl slowly towards the creature, look down, and gently stretch out her finger to poke the feathery bundle that was about the size of a small volleyball.

As it let out a small "Cheep," and large silver eyes met her emerald ones, she gave a bright smile at the **[Cosmic Phoenix]**. She didn't care if it did turn out to be a fluffy chicken, this was her Familiar, and she could already feel the bond sending feelings of love and acceptance between them. "Hello, lil birb, I'm Phoenix," she cooed.

She held out both of her hands together, palms up, in front of the round bird. After a couple of heavy blinks at her, it gave another *cheep* and hopped forward with a tiny flutter of its short wings to land in her grasp.

Phoenix sat back, crossing her legs under the folds of her dress, and lifted the bird up to her eyes to get a better look. It was lighter than she expected for how round it was, and she suspected the floofy feathers were to blame. Aside from the large silver irises of its eyes, its little beak was also a shimmery silver.

The little creature cocked its head to the side as it looked up at her and gave another curious *cheep.*

Dazien and Uriel sat down on either side of her to get a closer look at their newest party addition, and she grinned at both of them.

"Does it have a name?" Dazien asked. "Some of them already have one," he explained, "or a gender, for that matter?"

"Umm . . ." She stared at the speckled phoenix for a moment. "One chirp for 'girl,' two for 'boy,' three for 'both,' or four for 'none' or 'other.'"

The bird tilted its head in the other direction and gave another single *cheep.*

Dazien cut in. "How do you even know it understands what you're saying?"

"Uhh . . . two chirps for understanding what I'm saying?" she asked the creature hesitantly.

The phoenix gave two *cheep*s in quick succession before shaking its small body, causing the feathers to seem even more poofy than before.

Phoenix grinned and said, "See? She's a smart girl."

"So, does the little lady have a name?" Dazien asked the bird, leaning forward to get a closer look.

The newborn chick gave a single *cheep*, and the gemite looked at Phoenix.

"Was one chirp a yes or no?"

"Let's go with two for yes," she said and asked the same question, getting a single chirp once again. "Do you want a name?"

"Cheep, cheep."

All three of the young adults got a contemplative look on their faces as they thought about potential names, and Phoenix noticed that Paul was still leaning against the far wall, just watching the group carefully.

"What do you think, Paul?" she asked over to him, holding the poofy bird up for him to see better.

He shook his head and gave a wry grin. "I think that is for you and her to decide."

"I don't think either of us mind hearing suggestions," she pointed out.

"Cheep, cheep," the little phoenix said.

"See? She agrees," the larger Phoenix reaffirmed with a grin.

"What about Fluffball?" Dazien said, and somehow, both girls managed to roll their eyes at him. He laughed and tried again. "Okay then, how about Speckles? She has them all over her feathers."

"Starlight?" Uriel suggested.

"That's better," Phoenix said to the Mage, "but she's not just some pet. She's the newest member of our party, and I want her to have a name like any other person."

"You could pick any name then, like Bethel, or Vanessera, or Diana," Dazien listed off, not particularly enthused with those options.

"Actually, that last one reminds me of the mythos of my world," she said, perking up a bit. "We didn't have gods like you do here," she explained. "If they do exist there, they do a *very* good job of hiding. Anyways, I went through a period where I got super obsessed with all the different pantheons of deities, and I think I know the perfect name." She grinned and asked the little bird, "What do you think about 'Tala'? She's the goddess of stars in one of the pantheons."

"Cheep, cheep!" the little bird replied excitedly, bouncing up and down in Phoenix's palms.

They all laughed at the tiny Familiar's antics. Then Tala surprised them all by nuzzling down as though to roost, and she seemed to melt right into Phoenix's hands.

Phoenix became even more confused as she stared at her now empty hands and realized they were softly glowing. "What just happened?" she asked in a slight panic, "Did I just *melt* my Familiar?!"

Uriel chuckled and explained, "Every summoned Familiar can merge with their summoner like that. There's always some kind of visual component when they do. Changed color of the hair or eyes are most common, followed by markings on the skin, such as a tattoo or"—he gestured at her hands—"an overall shift in complexion."

As she stared at her now shining hands, she pulled back the sleeve that wasn't covering the bracelet over her Oathbond to confirm that her arm was also glowing with a soft light. She stared up at her companions. They were still staring at her, taking in her new appearance, and she asked in shock, "So this is *permanent?*"

"No, just when she's merged," Uriel clarified in that smooth bass that was fighting back the amused tint in it. "When she comes out to fight or support, or whatever it is she can do to help you, the glow *should* dissipate."

"*Should?*" she repeated, her voice going an octave higher.

Paul's chuckle came from across the room as he said, "Now you even shine like a star."

Her eyes went slightly wide, and she pulled out a hand mirror from her collection that she had snagged earlier when clothes shopping. She looked at her face, which was indeed also glowing softly, and it somehow managed to make her red hair and green eyes stand out even *more* than before.

"Oh, what in the abyss is this *nonsense*," she murmured, then clapped her hands together a few times. "Nope. Come out right now, Tala. I'm not walking around town like a freaking night-light."

"Hang on now," Dazien interjected, placing a hand on her arm, "can you tell what benefits you get from her like this?"

"Aside from not needing a glowstone," Uriel added with a smirk.

Phoenix glared at the Mage and replied sarcastically, "Ha. Ha." Then she closed her eyes to concentrate on the power of her Familiar nestled inside of her. It was an odd sensation to be two separate entities, yet not. Tala was now a part of her very being.

Once her mind was no longer consumed by the panic of going around town like a mobile Christmas tree, she realized that she already knew exactly what her new companion was capable of. Her eyes shot open as she muttered, "I think she just made me solar powered."

At the confused looks of her teammates, she elaborated. "I slowly charge up **[Starlight Qi]** and can release all of it to regenerate nearby allies' mana and stamina based on the amount of starlight my skin had absorbed up to that point while she's merged."

"Keep her inside," Paul said firmly, "you have a bad habit of close calls."

She gave him a flat look. "I am not *glowing* around the city," she argued and clapped her hands one more time. The little puffy bird slowly arose from her palm to look up at her with large, pleading eyes.

Phoenix rolled her own eyes, having seen it a million times before from the younger kids in the hospital. "Don't give me that look, Tala," she said, then plopped the blue and purple phoenix on top of her head. "You can stay up there. Still touching but no glowing."

Her companions chuckled at her as the small phoenix cheeped twice before settling into the red curls. She grinned at her teammates and Mentor, and with her newest companion, she started to feel like everything would be okay.

Character Profiles

Here is a quick reference for the character profiles, talents, titles, and abilities that were displayed during the book and their levels by the end of it.

Phoenix Fraser

Name: Phoenix Fraser
Species: Wayfarer
Caste: Crystal 1

Attributes
Strength (Sun): Crystal 1
Agility (Dark): Crystal 1
Fortitude (Star): Crystal 3
Mind (Moon): Crystal 1
Magic (Celestial Astromancer): Crystal 1

Natural Talents
Aetheric Transmigrator
Beacon of Hope
Collector
Guide Book
Waypoint

Divine Titles
Chosen One

Titles
Adventurer

<u>Aspects</u>
Star
- Guiding Stars (Aura Passive)
- Transversing the Stars - Crystal 5
- Wings of the Cosmos (Class) - Crystal 1

Dark
- Embrace of Shadows (Aura Passive)
- Night Blade - Crystal 3

Sun
- Radiant Sunlight (Aura Passive)
- Dawn Rises - Crystal 2

Moon
- Moonlit Eyes (Perception Passive)
- Lunar Dream - Crystal 2
- Celestial Astromancer (Class)
- Astral Oasis (Aura Passive)
- Ruler of Relativity - Crystal 3

Natural Talent: Aetheric Transmigrator
- Increased resistance to negative Dimension effects. Dimension abilities have an increased effect.
- You are a Natural Translator, allowing the understanding of languages you are exposed to.
- You can directly use Aspects and Spirit Gems without the need for an Absorption Ritual.

Natural Talent: Beacon of Hope
- You can unlock more than one Aura ability.
- Aspect abilities cultivate quicker than average.
- You can draw magic diagrams with conjured light, including ones that float in the air.

Natural Talent: Collector
- You have a personal dimensional storage space.
- You automatically loot slain enemies that have been touched by your Aura.
- Loot automatically goes into your collection.
- You can use material components for Spells, rituals, or enchantments directly from your collection.

Natural Talent: Guide Book
You can conjure a book that guides you and informs you about parts of the world that have been touched by your Aura.

Natural Talent: Waypoint
When suffering lethal damage, instead of crossing the Veil, your soul will be transported to the last place you designated as your Waypoint. Your body will be reconstituted there, regaining a state of full integrity. This effect can only be triggered once every twenty-four hours.

Divine Title: Chosen One
Your Aura has been altered by divine entities: Hero, Rebel, Scholar, Warrior, and Traveler. The alterations have enhanced the strength of your Aura, increasing its range and resistance to effects from higher Castes. Your soul has been marked as one who has been Chosen by the deities of Makera.

Title: Adventurer
Your Aura has been slightly modified by your accomplishment. The desire for adventure can be sensed within it. Your Aura has slightly increased effects when affecting a Mundane ally.

Passive Ability: Guiding Stars
Type: Aura (magical, light)
Crystal Effect: Allies within your Aura have increased stamina regeneration and will gain a **[Starlight Companion]**. Reconstructing a destroyed **[Starlight Companion]** expends a low amount of mana.
- Starlight Companion (construct, magical, light): A small Starlight Companion hovers around you, providing light and protection. This can intercept and negate Magical or Elemental projectiles.

Ability: Transversing the Stars
Type: Utility (construct, magical, dimension)
Cost: High mana.
Cooldown: 5 minutes.
Crystal Effect: Construct a stargate between two locations on a regional scale. The destination gate must appear in a location you have an aural imprint on.

Class Ability: Wings of the Cosmos
Type: Familiar (ritual, summon, magical, covenant, dimension)
Cost: Severe mana and stamina.
Cooldown: None.
Crystal Effect: Summon a [**Cosmic Phoenix**] to serve as a Familiar.

Passive Ability: Embrace of Shadows
Type: Aura (stealth, magical, dark)
Crystal Effect: Allies within your Aura are obscured by shadows, making attacks against them less likely to hit. The effectiveness of the shadows scales up with the level of darkness of the surrounding environment.

Ability: Night Blade
Type: Utility (construct, magical, dark)
Cost: Low mana.
Cooldown: None.
Crystal Effect: Constructs a magical dagger that inflicts additional Dark damage and an instance of [**Mana Siphon**].
- Mana Siphon (bane, drain, magical, arcane, stacking): Drains a low amount of mana over time.

Passive Ability: Radiant Sunlight
Type: Aura (magical, light)
Crystal Effect: Allies within your Aura gain a [**Sun Shell**]. Reconstructing a destroyed [**Sun Shell**] can be done after a short duration and costs a moderate amount of mana.
- Sun Shell (boon, construct, magical, light): A shield that blocks the next incoming physical attack with a chance to knock back and inflict [**Blind**] on the attacker.
- Blind (bane, magical, light): Hinders vision for a short duration.

Ability: Dawn Rises
Type: Spell (magical, life)
Cost: Variable mana.
Cooldown: Variable.
Crystal Effect: Can heal a touched target by activating for Low, Moderate, High, or Severe mana cost. The amount healed and respective cooldown time increase with cost.

Passive Ability: Moonlit Eyes
Type: Perception (magical, light)
Crystal Effect: The level of light does not hinder your sight.

Ability: Lunar Dream
Type: Spell (construct, magical, illusion)
Cost: Variable mana.
Cooldown: None.
Crystal Effect: Construct an illusory model. Cost varies based on scale and duration. The Illusion is semitransparent and intangible.

Passive Ability: Astral Oasis
Type: Aura (magical, arcane)
Crystal Effect: Allies within your Aura have increased regeneration to mana and abilities cost less mana.

Ability: Ruler of Relativity
Type: Utility (magical, covenant)
Cost: Variable mana.
Cooldown: None.
Crystal Effect: Change the gravitational relationship between you and a target within sight with mana cost dependent on the distance, speed, size, and Caste difference from the target.

Dazien Smithson

Name: Dazien Smithson
Species: Gemite (Amethyst)
Caste: Crystal 4

Attributes
Strength (Potent): Crystal 5
Agility (Sword): Crystal 3
Fortitude (Metal): Crystal 6
Mind (Noble): Crystal 6
Magic (Warrior King): Crystal 3

Natural Talents
Treasure Attunement
Drinking Buddy

Earthborn
Shiny
Right of Divinity

Titles
Orphan
Loyal Friend
Warrior Trainee
Slayer
Adventurer

Aspects
Potent
- Eagle Eye (Perception Passive)
- Duelist - Crystal 6
- Rallying Cry (Class) - Crystal 5

Sword
- Armory (Utility Passive)
- Accelerating Strikes - Crystal 7

Metal
- Tribute (Utility Passive)
- Stand Your Ground - Crystal 6
- To the Dungeon (Class) - Crystal 6

Noble
- Noble Subjects (Utility Passive)
- Lead the Charge - Crystal 7
- King's Banner (Class) - Crystal 6

Warrior King (Class)
- Monarch's Dominion (Aura Passive)
- Call of Fealty - Crystal 6

Passive Ability: Eagle Eye
Type: Perception
Crystal Effect: You have greater control over your vision and can focus on details from a great distance.

Ability: Stand Your Ground
Type: Utility (channel, elemental, metal)
Cost: Moderate mana per second.

Cooldown: None.
Crystal Effect: Become rooted in place, greatly increasing your resistance to physical damage, and gain an instance of **[Tenacity]** each second until your next movement.
* Tenacity (boon, elemental, metal, stacking): Increased **[Strength]** and resistance to Elemental damage. Instances are quickly lost when moving.

Uriel Karislian

Passive Ability: Scent in the Air
Type: Perception
Current Caste: Crystal 5
Crystal Effect: You have an extremely heightened and more controlled sense of smell.

Paul Wayland

Passive Ability: Penetrating Sight
Type: Perception (magical, covenant, light)
Crystal Effect: The level of light does not hinder your sight.
Sapphire Effect: You can see the types of magic a creature or item is attuned to.
Emerald Effect: The longer you focus your sight on a target, the easier it becomes to overcome their resistances and analyze their Aura. Looking away resets this effect.

Author's Note

Thank you so much for reading the first book of the Wayward series and supporting my stories. Having an epic fantasy adventure where the main protagonist and supporting cast of characters included representation of colorful people like me was a large driving force behind this, in addition to my love for LitRPG and Fantasy. I hope everyone reading has seen pieces of themselves reflected as well.

You can read more of the story by supporting me on Patreon at patreon.com /CasterCultivation, where you can also find the link to the Discord server where I welcome anyone to come chat, speculate, and build their own characters!

Acknowledgements

Special thanks to my life partner, Wraithian, for supporting me and putting up with my whims and self-doubts while keeping me well caffeinated. You are my Pillar.

Also to Karaaga Longtail for being my first fan—turned-alpha-reader—turned-friend for this story, offering Bliss for inclusion, keeping me in check with not breaking my own world rules, and motivating me to put in more effort. You are appreciated.

About the Author

T. A. Star is the author of the Wayward series, originally released on Royal Road. Star studied to be an actor and raised a family with their high school sweetheart before eventually becoming a software developer. Their long daily commute introduced a need for audiobooks, which in turn opened the door to the wonderful world of progression fantasy. Noticing a lack of LGBTQ+ protagonists they could better relate to, they decided to start writing their own stories. Star lives in Washington state.

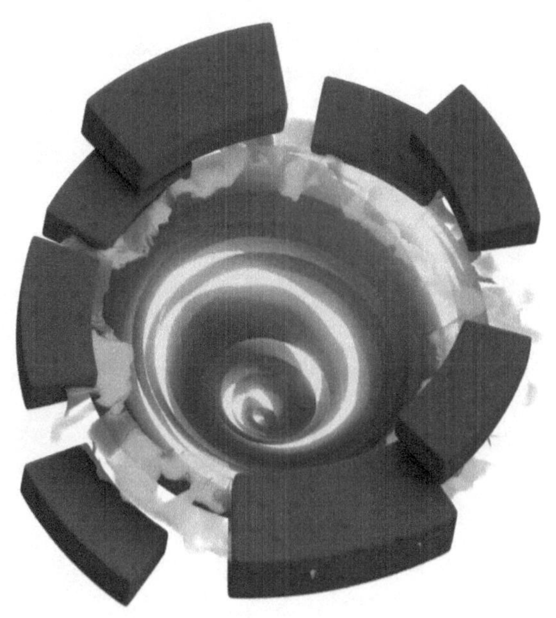

RESPAWN YOUR CURIOSITY

follow us on our socials

 podiumentertainment.com

 @podiumentertainment

 /podiumentertainment

 @podium_ent

 @podiumentertainment